MAR - - 2024

THE
PRISONER'S
THRONE

BY HOLLY BLACK

NOVELS OF ELFHAME

THE STOLEN HEIR DUOLOGY

The Stolen Heir
The Prisoner's Throne

THE FOLK OF THE AIR

The Cruel Prince
The Wicked King
The Queen of Nothing
How the King of Elfhame Learned to Hate Stories

The Darkest Part of the Forest

The Coldest Girl in Coldtown

THE
PRISONER'S
THRONE

A NOVEL OF ELFHAME

HOLLY BLACK

LITTLE, BROWN AND COMPANY

NEW YORK   BOSTON

Copyright © 2024 by Holly Black
Illustrations by Kathleen Jennings

Cover art copyright © 2024 by Sean Freeman. Cover design by Karina Granda.
Cover copyright © 2024 by Hachette Book Group, Inc.
Interior design by Karina Granda.

Little, Brown and Company
Hachette Book Group
1290 Avenue of the Americas, New York, NY 10104
Visit us at LBYR.com

First Edition: March 2024
Simultaneously published in 2024 by Hot Key Books in the United Kingdom

Little, Brown and Company is a division of Hachette Book Group, Inc.
The Little, Brown name and logo are registered trademarks of Hachette Book Group, Inc.

Library of Congress Cataloging-in-Publication Data
Names: Black, Holly, author. | Black, Holly. Stolen heir.
Title: The prisoner's throne : a novel of Elfhame / Holly Black.
Description: First edition. | New York : Little, Brown and Company, 2024. |
Series: The stolen heir ; 2 | Audience: Ages 14+ | Summary: "Prince Oak must find a way to stop a war between Elfhame and the north." —Provided by publisher.
Identifiers: LCCN 2023043868 | ISBN 9780316592710 (hardcover) |
ISBN 9780316592734 (ebook)
Subjects: CYAC: Fantasy. | Wars—Fiction. | Kings, queens, rulers, etc.—Fiction. | LCGFT: Fantasy fiction. | Novels.
Classification: LCC PZ7.B52878 Pr 2024 | DDC [E]—dc23
LC record available at https://lccn.loc.gov/2023043868

ISBNs: 978-0-316-59271-0 (hardcover), 978-0-316-59273-4 (ebook), 978-0-316-57588-1 (int'l), 978-0-316-56930-9 (B&N exclusive edition), 978-0-316-57888-2 (large print)

Printed in the United States of America

LSC-C

Printing 1, 2023

For Joanna Volpe, who is, as her last name suggests, every bit the charming and tricksy fox

I MET the Love-Talker one eve in the glen,

He was handsomer than any of our handsome young men,

His eyes were blacker than the sloe, his voice sweeter far

Than the crooning of old Kevin's pipes beyond in Coolnagar.

I was bound for the milking with a heart fair and free —

My grief! my grief! that bitter hour drained the life from me;

I thought him human lover, though his lips on mine were cold,

And the breath of death blew keen on me within his hold.

I know not what way he came, no shadow fell behind,

But all the sighing rushes swayed beneath a faery wind

The thrush ceased its singing, a mist crept about,

We two clung together — with the world shut out.

— Ethna Carbery,
"The Love-Talker"

SIX WEEKS BEFORE
IMPRISONMENT

Oak jammed his hooves into velvet pants.

"Have I made you late?" Lady Elaine asked from the bed, her voice full of wicked satisfaction. She propped up her head with an elbow and gave a little laugh. "It won't be too much longer before you don't have to do anything at their beck and call."

"Yes," Oak said, distracted. "Only yours, right?"

She laughed again.

Doublet only half-buttoned, he tried desperately to remember the fastest route to the gardens. He'd *meant* to be punctual, but then the opportunity to finally see the scope of the treasonous plot he'd been pursuing had presented itself.

I promise I will introduce you to the rest of my associates, she'd told him, her fingers sliding beneath his shirt, untucking it. *You will be impressed with how close to the throne we can get....*

Cursing himself, the sky, and the concept of time in general, Oak raced out the door.

"Hurry, you scamp," one of the palace laundresses called after him. "It will look ill if they begin without you. And fix your hair!"

He tried to smooth down his curls as servants veered out of his way. In the palace of Elfhame, no matter how tall he grew, Oak was forever the mischievous, wild-haired boy who coaxed guards into playing conkers with horse chestnuts and stole honey cakes from the kitchens. Faerie caught its inhabitants in amber, so if they were not careful, a hundred years might pass in the lazy blink of an eye. And so, few noticed how much the prince had changed.

Not that he didn't resemble his younger self right then, pelting down another corridor, hooves clattering against stone. He dodged left to avoid running into a page with an armful of scrolls, wove right so as not to knock over a small table with an entire tea tray atop it, then almost slammed into Randalin, an elderly member of the Living Council.

By the time he made it to the gardens, Oak was out of breath. Panting, he took in the garlands of flowers and musicians, the courtiers and revelers. No High King or Queen yet. That meant he had a chance to make his way to the front with no one the wiser.

But before he could slip into the crowd, his mother, Oriana, grabbed hold of his sleeve. Her expression was stern, and since her skin was usually ghostly white, it was easy to see the flush of anger in her cheeks. It pinked them so they matched the rosy color of her eyes.

"Where have you been?" Her fingers went to Oak's doublet, fixing his buttons.

"I lost track of time," he admitted.

"Doing what?" She dusted off the velvet. Then she licked her finger and rubbed a smudge on Oak's nose.

He grinned at her fondly, letting her fuss. If she thought of him as barely more than a boy, then she wouldn't look more deeply into any trouble he made for himself. His gaze went to the crowd, looking for his guard. Tiernan was going to be angry when he understood Oak's plan in full. But flushing out a conspiracy would be worth it. And Lady Elaine had been *so close* to telling him the names of the other people involved.

"We'd better head toward the dais," he told Oriana, catching hold of her hand and giving it a squeeze.

She squeezed back, swift and punishingly hard. "You are heir to all of Elfhame," she said as though he might have missed that bit. "It's time to start behaving like someone who could rule. Never forget that you must inspire fear as well as love. Your sister hasn't."

Oak's gaze went to the crowd. He had three sisters, but he knew which one she meant.

He put out his arm, like a gallant knight, and his mother allowed herself to be mollified enough to take it. Oak kept his expression every bit as grave as she could wish. That was easily done, because as he took the first step, the High King and Queen came into view at the edge of the gardens.

His sister Jude was in a gown the color of deep red roses, with high slashes on the sides so that the dress wouldn't restrict her movements. She wore no blade at her waist, but her hair was done up in her familiar horns. Oak was almost certain she hid a small knife in one of them. She would have a few more sewn into her garment and strapped beneath her sleeves.

Despite being the High Queen of Elfhame, with an army at her disposal and dozens of Courts at her command, she still acted as though she'd have to handle every problem herself—and that each one would best be solved through murder.

Beside her, Cardan was in black velvet adorned with even blacker feathers that shone like they'd been dragged through an oil spill, the darkness of his clothes the better to show off the heavy rings shining on his fingers and the large pearl swinging from one of his ears. He winked at Oak, and Oak smiled in return despite his intention to remain serious.

As Oak made his way forward, the crowd parted for him.

His other two sisters were among the throng. Taryn, Jude's twin, had clasped her son tightly by the hand, attempting to distract him from the running around he had probably been doing a moment before. Beside her, Vivienne giggled with her partner, Heather. Vivi was pointing to Folk in the audience and whispering into Heather's ear. Despite being the only one of his three sisters who was a faerie, it was Vivi who liked living in Faerie the least. She did, however, still keep up on the gossip.

The High King and Queen moved to stand before their Court, bathed in the light of the setting sun. Jude beckoned to Oak, as they'd practiced. A hush came over the gardens. He glanced to both sides, at the winged pixies and watery nixies, clever hobs and sinister fetches, kelpies and trolls, redcaps stinking of dried blood, silkies and selkies, fauns and brags, lobs and shagfoals, hags and treefolk, knights and winged ladies in tattered dresses. All subjects of Elfhame. All *his* subjects, he supposed, since he was their prince.

Not a one of them afraid of Oak, no matter what his mother hoped.

Not a one afraid, no matter the blood on his hands. That he'd tricked them all so handily frightened even him.

He halted in front of Jude and Cardan and made a shallow bow.

"Let all here bear witness," Cardan began, his gold-rimmed eyes bright, his voice soft but carrying. "That Oak, son of Liriope and Dain of the Greenbriar line, is my heir, and should I pass from this world, he will rule in my place and with my blessing."

Jude bent down to take a circlet of gold from the pillow a goblin page held up to her. Not a crown, but not quite *not* one, either. "Let all here bear witness." Her voice was chilly. She had never been allowed to forget that she was mortal, back when she was a child in Faerie. Now that she was queen, she never let the Folk feel entirely safe around her. "Oak, son of Liriope and Dain of the Greenbriar line, raised by Oriana and Madoc, *my brother*, is my heir, and when I pass from the world, he shall rule in my place and with my blessing."

"Oak," Cardan said. "Will you accept this responsibility?"

No, Oak yearned to say. *There is no need. The both of you will rule forever.*

But he hadn't asked Oak if he *wanted* the responsibility, rather if he would accept it.

His sister had insisted he be formally named heir now that he was of an age when he could rule without a regent. He could have denied Jude, but he owed all his sisters so much that it felt impossible to deny them anything. If one of them asked for the sun, he'd better figure out how to pluck it from the sky without getting burned.

Of course, they'd never ask for that, or anything like it. They wanted him to be safe, and happy, and good. Wanted to give him the world, and yet keep it from hurting him.

Which was why it was imperative they never discovered what he was really up to.

"Yes," Oak said. Perhaps he should make some kind of speech, or do something that would make him seem more suitable to rule, but his mind had gone utterly blank. It must have been enough, though, because a moment later, he was asked to kneel. He felt the cold metal on his brow.

Then Jude's soft lips were against his cheek. "You'll be a great king when you're ready," she whispered.

Oak knew he owed his family a debt so large he would never be able to repay it. As cheers rose all around him, he closed his eyes and promised he would try.

Oak was a living, breathing mistake.

Seventeen years ago, the last High King, Eldred, took the beautiful, honey-tongued Liriope to his bed. Never known for fidelity, he had other lovers, including Oriana. The two might have become rivals, but instead became fast friends, who walked together through the royal gardens, dipped their feet into the Lake of Masks, and spun together through circle dances at revels.

Liriope had one son already, and few faeries are blessed twice with progeny, so she was surprised when she found herself with child again. And conflicted, because she'd had other lovers, too, and knew the father of the child was not Eldred, but his favorite son, Dain.

All his life, Prince Dain had planned to rule Elfhame after his father. He had prepared for it, creating what he called his Court of

Shadows, a group of spies and assassins that answered only to him. And he had sought to hasten his ascension to the throne, poisoning his father by incremental degrees to steal his vitality until he abdicated. So, when Liriope fell pregnant, Dain wasn't going to let his by-blow mess things up.

If Liriope bore Dain's child, and his father discovered it, Eldred might choose one of his other children for an heir. Better both mother and child should die, and Dain's future be assured.

Dain poisoned Liriope while Oak was still in the womb. Blusher mushrooms cause paralysis in small doses. In larger ones, the body slows its movements like a toy with a battery running down, slower and slower until it moves no more. Liriope died, and Oak would have died with her if Oriana hadn't carved him from her friend's body with a knife and her own soft hands.

That's how Oak came into the world, covered in poison and blood. Slashed across the thigh by a too-deep cut from Oriana's blade. Held desperately to her chest to smother his squalling.

No matter how loud he laughed or how merry he made, it would never drown that knowledge.

Oak knew what wanting the throne did to people.

He would never be like that.

After the ceremony, there was, of course, a banquet.

The royal family ate at a long table partially hidden from view beneath the branches of a weeping willow, not far from where the rest of the Court feasted. Oak sat at the right of Cardan, in the place of favor.

His sister Jude, at the opposite head of the table, slumped in her chair. In front of family, she was totally different from the way she was in front of the Folk: a performer offstage, still wearing her costume.

Oriana was put at Jude's right. Also a place of honor, although Oak wasn't sure either of them was particularly happy to have to make conversation with the other.

Oak had an abundance of sisters—Jude, Taryn, Vivi—all of them no more related to him than Oriana or the exiled grand general, Madoc, who had raised them. But they were still his family. The only two people at the entire table who were kin to him by blood were Cardan and the small child squirming in the chair to his right: Leander, Taryn's child with Locke, Oak's half brother.

An assortment of candles covered the table, and flowers had been tied to the hanging branches of the weeping willow, along with gleaming pieces of quartz. They made a beautiful bower. He would have probably appreciated it more had it been in anyone else's honor.

Oak realized he'd been so lost in his thoughts that he'd missed the beginning of a conversation.

"I didn't enjoy being a snake, and yet I appear to be doomed to be reminded of it for all eternity," Cardan was saying, black curls falling across his face. He held a three-pronged fork aloft, as though to emphasize his point. "The excess of songs hasn't helped, nor has their longevity. It's been what? Eight years? Nine? Truly, the celebratory air about the whole business has been excessive. You'd think I never did a more popular thing than sit in the dark on a throne and bite people who annoyed me. I could have always done that. I could do that now."

"Bite people?" echoed Jude from the other end of the table.

Cardan grinned at her. "Yes, if that's what they like." He snapped his teeth at the air as though to demonstrate.

"No one is interested in that," Jude said, shaking her head.

Taryn rolled her eyes at Heather, who smiled and took a sip of wine.

Cardan raised his brows. "I could *try*. A small bite. Just to see if someone would write a song about it."

"So," Oriana said, looking down the table at Oak. "You did very well up there. It made me imagine your coronation."

Vivi snorted delicately.

"I don't want to rule anything, no less Elfhame," Oak reminded her.

Jude kept her face carefully neutral through what appeared to be sheer force of will. "No need to worry. I don't plan on kicking the bucket anytime soon, and neither does Cardan."

Oak turned to the High King, who shrugged elegantly. "Seems hard on pointy boots, kicking buckets."

When Oak was Leander's age, Oriana hadn't wanted him to be king. But the years had made her more ambitious on his behalf. Perhaps she'd even begun to think that Jude had stolen his birthright instead of saved him from it.

He hoped not. It was one thing to flush out plots against the throne, but if he found out his mother was involved in one, he didn't know what he'd do.

Don't make me choose, he thought with a ferocity that unsettled him.

This was a problem that ought to solve itself. Jude was mortal. Mortals conceived children more easily than faeries. If she had a baby, it would supplant his claim to the throne.

Considering that, his gaze went to Leander.

Eight, and adorable, with his father's fox eyes. The same color as

Oak's, amber with a lot of yellow in it. Hair dark as Taryn's. Leander was almost the same age Oak had been when Madoc had schemed to get him the crown of Elfhame. When Oak looked at Leander, he saw the innocence that his sisters and mother must have been trying to protect. It gave him an ugly feeling, something that was anger and guilt and panic all mixed up together.

Leander noticed himself being studied and pulled on Oak's sleeve. "You look bored. Want to play a game?" he asked, harnessing the guile of a child eager to press someone into the service of amusement.

"After dinner," Oak told him with a glance at Oriana, who was already looking rather pained. "Your grandmother will be angry if we make a spectacle of ourselves at the table."

"*Cardan* plays with me," Leander said, obviously well prepared for this argument. "And he's the *High King*. He showed me how to make a bird with two forks and a spoon. Then our birds fought until one fell apart."

Cardan was spectacle incarnate and wouldn't care if Oriana scolded him. Oak could only smile, though. He had often been a child at a table of adults and remembered how dull it had been. He would have loved to fight with silverware birds. "What other games have you played with the king?"

That launched a distractingly long catalog of misbehavior, from tossing mushrooms into cups of wine on the other ends of tables to folding napkins into hats to making awful faces at each other. "And he tells me funny stories about my father, Locke," Leander concluded.

At that, Oak's smile stiffened. He barely remembered Locke. His clearest memories revolved around Locke's wedding to Taryn, and even those were mostly about how Heather had been turned into a cat and got really upset. It had been one of the moments that had made Oak realize that magic wasn't fun for everyone.

On that thought, he looked across the table at Heather, suddenly wanting to reassure himself she was okay. Her hair was in microbraids with strands of vibrant, synthetic pink woven through them. Her dark skin glowed with shimmering pink highlights on her cheeks. He tried to catch her eye, but she was too busy studying a tiny sprite attempting to steal a fig off the center of the table.

His gaze went to Taryn next. Locke's wife and murderer, tucking a lacy napkin into Leander's shirt. It would be no wonder if Heather was nervous to sit at this table. Oak's family was soaked in blood, the lot of them.

"How's Dad?" Jude asked abruptly, raising her eyebrows.

Vivi shrugged and nodded in Oak's direction. He'd been the one to see their father last. In fact, he'd spent a lot of time with their father over the past year.

"Keeping out of trouble," Oak said, hoping it stayed that way.

After dinner, the royal family rejoined the Court. Oak danced with Lady Elaine, who smiled her cat-who-swallowed-a-mouse-and-is-still-hungry smile and whispered in Oak's ear about how she was arranging a meeting in three days' time with some people who believed in "their cause."

"You're certain you can go through with this?" she asked him, breath hot against his neck. Her thick red hair hung down her back in a single wide braid, strands of rubies woven into the plaits. She wore a dress adorned with threads of gold, as though already auditioning to become his queen.

"I've never thought of Cardan as any relation of mine, but I have often resented what he took from me," Oak reassured her. And if he shuddered a little at her touch, she might imagine it was a shudder of passion. "I have been looking for just this opportunity."

And she, misunderstanding in just the way he hoped, smiled against his skin. "And Jude isn't your real sister."

At that, Oak smiled back but made no reply. He knew what she meant, but he could never have agreed.

She departed after the end of the dance, pressing a last kiss on his throat.

He *was* certain he could go through with this. Though it led inexorably to her death and he wasn't at all sure what that meant about him.

He'd done it before. When he glanced around the room, he couldn't help noticing the absence of those whom he'd already manipulated and then betrayed. Members of three conspiracies he'd undone in the past, tricking members into turning against one another—and him. They'd gone to the Tower of Forgetting or the chopping block for those crimes, never even knowing they'd fallen into his trap.

In this garden full of asps, he was a pitcher plant, beckoning them to a tumble. Sometimes there was a part of him that wanted to scream: *Look at me. See what I am. See what I've done.*

As though drawn by self-destructive thoughts, his bodyguard, Tiernan, approached with an accusatory look, brows drawn sharply together. He was dressed in banded leather armor with the crest of the royal family pinning a short cape across one shoulder. "You're making a scandal of yourself."

Conspiracies were often foolish things, wishful thinking combined with a paucity of interesting Court intrigues. Gossip and too much wine and too little sense. But he had a feeling this one was different. "She's arranging the meeting. It's almost over."

Tiernan cut his glance toward the throne and the High King lounging on it. "He knows."

"Knows what?" Oak had a sinking feeling in the pit of his stomach.

"Exactly? I'm not sure. But someone overheard something. The rumor is that you want to put a knife in his back."

Oak scoffed. "He's not going to believe that."

Tiernan gave Oak an incredulous look. "His own brothers betrayed him. He'd be a fool if he didn't."

Oak turned his attention to Cardan again, and this time the High King met his eyes. Cardan's eyebrows rose. There was a challenge in his gaze and the promise of lazy cruelty. *Game on.*

The prince turned away, frustrated. The last thing he wanted was for Cardan to think of him as an enemy. He ought to go to Jude. Try to explain.

Tomorrow, Oak told himself. When it would not spoil her evening. Or the day after next, when it would be too late for her to prevent him from meeting the conspirators, when he still might accomplish what he had hoped. When he learned who was behind the conspiracy. After that, he'd do his usual thing—pretend to panic. Tell the conspirators he wanted out. Give them reason to become afraid he was going to go to the High King and Queen with what he knew.

Attempting *his* murder was what he planned on their going down for, rather than treason. Because multiple attempts on Oak's life allowed him to retain his reputation for fecklessness. No one would guess that he deliberately brought down this conspiracy, leaving him free to do it again.

And Jude wouldn't guess he'd been putting himself in danger, not now and not those other times.

Unless, of course, he had to confess to all of it in order to convince Cardan he wasn't against him. A shudder went through him at the thought of how horrified Jude would be, how upset his whole family would get. His well-being was the thing they all used to justify their own sacrifices, their own losses. *At least Oak was happy, at least Oak had the childhood we didn't, at least Oak...*

Oak bit the inside of his cheek so hard he tasted blood. He needed to make sure his family never truly knew what he'd turned himself into. Once the traitors were caught, Cardan might forget about his suspicions. Maybe nothing needed to be said to anyone.

"Prince!" Oak's friend Vier pulled free from a knot of young courtiers to sling an arm over Oak's shoulder. "There you are. Come celebrate with us!"

Oak pushed his concerns aside with a forced laugh. It was his party, after all. And so he danced under the stars with the rest of the Court of Elfhame. Made merry. Played his part.

A pixie approached the prince, her skin grasshopper green, with wings to match. She brought two friends with her, and they twined their arms around his neck. Their mouths tasted of herbs and wine.

He moved from one partner to another in the moonlight, spinning beneath the stars. Laughing at nonsense.

A sluagh pressed herself to him, her lips stained black. He smiled down at her as they were swept up into another of the circle dances. Her mouth had the sweetness of bruised plums.

"Look at my face and I am someone," she whispered in his ear. "Look at my back and I am no one. What am I?"

"I don't know," Oak admitted, a shiver running between his shoulders.

"Your mirror, Highness," she said, her breath tickling the hairs on his neck.

And then she slipped away.

Hours later, Oak staggered back to the palace, his head hurting and dizziness making his steps uneven. In the mortal world, at seventeen, alcohol was illegal and, by consequence, something you hid. That night, however, he'd been expected to drink with every toast—blood-dark wines, fizzing green ones, and a sweet purple draught that tasted of violets.

Unable to discern whether he already had a hangover, or if something still worse was yet to come once he slept, Oak decided to try to find some aspirin. Vivi had handed a bag from Walgreens to Jude upon their arrival, one which he was almost certain contained painkillers.

He staggered toward the royal chambers.

"What are we doing here, exactly?" Tiernan asked, catching the prince's elbow when he stumbled.

"Looking for a remedy for what ails me," said Oak.

Tiernan, taciturn at the best of moments, only raised a brow.

Oak waved a hand at him. "You may keep your quips—spoken and unspoken—to yourself."

"Your Highness," Tiernan acknowledged, a judgment in and of itself.

The prince gestured toward the guard standing in front of the entrance to Jude and Cardan's rooms—an ogress with a single eye, leather armor, and short hair. "She can look after me from here."

Tiernan hesitated. But he would want to visit Hyacinthe, bored and angry and fomenting escape, as he'd been every night since being bridled. Tiernan didn't like leaving him too long alone for lots of reasons. "If you're sure..."

The ogress stood up straighter. "The High Queen is not in residence."

Oak shrugged. "That's okay." It was probably better for him to get the stuff when Jude wasn't there to laugh at the state of him. And while the ogress appeared not to like it, she didn't stop him from walking past her, pushing open one of the double doors, and going inside.

The chambers of the High King and Queen were hung with tapestries and brocades depicting magical forests hiding even more magical beasts, with most surfaces covered in unlit, fat pillar candles. Those would be for his sister, who couldn't see in the dark the way the Folk could.

Oak found the Walgreens bag tossed onto a painted table to one side of the bed. He dumped the contents onto the elaborately embroidered blanket thrown across a low couch.

There were, in fact, three bottles of store-brand ibuprofen. He opened one, stuck his thumb through the plastic seal, and fished out three gelcaps.

There was a castle alchemist he could go to who would give him a terrible-tasting potion if he was really hurting, but Oak didn't want to be prodded, nor make conversation while the cure was prepared. He tossed the pills back and dry-swallowed them.

Now what he needed was a lot of water and his bed.

Swaying a little, he started shoving the contents back into the bag. As he did, he noticed a packet of pills in a paper sleeve. Curious, he turned it over and then blinked down in surprise that it was a prescription. Birth control.

Jude was only twenty-six. Lots of twenty-six-year-olds didn't want kids yet. Or at all.

Of course, most of them didn't have to secure a dynasty.

Most weren't worried about cutting their little brother out of the line of succession, either. He hoped he wasn't the reason she was taking these. But even if he wasn't the only reason, he couldn't help thinking he was in the mix.

And on that dismal thought, he heard steps in the hall. Cardan's familiar drawling voice carried, although he couldn't make out the words.

Panicking, Oak shoved the rest of the drugstore stuff back into the bag, flung it onto the table, and then scrambled beneath. The door opened a moment later. Cardan's pointy boots clacked on the tiles, followed by Jude's soft tread.

As soon as Oak's belly hit the dusty floor, he realized how foolish he was being. Why hide, when neither Jude nor Cardan would have been angry to find him there? It was his own shame at invading his sister's privacy. Guilt and wine had combined to make him absurd. Yet he would be even more absurd if he emerged now, so he rested next to an abandoned slipper and hoped they left again before he sneezed.

His sister sat on one of the couches with a vast sigh.

"We cannot ransom him," Cardan said softly.

"I know that," Jude snapped. "I am the one who sent him into exile. I *know that*."

Were they speaking of his father? And ransom? Oak had been with them most of the night, and no mention had been made of this. But who else had she exiled that she would care enough to want to ransom? Then he remembered Jude's question at dinner. Perhaps she hadn't been asking after Madoc at all. Perhaps she'd been trying to determine whether any of them knew something.

Cardan sighed. "Let it be some comfort that we don't have what Lady Nore wants, even should we allow ourselves to be blackmailed."

Jude opened something out of the line of Oak's sight. He crawled a little to get a better angle and see the box of woven branches she had in her hand. Tangled in her fingers was a chain, strung with a glass orb. Inside it, something rolled restlessly. "The message speaks of Mellith's heart. Some ancient artifact? I think she looks for an excuse to hold him."

"If I didn't know better, I might think this is your brother's fault," Cardan said in a teasing tone, and Oak almost banged his head against the wood frame of the table in surprise at hearing himself referenced. "First, he wanted you to be nice to that little queen with the sharp teeth and the crazy eyes. Then he wanted you to forgive that former falcon his bodyguard likes for trying to murder me. It seems too great a coincidence that Hyacinthe came from Lady Nore, spent time with Madoc, and had no hand in his abduction."

Those words were laced with suspicion, although Cardan was smiling. His mistrust hardly mattered beside the danger their father was in, though.

"Oak got mixed up with the wrong people, that's all," Jude said wearily.

Cardan smiled, a curl of black hair falling in front of his face. "He's more like you than you want to see. Clever. *Ambitious.*"

"If what's happening is anyone's fault, it's mine," Jude said with another sigh. "For not ordering Lady Nore's execution when I had the chance."

"All the obscene snake songs must have been greatly distracting," Cardan said lightly, moving on from the discussion of Oak. "Generosity of spirit is so uncharacteristic in you."

They were silent for a moment, and Oak saw his sister's face. There was something private there, and painful. He hadn't known, back then, how close she'd come to losing Cardan forever, and maybe losing herself, too.

Mind slowed by drink, Oak was still putting all this information together. Lady Nore, of the Court of Teeth, held Madoc. And Jude wasn't going to try to get him back. Oak wanted to crawl out from beneath the table and plead with her. *Jude, we can't leave him there. We can't let him die.*

"Rumor has it that Lady Nore is creating an army of stick and stone and snow creatures," Jude murmured.

Lady Nore was from the old Court of Teeth. After allying with Madoc and attempting to steal the crown of Elfhame, her entire Court had been disbanded. Their best warriors—including Tiernan's beloved, Hyacinthe—were turned into birds. Madoc had been sent into exile. And Lady Nore had been made to swear fealty to the daughter she tormented: Suren. The little queen with the sharp teeth that Cardan mentioned.

Oak felt a flush of an unfamiliar emotion at the thought of her.

Remembered running away to her woods and the rasp of her voice in the dark.

His sister went on. "Whether Lady Nore wishes to use them to attack us or the mortal world or just have them fight for her amusement, we ought to stop her. If we delay, she has time to build up her forces. But attacking her stronghold would mean my father's death. If we move against her, he dies."

"We can wait," Cardan said. "But not long."

Jude frowned. "If she steps from that Citadel, I will cut her throat from ear to ear."

Cardan drew a dramatic line across his throat and then slumped exaggeratedly over, eyes closed, mouth open. Playing dead.

Jude scowled. "You need not make fun."

"Have I ever told you how much you sound like Madoc when you talk about murder?" Cardan said, opening one eye. "Because you do."

Oak expected his sister to be angry, but she only laughed. "That must be what you like about me."

"That you're terrifying?" he asked, his drawl becoming exaggeratedly languorous, almost a purr. "I adore it."

She leaned against him, resting her head on his shoulder, and closed her eyes. The king's arms came around her, and she shivered once, as though letting something fall away.

Watching her, Oak turned his thoughts to what he knew would happen. He, the useless youngest child, the heir, would be protected from the information that his father was in peril.

Hyacinthe would be dragged away for questioning. Or execution.

Probably both, one following on the other. He might well deserve it, too. Oak knew, as his sister did not yet, that Madoc had spoken with the former falcon many times in recent months. If Hyacinthe *was* responsible, Oak would cut his throat himself.

But what would come after that? Nothing. No help for their father. Lady Nore bought herself time to build the army Jude described, but eventually Elfhame would move against her. When war came, no one would be spared.

He had to act quickly.

Mellith's heart. That's what Lady Nore wanted. He wasn't sure if he could get it, but even if he couldn't, that didn't mean there wasn't a way to stop her. Though he hadn't seen Suren in years, he knew where she was, and he doubted anyone else in the High Court did. They'd been friends once. Moreover, Lady Nore had sworn a vow to her. She had the power of command over her mother. One word from her could end this conflict before it started.

The thought of seeking Wren out filled him with an emotion he didn't want to inspect too closely, as drunk and upset as he already was. But he could plan instead how he would use the secret passageway to sneak out of his sister's room once she was asleep, how he would interrogate Hyacinthe as Tiernan packed up their things. How he would go to Mandrake Market and find out more about this ancient heart from Mother Marrow, who knew nearly everything about everything.

The conspiracy would wait. It wasn't as though they could make their move without a candidate for the throne standing by.

Oak would save their father. Maybe he could never fix his family, but he could try to make up for what he'd already cost them. He could try to measure up to them. If he went, if he persuaded Wren, if they succeeded, then Madoc would live and Jude wouldn't have to make another impossible choice.

They would have all forbidden him from going, of course. But before they had a chance, he was already gone.

CHAPTER

1

The cold of the prisons eats at Oak's bones, and the stink of iron scrapes his throat. The bridle presses against his cheeks, reminding him that he is shackled to an obedience that binds him more securely than any chains. But worst of all is the dread of what will happen next, a dread so great that he wishes it would just *happen* so he could stop dreading it.

On the morning after he was locked in his cell in the stone dungeons beneath the Ice Needle Citadel of the former Court of Teeth, a servant brought him a blanket lined in rabbit fur. A kindness he didn't know how to interpret. No matter how tightly he wraps it around himself, though, he is seldom warm.

Twice each day he is brought food. Water, often with a rime of ice on the surface. Soup, hot enough to make him comfortable for a scant hour or so. As the days stretch on, he fears that, rather than putting his torment off, as one puts a particularly delicious morsel to the side of one's plate to be saved for last, he has simply been forgotten.

Once, he thought he recognized Wren's shadow, observing him from a distance. He called to her, but she didn't answer. Maybe she'd never been there. The iron muddles his thoughts. Perhaps he only saw what he so desperately wanted to see.

She has not spoken with him since she sent him here. Not even to use the bridle to command him. Not even to gloat.

Sometimes he screams into the darkness, just to remind himself that he can.

These dungeons were built to swallow screams. No one comes.

Today, he screams himself hoarse and then slumps against a wall. He wishes he could tell himself a story, but he cannot convince himself that he is a brave prince suffering a setback on a daring quest, nor the tempestuous, star-crossed lover he has played at so many times in the past. Not even the loyal brother and son he meant to be when he set out from Elfhame.

Whatever he is, he's certainly no hero.

A guard stomps down the hall, driving Oak to his hooves. One of the falcons. Straun. The prince has overheard him at the gate before, complaining, not realizing his voice carries. He is ambitious, bored by the tediousness of guard duty, and eager to show off his skill in front of the new queen.

Wren, whose beauty Straun rhapsodizes over.

Oak hates Straun.

"You there," the falcon says, drawing close. "Be quiet before I quiet you."

Ah, Oak realizes. He's so bored that he wants to make something happen.

"I am merely trying to give this dungeon an authentic atmosphere," Oak says. "What's a place like this without the cries of the tormented?"

"Traitor's son, you think much of yourself, but you know nothing of torment," Straun says, kicking the iron bars with the heel of his boot, making them ring. "Soon, though. Soon, you'll learn. You should save your screams."

Traitor's son. Interesting. Not just bored, then, but resentful of Madoc.

Oak steps close enough to the bars that he can feel the heat of the iron. "Does Wren intend to punish me, then?"

Straun snorts. "Our queen has more important things to attend to than you. She's gone to the Stone Forest to wake the troll kings."

Oak stares at him, stunned.

The falcon grins. "Worry not, though. The storm hag is still here. Maybe *she'll* send for you. Her punishments are legendary." With that, he walks back toward the gate.

Oak sags to the cold floor, furious and despairing.

You have to break out. The thought strikes him forcefully. *You must find a way.*

Not easy, that. The iron bars burn. The lock is hard to pick, though he tried once with a fork. All he managed to do was snap off one of the tines and ensure that all subsequent food was sent only with spoons.

Not easy to escape. And besides, maybe, after everything, Wren still might visit him.

Oak wakes on the stone floor of his cell with his head ringing and his breath clouding in the air. He blinks in confusion, still half in dreams. He's seldom able to sleep deeply with so much iron around him, but that's not what woke him tonight.

A great cresting wave of magic washes over the Citadel, coursing from somewhere south, crashing down with unmistakable power. Then there is a tremble in the earth, as though something massive moved upon it.

It comes to him then that the Stone Forest is south of the Citadel. The trembling is not something moving upon the earth but something disgorged from it. *Wren did it.* She has released the troll kings from their bondage beneath the ground.

Broken an ancient curse, one so old that for Oak it seems woven into the fabric of the world, as implacable as the sea and sky.

He can almost hear the cracking sound of the rocks that imprisoned them. Fissures spider-webbing out from two directions at once, from both boulders. Waves of magical force flowing from those twinned centers, intense enough that nearby trees would split apart, sending the ice-crusted blue fruit to scatter on the snow.

He can almost see the two ancient troll kings, rising up from the earth, stretching for the first time in centuries. Tall as giants, shaking off all that had grown over them in their slumber. Dirt and grass, small trees, and rocks would all rain down from their shoulders.

Wren had done it.

And since that is supposed to be impossible, the prince has no idea what she might do next.

Since he's unlikely to be able to sleep again, Oak goes through the exercises the Ghost taught him long ago so that he could still practice while stuck in the mortal world.

Imagine you have a weapon. They had been in Vivi's second apartment, standing on a small metal balcony. Inside, Taryn and Vivi had been fussing over Leander, who was learning to crawl. The Ghost had asked about Oak's training and been uninterested in the excuse that he was eleven, had to go to school, and couldn't be swinging around a longsword in the common space of the lawn without neighbors getting worried.

Oh, come on! Oak laughed, thinking the spy was being silly.

The Ghost conjured the illusion of a blade out of thin air, its hilt decorated with ivy. His glamour was so good that Oak had to look closely to see that it wasn't real. *Your turn, prince.*

Oak had actually liked making his own sword. It was huge and black with a bright red hilt covered in demonish faces. It looked like the sword of someone in an anime he'd been watching, and he felt like a badass, holding it in his hands.

The sight of Oak's blade had made the Ghost smile, but he didn't laugh. Instead, he started moving through a series of exercises, urging Oak to follow. He told the prince he should call him by his nonspy name, Garrett, since they were friends.

You can do this, the Ghost—Garrett—told him. *When you have nothing else.*

Nothing else *to practice with,* he probably meant. Although right now, Oak has nothing else, full stop.

The exercises warm him just enough to be halfway comfortable when he wraps the blanket around his shoulders.

The prince has been imprisoned three weeks, according to the tallies he's made in the dust beneath the lone bench. Long enough to dwell on every mistake he has made on his ill-fated quest. Long enough to endlessly reconsider what he ought to have done in the swamp after the Thistlewitch turned to him and spoke in her raspy voice: *Didn't you know, prince of foxes, what you already had? What a fine jest, to look for Mellith's heart when she walks beside you.*

At the memory, Oak stands and paces the floor, his hooves clattering restlessly against the black stone. He should have told her the truth. Should have told her and accepted the consequences.

Instead, he convinced himself that keeping the secret of her origin protected her, but was that true? Or was it more true that he'd manipulated her, the way he manipulated everyone in his life? That was what he was good at, after all—tricks, games, insincerity.

His family must be in a panic right now. He trusts that Tiernan got Madoc to Elfhame safely, no matter what the redcap general wanted. But Jude would be furious with Tiernan for leaving Oak behind and even angrier with Madoc, if she guesses just how much of this is his fault.

Possibly Cardan would be relieved to be rid of Oak, but that wouldn't stop Jude from making a plan to get him back. Jude has been ruthless on Oak's behalf before, but this is the first time it's scared him. Wren is dangerous. She is not someone to cross. Neither of them are.

He recalls the press of Wren's sharp teeth against his shoulder. The nervous fumble of her kiss, the shine of her wet eyes, and how he repaid her reluctant trust with deception. Again and again in his mind, he sees the betrayal on her face when she realized what an enormous secret he'd kept.

It doesn't matter if you deserve to be in her prisons, he tells himself. *You still need to get out.*

Sitting in the dark, he listens to the guards play dice games. They have opened a jug of a particularly strong juniper liquor in celebration of Wren's accomplishment. Straun is the loudest and drunkest of the bunch, and the one losing the most coin.

Oak dozes off and wakes to the tread of soft footfalls. He surges to his hooves, moving as close to the iron bars as he dares.

A huldu woman comes into view, bearing a tray, her tail swishing behind her.

Disappointment is a pit in his stomach.

"Fernwaif," he says, and her eyes go to his. He can see the wariness in them.

"You remember my name," she says, as though it's some kind of trick. As though princes have the attention spans of gnats.

"Most certainly I do." He smiles, and after a moment, she visibly relaxes, her shoulders lowering.

He wouldn't have noted that reaction before. After all, smiles were *supposed* to reassure people. Just maybe not quite so much as his smiles did.

Maybe you can't help it. Maybe you do it without knowing. That's what Wren had said when he claimed he didn't use his honey-mouthed charm, his gancanagh ability, anymore. He'd stuck to the rules Oriana had given him. Sure, he knew the right things to say to make someone *like* him, but he'd told himself that wasn't the same as just giving himself over to the magic, not the same as enchanting them.

But sitting in the dark, he has reconsidered. What if the power leaches out of him like a miasma? Like a poison? Perhaps the seducing of conspirators he'd done wasn't his being clever or companionable; instead, he was using a power they couldn't fight against. What if he is a much worse person than he's supposed?

And as though to prove it, he presses his advantage, magical or not.

He smiles more broadly at Fernwaif. "You're far superior company to the guard who brought my food yesterday," he tells her with utter sincerity, thinking of a troll who wouldn't so much as meet his gaze. Who spilled half his water on the ground and then grinned at him, showing a set of cracked teeth.

Fernwaif snorts. "I don't know if that's much of a compliment."

It wasn't. "Shall I tell you instead that your hair is like spun gold, your eyes like sapphires?"

She giggles, and he can see her cheeks are pink as she pulls out the empty bowls near the slot at the bottom of the cell and replaces them with the new tray. "You best not."

"I can do better," he says. "And perhaps you might bring me a little gossip to cheer the chilly monotony of my days."

"You're very silly, Your Highness," she says after a moment, biting her bottom lip a little.

His gaze travels, evaluating the pockets of her dress for the weight of keys. Her blush deepens.

"I am," he agrees. "Silly enough to have gotten myself into this predicament. I wonder if you could take a message to Wr—to your new queen?"

She looks away. "I dare not," she says, and he knows he ought to leave it at that.

He remembers Oriana's warning to him when he was a child. *A power like the one you have is dangerous*, she said. *You can know what other people most want to hear. Say those things, and they will not only want to listen to you. They will come to want you above all other things. The love that a gancanagh inspires—some may pine away for desire of it. Others will carve the gancanagh to pieces to be sure no one else has it.*

He made a mistake when he first went to school in the mortal world. He felt alone at the mortal school, and so when he made a friend, he wanted to keep him. And he knew just how. It was easy; all he had to do was say the right things. He remembers the taste of the power on his tongue, supplying words he didn't even understand. Soccer and *Minecraft*, praise for the boy's drawings. Not lies, but nowhere near the truth, either. They had fun together, running around the playground, drenched in sweat, or playing video games in the boy's basement. They had fun together until he found that when they were apart, even for a few hours, the boy wouldn't speak. Wouldn't eat. Would just wait until he saw Oak again.

With that memory in his mind, Oak stumbles on, forcing his mouth into a smile he hopes looks real. "You see, I wish to let your queen know that I await her pleasure. I am hers to command, and I hope she will come and do just that."

"You don't want to be saved?" Fernwaif smiles. She's the one teasing him now. "Shall I inform my mistress that you are so tame she can let you out?"

"Tell her...," Oak says, keeping his astonishment at the news she's returned to the Citadel off his face through sheer force of will. "Tell her that I am wasted in all this gloom."

Fernwaif laughs, her eyes shining as though Oak is a romantic figure in a tale. "She asked me to come today," the huldu girl confides in a whisper.

That seems hopeful. The first hopeful thing he's heard in a while.

"Then I greatly desire your report of me to be a favorable one," he says, and makes a bow.

Her cheeks are still pink with pleasure when she leaves, departing with light steps. He can see the swish of her tail beneath her skirts.

Oak watches her go before bending down and inspecting his tray—a mushroom pie, a ramekin of jam, an entire steaming teapot with a cup, a glass of melted snow water. Nicer food than usual. And yet he finds he has little appetite for it.

All he can think of is Wren, whom he has every reason to fear and desires anyway. Who may be his enemy and a danger to everyone else he loves.

Oak kicks his hoof against the stone wall of his cage. Then he goes to pour himself a cup of the pine needle tea before it cools. The warmth of the pot on his hands limbers his fingers enough that, had he another fork, he would try that lock again.

That night, he wakes to the sight of a snake crawling down the wall, its black metal body jeweled and glittering. A forked emerald tongue tastes the air at regular intervals, like a metronome.

It startles him badly enough for him to back up against the bars, the iron hot against his shoulders. He has seen creatures like it before, forged by the great smiths of Faerie. Valuable and dangerous.

The paranoid thought comes to him that poison would be one straightforward way to solve the problem of his being held by an enemy of Elfhame. If he were dead, there'd be no reason to pay a ransom.

He doesn't think his sister would allow it, but there are those who might risk going around her. Grima Mog, the new grand general, would know *exactly* where to find the prince, having served the Court of Teeth herself. Grima Mog might look forward to the war it would start. And, of course, she answered to Cardan as much as Jude.

Not to mention there was always the *possibility* that Cardan convinced Jude that Oak was a danger to them both.

"Hello," he whispers warily to the snake.

It yawns widely enough for him to see silver fangs. The links of its body move, and a ring comes up from its throat, clanging to the floor. He leans down and lifts it. A gold ring with a deep blue stone, scuffed with wear. His ring, a present from his mother on his thirteenth birthday and left behind on his dresser because it no longer fit his finger. Proof that this creature was sent from Elfhame. Proof that he was supposed to trust it.

"Prinss," it says. "In three daysssss, you mussss be ready for ressssss-cue."

"Rescue?" Not here to poison him, then.

The snake just stares with its cold, glittering eyes.

Many nights, he hoped someone would come for him. Even though he wanted it to be Wren, there were plenty of times he imagined the Bomb blowing a hole in the wall and getting him out.

But now that it's a real possibility, he's surprised by how he feels.

"Give me longer," he says, no matter that it's ridiculous to negotiate with a metal snake and even more ridiculous to negotiate for his own imprisonment, just in order to get a chance to speak with someone who refuses to see him. "Two more weeks perhaps. A month."

If he could only *talk* to Wren, he could explain. Maybe she wouldn't forgive him, but if she saw he wasn't her enemy, that would be enough. Even convincing her that she didn't have to be an enemy to Elfhame would be something.

"Three daysssssss," it says again. Its enchantment is either too simple to decode his protests or it has been told to ignore them. "Be rehhhhdy."

Oak slides the ring onto his pinkie finger, watching the snake as it coils its way up the wall. Halfway to the ceiling, he realizes that just because it wasn't sent to poison him doesn't mean it wasn't sent to poison *someone*.

He jumps onto the bench and grabs for it, catching the end of its tail. With a tug, it comes off the wall, falling against his body and coiling around his forearm.

"Prinsssss," it hisses. As it opens its mouth to speak, he notes the tiny holes in the points of its silvery fangs.

When it does not strike, Oak pries the snake carefully from around his arm. Then, gripping the end of its tail firmly, he slams it down against the stone bench. Hears the cracking of its delicate mechanical parts. A gem flies off. So does a piece of metal. He whips it against the bench again.

A sound like the whistle of a teakettle comes from it, and its coils writhe. He brings its body down hard twice more, until it is broken and utterly still.

Oak feels relieved and awful at the same time. Perhaps it was no more alive than one of the ragwort steeds, but it had spoken. It had seemed alive.

He sinks to the floor. Inside the metal creature, he finds a glass vial, now cracked. The liquid inside is bloodred and clotted. Blusher mushroom. The one poison unlikely to harm him. Welcome proof that his sister doesn't want him dead. Maybe Cardan doesn't, either.

The snake is limp in his hands, the magic gone from it. He trembles to think of what could have happened had the creature been sent to visit Wren *before* finding him in the prisons. Or if his iron-addled mind had only realized the danger too late.

Three days.

He can no longer dawdle. No longer dread. No longer scheme. He has to act, and fast.

Oak listens for the changing of the guard. Once he hears Straun's voice, he bangs on the bars until the guard comes. It takes a long time, but not as long as it might have if Straun wasn't in a foul mood from a night of drinking and losing money at dice.

"Didn't I tell you to shut up?" the falcon roars.

"You're going to get me out of this cell," Oak says.

Straun pauses, then sneers, but there's a little wariness in it. "Have you run mad, princeling?"

Oak holds out his hand. A collection of gemstones rests in his scratched palm. He spent the better part of the night prying them out of the body of the snake. Each is worth ten times what Straun gambled away.

The falcon snorts in disgust but cannot disguise his interest. "You intend to bribe me?"

"Will it work?" Oak asks, walking to the edge of his cell. He's not sure if it's his magic urging him on or not.

Almost against his will, Straun steps closer. Good. The prince can smell the sharpness of the juniper liquor on his breath. Perhaps he is still a little drunk. Even better.

Oak reaches his right hand halfway through the bars, lifting it so the gems catch the faint edge of torchlight. He slides his other hand through, too, lower.

Straun smacks Oak's arm hard. His skin hits the iron bar on his cell, burning. The prince howls as the gems fall, most scattering across the corridor between the cells.

"Didn't think I was half so clever as you, did you?" Straun laughs as he gathers up the stones, not having promised a single thing.

"I did not," Oak admits.

Straun spits on the floor in front of the prince's cage. "No amount of gold or gems will save you. If my winter queen wants you to rot here, you're going to rot."

"*Your* winter queen?" Oak repeats, unable to stop himself.

The falcon looks a little shamefaced and turns to go back to his post. He's young, Oak realizes. Older than Oak, but not by so very much. Younger than Hyacinthe. It shouldn't be a surprise that Wren made such an impression on him.

It shouldn't bother Oak, shouldn't fill him with a ferocious jealousy.

What the prince needs to concentrate on is the key in his left hand. The one he grabbed from the loop at Straun's belt when the falcon smacked his right arm. Straun, who was, thankfully, *exactly* as clever as Oak had supposed him to be.

The key fits smoothly into the lock of Oak's cell. It turns so soundlessly it might as well have been greased.

Not that Straun is likely to come back to check on him, no matter how loud he bangs on the bars. The guard will be feeling smug. Well, let him.

The prince lifts a piece of cloth he's torn from his shirt and soaked in blusher mushroom liquid salvaged from the snake. Then he starts down the hall, his breath clouding in the cold air.

The Ghost taught him how to move stealthily, but he's never been very good at it. He blames his hooves, heavy and hard. They clack at the worst possible times. But he makes an effort, sliding them against the floor to minimize noise.

Straun is grumbling to another guard about how the others are cheats, refusing to play any more dice games. Oak waits until one leaves to bring back more refreshments and listens hard to the retreating steps of boots.

After he's sure there's only one guard there, he tries the gate. It's not even locked. He supposes there's no reason for it to be when there's only one prisoner, and he wears a bridle to keep him obedient.

Oak moves fast, jerking Straun backward and covering his nose and mouth with the cloth. The guard struggles, but inhaling blusher mushroom slows his movements. Oak presses him to the floor until he's unconscious.

From there, it's just a matter of arranging his body so that when the other guard returns, he might believe he's dozed off. It's hard for Oak to leave the guard's sword at his hip, but its absence would almost certainly give him away. He does, however, snatch up the cloak he finds hanging on a hook beside the door.

O ak takes the stairs, careful now.

He has the surreal feeling of being in a video game. He played enough of them, sitting on Vivi's couch. Creeping through pixelated rooms that had more of the appearance of Madoc's stronghold where he grew up than anywhere they went in the mortal world. Leaning on Heather's shoulder, controller in his hands. Killing people. Hiding the bodies.

This is a stupid, ugly, violent game, Vivi said. *Life isn't like that.* And Jude, who was visiting, raised her eyebrows and said nothing.

He recalls following Wren through these icy halls. Killing people. Hiding the bodies.

There are more visitors to the Citadel now than there were then; ironically, that makes it easier to be overlooked. There are so many new faces, neighboring Folk arriving to discover the nature of the new lady and curry her favor. Well-dressed nisse and huldufólk courtiers gather in knots, passing gossip. Trolls size one another up, and a few selkies hang around at the edges, no doubt gathering news of a rising power to take back to the Undersea.

Oak cannot blend in, not in his worn and filthy clothes, not with the straps of Grimsen's bridle tight to his cheeks. He sticks to the shadows, putting up the hood of the cloak and moving with slow deliberation.

After growing up with servants in his father's stronghold in Faerie and then without any when he was in the mortal world, the prince is very aware of what it takes to keep a castle like this one running. As a small child, he was used to his dirty clothing disappearing from his floor and returning to his armoire, cleaned and hung. But after he and Vivi and Heather had to carry bags of laundry to the basement of their apartment building and feed quarters into a machine, along with detergent and fabric softener, he realized that *someone* must have been performing a related service for him in Faerie.

And someone is performing that service here in the Citadel, washing linens and uniforms. Oak heads in the direction of the kitchens, figuring the flames of the ovens are likely the same ones used to heat the tubs of water necessary to clean fabric. Real fire would be easier to keep confined to the stone basements and first floor of the Citadel.

Oak keeps his head down, although the servants barely spare him a glance. They rush through the halls. He's sure the household is vastly understaffed.

It takes him a tense twenty minutes of creeping about before a change in the humidity of the air and the scent of soap reveal the laundry area. He pushes open the door to the room gingerly and is relieved to find no servant currently doing the wash. Three steaming vats rest on the black rock floor. Dirty bedding, tablecloths, and uniforms soak inside them. Clean linens hang from ropes strung overhead.

Oak pulls off his own filthy garments, dropping them into the water before stepping in, too.

He feels a bit foolish as he wades into a vat, naked. Should he be discovered, he will doubtless have to play the silly, carefree prince, so vain that he escaped his prison for a bath. It would be a crowning achievement of embarrassment.

The soapy water is merely warm, but it feels deliciously hot after being so chilled for so long. He shudders with the pleasure of it, the muscles in his limbs relaxing. He dunks himself, submerging his head and scrubbing at his skin with his fingernails until he feels clean. He wants to stay there, to float in water as it grows ever more tepid. For a moment, he allows himself to do just that. To stare at the ceiling of the room, which is black stone, too, although above this level, the walls, floors, and ceilings are all of ice.

And Wren, somewhere inside them. If he could just speak to her, even for a moment . . .

Oak knows it's ridiculous, and yet he can't help feeling as though they have an *understanding* of each other, one that transcends this admittedly not-great moment. She will be angry when he talks with her, of course. He deserves her anger.

He has to tell her that he regrets what he did. He's not sure what happens after that.

Nor is he sure what it means about him that he finds hope in the fact that Wren has *kept* him. Fine, not everyone would see being thrown into a dungeon as a romantic gesture, but he's choosing to at least consider the possibility that she put him there because she wants something more from him.

Something beyond, say, skinning him and leaving his rotting corpse for ravens to pick over.

On that thought, he splashes his way out of the tub.

Among the drying uniforms, he finds one that seems as though it will fit him—certainly fit better than the bloodstained one he used to get into the palace weeks ago. It's damp, but not so much as to draw notice, and only slightly too tight across his chest. Still, dressed this way and with the hood of the cloak pulled forward to hide his face, he might be able to walk straight out the door of the Citadel, as though he were going on patrol.

It would serve her right for never coming to see him, not even to use the bridle and command him to stay put.

He's not sure how far he could get in the snow, but he still has three of the stones from the snake. He might be able to bribe someone to take him in their carriage. And even if he didn't want to risk that, he might well find his own horse in the stables, since Hyacinthe was the one who stole Damsel Fly and Hyacinthe is now Wren's second-in-command.

Either way, he'd be free. Free to not need rescuing. Free to attempt to talk his sister out of whatever homicidal plan she might foment against the Citadel. Free to return home and go back to performing feckless-ness, back to sharing the bed of anyone he thought might be planning a political coup, back to being an heir who never wants to inherit.

And never seeing Wren again.

Of course, he might not make it to Jude in time for her to know he was free, to stop whatever plans she set in motion. Whatever murders her people would commit in his name. And then, of course, there would be the question of what Wren did in retaliation.

Not that he knows how to stop either of them if he remains here. He's not sure *anyone* knows how to stop Jude. And Wren has the power of annihilation. She can break curses and tear spells to pieces with barely any effort. She took apart Lady Nore as though she were a stick creature and spread her insides over the snow.

Really, that memory alone should send the prince out of the Citadel as quickly as his legs could carry him.

He pulls the hood of the cloak down over his face and heads toward the Great Hall. Getting a glimpse of her feels more like a compulsion than a decision.

He can feel the gaze of courtiers drift toward him—covering one's face in a hood is unusual, at the very least. He keeps his own eyes unfocused and his shoulders back, though his every instinct screams to meet their looks. But he is dressed like a soldier, and a soldier would not turn.

It is harder to pass falcons and to know they might spot his hooves and wonder. But he is hardly the only one to have hooves in Faerie. And everyone who knows that the Prince of Elfhame is in the Citadel believes him to be locked up tight.

Which doesn't make him any less of a fool for coming into the throne room. When everything goes wrong, he will have no one to blame but himself.

Then he sees Wren, and longing shoots through him like a kick to the gut. He forgets about risk. Forgets about schemes.

Somewhere in the crowd, a musician plucks at a lute. Oak barely hears it.

The Queen of the Ice Citadel sits upon her throne, wearing a severe black dress that shows her bare pale blue shoulders. Her hair is a tumble of azure, some strands pulled back, a few pieces braided through with black branches. On her head is a crown of ice.

In the Court of Moths, Wren flinched away from the gazes of courtiers as she entered the revel on his arm, as though their very notice stung. She curled her body so that, small as she was, she appeared even smaller.

Now her shoulders are back. Her demeanor is that of someone who does not consider anyone in this room—not even Bogdana—a threat. He flashes on a memory of her younger self. A little girl with a crown sewn to her skin, her wrists leashed by chains that threaded between bones and flesh. No fear in her face. That child was terrifying, but no matter how she seemed, she was also terrified.

"The delegation of hags has come," snaps Bogdana. "Give me the remains of Mab's bones and restore my power so that I can lead them again."

The storm hag stands before the throne, in the place of the petitioner, although nothing about her suggests submission. She wears a long black shroud, tattered in places. Her fingers move expressively as she speaks, sweeping through the air like knives.

Behind her are two Folk. An old woman with the talons of some bird of prey instead of feet (or hooves) and a man shrouded in a cloak. Only his hand is visible, and that is covered in what seems to be a scaled, golden glove. Or perhaps his hand itself is scaled and golden.

Oak blinks. He knows the woman with the feet like a bird of prey. That's Mother Marrow, who operates out of Mandrake Market on the isle of Insmire. Mother Marrow, whom the prince went to at the very start of his quest, asking for guidance. She sent him to the Thistlewitch for answers about Mellith's heart. He tries to recall now, all these weeks later, whether she'd said anything that might have put him in Bogdana's path.

Knots of courtiers are scattered around the room, gossiping, making it hard to hear Wren's soft reply. Oak steps closer, his arm brushing against a nisse. She makes an expression of annoyance, and he shifts away.

"Have I not suffered long enough?" asks Bogdana.

"You would speak to me of suffering?" Nothing in Wren's expression is soft or yielding or shy. She is every bit the pitiless winter queen.

Bogdana frowns, perhaps a little unnerved. Oak feels somewhat unnerved himself. "Once I have them, my might will be restored—me, who was once first among hags. That's what I gave up to secure your future."

"Not *my* future." There is a hollowness to Wren's cheeks, Oak notices. She's thinner than she was, and her eyes shine with a feverish brightness.

Has she been ill? Is this because of the wound in her side when she was struck by an arrow?

"Do you not have Mellith's heart?" demands the storm hag. "Are you not her, reborn into the world through my magic?"

Wren does not reply immediately, letting the moment stretch out. Oak wonders if Bogdana has ever realized that the trade she made must have ruined her daughter's life, long before it led to her horrible death. From the Thistlewitch's tale, Mellith must have been *miserable* as Mab's heir. And since Wren has at least some of Mellith's memories in addition to her own, she has plenty of reasons to hate the storm hag.

Bogdana is playing a dangerous game.

"I have her heart, yes," says Wren slowly. "Along with part of a curse. But I am not a child, no less *your* child. Do not think you can so easily manipulate me."

The storm hag snorts. "You are a child still."

A muscle jumps in Wren's jaw. "I am your queen."

Bogdana does not contradict her this time. "You have need of my strength. And you have need of my companions if you hope to continue as you are."

Oak stiffens at those words, wondering at their meaning.

Wren stands, and courtiers turn their attention to her, their conversations growing hushed. Despite her youth and her small stature, she has vast power.

And yet, Oak notices that she sways a little before gripping the arm of her throne. Forcing herself upright.

Something is very wrong.

Bogdana made this request in front of a crowd rather than in private and named herself as Wren's maker. Called Wren a child. Threatened her sovereignty. Brought in two of her hag friends. These were desperate, aggressive moves. Wren must have been putting her off for some time. But also, the storm hag may have thought she was attacking in a moment of weakness.

First among the hags. He doesn't like the thought of Bogdana being more powerful than she already is.

"Queen Suren," says Mother Marrow, stepping forward with a bow. "I have traveled a long way to meet you—and to give you this." She opens her palm. A white walnut sits at the center of it.

Wren hesitates, no longer quite as remote as she seemed a moment before. Oak recalls the surprise and delight in her face when he bought her a mere hair ornament. She hasn't been given many presents since she was stolen from her mortal home. Mother Marrow was clever to bring her something.

"What does it do?" A smile twitches at the corners of Wren's mouth, despite everything.

Mother Marrow's smile goes a little crooked. "I have heard you've been traveling much of late and spending time in forest and fen. Crack the nut and say my little poem, and a cottage will appear. Bring the two halves together again with another verse, and it will return to its shell. Shall I demonstrate?"

"I think we need not conjure a whole building in the throne room," Wren says.

A few courtiers titter.

Mother Marrow does not seem discomfited in the least. She walks to Wren and deposits the white walnut in her hand. "Remember these words, then. To conjure it, say: *We are weary and wish to rest our bones. Broken shell, bring me a cottage of stones.*"

The nut in Wren's hand gives a little jump at the words but then is quiescent once more.

Mother Marrow continues speaking. "And to send it away: *As halves are made whole and these words resound, back into the walnut shell shall my cottage be bound.*"

"It is a kind gift. I've never seen anything like it." Wren's hands curl around it possessively, belying the lightness of her tone. He thinks of the shelter she made from willow branches back in her woods and imagines how well she would have liked to have something solid and safe to sleep in. A well-considered gift, indeed.

The man steps forward. "Though I do not like to be outdone, I have nothing so fine to give you. But Bogdana summoned me here to see if I can undo what—"

"That is enough," Wren says, her voice as harsh as Oak has ever heard it.

He frowns, wishing she'd have let the man finish. But it was interesting that for all the damning things she allowed Bogdana to say, whatever he wanted to undo was the one thing she didn't want her Court to hear.

"Child," Bogdana cautions her. "If my mistakes can be unmade, then let me unmake them."

"You spoke of power," Wren snaps. "And yet you suppose I will let you strip me of mine."

Bogdana begins to speak again, but as Wren descends from the throne, guards gather around her. She heads toward the double doors of the Great Hall, leaving the storm hag behind.

Wren sweeps past Oak without a look.

The prince follows her into the hall. Watches the guards accompany her to her tower and begin to ascend.

He follows, staying to the back, blending in with a knot of soldiers.

When they are almost to her rooms, he lets himself fall behind farther. Then he opens a random door and steps inside.

For a moment, he braces for a scream, but the room is—thankfully—empty. Clothing hangs in an open armoire. Pins and ribbons are scattered across a low table. One of the courtiers must be staying here, and Oak is very lucky not to be caught.

Of course, the longer he waits, the luckier he will have to be.

Still, he can hardly barge into Wren's rooms now. The guards would not have left yet. And there would certainly be servants—even with so few in the castle—attending her.

Oak paces back and forth, willing himself to be calm. His heart is racing. He is thinking of the Wren he saw, a Wren as distant as the coldest, farthest star in the sky. He cannot even focus on the room itself, which he should almost certainly hunt through to find a weapon or mask or something useful.

But instead he counts the minutes until he believes he can safely—well, as safely as possible, given the inherent danger of this impulsive plan—go to Wren's rooms. He finds no guard waiting in the hall—unsurprising, given the narrowness of the tower, but excellent. No voices come from inside.

What is surprising is that when he turns the knob, the door opens.

He steps into her rooms, expecting Wren's anger. But only silence greets him.

A low couch sits along one wall, a tray with a teapot and cups on the table in front of it. In a corner beside it, the ice crown rests on a pillow atop a pillar. And across the room, a bed hung with curtains depicting thorned vines and blue flowers.

He walks to it and sweeps the fabric aside.

Wren is sleeping, her pale cerulean hair spread out over the pillows. He recalls brushing it out when they were in the Court of Moths. Recalls the wild tangle of it and the way she held herself very still while his hands touched her.

Her eyes move restlessly under their lids, as though she doesn't even feel safe in dreams. Her skin has a glassy quality, as though from sweat or possibly ice.

What has she been doing to herself?

He takes a step closer, knowing he shouldn't. His hand reaches out, as though he might graze his fingers over her cheek. As though to prove to himself that she's real, and there, and alive.

He doesn't touch her, of course. He's not that much of a fool.

But as though she can sense him, Wren opens her eyes.

Wren blinks up at Oak, and he gives her what he hopes is an apologetic grin. Her startled expression smooths out into puzzlement and some emotion he is less able to name. She reaches up, and he bends lower, going to one knee, so that she can brush her fingers over the nape of his neck. He shivers at her touch. Looking down into her dark green eyes, he tries to read her feelings in the minute shifts of her countenance. He thinks he sees a longing there to match his own.

Wren's lips part on a sigh.

"I want—" he begins.

"No," she tells him. "By the power of Grimsen's bridle, get on your knees and be silent."

Surprise makes him try to pull away, to stand, but he cannot. His teeth close on the words he now cannot say.

It's an awful feeling, his body turning against him. He was on one knee already, but his other leg bends without his deciding to move. As his calves strike the frozen floor, he understands, in a way that he never has before, Wren's horror of the bridle. Jude's need for control. He has never known this kind of helplessness.

Her mouth curves into a smile, but it isn't a nice one. "By Grimsen, I command you to do exactly as I say from here forward. You will stay on your knees until I say otherwise."

Oak should have left when he had the chance.

She rises from the bed and draws on a dressing gown. Walks over to where he kneels.

He looks at her slippered foot. Glances up at the rest of her. A strand of light blue hair has fallen across one scarred cheek. Her lips have a little pink at the inner edges, like the inside of a shell.

It is hard to imagine her as she was when they began their quest, a feral girl who seemed like the living embodiment of the woods. Wild and brave and kind. There is no shyness in her gaze now. No kindness, either.

He finds her fascinating. He's always found her fascinating, but he is not foolish enough to tell her that. Especially not in this moment, when he is afraid of her.

"You've gone to a lot of trouble to see me again, prince," Wren says. "I understand that you called for me in your cell."

He screamed for her. Screamed until his throat was hoarse. But even if he was allowed to speak, clarifying that would only compound his many, many mistakes.

She goes on. "How frustrating it must be not to have *everyone* eager to comply with your desires. How impatient you must have become."

Oak tries to push himself to his hooves.

She must note the impotent flex of his muscles. "How impatient you are even yet. Speak, if you wish."

"I came here to repent," he says, taking what he hopes will be a steadying breath. "I should never have kept what I knew from you. Certainly not something like that. No matter how I thought I was protecting you, no matter how desperate I was to help my father, it wasn't my place. I did you a grievous wrong, and I am sorry."

A long moment passes. Oak stares at her slipper, not sure he can bear to look into her face. "I am not your enemy, Wren. And if you throw me back into your dungeons, I won't have a chance to show you how remorseful I am, so please don't."

"A pretty speech." Wren walks to the head of her bed, where a long pull dangles from a hole bored into the ice wall. She gives it a hard tug. Somewhere far below, he can hear the faint ringing of a bell. Then the sound of boots on the stairs.

"I am already bridled," he says, feeling a little frantic. "You don't need to lock me away. I can't harm you unless you let me. I am entirely in your power. And when I did escape, I came directly to your side. Let me kneel at your feet in the throne room and gaze up adoringly at you."

Her green eyes are hard as jade. "And have you spending all your waking hours trying to think of some clever way to slither around my commands?"

"I have to occupy myself somehow," he says. "When I am between moments of gazing adoringly, of course."

The outer corner of her lip twitches, and he wonders if he almost made her smile.

The door opens, and Fernwaif comes in, a single guard behind her. Oak recognizes him as Bran, who occasionally sat at Madoc's dinner table when Oak was a child. He looks horrified at the sight of the prince on his knees, wearing the livery of a guard beneath a stolen cloak.

"How—" Bran begins, but Wren ignores him.

"Fernwaif," she says. "Go and have the guards responsible for the prisons brought here."

The huldu girl gives a small bob of her head and, with a wary glance at Oak, leaves the room. So much for her being on his side.

Wren's gaze goes to Bran. "How is it that no one saw him strolling through the Citadel? How is it that he was allowed to walk into my chambers with no one the wiser?"

The falcon steps up to Oak. The fury in his gaze is half humiliation.

"What traitor helped you escape?" Bran demands. "How long have you been planning to assassinate Queen Suren?"

The prince snorts. "Is *that* what I was trying to do? Then why, given everything I stole from that fool Straun and the laundry, didn't I bother to steal a weapon?"

Bran gives him a swift kick in the side.

Oak sucks in the sound of pain. "That's your clever riposte?"

Wren lifts a hand, and both of them look at her, falling silent.

"What shall I do with you, Prince of Elfhame?" Wren asks.

"If you mean for me to be your pet," he says, "there's no reason to return me to my pen. My leash is very secure, as you have shown. You have only to pull it taut."

"You think you know what it is to be under someone's control because I have given you a *single* command you were forced to obey," she says, heat in her voice. "I could give you a demonstration of what it feels like to own nothing of yourself. You are owed a punishment, after all. You've broken out of my prisons and come to my rooms without my permission. You've made a mockery of my guards."

A cold feeling settles in Oak's gut. The bridle is uncomfortable, its straps pulling tight against his cheeks, but not painful. At least not yet. He knows that it will continue to tighten and that if he wears it long enough, it will cut into his cheeks as it cut Wren's. If he wears it longer than that, longer than she did, it will eventually grow to be a part of him. Invisible to the world and impossible to remove.

That is why it was made. To make Wren eternally obedient to Lord Jarel and Lady Nore.

Wren hated that bridle.

"I grant you that I don't know what it feels like to be compelled to follow someone else's orders again and again," Oak says. "But I don't think you want to do that, not to anyone. Not even to me."

"You don't know me as well as you think, Greenbriar heir," she says. "I remember your stories, like the one about how you used a glamour against your mortal sister and made her strike herself. How would you like to feel as she felt?"

He confessed that when Wren won a secret from him in a game they played with three silver foxes, tossed in the dirt outside the war camp of the Court of Teeth. Another thing he maybe ought not to have done.

"I'll slap myself silly willingly, if you like," he offers. "No need for a command."

"What if, instead, I force you onto your hands and knees to make a bench for me to sit upon?" Wren inquires lightly, but her eyes are alight with fury and something else, something darker. She pads around his body, a prowling animal. "Or eat filth from the floor?"

Oak does not doubt that she saw Lord Jarel demand those things from people. He hopes that she was never asked to do those things herself.

"Beg to kiss the hem of my dress?"

He says nothing. Nothing he says could possibly help him.

"Crawl to me." Her eyes shine, fever bright.

Again, Oak's body moves without his permission. He finds himself writhing across the floor, his stomach against the carpet. He flushes with shame.

When he reaches her, he stares upward, rage in his eyes. He's humiliated, and she's barely begun. She was right when she said he didn't understand what it would feel like. He hadn't counted on the embarrassment, the fury at himself for not being able to resist the magic. He hadn't counted on the fear of what she would do next.

Oak cuts his gaze toward Bran, who has remained stiff and still, as though afraid to draw Wren's attention. The prince wonders how far she would go if he were not present.

How far she will go anyway.

Then the door opens.

Straun enters, along with a guard wearing battle-scraped armor and bearing a scar across the broadest part of his nose. He seems familiar, but Oak can't quite place him—he must have served with Madoc but not come to the house much. Straun looks as though he's fighting to move, and the scarred guard is looking as though he wants to murder Straun.

Straun steps forward, going to one knee. "Queen of winter, know that I only ever wished to serve—"

She holds up a hand, forestalling the groveling he seems to be working up to. "I have been tricked by the prince often enough to know how clever he can be. Now you will not be deceived again."

"I shall make a new oath to you," he declares. "That I will never—"

"Make no oaths you are not certain you can keep," she tells Straun, which is better advice than he deserves. Still, he looks chastened by it.

Oak pushes to his hooves, since she hadn't told him to stay there. Wren barely spares him a glance.

"Bind my prisoner's wrists," she tells the scarred guard.

"As you command, Queen." His voice is gruff.

He walks to Oak, pulling his arms behind him sharply. Tying his bonds uncomfortably tight. The prince's wrists are going to be sore by the time he makes it back to his cell.

"We were discussing how best to discipline Prince Oak," she says.

Straun and the other guard look a lot happier at that thought. Oak is certain that, after they were punished by the High Court for their treason, it would be at least a little satisfying to see a prince of Elfhame brought low. And that was before he gave them a reason to have a personal grudge.

Wren turns to him. "Perhaps I ought to have you sent to the Great Hall tomorrow and command that you endure ten strikes of an ice whip. Most barely get through five."

Bran looks worried. He might want Oak humiliated but perhaps didn't expect to see Madoc's son's blood spilled. Or maybe he is concerned that if they have to give back the prince, Elfhame will want him in one piece. Straun seems thrilled by the prospect of some suffering, however.

Dread and humiliation coil in Oak's stomach. He has been such a fool.

"Why not whip me now?" he asks, a challenge in his voice.

"Spending a night dreading what will come in the morning is its own punishment." She pauses. "Especially as you now know your own hand can be turned against you."

Oak looks directly into her eyes. "Why are you keeping me at all, Wren? Am I a hostage to be ransomed? A lover to be punished? A possession to be locked away?"

"That," she says, bitterness in her voice, "is what I am trying to figure out myself." She turns to the guards. "Take him back to his cell."

Bran reaches for him, and the prince struggles, pulling out of the guard's grasp.

"Oak," Wren says, pressing her fingers to his cheek. He goes still beneath her touch. "Go with Straun. Do not resist him. Do not trick him. Until you are confined again, you will follow these commands. And then you will stay in my prisons until you are sent for." She gives the prince a stern look and withdraws her hand. Turns to the soldiers. "Once Oak is in his cell, the three of you can go to Hyacinthe and explain how you allowed the prince to slip past you."

Hyacinthe. A reminder that the person in charge of the guards hates Oak more than the rest of them combined. As though he needed more miserable news.

"Will you send for me?" the prince asks, as though there's any room for bargaining. As though he has a choice. As though his body will not obey its own accord. "You said only *perhaps* you'd have me whipped."

Straun shoves him toward the door.

"Good night, Prince of Elfhame," Wren says as he is led from the room. He manages a single glance back. Her gaze locks with his, and he can feel the frisson of something between them. Something that might well be terrible, but that he wants more of all the same.

CHAPTER

4

The scarred-nose guard follows Straun and Oak down the stairs. Bran trails behind them. For a while, none of them speak.

"Let's take him to the interrogation room," the guard says, low-voiced. "Pay him back for the trouble we're going to be in. Find some information to make up for it."

Oak clears his throat loudly. "I'm a valuable possession. The queen won't thank you for breaking me."

One corner of the guard's mouth turns up. "Don't recognize me? But then, why would you? I'm just another of your father's people, just another one who fought and bled and nearly died to put you on the throne. All for you to throw it back in our faces."

I didn't want the throne. Oak bites the inside of his cheek to keep from shouting the words. That isn't going to help. Instead, he stares at the scarred man's face, at the dark eyes and auburn hair that hangs across his forehead. At the scar itself, which pulls his mouth up, as though his lip is perpetually curled.

"Valen," he prompts before Oak can recall his name. One of the generals who campaigned with Madoc for years. Not a friend, either. They vied against each other for the position of grand general, and Valen never forgave Madoc for winning. Madoc must have promised him something extraordinary to get Valen to betray the High King.

Oak could well believe that once coming to Madoc's side, Valen was unwilling to return to the military in Elfhame, tail between his legs. And now he is here, after spending perhaps *nine years* as a falcon. Oh, yes, Oak could well believe Valen despises him. Valen may actually hate him more than Hyacinthe does.

"I was a child," the prince says.

"A spoiled, disobedient boy. You still are. But that won't stop me from wringing every last drop of information out of you."

Straun hesitates, cutting his gaze toward Bran, still far enough back that he hasn't overheard their plan. "Aren't we going to get in more trouble? The prince said—"

"You take orders from a prisoner now?" Valen needles. "Perhaps you're still loyal to his father, despite being abandoned by him. Or the High Court? Maybe you think you made the wrong choice, not swearing fealty to that spoiled snake boy and his mortal concubine."

"That's not true!" Straun spits out, mightily offended. It's a fine piece of manipulation. Valen has made Straun feel as though he has to prove himself.

"Then let's go strap him down," Valen says with a crooked grin. Oak would be willing to bet that this is the soldier who took Straun's money playing dice.

"He's just goading you—" Oak manages to get out before he is shoved roughly forward. And, of course, he has been commanded not to resist.

"What's going on?" asks Bran, frowning at them.

"The boy has a smart mouth," Valen says, and Bran narrows his eyes in suspicion but doesn't ask any further questions.

Down they go, past the prisons. No matter how Oak tries to stop himself, his body moves like an automaton, like one of those stick soldiers Lady Nore created from Mab's bones. His heart thuds dully in his chest, his body alight with panic.

"Listen," he tries again. "Whatever you're thinking of doing to me—"

"Shut your mouth," snaps Valen, kicking the prince in the back of the leg.

"This isn't the right direction," Bran says, seeming to notice how far they've descended for the first time.

Oak hopes he will do something. Order them to stop. Tattle to Hyacinthe. It would be embarrassing to be saved by him, but the prince would far prefer that to whatever Valen is planning.

"We need information," the scarred guard says. "Something to give the queen so that we don't look like fools. You think you're not going to be demoted? Mocked? He got past all three of us."

Bran nods slowly. "I suppose there's something to that. And I am given to understand the interrogation rooms are well outfitted."

"You hardly need to strap me down. I will tell you how I stole the key, how I got into her tower, all of it." Oak can tell, though, how little they want to be convinced. "I—"

"Quiet." Straun shoves him hard enough for him to overbalance, arms behind his back as they are.

The prince hits the stone floor hard, smacking his head.

Valen laughs.

Oak pushes himself back up. A cut just above his left brow is bleeding, the blood dripping down over his eye. Since his hands are bound, he can't wipe it away. He flexes his wrists a little to test the bindings, but there is no give.

Fury chokes him.

A few more shoves and he's down the hall and into a room he's never seen before—one with manacles attached to a black stone table and instruments of interrogation in a glass-paned cabinet. Straun and Valen press Oak's back down onto the slab. They cut the bindings on his wrists, and for a moment, he's free.

Desperately, he tries to struggle, but he finds he cannot, not with the bridle's magic holding him down more firmly than they could. *Go with Straun. Do not resist him. Do not trick him.* The prince has to allow them to manacle his wrists and then his ankles.

He doesn't bother pretending he's not afraid. He's terrified.

"Hyacinthe has been dreaming of torturing me for years." The prince is unable to keep his voice from shaking a little. "I can't imagine what I know that would make him forgive you if you jump the line."

Bran squints in slight confusion as he parses the human phrase, looking more worried. "Maybe we should tell—"

Valen reaches for the small handheld crossbow on his hip.

"Bran!" Oak shouts in warning.

The falcon goes for his sword, unsheathing it in a single fluid movement. But the bolt from Valen's crossbow strikes him in the throat before he can so much as advance.

Go with Straun. Do not resist him. Do not trick him. Until you are
confined again, you will follow these commands.

Now that he is confined, Oak can finally resist. He pulls against
his bindings, writhing and kicking, shouting every filthy thing he can
think of—but, of course, it's too late.

Bran drops heavily to the floor as two more bolts lodge in his chest.

This doesn't seem like a good move. It doesn't seem clever, and Oak
doesn't like the idea that Valen may be desperate enough or paranoid
enough to make decisions that don't make strategic sense. He's not an
amateur. He must have really believed that Bran was about to betray him.

"Bar the door," Valen tells Straun.

Straun does it, stepping over Bran's body. He's breathing hard. If
he'd been asked to choose sides, he might have chosen Bran's. But no
one's asking him now.

"Well," says Valen, turning toward Oak. "Now you and I are finally
going to have a conversation."

Oak cannot repress the shudder that goes through him at those
words. He has been poisoned and stabbed many times over the course
of his short life. Pain is transient, he tells himself. He has endured it
before—broken bones and bled and survived. Pain is better than being
dead.

He tells himself a lot of things.

"It seems rude for me to be lying down during it," Oak says, but his
voice doesn't come out as calmly as he hoped.

"There are lots of ways to hurt us Folk," says Valen, ignoring the
prince's words as he draws on a brown leather glove. "But cold iron is
the worst. Burns through faerie flesh like a hot knife through lard."

"A grim topic to discuss, but if that's what you'd like to talk about, you are the host of this little get-together...." Oak tries to sound light, unconcerned. He's heard Cardan speak just this way on many occasions, and it disarms his audience. Oak can only hope it works that way now.

Valen's hand comes down hard on the corner of his mouth. It's more a slap than a blow, but it still stings. He tastes blood where a tooth cuts into his lip.

Straun gives a guffaw. Maybe he feels torture will be a proper vengeance for Oak's making him look like a fool. But with Bran's body lying by the guard's feet, Straun *is* a fool if he thinks himself safe.

Still, the game that has always served Oak best is seeming feckless, and he needs to play that up. Be that spoiled boy Valen expects.

At least until he can come up with something better.

"Let's talk about what your sister will do," says Valen, surprising Oak by not bothering to ask a single question about his escape. "Where were you planning on meeting her forces once you escaped your cell and murdered the queen?"

Clever of him to assume guilt and only press for details. Clever, but wrong.

With the stick creatures scattered into pieces, the falcons are the entire force of Wren's military. That gives Valen room to rise in the ranks, since those ranks are thin, but it puts him in danger, too. Whatever Elfhame sends at the Citadel, he and his falcons will have to meet it.

That's what Valen wants above all else, Oak realizes. Power. He's been simmering with that desire for as long as he's been laboring under the curse. And being Wren's military leader would have appeased him a little. But she passed him over, and now he is hungrier than ever.

"Sorry to disappoint, but I have no way to communicate with my sister," Oak says. That was true enough since he smashed the snake.

"You can't expect me to believe you were going to—what—murder the queen and then run off through the snow, hoping for the best?" Valen sneers.

"I'm glad you don't think that, though Bran certainly did," Oak says, keeping his gaze off the corpse on the floor. "I never wanted to hurt Wren, no less *murder* her."

Straun frowns at the familiar form of address—Wren, rather than Queen Suren or the Winter Queen or whatever fanciful title he thinks best suits her.

Can Straun truly believe he has a chance with her? There does not seem to be much guile in him. She may like that, even if Oak thinks he's dull as a toad.

Valen studies the prince's face, perhaps seeing the jealousy in it. "And you didn't intend to run, either?"

Oak isn't certain how to answer that. He's not sure he can explain his intentions, even to himself. "I was considering it. Prison isn't very nice, and I like nice things."

Valen's mouth turns down in disgust. This is what he expects a prince of Elfhame to be—vain and fussy and unused to suffering of any kind. The more Oak leans into that role, the more he will be able to hide himself.

"Although," Oak says, "freezing isn't particularly nice, either."

"So you drugged Straun and broke out of the prisons," Valen says slowly, incredulously, "with no plan at all?"

Oak cannot shrug, as tied down as he is, but he makes a gesture to indicate his nonchalance. "Some of my best ideas come to me in the moment. And I did get a bath."

"He must know *something*," Straun says, worried that they are risking all this for nothing. Worried, no doubt, about the corpse that will be hard to dispose of without anyone noticing.

Valen turns toward Oak, pressing a finger into his cheek. "The prince knows his sister."

Oak sighs dramatically. "Jude has an army. She has assassins. She has control of the Courts of other rulers who are sworn to her. She holds all the cards and could deploy any of them. You want me to tell you that in a duel, she turns her front foot inward while lunging, giving you an opening? I don't think you'll ever get close enough to find that information useful."

Straun's eyes narrow in calculation. "She turns her front foot?"

Oak smiles up at him. "Never."

Valen lifts an iron knife from the cabinet and presses the point of it to the hollow of Oak's throat. It sizzles against his skin.

The prince bites back a cry as his whole body jerks with pain.

Straun flinches despite his previous eagerness. Then he sets his jaw and makes himself watch as the prince's skin blisters.

"*Ouch*," Oak says, enunciating the word slowly and deliberately in a whiny sort of voice, despite how much the hot iron against his throat burns.

Straun is startled into a snort of laughter. Valen pulls the knife back, furious.

It's easy to make someone look foolish if you're willing to play the fool.

"*Leave*," shouts Valen, waving at Straun. "Guard from the other side of the door. Alert me if someone is coming."

"But—" Straun begins.

"Better do as he says," Oak tells him, breathing hard because despite his performance, the press of the iron is agony. "Don't want to end up like Bran."

Straun's gaze flicks guiltily to the floor, then back to Valen. He goes out.

Oak watches him with mixed feelings. The prince has few moves, and none of them are good. He can keep at getting under Valen's skin, but it's likely to cost him his own. Now that Straun is out of the room, though, he could try a different tack. "Maybe I could give you something better than impressing Hyacinthe, but I'd need something in return."

Valen smiles, letting his knife hover over Oak's face. "Bogdana told me that you inherited your mother's twisting tongue."

It takes all the prince's concentration not to look at the blade directly. He forces himself to stare up into the falcon's eyes. "Bogdana doesn't like me. I doubt she likes you much, either. But you want Hyacinthe's position, and I know a great deal about him...his vulnerabilities, the ways he is likely to fail."

"Tell me this," Valen says, looming over him. "Where did you get the poison you used on Straun?"

Well, crap. That's a very good question. Oak thinks of the jeweled snake. Imagines how he will look if he tries to explain.

"I thought I didn't need to torture you to get you to tell me whatever I wanted to know?" Valen turns the knife so that the point hovers over Oak's eye. He glances at it and sees the edge of one of the straps of the bridle reflected in the blade. A reminder that Wren didn't sanction this interrogation, that she doesn't know about it. She wouldn't need to torture him to find out any of this. All she'd have to do, with the bridle on him, was ask. He could no more deny her than he could stop his own heart from beating.

Of course, whether she'd care if Valen hurt him was another matter. He liked to think that she would, at least for her pride. After all, ten lashes from an ice whip wouldn't seem like much of a punishment if someone else had already gouged out one of his eyes.

He'd rather not lose the eye, though. Still, all he has going for him is his charm, and that's a double-edged sword. "You asked me about my sister—and you're right. I do know her. I know she's likely to send someone to negotiate for my return. Whatever you think of me, I am valuable to Elfhame."

"She'd pay a ransom?" Valen licks his lips. Oak can see his desire, a hunger for glory and gold and all the things that were denied him.

"Oh yes," Oak agrees. "But it hardly matters if Wren won't agree to give me up. Whatever my sister offers now could have always been Wren's, along with the Citadel, as a reward for removing Lady Nore."

Valen's mouth twists into a harsh smile. "But you seem to have made Queen Suren angry enough to prefer your being brought low to her own rise."

That stung, being uncomfortably true. "You could make your own bargain with the High Queen."

The tip of the iron knife presses against Oak's cheek. It burns like a lit match against his skin. He jerks again, a puppet on a string.

"How about you answer the question about the poison, and then we can discuss what deals I am going to make."

Panic floods Oak. He's going to refuse to talk. And he's going to be tortured until he gives in and talks anyway. Once Hyacinthe learns about the snake, he will tell Wren, and she'll believe Oak is her enemy, no matter what he says in his defense. And whatever his sister's plan is, it's sure to become exponentially more lethal.

But with enough pain and enough time, anyone will say almost anything.

Perhaps, Oak thinks, perhaps he can get himself hurt so badly the questioning *can't* continue. It's a terrible plan, but no other idea presents itself. He can hardly smile at Valen as he did at Fernwaif and have that be enough to persuade him to let Oak leave the dungeon.

Unless…

It's been a long time since he used his *twisting tongue*, as Bogdana put it. His true gancanagh power. Let his mouth speak for him, let the words come without his will. Say all the right things in the right way at the right time.

It's terrifying, like letting go in a sword fight and allowing pure instinct to take over, not being entirely sure whose blood will wind up on his hands.

But whatever Valen is going to do next is more terrifying. If Oak can escape this room in one piece and without putting anyone he cares about in danger, he can figure out the rest from there.

Of course, part of the problem is that his power isn't one of pure persuasion. He can't just make someone do what he wants. He can only make himself into what they want and hope that is enough. Worse, he is never sure what that will be. Once he gives in, his mouth makes the words, and he is left with the consequences.

"*The trolls of the Stone Forest have blusher mushroom. It's not so very hard to come by. Forget the poison. Think of your future,*" Oak says, his voice sounding strange, even to his own ears. There's a rough hum underneath and a buzz on his lips, like the sting of electricity. It's been a long time since he has reached for this power, but it uncurls languorously at his command. *"You only want command of Lady Wren's army? You were meant for greater things."*

Valen's eyes dilate, the irises blowing wide. He scowls in confusion, shaking his head. "The trolls? That's where you got the poison."

Oak doesn't like how eager the enchantment feels, now that it's awakened. How easily it flows through him. He's felt trickles of this magic before, but not since he was a child has he let himself feel the full force of it. *"I am closer to the center of power than anyone at this Citadel,"* he says. *"Madoc is out of favor, and many in the High Court do not like our armies being led by Grima Mog. Many would prefer you—and isn't that really what you want?"*

"I have lost all chance of that." Valen's words aren't scornful, though. He sounds frightened by his own hopes. The iron knife dips low enough in his gloved hand that he seems in danger of burning his own thigh with the tip.

"You have lived as a falcon for nine years," Oak says, the words dragging against his tongue. *"You were strong enough not to stagger beneath that burden. You are free, and yet if you are not careful, you will be caught in a new net."*

Valen listens as though fascinated.

"You are headed toward a conflict with Elfhame, yet you have no army of stick and stone and no authority of command. But with me, things could change. Elfhame could reward you instead of targeting you. I could help. Unbind me, and I will give you what you have long deserved."

Valen backs himself against the wall, breathing hard, shaking his head. "What are you?" he asks with a tremor in his voice and an ocean of wanting in his eyes.

"What do you mean?" The words come out of Oak's mouth without the basilisk charm in them.

"You—what did you do to me?" Valen growls, a spark of hot anger in his gaze.

"I was just talking." Oak reaches desperately for the honey-tongued roughness to his voice. He's too panicked to find it. Too unused to using it.

"I am going to make you *suffer*," Valen promises.

Back to Oak's first, worse plan, then. He gives Valen his most careless, insouciant grin. "I almost had you, though. You were almost mine."

Valen slams his forehead into the prince's face. Oak's skull snaps back to knock against the slab to which he's been bound. Pain blooms between his eyes, and his head feels as though it rattles on his neck. Valen's fist connects next, and Oak counts it as a win that the third blow is hard enough to knock him unconscious.

Oak is dreaming of a red fox that is also his half brother, Locke. They are in a forest at twilight, and things are moving in the shadows. Leaves rustle as though animals peer from between trees.

"You really screwed up this time," says the fox as he trots beside the prince.

"You're dead," Oak reminds him.

"Yes," agrees the fox who is also Locke. "And you're close to joining me."

"Is that why you've come?" Oak looks down at his muddy hooves. A leaf is stuck to the top of the one on his left.

The fox's black nose scents the air. Its tail is a wavering flame behind it. Its paws pad sure-footedly along a path that Oak cannot see. He wonders if he is being led somewhere that he doesn't want to go.

A breeze brings the scents of old, drying blood and weapon oil. It reminds Oak of the smell of Madoc's house, of home.

"I am a trickster, like you. I am here because it amuses me. When I am bored, I will go away."

"I'm not like you," Oak says.

He's *not* like Locke, even if they have the same power. Locke was Master of Revels, who spirited away his sister Taryn to his estate, where she drank wine and dressed in beautiful gowns and became sadder than he'd ever seen her.

Locke thought life was a story, and he was responsible for introducing the conflict. Oak had been nine when Taryn murdered Locke, with his tenth birthday soon after. He would like to say he hadn't known what she'd done, but he had. None of them tried to hide violence. By then, they were used to murder being an option that was *always* on the table.

At the time, though, he hadn't quite put together that Locke was his half brother.

Or quite how much Locke was a terrible person.

The fox's mouth opens, its pink tongue lolling out. It studies Oak with eyes that look alarmingly like his own. "Our mother died when I was just a child, but I still remember her. She had long red-gold hair, and she was always laughing. Everyone she met adored her."

Oak thought of Hyacinthe, whose father had loved Liriope too well and killed himself because of it. He thought of Dain, who had desired her and then murdered her.

"I am not like our mother, either," Oak says.

"You never met her," the fox tells him. "How do you know if you're like her or not?"

To that, Oak has no answer. He doesn't want to be like her. He wanted people to love him a normal amount.

But it was true that he wanted everyone to love him.

"You're going to die like her. And like me. Murdered by your own lover."

"I'm not dying," the prince snaps, but the fox scampers off, sliding between the trees. At first his bright coat gives him away, but then the leaves become scarlet and gold and withered brown. They fall in a great gust that seems to whirl around the prince. And in the shiver of the boughs, Oak hears laughter.

CHAPTER
6

Oak isn't sure how long he has lain on the cold stone tiles, dropping in and out of consciousness. He dreams of hunting snakes that glisten with gems as they whip through the night, of girls made of ice whose kisses cool his burns. Several times, he thinks he ought to crawl toward his blanket, but just contemplating the idea of moving hurts his head.

Whatever the prince thought of himself before, however skilled he claimed to be at evading traps and laughing in the face of danger, he isn't laughing now. He'd have been better off sitting in his cell and waiting. He'd have been better off if he ran out into the snow. He took a chance and lost, lost *spectacularly*, which is just about all he can say to his credit—at least it was spectacular.

It is the shift of shadows that causes him to realize someone is standing outside his cell. Feverishly, he looks up. For a moment, her face swims in front of him, and he thinks she must be part of another nightmare.

Bogdana.

The storm hag looms tall, her hair a wild mane around her head. She peers at him with black eyes that shine like chips of wet onyx.

"Prince Oak, our most honored guest. I was afraid you might have died in there," she says, kicking a tray beneath the door of his cell with her foot. On it rests a bowl of watery soup with scales floating on top, beside a carafe of sour-smelling wine. He has no doubt she selected the food personally.

"Well, hello," Oak says. "What an unexpected visit."

She smiles down in malicious glee. "You seem unwell. I thought a simple meal might be to your liking."

He pushes himself into a sitting position, ignoring how it makes his head pound. "How long was I out?" He isn't even sure how he got to the prisons. Had Straun been forced to carry him here, once Valen realized he wasn't going to wake anytime soon? Had Valen brought him back, in case he never woke?

"Somewhere you need to be, Prince of Elfhame?" Bogdana asks him.

"Of course not." Oak's hand goes to his chest. The burn by his throat is scabbed over. He can feel the wild beat of his heart beneath his palm. He couldn't have been unconscious long since Wren hadn't sent anyone to drag him before her Court for a whipping.

Bogdana's smile widens. "Good. Because I came to tell you that I will gut every servant you conscript, should you try to use one to escape your cell again."

"I didn't—" he begins.

She gives a harsh laugh, something that is half a snarl. "The huldu girl? You cannot truly expect me to believe you don't have her eating out of your hand. That you didn't put her under your spell?"

"You think Fernwaif helped me escape?" he snaps, incredulous.

"Feeling remorseful now, when it's too late?" The storm hag's lip curls. "You knew the risk when you used her."

"The girl did nothing." Fernwaif, who believed in romance, despite living in Lady Nore's Citadel. Who he hoped was still alive. "I got the key from Straun, and that's because he's a fool, not because I conscripted him."

Bogdana watches Oak's expression, drawing out the moment. "Suren interceded on Fernwaif's behalf. She's safe from me, for the moment."

Oak lets out a breath. "I shall be as unpleasant to the servants of the Citadel as you like hereafter. Now I hope our business is concluded."

Bogdana frowns down at him. "Our business won't be concluded until the Greenbriars have repaid their debt to me."

"With our lives, blah, blah, I know." Pain and despair have made the prince reckless.

The storm hag's eyes are bright with reflected light. Her nails tap against the iron of the bars as though contemplating shoving her hand inside and slashing him with them. "You desire something from Suren, don't you, prince? Perhaps it's that you aren't used to being rejected and it's not sitting well with you. Perhaps you see the greatness in her and want to ruin it. Perhaps you truly are drawn to her. Any which way, it will make the moment she bites out your throat all the sweeter."

Oak cannot help thinking of his dream and the fox walking beside him, prophesying his doom. Cannot help thinking of other things. "She's bitten me before, you know," he says with a grin. "It wasn't so bad."

Bogdana looks satisfyingly infuriated by the comment. "I am glad you're still locked up tight, little bait," she tells him, eyes flashing. "Were you less useful, I would flay your skin from your bones. I would hurt you in ways you cannot imagine." There is a hunger in her words that unnerves him.

"Someone beat you to that." Oak leans back onto the pillow of his own arm.

"You're still breathing," says the storm hag.

"If you were actually worried I was dead," he says, recalling the first thing she said to him when she came to his cell, "I must have looked pretty bad."

He may have been unconscious longer than he guessed. Is there still a day before Elfhame makes its move? Is it happening already? He really, really wishes the metal snake had been more specific about what Jude was planning. *Three daysssss* was just not enough information.

"I don't need you to last long," Bogdana says. "It's the High King I want."

Oak snorts. "Good luck with that."

"You're my luck."

"I wonder what Wren thinks," he says, trying to hide his discomfiture. "You're using her every bit as much as Lord Jarel and Lady Nore ever did. And you've been planning on using her for a long time."

Lightning sparks along Bogdana's fingers. "My revenge is hers as well. Her crown and throne were stolen."

"She's got both a crown and a throne now, hasn't she?" Oak asks. "And it seems you're the one likely to cost her them, *again.*"

The look the storm hag gives him could have boiled his blood. "For what Mab did, I will see the end of the Greenbriar reign," snaps Bogdana.

"You think you know Suren, but you do not. Her heart is that of my dead daughter. She was born to be the ruin of your kin."

"I know her well enough to call her *Wren*," he says, and watches the storm hag's eyes glisten with deeper malice. "And we don't always do the thing we were born for."

"Eat up, boy," Bogdana says, gesturing to the disgusting food she brought. "I'd hate to see you go to your slaughter hungry."

It's only hours later, when the footsteps of three guards wake him from another half sleep, that Oak realizes she may have meant those last words literally. His head still hurts enough that he thinks about just lying there and letting them do their worst, but then he decides that if he is going to die, at least he will do so standing.

He's up by the time they arrive. As they open the door to his cell, he uses the tip of his hoof to flip the bowl of soup into his hands. Then he slams it into the first guard's face.

The guard goes down. Oak kicks the second into the iron bars and, in a moment of hesitation from the third, grabs for the first guard's fallen sword.

Before he can get it, a club hits him in the stomach, knocking the air out of him.

He was faster, before the iron. Before his muscles got stiff. Before getting hit in the head several times by Valen. A few weeks ago, he would have had the sword.

They're crowded in the entrance of his cell; that's his main advantage. Only one can really come at him at a time, but all three have weapons drawn and Oak has only his hands and hooves. Even the bowl is lying on the ground, cracked in half.

But he refuses to be dragged back to the interrogation chamber. Panic fills him at the thought of Valen starting the torture over. At the strike of an ice whip. At Bogdana's nails peeling off his skin.

The second guard, the one who hit the bars, lunges at him with the sword. It's a small space, though, too small to get a real swing in, and the guard is slow as a consequence. Oak ducks and barrels into the first guard, who has managed to get onto his feet. The prince slams into him, and they both sprawl onto the cold stone tiles of the prison hall. Oak attempts to scramble up, only to be hit between the shoulder blades with the club by the third guard. He is knocked down again, falling heavily onto the second guard. He goes for a knife strapped to that one's belt. Drawing it, he rolls onto his back, ready to throw.

As he does, he feels a familiar shift in his mind. The shuttering of all other thoughts, the casting off of himself. There is a relief in letting go, allowing the future and past to drop away, to become someone without a hope or fear beyond this moment. Someone for whom there was only ever this fight and there will only ever be this fight.

It worries him, too, though, because every time it happens, he feels less and less in control of what he does when he's outside himself. How many times now has he found himself standing over a body with blood on his clothes, blood on his face and his sword and his hands—and no memory of what happened?

It makes him think of the gancanagh power, of all the warnings he doesn't seem able to heed anymore.

"*Oak!*" Hyacinthe shouts.

The prince lets his arm with the dagger in it sag. Somehow being yelled at by Hyacinthe brings him back to himself. Maybe it is just the familiarity of his scorn.

When he isn't hit again, he lets himself lie there, breathing hard. The other guard stands.

"She wants you to sit down to supper with her," Hyacinthe says. "I'm supposed to get you cleaned up."

"Wren?" Oak's sense of time is still very unclear. "I thought she was going to have me punished."

Hyacinthe raises both his eyebrows. "Yes, Wren. Who else?"

The prince looks at the guards, who glare at him resentfully. If he'd been thinking more clearly, he would have realized he had no cause to try to *murder* them. They weren't necessarily working for Valen or Bogdana, weren't necessarily leading him to his doom. He probably would have figured that out sooner had his head not hurt so much. Had Bogdana not come and threatened him.

"No one mentioned supper," Oak complains.

One of the guards, the one with the club, snorts. The other two wear scowls that remain unaltered.

Hyacinthe turns to all of them. "Find something else to do. I will escort the prince."

The guards depart, one spitting on the stone floor as he leaves.

"I warn you," Oak says. "If you are also planning on hitting me, it will have to be quite a blow to have any effect on the swelling and bruises already coming in."

"You might consider occasionally bowing to wisdom and keeping your tongue between your teeth," Hyacinthe says, reaching out a hand to pull Oak to his feet.

For a moment, the prince is certain he's going to open his mouth and say something Hyacinthe will not think is at all funny. Something that probably won't *be* at all funny.

"Unlikely, but we can both live in hope," Oak manages as he lets himself be levered up. He staggers a little and realizes that if he tries to catch himself, he will have to burn his hand on the iron bars. Dizziness washes over him. "If you intend to gloat, have at it."

Hyacinthe's mouth twists into a smile. "You're being paid, Prince of Elfhame. In exactly the coin you once demanded."

To that, Oak can make no refutation. He is staying upright by sheer force of will, taking deep breaths until he is sure he is going to stay that way.

"Well, come on," says Hyacinthe. "Unless you want me to carry you."

"Carry me? What a delightful offer. You can bear me in your arms like a maiden in a fairy tale."

Hyacinthe rolls his eyes. "I can throw you over my shoulder like a sack of grain."

"Then I suppose I shall walk," Oak says, hoping he can. He staggers after Hyacinthe, remembering how Hyacinthe was once his prisoner, feeling the poetic justice of the moment. "Are you going to bind my hands?"

"Do I need to?" Hyacinthe asks.

For a moment, Oak thinks he's referring to the bridle. But then the prince realizes Hyacinthe is simply offering him an opportunity to walk up the stairs without restraints. "Why are you—"

"A kinder captor than ever you were to me?" Hyacinthe supplies with a short laugh. "Maybe I am just a better person."

Oak doesn't bother to remind Hyacinthe of how he tried to *murder the High King* and, if Oak hadn't interceded, would have been executed or sent to the Tower of Forgetting. It doesn't matter. It is very possible that neither of them is a particularly nice person.

They move down the hall, past lit torches. Hyacinthe takes a long look at Oak and frowns. "You've got bruises, and it's too soon for them to have come from the fight I just saw. Those iron burns aren't fresh, either, and they're the wrong shape and angle to come from your prison bars. What happened?"

"I'm a miracle of self-destructiveness," Oak says.

Hyacinthe stops walking and folds his arms. The pose is so like one that Tiernan regularly makes that Oak is certain it's a copy, even if Hyacinthe isn't aware he's doing it.

Maybe that's what makes him talk, that familiar gesture. Or maybe it's that he's so tired and no small amount afraid. "You know a guy named Valen? Former general. Thick neck. More anger than sense?"

Hyacinthe's brow furrows, and he nods slowly.

"He wants your job," Oak says, and begins walking again.

Hyacinthe falls into step beside him. "I don't see what that has to do with you."

They come to the stairs and head up, out of the dungeons. The fading sunlight hits his face, hurting his eyes, but the only thing he feels is gratitude. He wasn't sure he'd ever see the sun again. "He may have told you something about a soldier named Bran deserting. He didn't. He's dead."

"Bran is—" Hyacinthe begins, and then lowers his voice to a whisper. "He's *dead*?"

"Don't look at me like that," Oak says quietly. "I didn't kill him."

Guards flank an entrance a few paces ahead, and by unspoken consensus, they both fall silent. Oak's shoulders tense as he passes them, but they do nothing to stop his progress through the halls. For the first time, as he steps into a high-ceilinged corridor, he is free to look around the Citadel without the danger of being caught. He catches the scent of melting wax and the sap of fir trees. Rose petals, too, he thinks. Without the persistent stink of the iron, his head hurts less.

Then the prince's gaze goes to one of the large, translucent walls of ice, and he stumbles.

As through a window, he can see the landscape beyond the Citadel and the troll kings moving across it. Although distant, they are far larger than the boulders in the Stone Forest, as if those massive boulders represented only the topmost portions of their bodies and the rest were buried beneath the earth. These trolls are larger than any giant Oak saw in the Court of Elfhame, or the Court of Moths, for that matter. He watches them lurch through the snow, dragging enormous chunks of ice, and mentally recalculates Wren's resources.

They are building a wall. A miles-wide defensive shield, encircling the Citadel.

In less than a month, between her own newfound power and her newfound allies, Wren has made the Court of Teeth more formidable and more forbidding than it ever was during Lord Jarel's reign. But when he thinks of her, he cannot help seeing the darkness beneath her eyes and the feverish shine of them. Cannot put aside the thought that something is wrong.

"Wren looks as though she's been unwell," Oak says. "Has she been sick?"

Hyacinthe frowns. "You can't really expect me to betray my queen by telling you her secrets."

Oak's smile is sharp-edged. "So there's a secret to tell."

Hyacinthe's frown deepens.

"I am a prisoner," Oak says. "Whether you have me in chains or no, I can't hurt her, and I wouldn't if I could. I warned you about Valen. About Bran. Surely, I have proved some measure of loyalty."

Hyacinthe huffs out a breath, his gaze going to the troll kings beyond the icy pane. "Loyalty? I think not, but I am going to tell you because you might be the one person who *can* help. Wren's power takes something terrible out of her."

"What do you mean?" Oak demands.

"It's eating away at her," Hyacinthe says. "And she's going to keep having to use it, again and again, so long as you're here."

Oak opens his mouth to demand further explanation, but at that moment, a knot of courtiers passes, all of them pale and cold-looking, their gazes sliding over Oak as though the very sight of him is an offense.

"You're going to the leftmost tower," Hyacinthe says.

Oak nods, trying not to be rattled by the hate in their eyes. The tower he's heading toward is, ironically, the same one he was caught in the day before. "Explain," he says.

"What she does—it's not just unbinding, it's *unmaking*. She became sick after what she did to Lady Nore and her stick army. *Harrowed.* And Bogdana was so insistent that Wren use it again to break the curse of the Stone Forest because she's going to need the trolls if Elfhame moves against us. But she's formed of magic herself, and the more she unmakes, the more she is unmade."

Oak recalls the strain in Wren's face as she looked down from the dais in the Great Hall, the hollows beneath her cheekbones as she slept.

He assumed that Wren didn't visit the prisons because she didn't want to see him out of uninterest or anger. But she might not have come if she was sick. As much as she knows that looking weak in front of her newly formed Court is dangerous, it's possible she feels it is similarly risky to look weak in front of him.

And if she doesn't keep using her power...

No matter how dangerous the magic, Oak can too easily imagine Wren believing that if she doesn't use it, she won't be able to keep her throne. This was a land of huldufólk, nisser, and trolls, used to bowing only to strength and ferocity. They followed Lady Nore, but they were willing to hail Wren, her murderer, as their new queen.

She may be inclined to push herself past her limits to keep that support. To prove herself worthy. Has he not witnessed his sister doing just that?

You know what would really impress them? his mind supplies unhelpfully. *Daring to skewer the heir to Elfhame.*

"Tonight, at dinner," Hyacinthe says, "persuade her to let you go. And if you can't, then leave. Go. Actually *escape* this time, and take your political conflict with you."

Oak rolls his eyes at the assumption that getting out of the prisons was easy and he could have done it at any time. "You could advise her to *let* me go. Unless she doesn't trust you, either."

Hyacinthe hesitates, not taking the bait. "She would trust me less if she knew we were having this conversation. Perhaps wisely, I am not sure she trusts anyone. All the Folk in the Citadel have their own agendas."

"I am last on the list of those whose advice she'd heed," Oak says. "As you well know."

"You have a way of persuading people."

It's a barbed comment, but the prince grits his teeth and refuses to be offended. No matter how barbed, it's also the truth. "It would be far easier if I wasn't wearing this bridle."

Hyacinthe gives him a sideways look. "You'll manage." He must have heard the specifics of her command. *You will stay in my prisons until you are sent for.*

Oak sighs.

"And in the interim, stop picking fights," Hyacinthe says, making Oak want to pick a fight with *him*. "Is there no situation you're not compelled to make worse?"

Oak climbs the steps of the tower, thinking of the dinner ahead of him with Wren. The idea of sitting across from her at a table seems surreal, part of his hectic, fox-filled dreams.

They come to a wooden door with two locks on the outside. Hyacinthe moves past the prince to fit a key inside the first one and then the other.

One key. Two locks. Oak notes that. And none of it iron.

The room it opens onto is well appointed. Low couches are arranged on a rug looking so much softer than anything he's seen in weeks that he could sink down onto that and be happy. Blue flames burn in the grate of a fireplace. They seem hot, and yet when he puts a hand to the ice wall above the fire, there is none of the slickness that would indicate melting. Where the rug doesn't cover, the floor is inset with stone. If you didn't look carefully, you could suppose that you weren't in an ice palace at all.

"A far finer class of prison," Oak says, moving to lean against one of the posts of the bed. While he was moving, he wasn't dizzy, but now that he's stopped, he feels the immense need to be supported by something.

"Get dressed," Hyacinthe says, pointing to a set of clothes laid out on the bed. He holds the key in his palm pointedly, then places it on the mantel. "If you can't persuade her, it may interest you to know there's a shift in the guard at dawn. I left you a book on the table over there as well. It's mortal literature, and I understand you like that sort of thing."

Oak stares at the key as Hyacinthe leaves. Part of him wants to dismiss this as a trick, a way for the former falcon to prove the prince untrustworthy.

His gaze goes to the clothing left for him and then the mattress beneath, stuffed with goose down or perhaps duck feathers. He feels almost sick with the desire to lie down, to allow his throbbing temple to rest on a pillow.

He takes a deep breath and forces himself to pick up the book that Hyacinthe indicated—a hardback with a dust jacket that proclaims *Magic Tricks for Dummies*. He ruffles the pages, thinking of how he once made a coin disappear and reappear in front of Wren. Remembering his fingers brushing against her ear, her surprised laugh.

He should have let her leave that night. Let her take the damned bridle, get on the bus, and go, if that was what she wanted.

But no, he had to show off. Be clever. Manipulate everyone and everything, just the way he'd been taught. Just the way his father had manipulated him to come here.

With a sigh, he frowns down at the book again. There doesn't seem to be anything tucked inside. He isn't sure what it means then, except that Hyacinthe thinks he's a dummy. Just in case, he goes through the pages again, more slowly this time.

On 161, he finds an almost thoroughly dried stalk of ragwort.

Guards wait for him in the hall when he emerges from the room, dressed in the clothes he was given.

The doublet is of some silvery fabric that feels sturdy and stiff, as though there might be silver threads woven into the cloth. His shoulders are a little broader and his torso a little longer than the original owner, and it feels even more uncomfortably tight than the uniform. The pants are black as a starless sky and have to be pushed up a little because of the curve of his leg above his hooves.

He says nothing to the guards, and their faces are grim as they escort him to a high-ceilinged dining room where their new queen is waiting.

Wren stands at the head of a long table in a dress of some material that seems to be black and then silver, depending on the light. Her hair is pulled away from her pale blue face, and while she does not wear a crown, the ornaments in her hair suggest one.

She looks every bit a terrifying Queen of Faerie, beckoning him to some final supper of poisoned apples.

He bows.

Her gaze rests on him, as though trying to decide if the gesture is mockery or not. Or maybe she's only inspecting his bruises.

He's certainly noting how fragile she looks. *Harrowed.*

And something else. Something he ought to have noted in her

bedroom, when she'd given him orders, but he'd been too panicked to think about. There's a defensiveness in her posture, as though she's bracing for his anger. After having held him prisoner, she believes he *hates* her. She might still be angry with him, but she quite obviously expects him to be furious with her.

And every time he behaves as though he isn't, she thinks he's playing a trick.

"Hyacinthe told me you were reluctant to explain how you came to be hurt," Wren says.

Oak doesn't need to glance at the entrances to note the guards. He saw them upon his arrival. Not knowing their loyalties, he can hardly mention Valen, or even Straun, without stripping Hyacinthe of the element of surprise. Did she know that? Was this a play put on for their benefit? Or was this another test? "What would you say if I told you I grew so bored that I hit myself in the face?"

Her mouth becomes an even grimmer line. "No one would believe that lie, could you even tell it."

Oak's head dips forward, and he cannot keep the despair out of his voice. This is off to a bad start, and yet he truly does seem unable to keep himself from making it worse. "What lie *would* you believe?"

CHAPTER

7

W ren stiffens. He can see the careful way she is holding herself. Transforming her habit for shyness into remoteness. He is all admiration, except for the part where this new queen might decide he is nothing but a thorn to be excised from her side.

"Am I to advise you how best to deceive me?" she says, and he knows they are no longer just talking about his bruises.

Oak walks to the end of the table opposite her. A servant comes and pulls out the chair for him. Dizzily, he drops into the seat, well aware that it probably makes him seem sulky.

He has no idea what to say.

He thinks of the moment in the Court of Moths when he was told that Wren betrayed him, when it seemed certain that she had. Used him as he was familiar with being used. Kissed him to distract from her true purpose. He was furious with her, certainly, and with himself for being a fool. He was angry enough to let them take her away.

It was only later when he understood the details that a terrible panic set in. Because she *had* betrayed him, but she did it to free those she felt were unfairly imprisoned. And she did it with no strategic or personal benefit, putting herself in danger for Folk and mortals she barely knew. Just as she helped all those mortals who made bad bargains with the Folk back in her town.

He hadn't found out her reasons before he'd let them take her. He recalls the uncomfortable mix of anger and fear over what might be happening to her, the horror of not being certain he could save her from Queen Annet.

He wonders if this dinner is because Wren heard he was hurt and regrets that, if nothing else. She certainly felt betrayed. But betrayal didn't stop one from feeling other things. "I do have some experience with deception," he admits.

She frowns at that unexpected confession, taking her seat as well.

Another servant pours black wine into a goblet in front of him, one carved of ice. Oak lifts it, wondering if there's any way to tell if the liquid within is poisoned. Some he can identify by taste, but plenty have either no flavor or one subtle enough to be masked by something more aromatic.

He thinks of Oriana, patiently feeding him a little bit of poison along with goat milk and honey when he was an infant, making him sicker to make him better. He takes a tentative sip.

The wine is strong and tastes of something like currants.

He notes that Wren has not touched her glass.

I have to show her that I trust her, he tells himself, even though he's not entirely sure that he does. After all, she wouldn't be the first person he liked who tried to kill him. She wouldn't even be the first person he *loved* who tried to kill him.

He pushes the thought away. Lifting his wineglass in salute, he takes a deep draught. At that, Wren finally brings her goblet to her lips.

Oak tries not to show his relief. "I asked you once about whether you might like to be queen in earnest. It seems you changed your mind." He manages to keep his voice light, although he still isn't sure why he's sitting here and not at the other end of an ice whip.

"Have you changed yours?" she asks.

He smiles. "Ought I? Tell me, Your Majesty, what is it like, now that you sit on a throne and have so many demands on your time and resources? Do you like having courtiers at your beck and call?"

Her returning smile is tinged with bitterness. "You know well, prince, that sitting at the head of the table does not mean your guests will not fall to bickering over the portions on their plates, the seating arrangements, or the polish on the silver. Nor does it mean they will not scheme for your seat."

As though part of her speech, two huldufólk servants enter the room and set the first course before Oak and Wren.

Thin slivers of cold fish on a plate of ice with a scattering of cracked pink peppercorns. Elegant and cold.

"As your guest," Oak says, lifting his fork, "I have few complaints. And I am, in fact, at your beck and call."

"Few complaints?" she echoes, one pale blue brow rising. "The prisons were just to your liking?"

"I would prefer not to return to them," Oak admits. "But if I had to remain there to be here, then I have none at all."

A faint flush comes into Wren's cheeks, and she frowns again. "You asked me what I wanted with you." She peers down the table at him with her moss-green eyes. A soft green, he always thought, but they are hard now. "But all that matters is that I *do* want you. And I have you." Though that seems like a confession, she delivers the words like a threat.

"I thought you believed that there could be no love where one person was bound. Isn't that what you told Tiernan?"

"You need not love me," she tells him.

"What if I did? If I do?" Oak has proclaimed his love to people before, but that felt like play and this feels like pain. Maybe it's because she sees him, and no one else has. The illusion he wears is much easier to love than what's underneath.

Wren laughs. "What if? Do not play word games with me, Oak."

He feels a hot flush of shame, realizing that was exactly what he was doing. "You're right. Let me be plain. I do—"

"*No,*" she says, cutting him off, her voice simmering with the magic of unmaking, sending one of the fruits on a footed tray to pulp and seeds, one of the platters to molten silver. It sears through the ice of the table to drip onto the floor in shining strings, cooling on the way down.

She looks as startled as he is, but she recovers quickly, pushing herself into a standing position. A strand of blue hair has come loose, falling over her face. "Do not think I will be flattered because you think me a better opponent and therefore set me a more careful romantic riddle to solve. I need no protestations of your feelings. Love can be lost, and I am done with losing."

He shivers, thinking of Lady Nore and Lord Jarel and how, though what was between them certainly was not love, it had something of love in it. He saw the former queens of the Court of Teeth immured inside the frozen walls of the Hall of Queens. That's what it was to want to possess another, being unwilling to let them go, even in death. To murder them when you decided it was time for them to be replaced, so that you could keep them still.

Oak hadn't thought Wren capable of wanting to possess someone that way, and he didn't want to believe it now.

But she may think—after throwing him in prison and leaving him there—they are enemies. That she made a choice in anger that cannot be taken back. That whatever else he says, he will always hate her.

And perhaps he would hate her, eventually. He blames himself for much, and is willing to endure much, but there's an end to his endurance.

"Perhaps you could remove the bridle, at least?" he asks. "You want me. You can have me. But will you kiss me even as I wear it? Feel the leather straps against your skin once more?"

A small shudder goes through her as she takes her seat again, and he knows he scored that point at least.

"What would you do to be freed from it?" she asks.

"Since you can use the bridle to make me do anything, it stands to reason that there ought to be nothing I wouldn't do to get it off," he says.

"But that's not the case." Her expression is canny, and he remembers how many bad bargains she has heard mortals make with the Folk.

He gives her a small, careful smile. "I would do *a lot*."

"Would you agree to stay here with me?" she asks. "Forever."

He thinks of his sisters, his mother and his father, his friends, and the idea of never seeing them again. Never being in the mortal world nor walking through the halls of Elfhame. He cannot imagine it. And yet, perhaps they could visit, perhaps in time he could persuade—

She must see the hesitation in his face. "I thought not."

"I didn't say no," he reminds her.

"I'll wager you were thinking of how you might bend the language in your favor. To promise something that sounded like what I asked for but had another meaning entirely."

He bites the inside of his cheek. That wasn't what he was thinking, but he would have eventually come around to it.

Oak stabs a piece of fish and eats it. It's peppery and has been splashed with vinegar. "What will you do when the High Court asks for me back?"

She gives him a mild look. "What makes you think they haven't already?"

He thinks of all the war meetings she was dragged to by a silver chain back in the Court of Teeth. She knows what a conflict with Elfhame means. "If you let me speak with my sister—" he begins.

"You would put in a good word?" There's a challenge in her voice.

Before, she played defensively. Her goal was to protect herself, but one cannot win that way.

I am done with losing.

He sees in Wren's face the desire to sweep the board.

He thinks of Bogdana, standing outside his cell, telling him that it is the High King she wants.

Was this all part of the storm hag's plan? His sister's lessons and his father's lessons come to him in a confusing rush, but they are all wrong for this.

"I could persuade Jude to give us a little longer to settle our differences. But I admit that it will be harder with this bridle on my face."

Wren takes another sip of her wine. "You can't stop what's coming."

"What if I promise to return if you let me go?" Oak asks.

She looks at him as though they are sharing an old joke. "Surely you don't expect me to fall for such a simple trick as that."

The prince thinks of the key on the mantel, of the possibility of escape. "I could have left."

"You wouldn't have gotten far." She sounds very sure.

Another course comes. This one is hot, so hot that the plate steams and the side of his ice wine goblet shines with melt. Deer hearts grilled over a fire, a sauce of red berries beneath them.

He wonders if Wren planned the progression of this meal. If not, someone in the kitchens has a truly grim sense of humor.

He doesn't lift his fork. He doesn't eat meat, but he's not sure he'd eat this even if he did.

She watches him. "You wish me to make you my advisor. To sit at my feet, tame and helpful. So advise me—I wish to be obeyed, even if I cannot be loved. I have few examples of queens that I might model myself after. Ought I rule like Queen Annet, who executes her lovers when she grows tired of them? Like your sister? I am told the High King himself called her method of diplomacy *the path of knives*. Or perhaps like Lady Nore, who used arbitrary and almost constant cruelty to keep her followers in line."

Oak sets his jaw. "I believe that you can be obeyed *and* loved. You don't need to rule like anyone other than yourself."

"Love, again?" Wren says, but the twist of her mouth softens. Some part of her must be frightened to be back in this Citadel, to be sovereign over those she was fighting mere weeks before, to have been ill, to have demands on her power. She doesn't behave as though she's afraid, though.

He looks across the table at the scars on her cheeks that came from wearing the bridle so long. At her moss-dark eyes. A feeling of helplessness sweeps over him. All his words tangle in his mouth, though he is used to having them come easily, tripping off his tongue.

He would tell her that he wants to stay with her, that he wants to be her friend again, wants to feel her teeth against his throat, but how can he possibly convince her of his sincerity? And even if she did believe him, what would it matter when his desires didn't keep her safe from his machinations?

"I never pretended to feelings that weren't real," he manages.

She watches him, her body tense, her eyes haunted. "Never? In the Court of Moths, would you really have endured my kiss if you didn't think you needed me on your quest?"

He snorts in surprise. "I would have *endured* it, yes. I would endure it again right now."

A slight rosiness comes into her cheeks. "That's not fair."

"This is nonsensical. Surely you could tell I liked it," he says. "I even liked it when you bit me. On the shoulder, remember? I might have a few tiny scars yet from the points of your teeth."

"Don't be ridiculous," she tells him, annoyed.

"Unfair," he says. "When I so love being ridiculous."

Servants come to collect their plates. The prince's food is untouched.

She looks down at her lap, turning enough away from him to hide her expression. "You cannot really expect me to believe you liked being bitten?"

He finds himself in the position he has so often put others, on his back foot. A hot flush creeps up his neck.

"Well?" she says.

He grins at her. "Didn't you mean for me to enjoy it a little?"

For a long moment, there's a silence between them.

The final course comes. Cold again, ice shaved into a pyramid of flakes, coated in a thin syrup as red as blood.

He eats it and tries not to shiver.

A few minutes later, Wren stands. "You will go back to the room in the tower, where I trust you will remain until I summon you again."

"To sprawl at your feet like a war prize?" he asks hopefully.

"That might amuse you enough to keep you from mischief." A small smile tugs at a corner of her mouth.

Oak pushes back his chair and walks to her, reaching for her hand. He is surprised when she lets him take it. Her fingers are cold in his.

She glances toward the guards. A red-haired falcon steps forward. Before Oak lets her hand go, though, he brings the back of it to his lips.

"My lady," he says, eyes closing for a moment when his mouth touches her skin. He feels as though he is attempting to cross a chasm on a bridge of razors. One misstep and he's going to be in a world of pain.

But Wren only makes a small frown, as though expecting to find mockery in his gaze. She takes back her hand, her face unreadable as the guards lead him to the door.

"I am not the person you believe me to be," she says in a rush.

He turns back to her, surprised.

"That girl you knew. Inside her was always this great rage, this emptiness. And now it's all I am." Wren looks wretched, her hands pressed together in front of her. Her eyes haunted.

Oak thinks of Mellith and her memories. Of her death and Wren's birth. Of the way she's watching him now.

"I don't believe that," he tells her.

She turns to one of the guards. "On the way to his rooms," she tells him, "make sure you pass the Great Hall."

One of the falcons nods, looking discomfited. The guards escort Oak out, marching him through the corridor. As they pass the throne room, they slow their steps enough for him to get a clear look inside.

Against the ice of the wall, as though a piece of decor, hangs Valen's body. For a moment, Oak wonders if this is Bogdana's handiwork, but the falcon is neither flayed nor displayed in the manner of the storm hag's other victims.

His throat is cut. A gruesome necklace of blood has dried along his collarbone. His clothing is stiff with it, as though starched. Oak can see the gape of flesh, cut cleanly with a sharp knife.

The prince glances back in the direction of where he had dinner with Wren.

When she noted his reluctance to name the person responsible for his bruises, she already knew. Hyacinthe must have conveyed Oak's words to her. She could have done this while the prince donned his clothes for their dinner.

It is not as if he hasn't seen murders before. In Elfhame, he saw plenty. His hands aren't clean. But looking at the dead falcon, displayed thus, he recognizes that, even without Mellith's memories, Wren saw things that were far more terrifying and cruel than anything he witnessed. And perhaps somewhere inside her, she is coming to learn that she can be all the things that once scared her.

Oak was a child when Madoc was exiled to the mortal world, and yet, no matter what anyone said, he still knew it was his fault.

Without Oak, there would have been no war. No plan to steal the crown. No family at one another's throats.

At least your father wasn't executed for treason, Oriana told Oak when he complained about not being able to see him. Oak laughed, thinking she made a joke. When he realized that really could have happened, the idea of Madoc's dying while he watched, powerless to stop it, haunted his nightmares. Beheadings. Drownings. Burnings. Being buried alive. His sisters, grim-faced. Oriana, weeping.

Those bad dreams made not seeing Madoc even harder.

It's not a good idea right now, Oriana told him. *We don't want to seem as though we're not loyal to the crown.*

And so he lived with Vivi and Heather in the mortal world, went to the mortal school, and during library time, compulsively looked up new, horrible details of executions. Sometimes Jude or Taryn would visit him at the apartment. His mother came often. Occasionally, someone like Garrett or Van would show up and instruct him in bladework.

No one thought he had any real talent for it.

Oak's problem was that he thought of sword fighting as a game and didn't want to hurt anyone. Games were supposed to be fun. Then, after a lot of scolding, he understood sword fighting as a deadly game and still didn't want to hurt anyone.

Not everyone needs to be good at killing things, Taryn told him with a pointed look at Jude, who was dangling a toy over baby Leander's head as though he were a cat ready to swat at it.

Sometimes after his nightmares, Oak would sneak out and stand on the lawn of the apartment complex and look up at the stars. Missing his mother and father. Missing his old house and his old life. Then he would walk into the woods and practice with his sword, even though he didn't know what he was practicing for.

A few months in, Oriana finally took him to see Madoc. There was no objection or interference from Jude. Either she didn't know—which was unlikely—or she looked the other way, reluctant to forbid the visits but unable to officially allow them.

Be nice to your father, Oriana warned. As though Madoc was ill, rather than exiled and bored and angry. But if Oriana taught Oak one thing, it was how to pretend everything was fine without actually lying about it.

Oak felt shy as he stood in front of his father after all this time. Madoc had a ground-floor apartment in an old brick building by the waterfront. It wasn't quite like Vivi's, since it was furnished with ancient pieces from their home in Elfhame, but it was clearly a mortal space.

There was a refrigerator and an electric stove. Oak wondered if his father resented him.

Madoc seemed mostly concerned about Oak becoming soft.

"Those girls were always fussing over you," his father said. "Your mother, too."

Because he was born poisoned and was sickly as a baby, Oriana was constantly worried that Oak would overextend himself or that one of his sisters would be too rough with him. He hated her fretting. He was forever running off and swinging from trees or riding his pony in defiance of her edicts.

After months apart from his father, though, he felt ashamed of all the times he went along with her wishes.

"I'm not very good with a sword," he blurted out.

Madoc raised his brows. "How's that?"

Oak shrugged. He knew that Madoc never trained him the way he trained Jude and Taryn, certainly not the way he trained Jude. If he'd come inside with bruises the way she used to, Oriana would have been furious.

"Show me," Madoc said.

Which is how he found himself on the lawn of a cemetery, blade raised, as his father walked around him. Oak went through the exercises, one after the other. Madoc poked him with a mop handle when he was in the wrong position, but it wasn't often.

The redcap nodded. "Good, fine. You know what you're doing."

That part was true. Everyone had seen to that. "I have a hard time hitting people."

Madoc laughed in surprise. "Well, that is a problem."

Oak made a sour face. Back then, he didn't like being laughed at.

His father saw the expression and shook his head. "There's a trick to it," he said. "One that your sisters never quite learned."

"*My* sisters?" Oak asked, incredulous.

"You need to let go of the part of your mind that's holding you back," Madoc said moments before he attacked. The redcap's mop handle caught Oak in the side, knocking him into the grass. By the conditions of his exile, Madoc wasn't allowed to hold a weapon, so he improvised.

Oak looked up, the breath knocked out of him. But when Madoc swept the wooden stick toward him, he rolled to one side, blocking the blow.

"Good," his father said, and waited for him to get up before striking again.

They sparred like that, back and forth. Oak was used to fighting, although not with this great intensity.

Still, his father wore him down, hit by hit.

"All the skill in the world doesn't matter if you won't *strike me*," Madoc shouted finally. "Enough. Halt!"

Oak let his blade sag, relieved. Tired. "I told you."

But his father didn't look as though he was going to let things go. "You're blocking my blows instead of looking for openings."

Barely blocking, Oak thought, but nodded.

The redcap looked like he was going to gnash his teeth. "You need to get some fire in your belly."

Oak didn't reply. He'd heard Jude tell him something similar many times. If he didn't fight back, he could die. Elfhame wasn't a safe place. Maybe there were no safe places.

"You need to turn off the part of you that's *thinking*," Madoc said.

"Guilt. Shame. The desire to make people *like* you. Whatever is getting in your way, you need to excise it. Cut it out of your heart. From the time your sword leaves your sheath, put all that aside and strike!"

Oak bit his lip, not sure if that was possible. He liked being liked.

"Once your sword is out of your sheath, you aren't Oak anymore. And you stay that way until the fight is over." Madoc frowned. "And do you know how to tell the fight is over? All your enemies are dead. Understand?"

Oak nodded and *tried*. He willed himself to forget everything but the steps of the fight. Block, parry, strike.

He was quicker than Madoc. Sloppier, but faster. For a moment, he felt as though he was doing okay.

Then the redcap came at him hard. Oak responded with a flurry of parries. For a moment, he thought he saw an opportunity to get under his father's guard but flinched from it. His nightmares flashed in front of him. He parried instead, harder this time.

"Halt, child," said Madoc, stopping, frustration clear on his face. "You let two obvious openings pass."

Oak, who had seen only one, said nothing.

Madoc sighed. "Imagine splitting your mind into two parts: the general and the foot soldier. Once the general gives an order, the foot soldier doesn't need to think for himself. He just has to do what he's told."

"It's not that I'm *thinking* I don't want to hit you," Oak said. "I just don't."

His father nodded, frowning. Then his arm shot out, the flat of the mop handle knocking Oak into the dirt. For a moment, he couldn't get his breath.

"Get up," Madoc said.

As soon as he did, his father was on him again.

This time Madoc was serious, and for the first time, Oak was scared of what might happen. The hits came hard enough to bruise and too fast to be stopped.

He didn't want to hurt his father. He wasn't even sure that he could.

His father wasn't supposed to *really* hurt him.

As the blows came relentlessly, he could feel tears sting his eyes. "I want to stop," he said, the words coming out in a whine.

"Then fight back!" Madoc shouted.

"No!" Oak threw his sword to the ground. "I give up."

The mop handle caught him in the stomach. He went down hard, scuttled back, out of his father's range. Only barely, though.

"I don't want to do this!" he shouted. He could feel that his cheeks were wet.

Madoc came forward, closing the distance. "You want to die?"

"You're going to *kill* me?" Oak was incredulous. This was his *father*.

"Why not?" Madoc said. "If you don't defend yourself, *someone* is going to kill you. Better it be me."

That made no sense. But when the mop handle hit him in the side of the head, he started to believe it.

Oak looked at his sword, across the grass. Pushed himself to his hooves. Ran toward it. His cheek was throbbing. His stomach hurt.

He wasn't sure he'd ever been scared like this, not even when he was in the Great Hall with the serpent coming toward his mother.

When he turned back to Madoc, his vision was blurry with tears. Somehow that made things easier. To not have to really see what was happening. He could feel himself slipping into that state of not quite awareness. Like times that he was daydreaming on the walk to school and got there without remembering being on the route. Like when he gave over to his gancanagh magic and let it turn his words to honey.

Like those things, except he was angry enough to give himself a single order: *win*.

Like those things, except when he blinked, it was to find the point of his blade nearly at his father's throat, held back only by the half-splintered end of the mop handle. Madoc was bleeding from a slash on his arm, one Oak didn't recall causing.

"Good," said Madoc, breathing hard. "Again."

CHAPTER

9

W hen Oak returns to the bedroom in the tower, two servants are
waiting for him. One has the head of an owl and long, gangly
arms. The other has skin the color of moss and small moth wings.

"We are to ready you for bed," says one, indicating the dressing gown.

After weeks wearing the same rags, this is a lot. "Great. I can take it
from here," he says.

"It is our duty to make sure you're properly cared for," says the other,
ignoring Oak's objections and shoving his arms into the positions necessary for the removal of his doublet.

The prince submits, allowing them to strip him down and put him
in the robe. It's a thick blue satin, lined in gold and warm enough that
he doesn't entirely begrudge the change. It is strange to have spent
weeks being treated as a prisoner, to now be treated as a prince. To be
pampered and bullied just as he would be in Elfhame, not trusted to do
basic tasks for himself.

He wonders if they do this to Wren. If she lets them.

He thinks of the rough silk of her hair slipping through his fingers. *All that matters is that I* do *want you.*

As he sat for those long weeks in the prisons, he dreamed of her speaking words like those. But if she truly desired him only to be a handsome object with no will of his own, sprawled at her feet like a lazy hound, he would come to hate it. Eventually, he would hate her, too.

He goes to the mantel and takes the key. The metal is cold in the palm of his hand.

If she wants more from him, if she wants *him*, then she has to trust that if he leaves, he'll return.

Taking a deep breath, he walks to the bed. The dressing gown is warm but won't be once he hits the wind. He takes the thickest of the blankets and wraps it over his shoulders like a cloak. Then, ragwort stalk in one hand, he opens the door and peers out into the corridor.

No guard waits for him. He supposes Hyacinthe made sure of that.

As lightly as he can with his hooves, he goes to the stairs and begins to ascend. Up the spiraling structure, avoiding the landings until at last he comes to the top of the parapet. He steps out into the cold and looks out on the white landscape below.

As high up as he is, he can see beyond the trolls' massive—and as yet unfinished—wall. He squints as he spots what appears to be a flickering flame. And then another. A sound comes to him with the wind. Metallic and rhythmic, at first it sounds like sheeting rain. Then like the early rumblings of thunder.

Below him, behind the battlements, guards shout to one another. They must have spotted whatever it is that Oak is seeing. There's a confusion of footsteps.

But it isn't until the prince hears the distant blare of a horn that he finally identifies what he's been looking at. Soldiers marching toward the Citadel. The snake promised that in three days' time, someone would rescue him. What he didn't expect was that it would be the *entire army of Elfhame*.

Oak paces back and forth atop the cold parapet, panic making it impossible to focus. *Think*, he tells himself. *Think*.

He could use the ragwort steed and fly to them—assuming they would know it *was* him and not shoot him out of the sky. But once he got there, then what? They marched here for a war, and he wasn't foolish enough to believe they would merely turn around and go home once he was safe.

No, once he was safe, they would have no reason to hold back.

He grew up in a general's home, so he has a sense of what's likely to happen next. Grima Mog will send ahead riders to meet with Wren. They will demand to see him and offer terms of surrender. Wren will reject that and possibly unmake the messengers.

He needs to do something, but if he goes there with the bridle cutting into his cheeks, that will end all hope of peace.

Closing his eyes, Oak thinks through his options. They're all terrible, but the sheer mad audacity of one has a particular appeal.

Is there no situation you're not compelled to make worse?

The prince hopes that Hyacinthe isn't right.

He doesn't have a lot of time. Dropping the blanket, he heads down the steps, not bothering to care how loud his hooves are on the ice. Any guard that hears him has bigger problems.

Halfway down the spiral stairs, he almost crashes into a nisse with hair the green of celery and eyes so pale they are almost colorless. The faerie is carrying a tray with strips of raw venison arranged on a plate beside a bowl of stewed seaweed. Startled, the nisse takes a step back and loses his balance. The whole tray crashes down, plate cracking, seaweed splashing onto the steps.

The terror on the nisse's face makes it clear that the punishment for such a mishap in the old Court of Teeth would have been terrible. But when the nisse realizes who is standing in front of him, he becomes, if anything, more afraid.

"You're not supposed to be out of your rooms," the nisse says.

Oak notes the raw meat. "I suppose not."

The nisse starts to move away, stepping down a stair, looking behind him in a nervous way that suggests he will run. Before he can, Oak presses his hand over the nisse's mouth, pushing the faerie's back to the wall, even as he struggles against the prince's grip.

Oak needs an ally, a willing one.

Hating himself, the prince reaches for the honey-mouthed power that stretches languorously at his summons. He leans in to whisper in the nisse's ear. "I don't want to frighten you," he says, his voice sounding strange to his own ears. "And I don't intend to hurt you. When you came here, I'll wager it was because of a bad bargain."

That's how it was in Balekin's house. And he didn't think anyone would stay working for Lord Jarel and Lady Nore if they had any other option.

The nisse doesn't respond. But something in his expression and his stance makes Oak understand that the servant has been punished before, has been badly hurt, more than once. No wonder Oak scares him.

"What did you promise? I can help," Oak asks, pulling his hand away slowly. The burr is still in his voice.

The nisse relaxes some, tipping his head back against the wall. "Mortals found my family. I don't know what they thought we were, but they killed two of us and caught the third. I got away and came to the only place I knew could get back the lover that was taken—the Ice Needle Citadel. And I promised that if they were returned to me, I would loyally work in the Citadel until one of the royal family thought I had repaid my debt and dismissed me."

Oak lets out a groan. That's the sort of desperate, foolish bargain he associates with mortals, but mortals are not the only ones who grow desperate or who can be foolish. "Is that *exactly* what you promised?" Again, his voice has lost its honey-tongued power. He became too distracted to maintain it, too interested in what he wants to remember to say the right thing.

The nisse winces. "I will never forget."

Oak thinks about being a child and reckless about magic. He thinks about Valen and how furious he was after he realized Oak was enchanting him.

When he speaks, he can feel the air thicken. "I am one of the royal family. Not the one you meant, but you didn't specify, so I ought to be able to free you from your debt. But I need your help. I need someone to act as a messenger." Oak can feel the moments his words sink in, like a fish biting a worm, only to have a hook sink through its cheek.

He remembers the feeling of his body betraying him, the feeling of his limbs fighting against his will. There's none of that here. This is the opportunity the nisse has been looking for.

"We could both get in a lot of trouble," he says with a nervous glance down the stairs.

"We could," Oak says in his regular voice.

The nisse nods slowly, pushing off from the wall. "Tell me what you will have me do."

"First, I need something other than this to wear."

The nisse raises his eyebrows.

"Yes, yes, you find me to be vain," says Oak. "But I'm afraid I still need to discover wherever it is that they keep Lord Jarel's old clothes."

The nisse flinches. "You'd wear them?"

Probably the dressing gown Oak has on once belonged to Lord Jarel, as well as what Oak was given to put on for dinner. There hadn't been time to commission whole new outfits, nor had they fit right. And if they had been fetched for him, then he could fetch something else for himself. "Let's just take a look. What ought I call you?"

"Daggry, Your Highness."

"Lead on, Daggry," Oak says.

It's easier to move through the Citadel with a servant able to scout ahead and report which ways are clear. They make it to a storeroom, slipping inside before they are spotted.

"This is very near my bedchamber," says Daggry. "Should you wish to visit me there tonight."

Oak makes his mouth curve, though guilt chokes him. "I don't think either one of us will have much time for sleeping."

Oak thinks of his mother's warning: *Say those things, and they will not only want to listen to you. They will come to want you above all other things.*

"No," Daggry says. "I was not proposing sleep."

The narrow room is piled with trunks, stacked haphazardly one on the next. And packed in them, the prince finds clothes spread with dried lavender and picked over for gold and pearl ornaments. Strings hang loose from the places where buttons and trims were cut away. He wonders if Lady Nore sold the missing pieces before she discovered the value of the bones she stole from the tombs underneath Elfhame. Before Bogdana began whispering in her ear, urging her on the path that would bring Wren back to the storm hag.

He finds paper and ink, books and pen nibs attached to owl feathers. At the very bottom of the trunk, Oak digs up a few scattered weapons. Cheap, flat ones, a few pitted or scratched where gems were obviously removed from hilts. He lifts up a small dagger, keeping it mostly hidden in the palm of his hand.

"I am going to write a note," he says.

Daggry watches him with unnerving eagerness.

Taking out the paper, pens, and ink, Oak braces against one of the chests and scratches out two messages. The owl feather pen stains his fingers and makes him wish for a Sharpie. "Take the first of these to Hyacinthe," Oak says. "And the second one to the army that waits beyond the wall."

"The High Court's army?" the nisse says with a squeak in his voice.

Oak nods. "Go to the stables of the Citadel. There you will find my horse. Her name is Damsel Fly. Take her, and ride as fast as you are able. Once you come to the army, tell them you have a message from Prince Oak. Do not let them send you back with a message. Tell them it wouldn't be safe for you."

Daggry frowns, as though thinking things through. "And you will be grateful?"

"Very," Oak agrees.

"Enough to—" the nisse begins to say as he tucks away the notes.

"As a member of the royal family, I deem the time you have served a fair recompense for what you were given, and I dismiss you from service at the Citadel," Oak tells the nisse, frightened of the low burr in his own voice, like the purr of a cat. Frightened of the way the nisse gives him a look so full of gratitude and longing that it feels like a lash.

"I will do just as you've asked," says the nisse as he leaves, closing the door behind him.

For a moment, Oak just rubs at his face, not sure if he should be ashamed of what he's done, and if so, how ashamed. Forcibly, he thrusts that confusion of guilt aside. He has made his choices. Now he must live with them and hope they were the right ones.

The army of Elfhame is in danger because of him. Planning to hurt Wren because of him. Perhaps about to die because of him.

He strips off the dressing gown, pulling out a more regal outfit, grateful for Lord Jarel's height. The clothes are still a little short on him, a little tight across the chest.

You are such a beanstalk, he remembers Heather's mother saying. *I remember when I could pick you up.* He is surprised by how much that memory hurts, since Heather's mother is still alive and still kind and would let him sleep in her guest room anytime he wanted. Of course, that's predicated on his leaving this Citadel alive.

Sometimes, Oak thinks, it's not in his best interest to investigate his feelings too closely. In fact, right now, perhaps he ought not investigate his feelings at all.

Oak puts on a blue doublet, threaded with silver, then the matching pants. The hem rips a little as he puts his left hoof through one leg, but it's not immensely noticeable.

He hides the knife in the waistband, hoping he won't need it.

I can still fix things. That's what he tells himself over and over. He has a plan, and it might be mad and desperate and even a little presumptuous, but it can work.

Despite the cold, he discovers only two cloaks in the pile of clothes. He rejects the one lined in sealskin on the theory it may be from a selkie. That leaves him with the other, lined in fox fur, though he likes it little better.

Oak draws the hood over his face and heads to the Hall of Queens, where he asked Hyacinthe to meet. The room is echoing and empty; as he waits, he stares at the two women frozen inside the walls, former brides of Lord Jarel. Former queens of the Court of Teeth. Their cold, dead eyes seem to watch him back.

The prince paces the floor, but minutes pass and no one comes. His breath steams in the air as he listens for footsteps.

As dawn breaks, through the wavy ice he can see riders passing through the gap in the ice wall. They thunder toward the Citadel with banners streaming behind them, on faerie steeds whose hooves are light on the frozen crust of the snow.

His plan—wobbly from the start, he now has to admit—feels as though it is capsizing.

"Why are you still here?" a gruff voice asks.

For a long moment, relief robs the prince of breath. When he can compose his face, he turns toward Hyacinthe. "If I run from the Citadel wearing this bridle," he says, "no one in command will care what I say. They will believe I am in Wren's power. I will have even less sway over the army than I do, and that isn't much. With Grima Mog in charge of them, and orders already in place from my sister, they'll be looking forward to a fight."

"All they want is you," Hyacinthe says.

"Maybe, but once they have me, what's the next thing they will want? If I am safe, they have no reason *not* to attack. Help me help Wren. Remove the bridle."

Hyacinthe snorts. "I know the words of command well. I could use them to order you to leave the Citadel and surrender yourself to Grima Mog."

"If you send me away with the bridle on, no one will ever believe that we are not at war," Oak says.

Hyacinthe crosses his arms. "Am I supposed to believe you're on Wren's side in this conflict? That escaping is somehow all for her?"

Oak wishes he could say that. Wishes he even believed in clear sides with defined borders. He had to give those up when his father crossed swords with his sister. "Even if Wren can unmake the entire army of Elfhame, pull them apart as easily as she might pull the wings off butterflies, it will cost her. Hurt her. Make her sicker."

"You're their prince," Hyacinthe says with a sneer. "You look to save your own people."

"How about no one dies? Let's try for that!" Oak snaps, his voice loud enough to echo in the room.

Hyacinthe looks at the prince for a long moment. "Very well. I'll take off the bridle and let you try whatever it is you're planning, so long as you promise no harm will come to Wren—and you agree to do something for me."

No matter how much he wants to, Oak knows better than to give his word without hearing the conditions. He waits.

"You thought I was foolish for going after the High King," Hyacinthe says.

"I still do," Oak confirms.

Hyacinthe gives him a frustrated look. "I admit that I'm impulsive. When the curse started again, when I could feel myself becoming a falcon again—I thought if Cardan were dead, it would end the curse. I blamed him."

Oak bites his tongue. Hyacinthe has not yet come to the favor part.

"There's something I want to know, but I am not crafty enough to discover it. Nor am I so well connected." Hyacinthe looks as though he hates admitting this. "But you—you deceive as easily as you breathe and with as little thought."

"And you want..."

"Revenge. I thought it was impossible, but Madoc told me something different," Hyacinthe says. "You should care, you know? You owe her a blood debt as well."

Oak frowns. "Prince Dain killed Liriope, and he's dead himself. I know you want to punish someone—"

"No, he *ordered* her killed," Hyacinthe says. "But he wasn't the one to administer the poison. Not the one to sneak past my father as he guarded her. Not the one to leave you both for dead. That is the person I can still kill for my father's sake."

Oak assumed that Dain administered the poison. Slipped it into a drink. Poured it over her lips while she slept beside him. He never imagined that her murderer was still alive.

"So I find the person who gave her the poison. Or try, at least—and you remove the bridle," Oak says. "I agree."

"Bring me the hand of the person responsible for her death," Hyacinthe says.

"You want a *hand*?" Oak raises both brows.

"That hand, I do."

Oak doesn't have time to negotiate. "Fine."

Hyacinthe gives a strange smile, and Oak worries that he's made the wrong decision, but it's too late to question it.

"*In Grimsen's name,*" Hyacinthe begins, and Oak jams his hand into the pocket of the cloak for the knife he found. His skin is clammy despite the cold. He cannot be sure that Hyacinthe won't use the command to do something other than unbind him. If so, Oak is going to try to cut the falcon's throat before he finishes speaking.

Probably there wouldn't even be time. Oak's fingers twitch.

"*In Grimsen's name, let the bridle no longer bind you,*" Hyacinthe says.

Oak takes his blade to the strap, but it doesn't cut. He nicks his own cheek for the effort. A moment later, though, he has unhooked the bridle with shaking hands. He pulls it off his face, throwing it to the ground. He can feel the indentations where the straps pressed into his cheek. Not sunken so deeply to scar, but tight enough to mark.

"A monstrous object," Hyacinthe says as he bends to pick up the bridle. He wore it long enough to hate it, perhaps even more than Oak. "Now what?"

"We go to the Great Hall to meet the riders." Oak traces his fingers over his cheeks, the cold of them a relief. He doesn't like the idea that Hyacinthe has the bridle, but even if the prince could wrest it from him, he dreads so much as touching it.

Hyacinthe frowns. "And...?"

"Attempt to seem convincingly happy to be Wren's guest," Oak says. "Then figure out how to send the army of Elfhame on its way."

"That's what you're calling a plan?" Hyacinthe snorts. "We can't be seen together, so give me a head start. I don't want anyone to guess what I've done, in case it doesn't work."

"It would be a lot easier to get into the Great Hall with your help," Oak points out.

"I'm sure it would be," says Hyacinthe.

The falcon stalks off, leaving Oak to wait. To pace the Hall of Queens some more. Count off the minutes. Trace his fingers over his cheek to feel for any trace of the straps. There's something there, but light, like the creases left from a pillow in the morning. He hopes these marks will disappear soon. Finally, he can bear to bide his time no longer. He pushes back the hood of his cloak and, head held high, walks toward the Great Hall.

If there is one thing he has learned from Cardan, it is that royalty inspires awe and awe can be cultivated easily into menace. It is with that in mind that he strides toward the guards.

Startled, they raise their spears. Two falcons, neither of whom he recognizes.

Oak looks at them blandly. "Well," he says with an impatient wave of his hand. "Open the doors."

He watches them hesitate. After all, he's dressed well and clean. He doesn't have on the bridle. And they must all know he is no longer being held in the prisons. They must all know Wren killed the last guard who put a finger on him.

"The emissaries of Elfhame are inside, are they not?" he adds.

One of the falcons nods to the other. Together, they open the double doors.

Wren sits on her throne; Bogdana and Hyacinthe stand beside her—along with a trio of heavily armored falcons.

And standing before her are four Folk—all of whom Oak recognizes. Unarmored, the Ghost appears to be playing the part of an ambassador. He's dressed in finery, and the slightly human cast of his features makes him look far less threatening than he is.

An actual ambassador, Randalin, one of the Living Council, bites off his words at Oak's arrival. Known as the Minister of Keys, he is short, horned, and even more beautifully dressed than the Ghost. As far as Oak is aware, Randalin can't fight and, given the danger, Oak is surprised he came. Jude never much liked him, though, so he can certainly see why she allowed—and even perhaps encouraged—it.

Behind them are two soldiers. Oak knows Tiernan instantly, despite the helmet hiding his face. He assumes Hyacinthe knows him, too. At his side is Grima Mog, the grand general who replaced Oak's father. A redcap, like Madoc, and the former general of the Court of Teeth. No one knows the defenses of the Citadel better than she does, so no one would have an easier time breaching them.

As Oak strides in, everyone becomes more alert. Tiernan's hand goes automatically to the pommel of his sword in a foolish rejection of diplomacy.

"Hello," the prince says. "I see you all started without me."

Wren raises both her brows. *Good game*, he imagines her saying. *Point to you.* Possibly right before she tells her guards to pop off his head like a wine cork.

And then the Ghost stabs her in the back. And everyone cuts everyone else to pieces.

"Your Highness," says Garrett, as though he really is some stuffy ambassador who hasn't known Oak half his life. "After receiving your note, we expected you to be in attendance. We were growing concerned."

Wren gives the prince a sharp look at the mention of a note.

"Hard to choose the right outfit for such a momentous occasion,"

Oak says, hoping that the sheer absurdity of his plan will help sell it. "After all, it's not every day that one gets to announce one's engagement."

At that, all of them stare at him agog. Even Bogdana seems to have lost the power of speech. But that is nothing to the way Wren is looking at him. It is as though she could immolate him in the cold green flame of her eyes.

Heedless of the warning, he walks to her side. Taking her hand, he slides the ring—the ring he was sent in the belly of an enchanted metal snake—off his pinkie finger and onto hers in the stealthy way the Roach taught him. So that it might be possible to believe she'd been wearing it the whole time.

He smiles up at her. "She's accepted my ring. And so, I would be delighted to tell you that Wren and I are to be wed."

O ak keeps his gaze on Wren. She could deny him, but she remains
silent. Hopefully she sees that in the face of their *engagement*, it
will be possible to avoid a war. Or, since she holds all the cards, maybe
she finds it amusing to let him reshuffle a little.

A wordless growl comes from deep in Bogdana's throat.

Hyacinthe gives Oak an accusatory look that seems to say, *I can't
believe you talked me into helping you with such a stupid plan.*

This was the gamble. That Wren didn't want to fight. That she'd see
the path to peace with Elfhame was through playing along with him.

"Quite a surprise," the Ghost says, voice dry. Hyacinthe's gaze drifts
to him, and his expression stiffens, as though he recognizes the spy and
understands the danger of his being here.

Tiernan's hand has yet to leave his sword hilt. Grima Mog's eyebrows are raised. She seems to be waiting for someone to tell her this is
all a joke.

Oak goes on smiling, as though everyone has been expressing only their utmost delight.

Randalin clears his throat. "Let me be the first to offer my felicitations. Very wise to secure the succession."

Although the councilor's reasoning seems muddled, the prince is happy for any ally. Oak makes a shallow bow. "I can occasionally be wise."

Eyebrows raised, the Ghost moves his gaze from Wren to Oak. "Your family will be pleased to know you are well. The reports... let's say they suggested otherwise."

At that, Bogdana manages a toothy smile. "Your besotted princeling seems none the worse for wear. Accept our hospitality. We offer you rooms and repast. Stay the night, then take your army and toddle back to Elfhame. Perhaps send the king and queen for a little visit."

"I didn't realize you were empowered to offer us much of anything, storm hag." Grima Mog makes the words sound almost as though they were spoken in honest confusion. "Is it not Queen Suren alone who rules here?"

"For now," says the storm hag with an almost gracious nod toward Oak, as if she were indicating he would rule beside Wren rather than asserting her own power.

Wren motions toward a servant and then turns back to the Minister of Keys. "You must be tired after your travels, and cold. Perhaps a hot drink before you are led to your rooms."

"We would be honored to accept your accommodation," Randalin says, puffing himself up. He accompanied the army, so he must have thought there would be some kind of negotiation for him to lead. Maybe he convinced himself this would be an easy situation to resolve and is gratified to believe himself correct. "On the morrow, we must discuss your plans to return to Elfhame. The prince returning with his bride-to-be will be glad tidings indeed and a cause for much celebration. And of course, there will be a treaty to negotiate."

Oak winces. "A treaty. Of course." He cannot help but cut a glance in Wren's direction, trying to gauge her reaction.

The Ghost tilts his head as he regards Wren. "Are you certain about accepting the young prince's proposal? He can be something of a fool."

Her lips twitch.

Randalin draws in a shocked breath.

Oak gives the Ghost a speaking look. "The question is whether she will have me be *her* fool."

Wren smiles. "I'm certain."

Oak glances at her in surprise, unable to help himself. He attempts to smooth out his expression but is certain he's too late. Someone saw. Someone knows he isn't sure of her love.

"We have a great deal in common, after all," Wren affirms. "Especially a love of games."

She's good at them, too. Quick to pick up on his plan, to measure its worth, and play along. They've been working against each other for so long that he forgot how easy it was to work together.

"We can unravel the details of the treaty in Elfhame," Randalin says. "It will be easier with all parties present."

"I am not sure I'm ready to leave my Citadel," says Wren, and she glances at Oak. He can see her weighing the choice to let him return with them. Can see the calculation in her face as to whether this was his intention all along.

Two servants enter the room bearing a large wooden tray with steaming silver goblets atop it.

"Please, take one," Wren offers.

Do not try to poison them, he thinks, staring at her as though he can somehow speak through his gaze. *Garrett will switch cups with you, and you'll never guess it.*

The Ghost takes the hot drink. Oak lifts one, too, the metal warm in his hand. He catches scents of barley and caraway.

Randalin raises his glass. "To you, Lady Suren. And to you, Prince Oak. In the hopes you will reconsider and join us in returning to Elfhame. Your family will insist on it, prince. And I was meant to remind you, should I be so fortunate as to have an audience with *you*, Lady Suren, that you made vows to the High Court."

"If they mean to give me orders, let them come here and do so," Wren says. "But perhaps I can sweep aside a promise like I would a curse. Pull it apart like a cobweb."

The Folk stare, horrified by even the possibility that someone in Faerie could not be bound by her word. Oak never thought of the promises they made as *magic*, but he supposes they are a kind of binding.

"You ought not want things to start off on the wrong foot," Randalin warns, sounding as though he were reprimanding a student who gave a wrong answer. The councilor seems unaware of how quickly this conversation might devolve into violence.

Grima Mog cracks her knuckles. She is very aware.

"Randalin—" Oak begins.

Bogdana interrupts him. "The councilor is correct," she says. "Wren ought to be properly wed to the heir of Elfhame, with all the pomp and circumstance appropriate to such a union. Let us journey together to the Shifting Isles."

Wren gives the storm hag a sharp look but doesn't contradict her. Doesn't say she won't go. Instead, her fingers linger on the ring sitting loosely on her hand. She turns it anxiously.

Oak recalls Wren coming to the gardens of Elfhame years and years ago, where Jude had received her, along with Lord Jarel, Lady Nore, and Madoc. Recalls that one of them had proposed a truce, cemented with a marriage between him and Wren.

He was a little afraid of her, with her sharp teeth. He had yet to hit the growth spurt that came at thirteen and pulled his body like taffy; she almost certainly was taller than him. He didn't want to marry her—he didn't want to marry *anyone*—and was relieved when Jude refused.

But he saw the expression in Wren's face when Vivi referred to her as *creepy*. The sting of hurt, the flash of rage.

She is going to destroy Elfhame. It's what she was born to do. That's what Bogdana believes, what she wants. And maybe Wren wants it a little bit, too. Maybe Oak has made a horrifically large mistake.

But, no. Wren couldn't have known he would do anything like this. Still, whatever Bogdana favors is unlikely to be a good idea.

"We don't need to depart immediately," the prince hedges. "No doubt you will need time to get together your trousseau."

"Nonsense," says Bogdana. "I know a hag who will enchant Queen Suren three dresses, one for every day in Elfhame before her wedding. The first shall be the pale colors of morning, the second the bright colors of the afternoon, and the last spangled with the jewels of night."

"Three days won't be enough time," says Randalin, frowning.

"Now who is trying to delay?" the storm hag demands, as though the councilor has committed a grave offense. "Perhaps none of this is necessary. He could marry her now, with those gathered here as witnesses."

"*No*," says Wren firmly.

A shame, because Oak doesn't think it's such a bad idea. If they were married, then surely his sister couldn't attempt to burn the Citadel to the ground. Her troops would have to pull back while Oak could keep the ragwort stalk safely in his pocket and bide his time.

"We would not want to disrespect the High Court," Wren says. "We will return with you to Elfhame so long as you withdraw your army from this territory. Whatever preparations are necessary, we will manage."

The Ghost smiles enigmatically. "Excellent. Randalin, your ship is small and swift and well outfitted for traveling in comfort. We can use it to return to Elfhame ahead of the army. If you expect to be ready within a day or two, I will send the message right now."

"You may do so," Wren tells him.

"No, no need," Grima Mog interrupts them gruffly. "I am here to negotiate over battles, not withdrawals. I will return to my army and inform them that no blood will be shed upon the morrow, nor possibly at all." She says this as though they are to be deprived of a great treat. She's a redcap; she might actually believe that.

Her leaving is also almost certainly a test, to see if her departure will be allowed.

As she stomps out, the rest of them drink the contents of their steaming goblets. Randalin makes an officious and confusing speech that manages to be partially about his grievances over the discomforts he endured on the journey, his loyalty to the throne and to Oak, and his belief that alliances are very important. By the time he's done, he's behaving as though he negotiated the marriage himself.

After that, servants make ready to lead each of them to rooms.

The Ghost catches Wren's eye. "We hope that you will choose wisely when you select your retinue." He gives a pointed look in the direction of the storm hag.

A small smile pulls at the corner of Wren's mouth, making her sharp teeth evident. "Someone will have to remain here and watch over the Citadel."

After the Elfhame ambassadors and their guards depart, Wren puts a hand on Oak's arm, as though she needs to draw his attention. "What kind of game is this?" She lowers her voice, although Bogdana is watching them closely. Hyacinthe and the other guards are pretending they are not.

"The kind where no one loses so badly that they have to throw away all their cards," Oak says.

"You only delay the inevitable." She turns from him, her skirts whirling around her.

He wonders how she must have felt when the army of Elfhame arrived. She seems to have resigned herself to the battle with a certain hopelessness, as though she couldn't imagine a way out.

"Maybe I can keep delaying it." Daringly, he walks after her, stepping in front so that she's forced to look up at him. "Or maybe it isn't inevitable."

A few strands of light blue hair have fallen around her face, lessening the severity of the style. But nothing can alter the hardness in her expression. "Hyacinthe," she says.

He steps forward. "My lady."

"Take the prince back to his rooms. And this time, make sure he actually stays there." It's not an accusation, but it's close.

"Yes, my lady," Hyacinthe affirms, taking Oak by the arm and tugging him in the direction of the hall.

"And bring the bridle to my chambers immediately after," she says.

"Yes, my lady," Hyacinthe says again, his voice remarkably even.

The prince goes along willingly. At least until they enter the stairwell and Hyacinthe shoves him against the wall, hand to his throat.

"What exactly do you think you were doing?" Hyacinthe demands.

The prince holds his hands out in surrender. "It worked."

"I didn't expect you to . . . ," he starts, but cannot seem to finish the sentence. "I should have, of course. Do you think that traveling to Elfhame will help her use her power less?"

"Than fighting a war?" Oak asks. "I do."

"And whose fault is it that she's in this position in the first place?"

"Mine," Oak admits with a wince. "But not just mine. You were the one who put the idea of defeating Lady Nore in order to end his exile into my father's head. If Madoc had never come here, then none of this would have ever happened."

"You're blaming me for the former grand general's schemes. I ought to be flattered."

"My sister would have *executed* you for your part in those schemes," Oak tells Hyacinthe. "Had we not taken you that night, at best, you would have been locked in the Tower of Forgetting. But most likely she would have had your head. And then Tiernan's for good measure."

"Is that how you justify manipulating all the people around you like pieces on a chessboard?" Hyacinthe accuses. "That you're doing the best for them?"

"As opposed to you, who doesn't care how much Tiernan suffers for your sake? I suppose you think that makes you honest, rather than a coward." Oak isn't thinking about what he's saying anymore. He's too angry for that. "Or maybe you want to cause him pain. Maybe you're still furious with him for not following you into exile. Maybe making him miserable is your way of having revenge."

Hyacinthe's punch sends Oak staggering back. He can taste blood where a tooth caught on the inside of his mouth. *Is there no situation you're not compelled to make worse?*

"You have no right to *speak* of my feelings for Tiernan." Hyacinthe's voice is raw.

For a moment, in the hot flush of his anger, Oak wonders what would happen if he said all the right things now, instead of the wrong ones. It would serve Hyacinthe right to *have* to like him.

But it was so satisfying to do just the opposite.

"You've been wanting to hit me for a long time." Oak spits blood onto the ice steps. "Well, come on, then."

Hyacinthe punches him again, this time connecting with his jaw, knocking him against a wall.

When Oak looks up, it's as though he's seeing through a haze. *Oh, this was a bad idea.* There's a roaring in his ears.

He's afraid suddenly that he cannot hold back.

"Fight, you coward," Hyacinthe says, punching him in the stomach.

Oak's hand goes to his side, to the knife he concealed there, wrapped tight enough not to muss the line of the doublet. He doesn't remember deciding to draw it before it's in his hand, sharp and deadly.

Hyacinthe's eyes widen, and Oak is very afraid that he is about to lose time again.

He lets the blade drop.

They stare at each other.

Oak can feel the pulse of his blood, that part of him that's eager for a *real* fight, that wants to stop thinking, stop feeling, stop doing anything but make the cold calculations of combat. His awareness of himself flickers like a light, warning that it's about to cut out and welcome in the dark.

"Well," says a voice from behind the prince. "This is not at all what I expected to find when I went looking for both of you."

He whirls to see Tiernan standing there, sword drawn.

A flush creeps up Hyacinthe's neck. "You," he says.

"Me," says Tiernan.

"Be flattered." Oak wipes blood off his chin. "I think we were fighting over you."

Tiernan looks at Hyacinthe with frightening coldness. "Striking the heir to Elfhame is treason."

"Good thing I am already well known to be a traitor," Hyacinthe growls. "Allow me to remind you, however. This is my Citadel. I am in charge of the guard here. I am the one who enforces Wren's will."

Tiernan bristles. "And I am responsible for the prince's well-being, no matter where we are."

Hyacinthe sneers. "And yet you abandoned him."

Tiernan's jaw is tight with the force of his restraint. "I assume you have no objections to the prince finding his own way back to his rooms. We can handle what is between us without him."

Hyacinthe glares at Oak, perhaps thinking of Wren ordering him to make sure the prince didn't wind up wandering the Citadel again.

"I'll be good," Oak says, heading up the stairs before Hyacinthe decides to stop him.

When he glances back, Tiernan and Hyacinthe are still staring at each other with painful suspicion, in a standoff that he doesn't think either of them knows how to end.

Oak climbs two floors before he stops and listens. If he hears the clang of metal on metal, he's going back. He must have missed something, because Hyacinthe speaks as though replying to Tiernan.

"And where am I in this reckoning?" Hyacinthe asks.

"Three times I put aside my duty for you," Tiernan says, as angry as Oak has ever heard him. "And three times you spurned it. Once, when I went to you in the prisons before you were to be judged for following Madoc. Do you remember? I promised that were you sentenced to death, I would find a way to get you out, no matter the cost. Second, when I persuaded the prince, *my charge*, to use his power to mitigate the curse you wouldn't even have had if you had simply repented your betrayal of the crown. And let's not forget the third, when I pleaded for you to wear the bridle instead of being put to death for an attempted assassination. Do not ask me to do so again."

"I wronged you," Hyacinthe says. Oak shifts on the stairs so he can see just a bit of him—his shoulders are slumped. "You have put aside your duty more than I have put aside my anger. But I—"

"You will never be satisfied," Tiernan snaps. "Joining Madoc's falcons and turning on Elfhame, spitting on mercy, blaming Cardan and Oak and Oak's dead mother and everyone except your father.

"No vengeance will ever be enough, because you want to punish his murderer, but he *died by his own hand*. You refuse to hate him, so you hate everyone else, including yourself."

Tiernan didn't raise his voice, but Hyacinthe makes a sound as though struck.

"Including me," says Tiernan.

"Not you," Hyacinthe says.

"You didn't punish me for being like him, for guarding her son? You didn't hate me for that?"

"I believed I was doomed to lose you," Hyacinthe says, voice so soft that Oak can barely hear it.

For a long moment, they are quiet.

It seems unlikely they are going to break into violence. Oak should go up the rest of the stairs. He doesn't want to invade their privacy more than he already has. He needs to go slowly, though, so they don't hear his hooves.

"Joy is never guaranteed," Tiernan says, his voice gentle. "But you can wed yourself to pain. I suppose, at least in that, there is no chance of surprise."

Oak winces at those words. *Wed yourself to pain.*

"Why would you want me after all I have done?" Hyacinthe asks, anguished.

"Why does anyone want anyone else?" Tiernan answers. "We do not love because people deserve it—nor would I want to be loved because I was the *most deserving* of some list of candidates. I want to be loved for my worst self as well as my best. I want to be forgiven my flaws."

"I find it harder to forgive your virtues," Hyacinthe tells him, a smile in his voice.

And then Oak is up the stairs far enough to be unable to hear the rest. Which is good, because he hopes it involves a lot of kissing.

When Oak was a child, he came down with fevers that laid him up for weeks. He would thrash in bed, sweating or shivering. Servants would come and press cold cloths to his brow or put him in baths stinking with herbs. Sometimes Oriana would sit with him, or one of his sisters would come and read.

Once, when he was five, he opened his eyes to see Madoc in the doorway, regarding him with an odd, evaluating expression on his face.

Am I going to die? he asked.

Madoc was startled out of whatever he was thinking, but there was still something grim in the set of his mouth. He walked to the bed and placed his large hand on Oak's brow, ignoring his small horns. *No, my boy,* he said seriously. *Your fate is to cheat death like the little scamp you are.*

And because Madoc could not lie, Oak was comforted and fell back to sleep. The fever must have broken that night, because when he woke, he was well again and ready for mischief.

This morning, Oak feels like a scamp who's cheated death again.

Waking to warmth and softness is such a delicious luxury that Oak's burns and bruises cannot dent the pleasure of it. There is a taste on his tongue that is somehow the flavor of sleep itself, as though he went so deep into the land of dreams that he brought some of it back with him.

He looks at his little finger, bare now, and smiles up at the ice ceiling.

There is a knock on the door, shaking him out of his thoughts. Before he realizes he's not wearing much in the way of clothes, Fernwaif bustles in with a tray and a pitcher. She's got on a brown homespun dress and an apron, her hair pulled back in a kerchief.

"Still abed?" she asks, plopping down the tray on his coverlets. It contains a teapot and cup, along with a plate of black bread, butter, and jam. "You're leaving with the tide."

The prince feels oddly self-conscious at sleeping late, although lounging around at all hours is part of the self-indulgent persona he's played for years. He's not sure why that role feels so suffocating this morning, but it does.

"We're leaving *today*?" He pushes his back against the headboard so he can sit upright.

Fernwaif gives a little laugh as she pours water into a bowl on a washing stand. "Will you miss us when you're in the High Court?"

Oak will not miss the endless boredom and despair of his prison cell, or the sound of cold wind howling through trees, but it occurs to him that while he's glad to be headed home, being with Wren there will be complicated in new ways. The High Court is a place full of intrigues and ambition. Once Oak returns, he will be at the swirling center of at least one conspiracy. He has no idea if it will even be *possible* to play the feckless, merry courtier while winning Wren's goodwill.

And he is even less sure that's who he wants to be.

"Fate may bring me again to these shores," Oak says.

"My sister and I will look forward to tales of the great feasts and dances," Fernwaif says, looking wistful. "And how you honored our lady."

Oak can only imagine what Wren might say if somehow she found herself having to actually exchange vows with him. *I pledge my troth to thee and promise to turn thy guts inside out if you deceive.* Oh yes, this is going well.

What was it that Hyacinthe said? *You deceive as easily as you breathe and with as little thought.* Oak very much hopes that's not true.

He doesn't hear the turn of the lock as Fernwaif leaves. He supposes there's no point in restricting his movements now, when they're planning on his leaving.

Rising, Oak splashes his face with the water from the washing stand, slicking back his hair. He manages to pull on Lord Jarel's pants before heavy footsteps on the stairs herald the appearance of five knights. To his surprise, they wear the livery of Elfhame—the crest of the Greenbriar line imprinted on their armor with its crown, tree, and grasping roots.

"Your Highness," one says, and Oak feels disoriented at the sound of his title, spoken without hostility. "Grima Mog sent us. Our commander wishes you to know that the boat awaits you and that we will accompany you on your return to the isles."

They have more appropriate garments for him, too—a green cloak embroidered in gold, heavy gloves, and a woolen tunic and trousers.

"Do you have anything here you wish us to pack?" one of the knights asks. She has eyes like those of a frog, gold-flecked and wide.

"I seem to have . . . misplaced my armor and my sword," Oak admits.

No one questions the strangeness of that. No one questions him at all. A knight with sharply pointed ears and moonlight-colored hair passes over his own curved blade—a cutlass—along with its sheath.

"We can find some armor for you among our company," the knight says.

"That's not necessary," Oak says, feeling very self-conscious. They are looking at him as though he has endured a terrible trial, even though they must know he's betrothed. "You really ought to keep your sword."

"Return it to me once you've found one better," says the knight, crossing to the door. "We will await you in the hall."

Quickly, the prince changes clothes. The fabric carries the scent of the air that blew across the line where it was hung to dry—sweetgrass and the salty tang of the ocean. Breathing it in fills him with homesickness.

Outside the Citadel, more soldiers of Elfhame wait, bundled up in heavily padded and fur-trimmed armor, their cloaks whipping behind them. They glare across the snow at the former falcons.

One of them holds Damsel Fly's reins. His horse's legs are wrapped against the snow, and a blanket hangs over her back. When the prince draws close, she frisks up to him, butting her head against his shoulder.

"Damsel!" Oak exclaims, stroking his hand over his horse's neck. "Was there a messenger from the Citadel with her?"

The soldier looks surprised to be asked for information. "Your Highness, I believe so. He rode into the camp yesterday. We recognized your steed."

"Where is that messenger now?" Valen became violent when Oak stopped actively using enchantment against him—but Valen *hated* Oak. Hopefully Daggry felt their transaction benefited them both. Hopefully Daggry was well on his way back to the lover he sacrificed so many years to save.

"I'm not sure—" the soldier begins.

From inside the stable comes the sounding of a horn, and he sees an open-topped carriage roll out, pulled by elk. It is all of black wood, looking as though it wasn't painted that way but scorched instead. The wheels are as tall as one of the soldiers standing beside it, the spokes slender as spun sugar. A groom perches on the back, all in white with a mask in the shape of a falcon, the leather twisting like branches over his eyebrows. A similarly masked driver—this one wearing the mask of a wren—sits in the front, urging the elk on with a whip.

They stop and open the door to the carriage, standing at attention.

Wren walks from the Citadel, unaccompanied by guards or ladies-in-waiting. Her gown is all black, and the toothlike, obsidian crown of the Court of Teeth rests on her head. Her feet are bare—perhaps to show that the cold cannot harm her or because she prefers it. After all, she went barefoot for many years in the woods.

She allows her groom to hand her into the carriage, where she sits, back straight. Her blue skin is the color of the clear sky. Her hair blows in a wild nimbus around her face, and her gown billows, making her seem elemental. One of the Folk of the Air.

Wren's gaze goes to him once, then darts away.

The rest of Wren's retinue assembles around her. Hyacinthe rides a large, shaggy deer, which seems as though it will be far better in picking its way through the snow than the delicate hooves of Oak's faerie horse.

Half a dozen falcons accompany him, wearing livery all of a shimmering gray. Bogdana rides a bear, which lumbers around, unnerving everyone.

Tiernan rides up to where Oak has mounted Damsel Fly. His jaw is tight with tension. "This doesn't feel right."

Randalin arrives a moment later, the Ghost beside him.

"Your betrothed really is remarkable," the Minister of Keys says. "Do you know she has two ancient troll kings swearing fealty to her?"

"I certainly do," Oak says.

"It would be better for everyone if we move now," says the Ghost.

"I suppose," Randalin says with a long-suffering sigh, somehow oblivious to the danger all around him. "We were in such a hurry to march here, and now we're in such a hurry to leave. I personally would be interested in sampling local dishes."

"The kitchens are somewhat understaffed," Oak says.

"I am going to check on the queen's party," the Ghost says, then rides off in that direction.

"When did the knights arrive?" Oak asks Tiernan, gesturing toward the Folk swarming around the castle.

"This morning. Courtesy of Grima Mog. To escort us to the boat," Tiernan says mildly since Randalin is beside them.

Oak nods, taking that in.

The horn blows again, and they begin to move.

It takes them more than an hour to arrive at the rough-hewn ice wall built by the troll kings. As they draw closer, Oak is awed by the sheer scale of it. It towers over them as they ride into the gap.

And then past the army of Elfhame.

Fires dot the landscape, burning where soldiers crowd around them for warmth. Several knights sit alone on makeshift stools, polishing weapons, while larger groups gather to drink barley tea and smoke pipes. Although a few call out cheerfully at the sight of Oak, he notes something ugly in their gaze when they see Wren's carriage.

A loud sound like a clang of metal on metal rings across the snow, and the group comes to an abrupt halt. Bogdana's bear growls. Wren's guards crowd around her carriage, hands on their weapons. She says something to them, low. The air is thick with the threat of violence.

Grima Mog and a group of armored soldiers walk toward the procession. Oak spurs Damsel Fly toward the grand general, his heart beating hard.

Do they mean to betray Wren? Make a captive of her? If they try, he'll invoke his authority as Cardan's heir. He will find out the extent of all his powers. He will do *something*.

"Greetings, Prince Oak," says Grima Mog. She wears a hat, clotted and black with blood. Armor covers the rest of her, and she has a massive, two-handed sword strapped to her back. She passes a scroll up into his hands. It's sealed with a ribbon and wax. "This explains to the High King and Queen that we will remain here until a treaty is signed."

The entire army, camped in the cold just beyond the wall, waiting and planning.

"Word will come soon," Oak promises.

Grima Mog gives a half smile, lower canine escaping her lip. "Waiting is dull business. You wouldn't want us to grow restless."

Then, taking a step back, Grima Mog gives a signal. Her people fall back. The soldiers of Elfhame who were part of Oak's procession begin to move again. The wheels of Wren's carriage roll forward. The bear plods on.

Oak is immensely relieved to leave the army behind.

Next, they draw close to the Stone Forest, the trees hanging heavy with their strange blue fruit. Wind whistles through branches, making an eerie tune.

The Ghost rides up to Oak, reining in his horse. "I wasn't sure how to interpret your note," the spy says quietly.

"I meant it quite literally," Oak returns.

He wrote it in haste, sitting on the floor of the storage room, with Daggry watching him. Certainly it could have been better, but he thought it was quite clear:

*Things are not as they seem. Call off the battle.
Send someone to the Citadel, and I will explain.*

"Although I admit not to fully understanding how you accomplished what you did," the Ghost says, "I am impressed."

Oak frowns, not liking what the spy is implying. That Oak's offer of marriage is insincere, a lure. That the prince has set and sprung a trap. Oak doesn't want Wren cast in the role of their enemy, nor that of a mark.

"When one is charmed," the prince says, "it's easy to be charming."

"You worried your sisters," the Ghost counters.

Oak notes the plural. The spy has been close to Jude's twin, Taryn, for years, leaving *how close* as a matter of speculation among the family.

"They ought to recall what they were doing when they were my age," Oak says. Jude has been worrying the rest of them for years.

The spy gives a half smile. "Perhaps that's what stopped the High

Queen from hanging Tiernan up by his toes for going along with your plan instead of stopping you."

No wonder Tiernan was so stiff with Oak. He must have been interrogated, insulted. "Perhaps she remembered that if Tiernan had stopped me, that would have meant letting our father die."

The Ghost sighs, and neither of them speaks for the rest of the ride to the shore.

A ship made of pale wood is anchored out past the black stones and shallow waters of the beach. Long and slender, with both bow and stern tapered to points that curl like the stems of leaves, she is a proud ship. Two masts rise from her deck, and around their bases, Oak can see puddles of the white sails that will be hoisted to catch the wind. The name *Moonskimmer* is emblazoned along the side in carved letters.

And from the other direction, he sees the troll kings, stepping through the snow toward them. Their skin is the deep gray of granite, riddled with what appear to be cracks and fissures. Their faces look more sculpted than alive, even as their expressions shift. One has a beard, while the other's face is bare. Both wear old and tattered scale armor, marbled with tarnish. Both have circlets on their brows of rough, dark gold. One has a club made from most of a fir tree attached to a leather belt that must have been sewn from the whole hides of several bears.

Oak draws Damsel Fly up short. The others stop as well; even Wren's carriage skids to a halt, the elk pawing at the ground and shaking their heads as though wishing they could pull free from their harnesses.

Wren hops down fearlessly, her bare feet in the snow.

Alone, she walks toward them. Her dress furls around her as the wind whips at her hair.

Oak slides off his horse, sinking his nails into the palm of his hand. He wants to run after Wren even though he knows this would be a terrible moment to undermine her authority. Still, it's hard to watch her, small and alone, standing before these massive, ancient beings.

One begins to speak in an old tongue. Oak sort of learned it in the palace school, but only ever as a language used to read equally old books. No one spoke it conversationally. And it turned out his instructor's pronunciations were waaaaay off.

The prince is able to understand only the vaguest gist. They promise to watch over her lands until she returns. They agree to stay clear of the army but don't seem to like the idea. Oak isn't sure *how* Wren understands them—perhaps Mellith knew their speech—but she clearly does.

"We entrust these lands to you while we are away," she says. "And if I do not return, make war in my name."

Both troll kings sink to one knee and bow their heads to her. A deeper hush falls over the Folk standing witness. Even Randalin looks more awed than delighted.

Wren touches the hand of each king, and they rise at the press of her fingers.

Then she walks back, barefoot, to her carriage. Halfway there, she glances at Oak. He gives her a smile, a small one because he's still a bit stunned. She doesn't return it.

The procession moves on to the coastline. Oak rides alone and speaks to no one.

At the edge of the black rocks, where the waves crash, Tiernan dismounts. He says something to the Ghost, who signals to the ship with a waved hand. They cast off a rowboat to ferry the passengers aboard in groups.

"You should head over first, Your Highness," the Ghost says.

Oak hesitates, then shakes his head. "Let the queen's party go."

Tiernan sighs with annoyance at what he no doubt sees as Oak's objection to reasonable security. Oak is aware that it seems he's just being contrary, but he refuses to give them an opportunity to sail once he's aboard, leaving Wren to Elfhame's army.

The Ghost gestures toward Hyacinthe, indicating Wren's people should take precedence.

It's a strange feeling, after being in captivity for weeks, to realize that no one here has the authority to make him do anything. People have been thrusting power at Oak since the beginning of Cardan's rule, and he's been avoiding it for just as long. He wonders if, after being stripped of so many choices, he has finally grown a taste for it.

Hyacinthe hands Wren into the boat. Her masked driver stays with the coach, though the footman climbs down and joins her, taking a seat in the front. The rest of her soldiers remain on the rocks as the crewperson who rowed to shore casts off again.

Oak watches in puzzlement. Surely, she isn't going with that few attendants?

The storm hag dismounts from her bear. With a twist of her head, she transforms herself into a massive vulture. Giving a screech, she flies out to the ship, alighting atop the mast. And then, as if responding to some unseen signal, Wren's soldiers become falcons. They soar up into the sky, leaving the sound of feathered wings echoing all around Oak.

"What has she done?" Tiernan mutters.

Oh, no one in Elfhame is going to like this. Wren didn't just break the curse on the traitors; she turned it into a boon. She gave them the ability to turn into their cursed form *at will*.

The falcons fly to the ship, landing on the boom, where, one by one, they drop to the deck as Folk again.

Oak wonders if Hyacinthe can do that. He's in a boat, so perhaps not. She broke his curse before she discovered the extent of her power.

When the rowboat returns, Oak gets in with half the knights of Elfhame accompanying him. At the ship, sailors help him aboard, then bow low. The captain introduces himself—he is a wizened man with wild white hair and skin the color of rich clay.

"Welcome, Your Highness. We're all so glad the rescue was successful."

"I wasn't precisely saved," Oak says.

The captain glances in Wren's direction, a flicker of unease in his face. "Yes, we understand."

As the captain moves to greet the Minister of Keys, Oak admits to himself that went poorly.

Then there is a great deal of negotiation over accommodations and storage, most of which the prince ignores. As the billowing white sails marked with the sigil of Elfhame rise, and the ship steers out into the sea, his heart speeds with the thought of going home.

And with what he will find when he gets there.

He stopped a war—or at least *paused* one. And yet, he is aware that bringing Wren into the heart of Elfhame puts the people there—people he loves—at risk. At the same time, spiriting Wren from her stronghold and separating her from the largest part of her defenders put her in an equally vulnerable position.

Wren knows that. And so does Jude. He must be very careful to keep either of them from feeling they must act on that knowledge.

He understands—or at least thinks he does—why Wren went along with his plan. She used up a lot of her power freeing the troll kings from their curse, and an engagement with the army of Elfhame, an army that could continuously replenish soldiers from the lower Courts, would be nearly impossible to win. After all, that's what he'd been counting on when he put his ring on her finger.

And after some consideration, he believes he also understands why Bogdana wants them to go to Elfhame. She hates the Greenbriars, hates the High Court, and yet has long desired to see her daughter on the throne. If she was willing to trade a portion of her own power for Mellith to be Mab's heir, then as much as she desires revenge, she must also long for a do-over. If Wren marries Oak, she will be in line to be High Queen. That has to have some appeal.

And if not, Cardan will be in Bogdana's sights. She will have gotten closer to him than would be possible otherwise.

And Wren herself? He suspects she's venturing to the High Court because she wants the Court of Teeth made officially hers. But, of course, he hopes that some part of it has to do with him. He hopes that some part of her wants to see where this goes. The last time they were together in the Court of Elfhame, they'd been children. He hadn't been able to do much for her. Neither of them is a child now, and he can do better. He can show her he cares about her. And he can show her some fun.

Of course, Oak will have to keep his family from making things extra complicated. Jude will want to punish Wren for holding Oak captive. Cardan will probably still be a bit resentful if he thinks Oak is plotting against him. Cardan may even think Wren is part of a new plot.

And so Oak needs to show his loyalty to a lot of different people, keep Bogdana from hurting anyone, and get a treaty signed before a battle breaks out in the heart of Elfhame. Not to mention he has to do that while proving to Wren he isn't out for revenge—and that if she forgives him, he won't see it as a chance to hurt her.

Well, no time like the present to begin. Oak moves across the deck toward her. Two falcons step in his way.

"She is my betrothed," Oak says, as though there is merely some misunderstanding.

"You ought to be her *prisoner*," says one, low enough that he will not be overheard by the Elfhame contingent.

"Both those things can be true," Oak tells him.

Wren frowns at the guards and the prince both. "I will receive him. I wish to hear what he has to say."

Her guards step away, but not far enough to be out of earshot.

Oak smiles and attempts to find a tone to communicate his sincerity. "My lady, I wished to tell you how glad I was that you decided to accept my suit and return to Elfhame by my side. I hope you do not begrudge too greatly the manner in which the proposal was given."

"Should I?" she asks.

"You might consider it romantic," he suggests, but he knows what she really thinks—that this is a game. And should he claim otherwise, she will be insulted that he thinks her such a poor opponent as to fall for that.

And it is not as though there is *no* strategy behind his offer, but he feels more like a hopelessly besotted ninny than a master strategist. He'd marry her, and happily.

She gives him a chilly little smile. "However I might feel, I will keep my word."

Though you may not is heavily implied.

"We need not forever be at daggers drawn," he says, and hopes she will believe him. "To that end, I did hope that Bogdana would not be accompanying us, since she wants to murder the High King—and me. I think that could complicate our visit."

To his surprise, Wren glances up at the vulture in frustration. "Yes," she says. "I told her to stay behind, but apparently I wasn't clear enough. That's why she's hiding up there. If she came down, I could order her to go home."

"She can't hide from you forever," Oak says.

The corners of Wren's mouth twitch. "What do you think we will find when we arrive in Elfhame?"

An excellent question. "The High King and Queen will throw us some sort of party. But I suppose they may have a few concerns for me to allay first."

Her lip lifts, showing off sharp teeth. "A polite way of putting it. But you are ever charming."

"Am I?" he asks.

"Like a cat lazing in the sun. No one expects it to suddenly bite."

"I am not the one fond of biting," he says, and is gratified when she blushes, the pink coming up bright enough to show through the pale blue of her skin.

Not waiting to be dismissed, he takes that victory, makes a shallow bow, and departs, heading in the direction of Tiernan.

Her guards watch him go with angry looks. They probably blame him for Valen. Perhaps they blame him for all the things that Valen blamed him for. Might there really be some day that he and Wren were not at daggers drawn? He believed it enough to say it, but he was an eternal optimist.

"You've got a bruise on your face," Tiernan says.

Oak reaches up self-consciously and prods around until he finds it, to the left of his mouth. It joins the bump on his head and the burns from the iron knife hidden by his collar. He's a mess.

"How is my father?" he asks.

"Allowed back into Elfhame, just as he planned," Tiernan says. "Giving your sister lots of unsolicited advice."

Just because I'm bad doesn't mean the advice is. That's what Madoc told Wren, although Oak isn't so sure he agrees on that point. Still, his father must be doing well, to be behaving like himself. That is the main thing.

He lets out a sigh of relief, his gaze going to the horizon, to the waves. His mind wanders to the last time they crossed this water and how Loana tried to distract him with a kiss and then drag him down to the watery depths. That was the second time she tried to drown him.

Drown me once, shame on me... He decides he doesn't like the direction his thoughts are taking him. Nor does he like acknowledging that he has a particular sort of taste for paramours—the more dangerous, the better.

"Do you still love Hyacinthe?" the prince asks.

Tiernan looks at him in surprise. It isn't that they never talk about their feelings, but Oak supposes it isn't the second thing Tiernan expected him to ask about.

Or perhaps it isn't something that Tiernan is prepared to think too closely on, because he shrugs. When Oak does not retract the question, Tiernan shakes his head, as though at the impossibility of answering. Then, finally, he gives in and speaks. "In ballads, love is a disease, an affliction. You contract it as a mortal might contract one of their viruses.

Perhaps a touch of hands or a brush of lips, and then it is as though your whole body is fevered and fighting it. But there's no way to prevent it from running its course."

"That's a remarkably poetic and profoundly awful view of love," Oak says.

Tiernan looks back at the sea. "I was never in love before, so all I had were ballads to go by."

Oak is silent, thinking of all the times he thought himself to be in love. "Never?"

Tiernan gives a soft huff of breath. "I had lovers, but that's not the same thing."

Oak thinks about how to name what he feels about Wren. He does not wish to write her ridiculous poems as he did for so many of the people with whom he thought he was in love, except that he does wish to make her laugh. He does not want to give her enormous speeches or to make grand, empty gestures; he does not want to give her the *pantomime* of love. He is starting to suspect, however, that pantomime is all he knows.

"But...," Tiernan says, and hesitates again, running a hand through his short blackberry hair. "What I feel is not like the ballads."

"Not an affliction, then?" Oak raises an eyebrow. "No fever?"

Tiernan gives him an exasperated look—one with which the prince is very familiar. "It is more the feeling that there is a part of me I have left somewhere and I am always looking for."

"So he's like a missing phone?"

"Someone ought to pitch you into the sea," Tiernan says, but he has a small smile in the corner of his mouth. He doesn't seem like someone who would like being teased. His grimness is what often allows him to be mistaken for a knight, despite his training as a spy. But he does like it.

"I think he's rather desperately in love with you," Oak says. "I think that's why he was punching me in the mouth."

When Tiernan sighs and looks out at the sea, Oak follows his example and is silent.

CHAPTER

12

Three days, they are supposed to spend at sea. Three days before they land on the isles and Oak must face his family again.

As the prince drowses in a hammock with the stars far above him on the first night, he hears Randalin boasting loudly that of course he was willing to give up his private cabin to Wren, as a queen *needed* privacy for travel, and that he *hardly* minded the hardship. Of course, she *nearly* persuaded him not to *inconvenience* himself, which was quite *gracious* of her. And she *insisted* on keeping him there for several hours to eat, drink, and speak with her of the Shifting Isles and his own *loyalty* to the prince, whereupon she *praised him* greatly, one might even say *excessively*.

Oak is certain that her evening was stultifyingly dull and yet he can't help wishing he'd been there, to share a glance over the obsequious councilor's head, to watch her smother her smiles at his puffery. He craves her smiles. The shine of her eyes when she is trying to hold back laughter.

He is no longer locked in a cell, no longer barred from seeing her. He may go to the door of the room where she is resting and bang on it until she opens up. But somehow knowing that he can and being afraid he wouldn't be welcome make her seem even farther away.

And so he lies there, listening to Randalin going on and on about his own consequence. The councilor falls silent only after the Ghost throws a balled-up sock at him.

That reprieve lasts only the night.

Invigorated by the success of their mission and certain of his elevated status with Wren, Randalin spends much of the second day trying to talk everyone into a version of the story where he can take credit for brokering peace. Maybe even for arranging a marriage with Oak.

"Lady Suren just needed a little *guidance*. I really see the *potential* in her to be one of our great leaders, like a queen of old," he is saying to the captain of the ship as Oak passes.

The prince's gaze goes to Wren, standing at the prow. She wears a plain dress the color of bone, dotted with sea spray, its skirts fluttering around her. Her hair is blown back from her face, and she bites her lower lip as she contemplates the horizon, her eyes darker and more fathomless than the ocean.

Above them, the sky is a deep, bright blue, and the wind is good, filling the sails.

"I *told* Jude," Randalin goes on. "She proposed *violent* solutions, but you know *mortals*, and her in particular—no patience. I *never* supported her elevation. Neither kith nor kin to *us*."

Oak sets his jaw and reminds himself that nothing good will come of punching the councilor in his smug little horned face. Instead, the prince tries to concentrate on the feeling of the sun on his skin and the knowledge that things could have turned out much worse.

Later that afternoon, when Oak is summoned to Wren's cabin, he is particularly glad he didn't hit anyone.

The guard who leads him to her chambers isn't one the prince knows, but he's had enough experience of her falcons for just the uniform to put him on edge.

Wren sits on a chair of white wood, beside a marble-topped side table and a settee upholstered in scarlet. Small, round windows high on the walls illuminate the space. A bed was built in to a corner, wood frame keeping the cushions from shifting with the swells, a half-open curtain for privacy. When he enters, she makes a movement with her hand and her guard leaves.

Fancy, he thinks. *I should work out a signal like that with Tiernan.* Of course, he doubts Tiernan would leave if there was a gesture he could just ignore.

"May I sit?" Oak asks.

"Please," she says, her fingers anxiously turning the ring he gave her. "I summoned you to talk about the dissolution of our engagement."

His heart sinks, but he keeps his voice light. "So soon? Shall we turn the ship around?" He settles himself grimly on the settee.

She gives a little sigh. "Too soon, yes, I agree. But we will have to break it off eventually. I understand what you did at the Citadel. You managed to keep a battle from happening and bloodshed at bay with your lies, and you managed to remove yourself from my clutches. It was nicely done."

"I can't lie," he objects.

"You lived in the mortal world," Wren says. "But you never had a mortal mother. Mine would have called that a *lie of omission.* But name it a trick or a deception, name it whatever you will. What matters is that this betrothal cannot continue too long or we shall be wed and you, tied to me forever."

"A terrible fate?" Oak inquires.

She nods briskly, as though he's finally understanding the seriousness of the problem. "I suggest that you allow your family to persuade you to put off the ceremony for months. I will agree, of course. I can conclude my visit to Elfhame and return north. You will strongly suggest that your sister give me what was once the Court of Teeth to rule."

"Is that what you want?" he asks.

She looks down at her hands. "Once, I thought I might return to my mortal home, but I cannot imagine it now. How could they see me as that child, when I would frighten them, even without knowing the nature of my magic?"

"They don't have to see you as a child to care for you," he says.

"They would never love me as much as I want to be loved," she tells him with painful honesty. "I will do well in the north. I am well suited to it."

"Do you—" he begins, not sure how to ask this question. "Do you remember much of being Mellith?"

She starts to shake her head and then hesitates. "Some things."

"Do you remember Bogdana being your mother?"

"I do," she says, so softly he can barely hear it. "I remember believing she loved me. And I remember her giving me away."

"And the murder?" he asks.

"I was so happy to see her," she says, fingers going almost unconsciously to her throat. "I almost didn't notice the knife."

For a moment, the sadness of the story robs him of speech. His own mother, Oriana, is so fiercely protective of him that he cannot imagine being pushed out on his own, among people who hate him enough to arrange his death. And yet, he recalls sitting at the end of his bed and hearing Vivi explain how it was a miracle Jude was alive after the way their father carved her up. And from the time he learned that he had a first father, he knew that person tried to kill him.

Maybe he doesn't understand how she feels exactly, but he understands that familial love isn't guaranteed, and even when you have it, it doesn't always keep you safe.

Wren watches him with her fathomless eyes. "It seems as though it should change me, to have those memories, but I do not feel much changed." She pauses. "Do I seem different?"

He notes the careful way she's holding herself. Stiff, her back upright. She seems wary, yet underneath there's a hunger in her. A spark of desire she cannot mask, although whether it is for him or power, he cannot say.

"You seem more like yourself than ever before," he says.

He can see her considering that but not misliking his words. "So we are agreed. We delay the exchange of vows. Your sister will have a reason to send me back north with a kingdom of my own, and we will let her believe that her plan to separate us has worked. You can take up with any number of courtiers to drive the point home. Drown whatever lingering feelings you have for me in a new love, or ten." She says the last bit with some asperity.

He puts a hand to his chest. "Have you no feelings to drown?"

Wren looks down. "No," she says. "Nothing I have would I ever want to give away."

After a dinner of kelp and cockles, which the cook serves up in wooden bowls with no spoons, the captain invites them to sit on the deck and tell tales, as is his crew's tradition. Wren arrives with Hyacinthe by her side, settling some distance from the prince. When her gaze meets his, she tucks a long strand of hair behind her ear and gives him a hesitant smile. Her green eyes shine as one of the crew begins to speak.

She loves a story. He remembers that, remembers their evenings around the fire as they traveled north. Remembers her talking about Bex, her mortal sister, and their games of pretend. Remembers how she laughed when he retold some of his own antics.

The prince listens as crew members speak of far-off shores they've visited. One tells of an island with a queen who has the head and torso of a woman and the appendages of an enormous spider. Another, of a land so thick with magic that even the animals speak. A third, of their adventures with merfolk and how the captain wed a selkie without stealing its skin.

"We avoid talking politics," the captain qualifies with a puff on a long, thin pipe of carved bone.

In a lull, the storm hag clears her throat.

"I have a tale for you," says Bogdana. "Once, there was a girl with an enchanted matchbook. Whenever she lit one—"

"Is this a true story?" the Ghost interrupts.

"Time will tell," the storm hag answers, giving him a lethal look. "Now, as I was about to say—when this girl struck a match, a thing of her choosing was destroyed. This made all of those in power want her on their side, but she fought only for what she herself considered right."

Wren looks down at her hands, strands of hair falling to shield her face. Oak supposes there's going to be a lesson in this, one that no one will like.

"The more terrible the destruction, the more matches needed to be struck. And yet, each time the girl looked in the matchbook, there were at least a few new matches within. To have such vast power was a great burden for the girl, but she was ferocious and brave in addition to being wise, and shouldered her burden with grace."

Oak sees the way Hyacinthe is frowning at the storm hag, as though disagreeing with the idea that Wren's "matches" are so easily replaced. When Oak thinks of the translucency of her skin, the hollowness beneath her cheekbones, he worries. But he believes that Bogdana very much wants to believe this is how Wren's magic works.

"Then the girl met a boy with a shining brow and an easy laugh." The storm hag's eyes narrow, as though in warning of what is to come. "And she was struck low by love. Though she ought to fear nothing, she feared the boy would be parted from her. Not wisdom, nor ferocity, nor bravery saved her from her own tender heart."

Ah, so this isn't going to be about Wren's magic. This is going to be about him. Great.

"Now, our girl had many enemies, but none of those enemies could stand against her. With a single match, she caused castles to crumble. With a handful of matches, she burned whole armies to the ground. But in time the boy tired of that and persuaded her to put away her matchbook and fight no more. Instead, she would live with him in a cottage in the woods, where no one would know of her power. And though she ought to have known better, she was beguiled by him and did what he wished."

The ship goes quiet, the only sounds the slap of water against wood and the luff of the sails.

"For some time they lived in what passed for happiness, and if the girl felt as though there was something missing, if she felt as though to be loved he must look through her and not at her, she pretended that away."

Oak opens his mouth to object and at the last moment bites his tongue. He would only make himself seem like a fool, and a guilty one at that, to argue with a story.

"But in time, the girl was discovered by her enemies. They came for her together and caught her unawares, locked in an embrace with her beloved. Still, in her wisdom, she always kept her matchbook in a pocket of her dress. Under threat, she drew it out and struck the first match, and those who came for her fell back. The flames that consumed them consumed her cottage, too. Yet still more enemies came. Match after match was struck and fire raged all around her, but it was not enough. And so the girl struck all the remaining matches at once."

Oak glares at the storm hag, but she seems too swept up in her tale to even notice. Wren is plucking at a thread of her dress.

"The armies were defeated and the land scorched black. The girl went up in flames with them. And the boy burned to cinders before he could pull free from her arms."

A respectful silence follows her final words. Then the captain clears his throat and calls for one of his crewmen to take up a fiddle and play a merry tune.

As a few begin to clap along, Wren stands and moves toward her cabin.

Oak catches up at her door, before her guards seem to have realized his intention. "Wait," he says. "Can we speak?"

She tilts her head and regards him for a long moment. "Come in."

One of her guards—Oak realizes, abruptly, that it's Straun—clears his throat. "I can accompany you and make sure he doesn't—"

"There is no need," she says, cutting him off.

Straun attempts to keep the sting of her words from showing on his face. Oak almost feels sorry for him. Almost, except for the memory of his being party to the prince's torture.

Because of that, he gives Straun an enormous, irritating grin as he follows Wren across the threshold and into her room.

Inside, he finds the chamber much as it was before, except that a few dresses have been spread out on her bed and a tray with tea things rests on the marble table.

"Is that what your power is like?" Oak asks. "A book of matches."

Wren gives a soft laugh. "Is that truly why you've followed me? To ask that?"

He smiles. "It's hardly a surprise that a young man would want to spend time with his betrothed."

"Ah, so this is more playacting." She moves across the floor gracefully, the pitch and roll of the ship not causing her a single stumble. Finding her way to the upholstered settee, she takes a seat, indicating with a gesture that he should take the chair across from her. A reversal of their positions the last time he visited this room.

"I *do* wish to spend time with my betrothed," he says, going to sit.

She gives him a look of disdain, but her cheeks have a flush of pink on them. "My magic might be like the matches in the story, but I think it burns me, too. I just don't know how much yet."

He appreciates her admitting that to him. "She's going to want you to keep using it. If there's one thing I took away from her story, it's that."

"I do not plan on dancing to her tune," Wren says. "Not ever again."

His father has managed to manipulate him cannily, without Oak ever once agreeing to a single thing that Madoc proposed out loud. "And yet you haven't ordered her to go home."

"We're far from shore," Wren says with a sigh. "And she promised to be on her best behavior. Now, to be fair, since I told you about my magic, tell me about yours."

Oak raises his brows in surprise. "What do you want to know?"

"Persuade me of something," she says. "I want to understand how your power works. I want to know what it feels like."

"You want me to charm you?" This seems like a terrible idea. "That suggests a great deal more trust on your part than you've indicated you're willing to extend to me."

She leans back on her cushions. "I want to see if I can break the spell."

He thinks of all the matches set ablaze. "Won't it hurt you to do that?"

"It should be a small thing," she says. "And in return, you can obey an order."

"But I'm not wearing the bridle," he protests, hoping that she isn't going to ask him to put it on. He won't, and if it's a test, it's one he's going to fail.

"No," she says. "You're not."

Willingly following a command seems interesting and not *too* dangerous. But he doesn't know how to make his gancanagh magic tame. If he tells her what she most wants to hear and it is a distortion of the truth, what then? And if the words are ones he means, how will they ever seem true when they've first come from his mouth as persuasion?

"Are you doing it?" Her body is slightly hunched as though against some kind of attack.

"No, not yet," he says with a surprised laugh. "I have to actually *say* something."

"You just *did*," she protests, but she's laughing a little, too. Her eyes glitter with mischief. She was right when she said they both loved games. "Just do it. I'm getting nervous."

"I'm going to try to persuade you to pick up that teacup," he says, waving toward a clay vessel with a wide base and a little bit of liquid still at the bottom. It's resting on the marble-topped table, and with all the rocking the boat has done as it goes over swells, he's surprised it hasn't slid to the floor already.

"You're not supposed to tell me," she says, smiling. "Now you'll never manage it."

He finds himself filled with a strange glee at the challenge. At the idea he could share this with her and it could be fun instead of awful.

When he opens his mouth again, he allows the honey-tongued words to spill out.

"When you came to Elfhame as a child," he says, his voice going strange, "you never got to see the beauty of it. I will show you the silvery white trees of the Milkwood. We can splash in the Lake of Masks and see the reflections of those who have looked into it before us. I will take you to Mandrake Market, where you can buy eggs that will hatch pearls that shine like moonlight."

He can see that she's relaxed, sinking back onto the cushions, eyes half-closed as though in a daydream. And although he wouldn't choose those words, he does plan to take her to all those places.

"I look forward to introducing you to each of my sisters and reminding them that you helped our father. I will tell the story of how you single-handedly defeated Lady Nore and bravely took an arrow in the side." He's not sure what he expects from his magic, but it isn't this rush of words. Not a single thing he said is anything other than true. "And I will tell them the story of Mellith, and how wronged she was by Mab, how wronged you were and how much I want—"

Wren's eyes open, wet with unshed tears. She sits up. "How dare you say those things? How dare you throw everything I cannot have in my face?"

"I didn't—" he starts, and for a moment, he isn't sure if he's speaking as himself. If he's using his power or not.

"Get out," she growls, standing.

He holds up his hands in surrender. "Nothing I said was un—"

Wren hurls the teacup at him. It smashes against the floor, jagged bits of pottery flying. "Get out!"

He stares at the shards in horror, realizing what it means. *She picked up the cup. I persuaded her to pick up the cup.* This is the exact problem with being a love-talker. His power cares nothing for consequences.

"You told me you'd give me an order after I tried to persuade you." Oak takes a step toward the door, his heart beating painfully hard. "I shall obey."

When he passes Straun, the guard snorts, as though he believes Oak had his chance and blew it.

The prince stands on the deck for the better part of the night, staring numbly into the sea as dawn blushes on the horizon. He's still there when he hears a scream behind him.

At the cry, he whirls, hand already going to the blade at his hip—finding not the needle-thin rapier he's used to wielding but a borrowed cutlass. The curved blade rattles in its scabbard as he pulls it free—just as a thick black tentacle sprawls across the deck.

It wriggles toward the prince like some disembodied finger, dragging itself forward. Oak takes several steps back.

Another tentacle rises from the water to twine around the prow, ripping through one of the sails.

A troll sailor, interrupted from a game of Fidchell with an ogre, scrambles to his feet and up the rigging in horror. Shouts ring out.

"The Undersea! The Undersea is attacking!"

The ocean churns as seven sharks surface with merrows astride their backs. All the merrows are different shades of mottled green and wield jagged-looking spears. They are armored in pearlescent scales of shells and draped in woven ropes of seaweed. The expression in their cold, pale eyes makes it clear they have come to fight.

The captain blows on a crooked pipe. Sailors run to positions, beginning to haul out massive harpoons from hatches beneath the deck, each weapon heavy enough to take several of them to move.

The knights and falcons spread out, swords and bows to hand.

"Subjects of Elfhame," a merrow shouts. Like the others, he is clad in shells cut into discs that overlap one another to make a sort of scale armor, but his bare arms are encircled in bracelets of gold, and his hair is knotted into thick braids, decorated with the teeth of sea creatures. "Know the power of Cirien-Cròin, far greater than the line of Orlagh."

Oak steps toward the gunwale, but Tiernan grabs his shoulder and squeezes it hard. "Don't be a fool and draw their eye. Perhaps they won't recognize you."

Before Oak can argue, Randalin raises his voice. "Is that your name? The name of your monster?" He sounds somewhere between stern lecturer and on the verge of panic.

The merrow laughs. "The name of our master, who has gone courting. He sends us with a message."

"Deliver it, and go on your way," says Randalin, making a shooing motion toward the tentacle. "And get that thing off our deck."

Oak spots Wren, not sure when she left her chambers. He catches her gaze, remembering the warning she was given by the merrow she freed from the Court of Moths—that a war was coming for control of the Undersea. And Loana mentioned that Nicasia was having a contest for her hand and, with it, her crown. Then Loana tried to drown him, which overshadowed the warning. But he recalls it vividly now.

Wren widens her eyes, as though trying to tell him something. Probably that they're screwed. If she unmakes the tentacle, she might unmake the ship along with it.

At least this seems to have put their disastrous game out of her mind.

"You are the message," the merrow says. "You, at the bottom of the sea with crabs picking out your eyes."

Another tentacle rises from the waves, slithering up the side of the boat. Well, this is very, very bad.

Seven merrows and one monster. The thing with the tentacles doesn't seem to have any particular cleverness. As far as Oak can tell, it can't even see what it is grabbing for. If they can get rid of the merrows, there is a chance that without anyone commanding it to strike, the thing will go away. Of course, there is also a chance it may decide to rip the ship to teeny, tiny pieces.

"Queen Suren," the merrow says, spotting her. "You should have taken our offer and given us your prize. I see you lost your war. Here we find you in the hands of your enemy. Were you our ally, we would save you, but now you will die with the others. Unless..."

"Your Highness," Tiernan hisses at Oak. His sword is drawn and his jaw set. "Get below."

"And how will that help, exactly?" Oak demands. "Will waiting to drown make the experience better?"

"For once, just—" Tiernan begins.

But Oak has already come to a decision. "Hello there!" he says, striding toward the merrow. "Looking for a prize? What did you have in mind?"

From behind him, he thinks he hears Tiernan muttering about how strangling Oak himself may be a kindness. At least it would be a merciful death.

"Prince Oak of Elfhame," the merrow says with a scowl. As though he is finding this much too easy. "We're taking you to Cirien-Cròin."

"Wonderful plan!" says Oak. "Did you know that she chained me up? And now I'm supposed to marry her unless *someone* takes me away. Come aboard. Let's go."

Wren's expression has gone shuttered. She can't possibly believe he's serious, but that doesn't mean his words don't cut close to the bone.

"You can't mean to go with them," Randalin says, because Randalin is an idiot.

The merrow signals, and six of the sharks swim closer so that the merrows on their backs can climb onto the deck. One has a silver net in his hands. It gleams in the morning light.

Six. That's almost all of them.

"Take the queen, too," commands the merrow leader. "Leave the rest to Sablecoil."

Sablecoil. That must be the monster.

"You're not taking anyone," says one of the knights. "If you board the ship, we'll—"

"Oh, let them come," Oak interrupts with a speaking look. "Maybe they'll take her and allow the rest of us to go."

"Your Highness," says another knight, his voice respectful but slow, as though Oak is a greater fool than the councilor. "I very much doubt that's their plan. If it were, I would hand her over in a heartbeat."

The prince glances toward Wren, hoping she didn't hear. Randalin has caught hold of her hand and is attempting to drag her toward the stateroom near the helm of the ship, in what appears to be an act of actual valiance on his part.

"Perhaps we can come to some arrangement," the merrow commander says. "After all, who can speak of Cirien-Cròin's might if all who witness it are dead? We will take the prince and the queen, then Sablecoil will release you while we treat with one another."

That's a terrible deal. That's such a bad deal even Sablecoil would know better than to take it.

"Yes, yes!" Oak says cheerily. "I look forward to discussing this Cirien-Cròin's wooing of Nicasia. I might have some insights to share. My half-brother seduced her, you know."

A nearby sailor makes a startled noise. None of them would speak of her that way while they crossed her waters.

The merrow commander, still on his shark, smiles, showing thin teeth, like those of some deepwater fish. The six merrows on the deck split up, four heading toward Wren and two toward the prince. They don't expect Oak to be difficult to subdue, even if he resists.

As the merrows get closer, he feels a momentary spike of panic.

Most of the people on this boat don't expect him to be hard to subdue, either, or anything other than a fool. That's the reputation he's painstakingly built. A reputation he's about to throw away.

He tries to push that out of his mind, to concentrate on sinking into the moment. The merrows are perhaps five feet from him and seven feet from Wren when he attacks.

He slashes the throat of the first, spraying the deck with thin, greenish blood. Twisting around, he sinks the edge of the cutlass into the second merrow's thigh, slicing open the vein. More blood. So much blood. The deck is slippery with it.

Arrows fly. The massive harpoons fire.

Oak runs across the deck toward the four bearing down on Wren. A pair of her falcons match blades with one merrow. A lone falcon flies up in bird form and lands behind another, transforming in time to stab a knife into his back. Wren herself has thrown a knife at one fleeing across the deck. Oak gets there in time to dispatch the last by cleaving his head clean from his shoulders.

There are a lot of screams.

From the top of the mast, Bogdana descends on black wings. Oak glances toward Wren.

In that moment of inattention, he is knocked off his hooves by a sinuous tentacle that wraps around his calf. He tries to pull free, but it yanks him across the deck fast enough that his head slams against the wooden boards.

He kicks out with a hoof at the same time he stabs the blade of his cutlass deep into Sablecoil's rubbery flesh, pinning the tentacle to the deck. Writhing, it drops the prince. He stumbles to his hooves.

Tiernan hacks at the tentacle, trying to sever it from the body of the monster.

With a shudder, it rips free from the deck. The cutlass is still stuck in it when it wraps around Tiernan. Then it hauls him backward into the sea.

"Tiernan!" Oak runs to the gunwale of the ship, but Tiernan has disappeared beneath the waves.

"Where is he?" Hyacinthe shouts. There's black blood smeared across his face and a bow in his hand.

Before Oak can get any words out, Hyacinthe has dropped the bow and jumped off the side. The ocean swallows him whole.

No, no, no. Oak is wild with panic. He can swim, but certainly not well enough to haul both of them out.

All around him, there's fighting. The fleeing merrow is cut down. The Ghost slashes at another enormous tentacle, battling to save one of the fallen falcons. Three more tentacles curl around the prow. From everywhere, there are cries. From some places, screams.

Oak wants to scream, too. If Tiernan dies, it will be because of Oak.

This is why he never wanted a bodyguard. This is why he should never have been given one.

The prince loosens a rope from a cleat, wrapping one end around his waist and knotting it there. Once tied, the prince gives a hard tug to test whether it can bear his weight.

He looks into the waves. This close, he can see shapes moving in the deep.

He sucks in a breath and prepares to join them when a crack of lightning draws his attention back to the deck. Fog is rolling toward the ship, along with higher swells.

Bogdana has brought a storm.

Well, that seems completely unhelpful.

Taking another breath, Oak drops himself down, rappelling off the side of the boat. As his hoof hits the water, Hyacinthe surfaces, Tiernan limp in his arms. Oak reaches for him automatically, afraid it's too late.

"Highness," Hyacinthe says, relief in his voice. Tiernan's head lolls against his shoulder.

Waves splash Oak's face as he grabs hold of his bodyguard. The sky overhead has darkened. He hears a crack of thunder behind him and sees another bright streak of lightning reflecting in Hyacinthe's eyes.

Tiernan's body is heavy in his arms. He tries to find a way to hold him securely enough that he won't slip, tries to find a way to haul them all back up onto the deck.

He lifts himself upward, one-handed. He gets a few inches higher, but it's slow and he's not sure his strength will hold.

And then Garrett is there, peering down.

"Hold on," he calls. "Hold him."

Swells roll against the side of the ship. The Ghost is stronger than he seems, and yet Oak can see how hard it is to pull them up. As soon as he's over the gunwale, the prince rolls himself and Tiernan onto the deck. A sailor is already tossing another rope over the side to Hyacinthe.

Tiernan coughs up water, then lies still again.

When Oak looks up, he sees one of the tentacles slide across the deck toward Wren. The wind steals his cry of warning. He tries to rise to his hooves in time, but he is too slow and has no sword anyway. Hyacinthe, just making it over the side, shouts in horror.

Wren lifts her hand. As she does, the skin of Sablecoil peels back from the muscle, the tentacle going limp and shriveled. A horrible shuddering goes through the ship as all the tentacles detach at once. The boards creak.

The last of the merrows disappears beneath the waves, whatever last taunt he may have spoken dying on his lips.

The storm hag, in vulture form, makes a guttural sound as she flies. The wind rises higher, blowing all around them, as though she is conjuring a shield of rain and wind.

Wren stumbles, reaching for Oak's arm. He puts it around her waist, holding her upright.

"I killed it." Already, her skin has a waxy appearance.

He thinks about Bogdana's story. About how if Wren's power really works like matches, she keeps taking handfuls of them and setting them alight. "Killing is my thing," he tells her. "You should get your own thing."

Her lip quirks. Her gaze seems a little unfocused.

The wind lifts the sail, snapping ropes that were already frayed. The hull of the ship seems to rise above the slap of the waves.

Oak's gaze goes to Tiernan, still as stone, with Hyacinthe bent over him. To the blood washing the deck. To the wounded falcons and knights and sailors. Then to the purpling cast, not unlike a bruise, creeping over Wren's pale blue skin.

The ship rises higher. Abruptly, Oak realizes that it's *above the waves*. Bogdana has used her storm to make their ship fly.

If she devoured the remains of Mab's bones, perhaps she really did have a large portion of her old power back. And perhaps she really was first among hags.

Wren leans more heavily against him, the only warning before she collapses. He catches her in time to swing her up into his arms, her head lying against his chest. Her eyes remain open, but they are fever bright, and though she blinks up at him, he's not sure she sees him.

A few of her guards frown, but not even Straun tries to stop Oak from pushing the door of her room open with one hoof and carrying her inside.

Her sofa and the small table have been tipped over. The rug beneath them is wet, and shards of pottery are scattered over it—the remains of her teapot have joined her broken teacup.

Oak crosses the room and places Wren down gently on her coverlets, her long hair spreading over the pillow. Her deep green eyes are still glassy. He recalls what Hyacinthe said about her power. *The more she unmakes, the more she is unmade.*

A moment later, her hand comes up, running over his cheek. Her fingers push into his hair, then slip over his nape to his shoulder. He goes very still, afraid that if he moves, it will startle her into pulling back. She has never touched him this way, as though things could be easy between them.

"You must stop," she says, her voice little more than a whisper. Her expression is fond.

He frowns in puzzlement. Her hand has dipped down to his chest, and even as she speaks, she opens her palm over his heart. He has barely moved. "Stop what?"

"Being kind to me. I can't bear it."

He tenses.

She withdraws her hand, letting it fall to the coverlet. The blue stone in the ring he gave her glints up at him. "I'm not...I am not good at pretending. Not like you."

If she is speaking of her coldness toward him, she is far better than she believes. "We can stop. We can call a truce."

"For now," she says.

"Then today, my lady, speak freely," he tells her with what he hopes is a reassuring smile. "You can deny me tomorrow."

She looks up at him, her lashes falling low. She seems to be half in a dream. "Is it exhausting to be charming all the time? Or is it just the way you're made?"

His grin fades. He thinks of the magic leaching out of him. He can control his charm, sort of. More or less. And he can resist using it. He will.

"Have you ever wondered if *anyone* truly loved you?" she asks in that same fond, unfocused voice.

Her words are a kick to the stomach, the more because he can tell she doesn't mean to be cruel. And because he *hadn't* thought of it. He sometimes wondered if gancanagh blood meant Folk liked him a little better than they might have otherwise, but he was too vain to think of it affecting Oriana or his sisters.

Oriana, who loved his mother so well that she took Liriope's son and raised him as her own, risking her life to do so. Jude and Vivi, who sacrificed their own safety for him. Jude, who was still making sacrifices to ensure he would someday be the High King. If magic is the cause of that loyalty, instead of love, then he is a curse on the people around him.

A part of him must have suspected, because why else keep himself so apart? He told himself that it was because he wanted to repay them for all the sacrifices they made, told himself that he wanted to become as great as they were, but maybe it had always been this.

He feels sick.

And sicker still when his mouth curves unconsciously into a smile. It has become such an automatic reaction to pain, for him to mask it with a grin. Oak, laughing all the time. Pretending nothing hurts. A false face hiding a false heart.

He can't blame her for saying what she did. Probably someone should have said it to him much sooner. And how could he have ever supposed she would come to care for him? Who can love someone who is empty inside? Someone who steals love instead of earning it?

The prince recalls lying on the ground after drinking several cups of liquor laced with blusher mushroom, back in the troll village. That was the last time he felt Wren's hand on his flushed cheek, her skin cool enough to ground him in that moment, to keep him hanging on to consciousness.

I am poison, he told her then. And he didn't even know the half of it.

Oak sits with Wren until she falls asleep. Then he spreads a blanket over her and stands. Inside, the horror he felt when she spoke those words— *have you ever wondered if* anyone *truly loved you*—hasn't faded, but he can hide that. Easily. For the first time, he hates how easily. He hates that he can fold himself up so tightly in his own skin that there's nothing real about him on the outside.

He climbs the step. Standing on the deck, he looks at the ocean far below. It seems as though they're sailing through a sea of clouds.

Soldiers are attempting to repair the gunwale, shattered by tentacles. Others are trying to smooth out the raw, splintered bits of wood where spearpoints gouged the deck, a faint spatter of blood marring the light color of it.

The ship flies high enough for sailors and soldiers to trail their fingers through clouds and let the mist wet their skin. High enough for seabirds to soar beside them; a few even rest on the mast and rigging.

Bogdana stands at the helm. Her expression is strained, and when she sees him, her eyes narrow. Whatever she wishes to say to him, though, it seems she cannot move away from directing the storm that propels them in order to do it.

Scanning the ship, Oak spots Tiernan near the mast, beneath the netting running up to the base of the sail. His head is pillowed on a cloak, his blackberry hair still damp and stiff with salt. His eyes are shut, his skin gone very pale.

Hyacinthe sits beside him, long fall of dark hair over his face. When Oak squats nearby, Hyacinthe pushes it back to reveal his pained expression. He looks as though he is losing blood from some invisible wound.

"She woke up enough to speak with me," Oak tells him so at least he doesn't have Wren to worry about. "Told me some very unpleasant things about myself."

"He's breathing," says Hyacinthe, nodding toward Tiernan.

For a long moment, they watch the rise and fall of Tiernan's chest. Each inhalation comes with what seems like a lot of effort. As he watches, the prince doesn't trust that one breath will follow the next.

"His loyalty to me might cost him his life," Oak says.

To his surprise, Hyacinthe shakes his head. His hand goes to the other man's chest, coming to rest over his heart. "It was my lack of loyalty to him that was the problem." His voice is so soft that the prince isn't sure he heard the words correctly.

"You couldn't have—" Oak begins, but Hyacinthe cuts him off.

"I could have loved him better," Hyacinthe says. "And I could have better believed in his love."

"How could that have helped against a monster?" the prince asks. He's in the mood for an argument and beginning to hope that Hyacinthe might give him one.

"You don't think what I said is true?"

"Of course I do," Oak says. "You should better believe in his love—you should beg him for another chance. But that wouldn't have saved him from drowning. You jumping in after him *did* save him."

"And you being there to pull us back onto deck saved us both." Hyacinthe shoves his hair behind his ear and gives a shuddering sigh. His gaze snags on Tiernan as he shifts a little. "Perhaps I have had enough of vengeance. Perhaps I need not make things so hard." As Oak begins to stand, though, the former falcon looks up at him. "That doesn't mean I release you from your promise, prince."

Right. He'd promised to cut off someone's hand.

As afternoon moves toward night, Tiernan finally wakes. Once he understands what happened, he's furious with Oak and Hyacinthe both.

"You shouldn't have gone after me," he tells Hyacinthe, then turns to the prince. "And you *certainly* shouldn't have."

"I barely did anything," says Oak. "While it's possible that Hyacinthe battled a shark for you."

"I did *not*." For all Hyacinthe's talk of love, the evening finds him sullen.

Oak stands. "Well, I leave you two to that argument. Or some other argument."

The prince heads to the helm, where he finds the Ghost sitting alone, watching the sails billow. He has a staff beside him. Like Vivi, the Ghost had a human parent, and it's visible in the sandy brown of his hair, an unusual color in Faerie.

"There is a tale about hags to which you might hearken," Garrett says.

"Oh?" Oak is almost certain he's not going to like this.

The Ghost gazes past the prince, at the horizon, the bright blaze of the sun fading to embers. "It is said that a hag's power comes from the part of them that's missing. Each one has a cold stone or wisp of cloud or ever-burning flame where their hearts ought to be."

Oak thinks of Wren and her heart, the only part of her that was ever flesh, and doesn't think that can be true. "And?"

"They are as different from the rest of the Folk as mortals are from faeries. And you're bringing two of the most powerful of their kind to Elfhame." The Ghost gives him a long look. "I hope you know what you're doing."

"So do I," Oak says, sighing.

"You remind me of your father sometimes, though I doubt you would like to hear it."

"Madoc?" No one has ever said that to him before.

"You're very like Dain in some ways," says the Ghost.

Oak frowns. Being compared to Dain can be no good thing. "Ah yes, my father who tried to kill me."

"He did terrible things, brutal things, but he had the potential in him to be a great leader. To be a great king. Like you." Garrett's gaze is steady.

Oak snorts. "I am not planning on leading anyone."

The Ghost nods toward Wren. "If she's a queen and you marry her, then you'd be a king."

Oak stares at him in horror because he's right. And Oak didn't really consider that. Possibly because he still thinks it's unlikely that Wren will go through with it. Possibly also because Oak is a fool.

Across the ship, Hyacinthe is leading Tiernan toward a cabin. Hyacinthe, who hasn't really let Oak off the hook. "Since you knew Dain so well, can you tell me who really poisoned Liriope?"

The Ghost's brows rise. "I thought you believed *he* did?"

"Possibly there was someone else who helped him," Oak presses. "Someone who actually slipped the blusher mushroom into her cup."

Garrett looks genuinely uncomfortable. "He was a prince of Elfhame, and his father's heir. He had many servants. Plenty of help with whatever he attempted."

Oak doesn't like how many of those words also apply to him. "Have you heard there was someone else involved?"

Garrett is silent. Since he cannot lie, the prince assumes he has.

"Tell me," Oak says. "You owe me that."

The line of the Ghost's mouth is grim. "I owe many people many things. But I know this. Locke had the answer you seek. He knew the name of the poisoner, much good it did him."

"I am cleverer than Locke." But what Oak thinks of is his dream and the fox's laughter.

The Ghost stands and dusts off his hands on his pants. "That doesn't take much."

Oak can't tell if Garrett knows the name or only knows that Locke did. Taryn may have told him any secrets that Locke told her. "Does my sister know?"

"You should ask her," says the Ghost. "She's probably waiting for you on the shore."

The prince lifts his eyes and sees the Shifting Isles of Elfhame in the distance, breaking through the mist shrouding them.

The Tower of Forgetting rises like a black and forbidding obelisk from the cliffs of Insweal, and beyond it he can make out the green hill of the palace on Insmire, the blaze of the sunset making it look as though it caught fire.

*O*nce upon a time, there was a woman who was so beautiful that none could resist her.

That was how Oriana told the story of Liriope to Oak once he crowned Cardan as the new High King. It sounded like a fairy tale. The kind with princes and princesses that mortals told to one another. But this fairy tale was about how Oak had been told a lie, and that lie was the story of his life.

Oriana was and wasn't his mother. Madoc was and wasn't his father.

Once upon a time, there was a woman who was so beautiful that none could resist her. When she spoke, it seemed that the hearts of those who listened beat for her alone. In time, she caught the eye of the king, who made her the first among his consorts. But the king's son loved her, too, and wanted her for his own.

Oak hadn't known what consorts were, and because it was Faerie and sex didn't embarrass them, Oriana explained that a consort was someone the king wanted to take to bed. And if they were boys like Val Moren, it was for delight; if they were girls like herself, then it was for delight, but also might yield babies; and if the lover were of some other gender, that was for delight and the part about the babies could be a surprise.

"But you didn't have the king's baby," he said. "You only have me."

Oriana smiled and tickled him in the crook of his arm, making him shriek and pull away.

"Only you," she agreed. "And Liriope wasn't going to have the king's child, either. The baby in her belly was sired by his son, Prince Dain."

Once upon a time, there was a woman who was so beautiful that none could resist her. When she spoke, it seemed that the hearts of those who listened beat for her alone. In time, she caught the eye of the king, who made her the first among his consorts. But the king's son loved her, too, and wanted her for his own. When he got a child on her, however, he was afraid. Although the king favored his son, he had other sons and daughters. His favor might change if he knew that his son had taken the king's consort to bed. And so the prince slipped poison into the woman's cup and left her to die.

"I don't understand," said Oak.

"People can be greedy about love," Oriana said. "It's all right if you don't understand, my darling."

"But if he loved her, why did he kill her?" The story made Oak feel strange, as though his life didn't quite belong to him.

"Oh, my sweet boy," his mother told him. His second mother, the only mother he would ever know. "He loved power best, I'm afraid."

"If I love someone—" he started, but he didn't know where to go from there. *If I love someone, I won't kill them* was a poor vow. Besides, he loved lots of people. His sisters. His father. His mother. His other mother, though she was gone. He even loved the ponies in the stables and the hunting dogs his father told him weren't pets.

"When you love someone," Oriana told him, "be better than your father was."

Oak shuddered at the word *father*. He'd accepted that he had two mothers and that he might act like or look like Liriope because he inherited part of himself from her, but until that moment, he'd never thought of the villain of the story, the "king's favored son," as someone with whom he shared anything other than blood.

He looked down at his hooves. The Greenbriars were noted for their animal traits. Those must have come from Dain, along with his horns. Maybe along with things he couldn't see.

"I—"

"And be more careful than your mother. She had the power to know what was in anyone's heart and to say the words they most wanted to hear." She gave him a look.

He was silent, afraid. Sometimes he knew those words, too.

"You can't help what you are. You can't help being charming. But look into too many other hearts, and you may lose your way back to your own."

"I don't understand," he said again.

"You can become the embodiment of someone's—oh, you're so young, I don't know how to say this—you can make people see you the way they want to see you. This seems harmless, but it can be dangerous to become *everything* a person wants. The embodiment of all their desires. And more dangerous for you to twist yourself into shapes others choose for you."

He looked up at her, still confused.

"Oh, my darling, my sweet child. Not everyone needs to love you." She sighed.

But Oak liked everyone loving him. Oak liked it so much that he didn't understand why he would want it to be otherwise.

CHAPTER

14

Half the Court seems to have come out to watch the ship touch down in the water near Mandrake Market. When the hull drops with a splash, it sends salt spray high into the air. The sail luffs, and Oak hangs on to the rigging to keep from stumbling around the deck like a drunk.

He can guess that the onlookers have come, in part, to see the Crown Prince home and, in part, to get a look at the new northern queen, to decide if she and Oak might really be in love, to determine if this is meant to be a marriage, or an alliance, or the prelude to an assassination.

The Living Council stands near the back of the crowd in a knot. Baphen, the Minister of Stars, strokes a blue beard threaded with celestial ornaments. Beside him, Fala, the Grand Fool, dressed in purple motley, pulls a matching purple rose from his hair and chews on the petals, as though he has been waiting long enough for their landing to need a snack. Mikkel, the troll representative of the Unseelie Courts, looks intrigued by the flying ship, while insectile Nihuar, the representative of the Seelie Courts, blinks blankly. With her bug-like eyes, Oak has always found her to be eerily inscrutable.

Oak's family members aren't far off. Taryn's skirts blow around her from the last of the wind that propelled the ship. Her head is bent toward Oriana while Leander runs in circles, as restless as Oak was as a child, playing while dull, important things happened around him.

Sailors aboard the ship throw down the anchor. Small boats launch off the shore of Insmire to ferry the passengers home. A collection of vessels—none of the armada, but pleasure boats. One in the shape of a swan, two carved to appear like they are fishes, and a silvery skiff.

As Oak watches, Jude emerges from a carriage. Ten years into her reign, she doesn't bother waiting for a knight or page to hand her down as would be proper, but simply jumps out. She hasn't bothered with a gown today, either, but wears a pair of high boots, tight-fitting trousers, and a vestlike doublet over a shirt poufy enough that it may have been borrowed from Cardan. The only sign that she is the High Queen is the crown on her head—or perhaps the way the crowd quiets upon her arrival.

Cardan emerges from the carriage next, wearing all the finery she eschewed. He is in a black doublet as ink dark as his hair with lines of scarlet thorns along the sleeves and across the chest. As if the suggestion of prickliness isn't enough, his boots come to stiletto points. The smirk on his face manages to convey royal grandeur and boredom all at once.

Knights swarm around them, full of the alarm the king's and queen's expressions hide.

After the pleasure boats arrive at the ship, Hyacinthe goes below and emerges with Wren at his side. She has recovered enough to dress for the occasion in a gown of cloud gray, which sparkles when she moves. Her feet remain bare, but her hair has been braided high on her head, woven between the tines of the jagged onyx crown. And if she leans heavily on Hyacinthe, at least she is dressed and upright.

"I will go across first," Randalin informs the prince. "And you may proceed next, with the queen. I have taken the liberty of instructing your armsfolk to bring up the rear, with Bogdana. That is, of course, if you approve?" The question is clearly meant as a formality. The command was already issued, the procession set. The Minister of Keys may have been unusually quiet since the ship was attacked, but that hasn't cut down on his pompousness.

Once, Oak would have been amused rather than annoyed. He knows the councilor is harmless. Knows his annoyance is overreaction. "Go ahead," the prince says, trying to get back his equilibrium.

When the councilor heads off toward shore, Oak heaves a sigh and stalks toward Wren. Hyacinthe is whispering something in her ear while she shakes her head.

"If you're well enough—" Oak begins.

She cuts him off. "I am."

"Then, Your Majesty," says the prince, "will you take my arm?"

She looks up at him, as remote and impenetrable as the Citadel itself. Oak feels a little awed by her and then angry on her behalf. He hates that she must wear a mask, no matter how much it costs her, no matter what she's been through.

As you must.

She nods, placing her hand lightly atop his. "I shall be the politest of monsters."

For a moment, in the flash of her eyes, in the lifted corner of her mouth, and the glint of a sharp tooth, he sees the girl who quested with him. The one who was fierce and kind, resourceful and brave. But then she is gone again, submerged into cold stiffness. No longer looking like the girl he loved in the weeks leading up to this, but very like the one he loved as a child.

She's nervous, he thinks.

As Oak leads her ashore, toward the onlookers, he hears whispers.

Witch Queen. Hag Queen.

Still, he is their prince. Their whispers fade as the crowd dutifully parts around him. Tiernan and Hyacinthe both follow, one on each side.

When Oak comes to his sister, he bows. Wren, seeming unsure of the etiquette, bobs in a shallow curtsy.

Despite how much magic it must have taken to destroy that monster in the sea, despite how sick she was after, she appears remarkably composed.

"Welcome home, Prince Oak," Jude says formally, and then her mouth twists into a wry smile. "And congratulations on the completion of your epic quest. Remind me to knight you when I get the chance."

Oak grins and bites his tongue. He is certain she will have much more to say to him later when they are alone.

"And you, Queen Suren of the former Court of Teeth," says Cardan in his silky voice. "You've changed quite a bit, but then you would have, I suppose. Felicitations on the murder of your mother."

Wren's body stiffens with surprise.

Oak desperately wants to stop Cardan from talking, but short of kicking him or throwing something at his head, he has no idea how.

"The Ice Needle Citadel is full of old nightmares," Wren says after a beat of silence. "I look forward to making new ones."

Cardan gives her a half smile of appreciation for that line. "We shall dine together at dusk tomorrow to celebrate your arrival. And betrothal, if the frantic messages we received from Grima Mog were accurate."

Oak's mind spins, trying to figure out if he should object to any part of this. "We are, indeed, betrothed," he confirms.

Jude looks over at him, studying his face. Then she turns to Wren. "So you're to be my new sister."

Wren flinches, as though her words are the opening move of some kind of cruel game. Oak wants to put his hand out, to touch her arm, to reassure her, except he knows better than to make Wren look as though she needs reassurance.

Besides, he's not entirely sure what his sister *did* intend with those words.

A moment later, the black vulture lands on the dirt beside them and transforms into Bogdana, dark feathers becoming her dress and hair.

All around, there is the rattle of swords coming free of sheaths.

"What an appropriate greeting, Your Majesties," says the storm hag. She does not bow. Nor does she curtsy. She doesn't even incline her head.

"Bogdana," Jude says, and there is something that is possibly admiration in her voice. "Your reputation precedes you."

"How pleasing," says the storm hag. "Especially since I saved your ship from certain destruction."

Jude looks toward the Ghost—then checks herself and turns to Randalin instead.

"It is even so, Your Majesty," the councilor affirms. "The Undersea launched an attack on us."

A ripple of surprise goes through the crowd.

Cardan raises his brows, looking skeptical. "The Undersea?"

"One of the contenders for Queen Nicasia's hand," Randalin clarifies.

The High King turns to Oak with an amused smirk. "Perhaps they were worried you might throw your hat into that ring."

"They wanted to send a message," Randalin goes on, as though arguing the case, "that the land ought to keep to itself and let the Undersea work out its ruler business on its own. If we act otherwise, we will have made a powerful new enemy."

"Their dim view of treaties gives me a dim view of them," says Cardan. "We will give Nicasia aid, as she once aided us, and as we swore to do."

It was the Undersea who'd rallied to Jude's side when Cardan had been enchanted into a serpent, while Madoc and his allies conspired to take crown and throne, and while Wren hid in Oak's room.

"We are grateful to you for your help," Jude tells Bogdana.

"I saved the ship, but Wren saved those on board," the storm hag says, curling her long fingers possessively on the girl's shoulder.

Wren tenses at the touch or the praise.

"And saved our father as well," Oak affirms, because he has to make his sister understand that Wren isn't their enemy. "I couldn't have gotten to Madoc without her, nor gotten him out—but I'm sure he told you as much."

"He told me many things," says Jude.

"I hope we will see him at the wedding," says Bogdana.

Jude raises her eyebrows and glances in the High King's direction. It's obvious they thought Oak being betrothed was a long way from an exchange of vows. "There are several celebrations that ought to precede—"

"Three days' time," Bogdana says. "No longer."

"Or?" Cardan asks, voice light. A dare.

"Enough," Wren hisses under her breath. She cannot quite call the storm hag to account in front of everyone, and Bogdana knows it, but past a certain point, she will have to do something.

The storm hag places both hands on Wren's shoulders. "Prince?"

They all look at him, all weighing his loyalty. And while he would marry Wren right then if it were only up to him, he can't help thinking that anything Bogdana is this eager for can't be good. Maybe she's guessed that Wren doesn't intend to ever go through with it.

"It would pain me to wait even three days," Oak says, lightly, deflecting. "But if we must, for the sake of propriety, better the thing is done right...."

"There are rituals to complete," Jude says. "And your family to gather." She is certainly stalling, as Wren hoped she would.

Cardan watches the interaction. Most particularly, he watches Oak. He suspects the prince of something. Oak has to get him alone. Has to explain.

"We have rooms ready at the palace—" Jude begins.

Wren shakes her head. "There is no need to trouble yourself for my sake. I can keep and quarter my own people." From a pocket in her shimmering gray dress, she takes out the white walnut.

Jude frowns.

Oak can well believe Wren doesn't want to be at the palace, to have them observe her every weakness. Still, to refuse the hospitality of the rulers of Elfhame makes a statement about her loyalties.

Cardan seems distracted by the walnut itself. "Oh, very well, I will be the one to ask the obvious question—*what have you there?*"

"If you will allow us a patch of grass, this is where myself and my people will stay," Wren says.

Jude glances toward Oak, and he shrugs.

"By all means," says the High Queen, gesturing toward the guard. "Clear a space."

A few of her knights disperse the crowd until there is an expanse of grass near the edge of the black rocks overlooking the water.

"Is this enough room?" Jude asks.

"Enough and more than enough," says Bogdana.

"We can be generous," says Cardan, clearly choosing his words to irritate the storm hag.

Wren takes a few steps away from them, then tosses the walnut against a patch of mossy earth, reciting the little verse under her breath. Cries of astonishment ring out around them as a pavilion the white of swan feathers, with golden feet like those of a crow, rises from the dirt.

It reminds him of one of the tents in the encampment of the Court of Teeth. He recalls seeing something very like it when he came to cut through the ropes that tied Wren to a post. Recalls listening for Madoc's voice among those of the other soldiers, half in longing and half in fear. He'd missed his father. He'd also been afraid of him.

The prince wonders if Wren is reminded of the encampment, too, not far from where they currently stand. Wonders if she hates being back here.

Mother Marrow was the one who gave her the magic walnut. Mother Marrow, who keeps a place at Mandrake Market. Who gave Oak the advice that sent him off to the Thistlewitch, who sent him straight to Bogdana, in turn. Passed him from hag to hag, perhaps with a specific plan in mind. A specific version of a shared future.

All his thoughts are disturbing.

"What a clever nut," says Cardan with a smile. "If you will not stay in the palace, then we have no recourse but to send you refreshments and hope to see you tomorrow." He gestures toward Oak. "I trust that you don't also have a cottage in your pocket. Your family is eager to spend some time with you."

"A moment," the prince says, turning to Wren.

It's almost impossible to say anything meaningful to her here, with many eyes on them both, but he can't leave without promising that he will see her. He needs her to know he's not abandoning her.

"Tomorrow afternoon?" he says. "I will come and find you."

She nods once, but her face seems braced for betrayal. He understands that. Here, he has power. If he was going to hurt her, this would be the time to do it. "I really do want to show you the isles. We could go to Mandrake Market. Swim in the Lake of Masks. Picnic on Insear, if you're feeling up to it."

"Perhaps," she says, and lets him take her hand. Even lets him press a kiss to her wrist.

He isn't sure what to make of the tremble in her fingers as he releases them.

And then Oak is herded toward the palace, with Tiernan behind him and Randalin complaining vociferously to the High King and Queen about the discomforts of the journey.

"*You* insisted on going north," Jude reminds the councilor.

As soon as they pass through the doors of the Palace of Elfhame, Oriana embraces Oak, hugging him tightly. "What were you thinking?" she asks, which is so exactly what he expects her to say that it makes him laugh.

"Where's Madoc?" he asks between being released by his mother and Taryn sweeping him into another hug.

"Probably waiting for us in the war room," Jude says.

Leander comes up to Oak, demanding to be swung around. He lifts the boy in his arms and whirls, rewarded with the child's laughter.

Cardan yawns. "I hate the war room."

Jude rolls her eyes. "He's probably arguing with Grima Mog's second-in-command."

"Well, if there's an actual *fight* to watch, that's different, obviously," Cardan says. "But if it's just pushing little wooden people around on maps, I will leave that to Leander."

At the mention of his name, Leander capers over. "I'm bored and you're bored," he says. "Play with me?" It's half request, half demand.

Cardan touches the top of the child's head, brushing back his dark coppery hair. "Not now, imp. We have many dull adult things to do."

Oak wonders if Cardan sees Locke in the boy. Wonders if he sees the child he and Jude do not—and will not anytime soon, it seems—have.

When she turns toward him, Oak holds up a hand to forestall whatever his sister is about to say. "May I speak with Cardan for a moment?"

The High King looks at him with narrowed eyes. "Your sister has precedence, and she would like some time with you."

At the thought of Jude's lecture and then the lectures of all the other family members who took precedence, Oak feels exhausted.

"I haven't been home in almost two months and am sticky with salt spray," he says. "I want to take a bath and put on my own clothes and sleep in my own bed before you all start yelling at me."

Jude snorts. "Pick two."

"What?"

"You heard me. You can sleep and then have a bath, but I am going to be there the moment you're done, not caring a bit about your being naked. You can bathe and put on fresh clothes, and see me before you sleep. Or you could sleep and change your garments, no bath, although I admit that's not my preference."

He gives her an exasperated look. She smiles back at him. In his mind, she has always been his sister first, but right at that moment it's impossible to forget that she's also the Queen of Elfhame.

"Fine," he says. "Bath and clothes. But I want coffee and not the mushroom kind."

"Your wish," she tells him, like the liar she is, "is my command."

"Explain this to me from the beginning," Jude says, sitting on a couch in his rooms. Her arms are crossed. On the table beside her is an assortment of pastries, a carafe of coffee, cream so fresh that it is still warm and golden, along with bowls of fruit. Servants keep coming with more food—oatcakes, honey cakes, roasted chestnuts, cheeses with crystals that crunch between his teeth, parsnip tarts glazed in honey and lavender—and he keeps eating it.

"After I left Court, I went to see Wren because I knew she could command Lady Nore," he begins, distracted by someone putting a cup of hot coffee into his hand. His hair is wet and his body relaxed from soaking in hot water. The abundance that he has taken for granted all his life surrounds him, familiar as his own bed.

"You mean *Suren?*" Jude demands. "The former child-queen of the Court of Teeth? Whom you call by a cute nickname."

He shrugs. *Wren* is not precisely a nickname, but he takes his sister's point. His use of it indicates familiarity.

"Tiernan says that you've known her for years." He can see in Jude's face that she believes he took a foolish risk recruiting Wren to his quest, that he trusts too easily, and that's why he often winds up with a knife in his back. It's what he wants her to believe about him, what he has carefully made her believe, and yet it still stings.

"I met her when she came to Elfhame with the Court of Teeth. We snuck off and played together. I told you back then that she needed help."

Jude's dark eyes are intent. She's listening to all the nuances of what he says, her mouth a hard line. "You snuck off with her during a *war?* When? Why?"

He shakes his head. "The night you and Vivi and Heather and Taryn were talking about serpents and curses and what to do about the bridle."

His sister leans forward. "You could have been killed. You could have been killed by *our father.*"

Oak takes an oatcake and begins tearing it apart. "I saw Wren once or twice over the years, although I wasn't sure what she thought of me. And then, this time..."

He sees the change in Jude's face, the slight tightening of the muscles of her shoulders. But she's still listening.

"I betrayed her," Oak says. "And I don't know if she'll forgive me."

"Well, she's wearing your ring on her finger," Jude says.

Oak takes one of the shredded pieces of oatcake and puts it into his mouth, tasting the lie he can't tell.

His sister sighs. "And she came here. That has to be worth something."

And she held me prisoner. But he isn't sure that Jude will be at all moved by that as proof of Wren's caring about him.

"So do you really intend to go through with this marriage? Is this real?"

"Yes," Oak says, because none of his concerns are about his own willingness.

Jude doesn't look happy. "Dad explained that she has a unique power."

Oak nods. "She can unmake things. Magic, mostly, but not exclusively."

"People?" Jude asks, although if Cardan can congratulate Wren on the death of Lady Nore, he clearly knows the answer, which means she knows, too.

Still, his sister wants to hear it from him. Maybe she just wants to make him admit it. He nods.

Jude raises a brow. "And that means what exactly?"

"Scattering our guts across the snow. Or whatever landscape she has to hand."

"Lovely," she says. "And are you going to tell me she's our ally? That we're safe from that power?"

He licks dry lips. No, he cannot say that. Nor does he want to confess that he's worried Wren will take herself apart without meaning to.

Jude sighs again. "I am going to choose to trust you, brother mine. For now. Don't make me regret it."

CHAPTER

15

O ak wakes in his familiar bedroom, among a familiar mess. Papers
cover his dresser and desk. Books are piled in untidy stacks,
shoved back into their shelves at odd angles. On his bedside table, a vol-
ume is open facedown, its spine cracked.

The prince has very poor book etiquette. It has been remarked on
before by his tutors.

Tacked up on the wall is a collage of drawings and photographs and
other artifacts from both worlds that Oak occupies. A bright orange
ticket from a fair hangs beside a riddle on a piece of vellum found in
the gullet of a fish. A napkin with the number of a boy he met at a
movie theater written in ballpoint pen. A sticky note with three books
he means to pick up from a library. A golden necklace in the shape of an
acorn, given by his first mother to his second and then to him, attached
with gum to the wall. A silver fox figurine with twine around its middle, twin to the one Wren has. A manga-style portrait of Oak done by

Heather in markers. A pencil sketch for a formal portrait of the family that hangs in one of the halls.

It all is just as it was when he left. Looking around makes him feel as though time telescoped, as though he stepped out for only a few hours. As though he couldn't have come back so changed.

Oak hears a sound from the sitting room outside his bedroom—part of the chambers that ought to be his alone. He comes fully awake, sliding out of bed, his hand going automatically to the dagger beneath his mattress.

That's right where he left it as well.

He creeps along the wall, careful with his hooves against the stone floor. He peers through the gap between door and frame.

Madoc is picking over the remainder of the food on the table.

With a sigh of disgust—at himself, his father, and his apparent paranoia—he stabs the dagger into the wall and grabs a robe. By the time he comes out, Madoc is sitting on a couch and drinking cold, leftover coffee from the night before. An eye patch covers a quarter of his face, and a twisted black cane rests against a side table. The reminders of his father's suffering in the Citadel temper Oak's rage toward him but don't rid him of it.

"You're alive," Madoc says with a grin.

"I might say much the same of you," Oak points out, sitting across from his father. He's in a dressing gown embroidered with a pattern of deer, half of them shot with arrows and bleeding red thread on the golden cloth. Everything in Elfhame feels surreal and sinister at the moment, and the dying deer on his robe aren't helping. "And before you make *any* point about *anything* I've done that you believe was risky, I suggest you recall you did something riskier and far more foolish."

"I am chastened," Madoc says, and then his mouth lifts in a grin. "But I did get what I wanted."

"She pardoned you?" Oak isn't entirely surprised. His father is here in the palace, after all.

The redcap shakes his head. "Your sister rescinded the exile. *For now.*" He snorts, and Oak understands that's all Jude could do without looking as though he was getting some kind of special favor out of her. But it was enough.

"And you're done with scheming?" Oak asks him.

Madoc waves a hand in the air. "What would I need to scheme for when my children control everything I ever wanted for them?"

In other words, no, he's not done.

Oak sighs.

"So let's discuss your wedding. You know several factions here are enthusiastic about it."

Oak's eyebrows go up. People who want him out of the way?

"If you had a powerful queen, it would be more possible to support you against the current occupants of the thrones."

Oak should have known better. "Since I haven't made myself look as though I would make a competent ruler."

"Some Folk prefer incompetence. Their desire is for their rulers to have enough power to hold the throne and enough naivete to listen to those who put them there. And your queen exudes both."

"Oh?" Madoc holding forth about politics is comforting in its familiarity, but it bothers him that Madoc so quickly identified the factions at Court that were up for treachery. It worries Oak how Madoc might respond if Oak ever indicated he *was* interested in becoming

High King. He's concerned that the redcap might prize naivete in Oak as much as any conspirator.

"They will sidle up to your little queen tonight," his father goes on. "They will introduce themselves and curry her favor. They will attempt to ingratiate themselves with her people and compliment her person. And they will gauge just how much she hates the High King and Queen. I hope her vows were ironclad."

Oak can't help recalling the way she told Randalin she might be able to break her vows like she broke a curse. *Pull it apart like a cobweb.* He doesn't like thinking how intrigued his father would be by that information. "I better get dressed."

"I'll ring the servants," Madoc says, reaching for his cane and pushing himself to his feet.

"I can manage," Oak tells his father firmly.

"They ought to clear these platters and bring you some breakfast." His father is already moving toward the pull beside the door. As with so many things, it is not as though Oak *couldn't* stop him, but it would take so much effort that it doesn't seem worth doing.

Oak's family is used to thinking of him as someone who needs to be taken care of. And for all that Madoc knew that Oak was dangerous enough to spring him from the Ice Needle Citadel, he suspects Madoc would be surprised about the prince's machinations at Court.

Before a servant can be called in to give him help he neither wants nor needs, Oak goes back to his bedroom and hunts through his armoire for something to wear. As soon as he finishes with his father, he will steal a basket of food from the kitchens and go to Wren's clawfooted cottage, so there's no need for anything fussy. He chooses a plain woolen green jacket and dark pants that stop at the knee. He's going to tempt Wren to run wild in Elfhame. Leave their guards behind and politics behind, too. He's determined to make her laugh. A lot.

A fierce knock on the door brings him out of his bedroom. Despite having gorged the night before, and despite telling his father not to bother summoning more food, his stomach growls. Probably he has some meals to catch up on. Possibly he can take this food and not bother robbing the kitchens.

"Ah," Madoc says. "That would be your mother."

Oak gives the redcap a look of betrayal. There would have been no avoiding Oriana for long, but he could have managed a little longer. And his father could have warned him. "What about breakfast?"

"She'll have brought you something." He supposes they had some kind of prearranged signal when Madoc was done with Oak—the bell pull, a servant to run and alert her.

With a sigh, the prince opens the door, then moves to one side as his mother sweeps into the room. She has a tray in her hands. On it rests a teapot and some sandwiches.

"You're not going to marry that girl," Oriana says, fixing him with a glare. She sets down the tray sharply, ignoring the loud sound of it hitting the table.

"Careful," Oak warns.

Madoc rises, leaning heavily on his black cane. "Well, I will leave you two to catching up." His expression is mild, fond. He is not fleeing conflict. He loves conflict. But perhaps he doesn't want to be in the position of openly telling Oriana that her priorities do not match his own.

"Mom," Oak says.

She makes a face. She is dressed in a gown of white and rose, a frothy ruff at her throat and the ends of her sleeves. With her pink eyes and pale skin and petallike wings on her back, she sometimes looked like a flower to him—a snapdragon. "You sound like a mortal. Is it so hard to say in full?"

He sighs. *"Mother."*

She presents her cheek to be kissed, then presses the backs of his hands to her lips. "My beauty. My precious child."

He smiles automatically, but her words hurt. He never before doubted her love for him—she turned her life upside down, even marrying Madoc, for the sake of Oak's protection. But if that love was something forced on her, some enchantment, then it wasn't real and he would have to find a way to free her from the burden of it.

"You worried me when you left," she says. "I know you adore your father, but he wouldn't want you to risk your life for him."

Oak bites his tongue to keep from answering that. Not only was Madoc willing to let Oak risk his life, but he was counting on it. Perhaps Oak should be grateful, though. At least he was certain Madoc's feelings were real—he was far too manipulative to have been manipulated by magic. "Father looks well."

"Better than he was. Not resting enough, of course." She looks up at Oak, impatience in her face. Normally, she is rigid about etiquette, but he can tell she's not interested in small talk now. He's only surprised that she allowed Madoc and Jude to get at him first. Of course, by buttonholing him after they left, she had the advantage of being able to lecture him as long as she liked without the worry of being interrupted. "Questing I understand, even if I didn't like the thought of you in danger, but not this. Not offering this girl marriage when she has none of the qualities anyone might look for in a bride."

"So let me get this straight," Oak says. "You understand the part where I might have had to kill a lot of people, but you think I chose the wrong girl to kiss?"

Oriana gives him a sharp look, then pours him some tea.

He drinks. The tea is dark and fragrant and almost washes the taste of bitterness from his mouth.

"You were in her prisons. I have spoken with Tiernan many times since he returned. I asked him dozens of questions. I know you sent him away with Madoc to save them both. So tell me, are you marrying her because you care for her or because you want to save the world from her?"

Oak grimaces. "You didn't include saving her from the world as a possibility."

"Is that your reason?" Oriana inquires.

"I care for her," Oak says.

"As the Crown Prince, you have a responsibility to the throne. When you—"

"No." A thin tendril of worry uncurls inside him at the thought she, like Madoc, might grow too ambitious on his behalf. "There's no reason to believe I will outlive either Jude or Cardan. No reason for me ever to wear the crown."

"I admit that once I dreaded the possibility," Oriana says. "But you're older now. And you have a kind heart. That would be a great boon to Elfhame."

"Jude is doing just fine. And it's not like she doesn't have a kind heart."

Oriana gives him an incredulous look.

"Besides, Wren is a queen in her own right. If you want me to wear a crown, there you go. If I marry her, I get one by default." He takes one of the sandwiches and bites into it.

Oriana is not appeased. "This is nothing to take lightly. Your sister certainly doesn't. She sent her people to bring you back the moment she found that you'd gone after your father. And though she failed to get hold of you, her people brought back one of your traveling companions—a kelpie."

"Jack of the Lakes," Oak says, delighted until the rest of what Oriana is saying catches up with him. "Where is he? What did she do to him?"

Oriana gives a minute shrug. "What is it you were saying about your sister having a kind heart?"

He sighs. "Your point is made."

"Jack was hauled before us and made to tell us all he knew of your journey and its intention. He's still in the palace—a guest of the Court, not *exactly* a prisoner—but he described Suren as more animal than girl, rolling in mud. And I remember how she was as a child."

"*Tortured* is how she was as a child. Besides, how can he call anyone an animal when he turns into a literal horse?"

Oriana presses her lips together. "She is not for you," she says finally. "Feel as sorry for her as you like. Desire her if you must. But do not marry her. I will not have you stolen from us again."

Oak sighs. He owes his mother so much. But he does not owe her this. "You want to rule over me as though I were a child. But you also want me to be a ruler. You will have to trust me when I say that I know what I want."

"You have grown tired of far more fascinating girls," Oriana says with a wave of her hand. "A few boys, too, if Court rumors are true. Your Suren is dull, without grace or manners, and furthermore—"

"Enough!" Oak says, surprising both of them. "No, she is not going to become the Mistress of Revels and have all of Court eating out of her hand. She's quiet. She doesn't love crowds or people staring at her or having to find things to say to them. But I don't see what that has to do with my loving her."

For a moment, they just stare at each other. Then Oriana goes to his wardrobe and riffles through the clothes.

"You ought to change into the bronze. Here, this." She holds up a doublet shining with metallic thread. It is the brown of dried blood, and velvet leaves have been sewn on it as though they were blown in a great gust across its surface. Most of them are various shades of brown and gold, but a few green ones catch the eye with their brightness. "And perhaps the golden horn and hoof covers. Those are lovely in candlelight."

"What's wrong with what I'm wearing?" he asks. "I am going out for the rest of the afternoon, and tonight it's only dinner with the family and a girl you don't want me to impress."

Oriana gives him an incredulous look. "Dinner? Oh no, my darling. It's a *feast*."

CHAPTER

16

O *f course*, when Cardan invited Wren to dinner, he didn't mean dining together at a table. He meant attending a feast held in her honor. *Of course he did.*

Oak forgot how things worked, how people behaved. After being away from Elfhame for so long, he is being crammed back into a role he no longer remembers how to fit into.

Once he's dressed, scolded, and kissed by his mother, he manages to make it out the door. On his way to the kitchens, he runs into his nephew, who demands a game of hide-and-seek and chases after a palace cat when he's put off. Then, as the prince packs a basket, he endures being good-naturedly fussed over by several of the servants, including the cook who sent up little iced cakes. Finally, having obtained a pie, several cheeses, and a stoppered bottle of cider, he slips away, his cheeks stinging only a little from the pinching.

Still, the sky over Insmire is the blue of Wren's hair, and as he makes his way to her cottage, he cannot help feeling hopeful.

He is most of the way there when a girl darts from the trees.

"Oak," Wren says, sounding out of breath. She's clad in a simple brown dress with none of the grandeur of the clothes he's seen her in since she took over the Court of Teeth. It looks like something she threw on in haste.

"I love you," Oak says, because he needs to say it simply, so she can't find a way to see a lie in it. He's smiling because she came through the woods in a rush, looking for him. Because he feels ridiculously happy. "Come have a picnic with me."

For a moment, Wren looks utterly horrified. The prince's thoughts stagger to a stop. He feels a sharp pain in his chest and fights to keep the smile on his lips.

It's not as though he expected her to return the sentiment. He expected her to laugh and perhaps be a little flattered. Enjoy the thought of having a little power over him. He thought she *liked* him, even if she found him hard to forgive. He thought she *had* to like him some to *want* him.

"Well," he manages, hefting the basket with false lightness. "Luckily, there's still the picnic."

"You fall in love with the ease of someone slipping into a bath," she tells him. "And I imagine you extricate yourself with somewhat more drama, but no less ease."

Now that was more the sort of thing he was prepared to hear. "Then I urge you to ignore my outburst."

"I want you to call off the marriage," she says.

He sucks in a breath, stung. Truly, he didn't expect her to rub salt in so fresh a wound, although he supposes she gave him no reason to think she wouldn't. "That seems like an excessive response to a declaration of love."

Wren doesn't so much as smile. "Still, call it off."

"Call it off yourself," he snaps, feeling childish. "As I remember from the ship, we had a plan. If you wish to change it now, go right ahead."

She shakes her head. Her hands are clenched into fists at her sides. "No, it must be you. Come on, it's not as though a marriage is what you want, not really, right? No matter how you say you feel. It was a clever thing to do—a clever thing to say. You've always been clever. Be clever now."

"And break things off with you? Cleverly?" He sounds brittle, resentful.

She actually looks hurt by his tone. Somehow that makes him angrier than anything else. "I should never have come here," she tells him.

"You can go," he reminds her.

"You don't understand." She wears a pained expression. "And I can't explain."

"Then it seems we are at an impasse." He folds his arms.

She glances down at her hands, which are gripping each other tightly, fingers threaded together. When she looks back up into his eyes, she seems sorrowful.

"I shall see you at the feast," he says, attempting to regain his dignity.

Then he turns and stomps off toward the woods, before he can say more things he will regret. Before she takes the chance to hurt him worse. He feels petty, petulant, and ridiculous.

Rubbing the heel of his hand over one eye, he doesn't look back.

Striding toward Mandrake Market with a picnic basket in his hand, Oak feels a perfect fool.

Several people bow low when he passes, as though sharing the same path is a singular honor. He wonders if he would feel less awkward if he had grown up entirely on the isles and wasn't used to being treated as nothing special in the mortal world.

He gloried in it when he was younger. Loved how all the children here wanted to play with him, how everyone had smiles for him.

And yet you knew it was false. That was part of what drew you to Wren—she had your measure from the first.

But though she had his measure, he wasn't sure he had hers. Mother Marrow was summoned north by Bogdana. Mother Marrow gave Wren the gift of that cottage where she and her people spent the night.

Mother Marrow knew *something* of their plans.

Mandrake Market, on the tip of Insmoor, used to be open only on misty mornings, but it's grown into a more permanent fixture. There, one can find everything from leather masquerade masks to charms for the bottoms of shoes, swirling tinctures of everapple, potion-makers, and even poisons.

Oak passes maple sugar in the shape of strange animals, a lace-maker weaving skulls and bones into her patterns. A shopkeeper sets out trays of acorn cups full to their tiny brims with blood-dark wine. Another offers to tell fortunes from the pattern of spit on a page of fresh parchment. A goblin grills fresh oysters over an outdoor fire. The midday sun stains everything gold.

Like the growth of the market, stalls and tents have given way to more permanent structures. Mother Marrow's house is a sturdy stone cottage with none of the fancifulness of walls shingled in candy. Out front, an herb garden grows wild, vines tied so they weave over the top of a diamond-paned window.

Steeling himself, he raps on the wooden planks of her door.

There is a shuffling from the other side, and then it opens, squeaking on dry hinges. Mother Marrow appears in the doorway, standing on clawed feet, like those of a bird of prey. Her hair is gray as stone, and she wears a long necklace of rocks carved with archaic symbols on them, ones that puzzle the eye if you look too long.

"Prince," she says, blinking up at him. "You look far too fine for a visit to poor Mother Marrow."

"Could any grandeur be great enough to properly honor you?" he asks with a grin.

She huffs, but he can tell she's a little pleased. "Come in, then. And tell me of your adventure."

Oak moves past her into her cottage. There is a low fire in the grate and several stumps before it, along with a wooden chair. Another threadbare chair sits off to one side with knitting equipment piled in a basket at its feet. The yarn seems freshly spun, yet not carded well enough to remove all the bits of thistle. On the wall, a large, painted curio cabinet contains an array of things that don't reward observing too closely. Tiny skeletons covered in a thin layer of dust. Viscous fluids half-dried in ancient bottles. Beetle wings, shining like gems. A bowl of nuts, a few shaking and one hazelnut rolling back and forth. Beyond the cabinet, the prince can see a passageway into a back room, perhaps a bedroom.

She urges him to sit in the wooden chair by the fire, the back carved in the shape of an owl.

"Tea?" she offers.

Oak nods, to be polite, although he feels as though he's been swimming in tea since his homecoming.

Mother Marrow tops off a pot from the kettle hanging over the fire and pours him a cup. It's a blend of some kind, carrying the scent of kelp in it, and anise.

"This is very kind," he says, because the Folk do not like to have their efforts dismissed with mere thanks and take hospitality very seriously.

She grins, and he notes a cracked tooth. She picks up her own cup, which she has freshened, using it to warm her hands. "I see the advice I gave you was useful. Your father has returned. And you have won yourself a prize."

He nods, feeling as though he's on unsteady ground. If she's referring to Wren, it seems dismissive to call her a prize, as though she were an object, but he can't think what else she could be talking about. Perhaps Mother Marrow has a reason to appear not to care too much for Wren. "Leaving me to seek your guidance again."

She raises her eyebrows. "On what subject, prince?"

"I saw you in the Ice Citadel," he says.

She stiffens. "What of it?"

He sighs. "I want to know why Bogdana brought you there. What she hoped you were going to do."

Silence stretches out for a long moment between them. In it, he hears the boiling of the water and the clack of the nuts as they move in her cabinet.

"Did you know I have a daughter?" she asks finally.

Oak shakes his head, although now that she mentions it, he does remember something about her having a child. Perhaps someone referred to the daughter before, although the context eludes him.

"I tried to trick the High King into marrying her."

Oh, right. That was the context. Mother Marrow gave Cardan a cape that, when worn, makes him immune to most blows. It's said to be woven of spider silk and nightmares, and although Oak has no idea how that could be done, he doesn't doubt the truth of it. "So you have some interest in your line ruling."

"I have some interest in my *kind* ruling," she corrects him. "I would have liked to see my daughter with a crown on her head. She's very beautiful and quite clever with her fingers. But I will be glad to see any hag daughter on the throne."

"I don't intend to be High King," he informs her.

At that, she smiles, takes a sip of her tea, and says nothing.

"Wren?" he prompts. "The Citadel? Bogdana's request?"

Her smile widens. "We hags were the first of the Folk, before those of the air alighted and claimed dominion, before those of the Undersea first surfaced from the deep. We, like the trolls and the giants, come from the earth's bones. And we have the old magic. But we do not rule. Perhaps our power makes other Folk nervous. Little wonder that the storm hag was tempted by Mab's offer, though in the end the cost was high."

"And now she bears a grudge against my family," he says.

Mother Marrow snorts, as though at the delicacy of his phrasing. "So she does."

"Do you?" he asks.

"Have I not been a loyal subject?" she asks him. "Have I not served the High King and his mortal queen well? Have I not served you, prince, to the best of my poor abilities?"

"I don't know," he says. "Have you?"

She stands—acting offended to cover that she does not—and perhaps dares not—answer. "I think it's time you go. I am sure you are wanted at the palace."

He sets down his untouched cup of tea and rises from the chair. She's intimidating, but he's taller than her and royal. He hopes he seems more formidable than he feels. "If Bogdana has a plan to move against Jude and Cardan, and you're a part of it, the punishment will not be worth whatever reward you've been promised."

"Is that so? Rumors abound about *your* loyalties, prince, and the company *you* keep."

"I am loyal to the throne," he says. "And to my sister, the queen."

"What about the king?" asks Mother Marrow, her eyes like flint.

Oak's gaze doesn't waver. "So long as he doesn't cross Jude, I am his to command."

She scowls. "What about the girl? What loyalties do you owe her? Would you give her your heart?"

An ominous question, given what he knows of Mellith's history.

He hesitates, wanting to give a real answer. He is drawn to Wren. He is consumed by thoughts of her. The rough silk of her voice. Her shy smile. Her unflinching gaze. The memory of fine, wispy strands of her hair under his hands, the nearness of her skin, her indrawn breath. Memory of the way she sparred with him across that long table in the Citadel—the familiarity of it, so like many of his own family meals. But the sting of his confession and her rejection is fresh. "I would give her whatever she wanted of me."

Mother Marrow raises her brows, looking amused. Then her smile dims. "Poor Suren."

Oak puts a hand to his heart. "I think I'm offended."

She gives a little laugh. "Not that, foolish boy. It's that she should have been one of the greatest of hags, an inheritor of her mother's vast power. A maker of storms in her own right, a creator of magical objects so glorious that the walnut I gave her would be a mere trinket. But instead, her power has been turned inside out. She can only absorb magic, break curses. But the one curse she cannot break is the one on herself. Her magic is warped. Every time she uses it, it hurts her."

Oak thinks of the story Bogdana told, of a girl whose magic burned like matches, and considers that Bogdana's own magic doesn't work in that way. The storm hag was exhausted, perhaps, after she made the ship fly, but not sick. When Cardan brought a whole island from the bottom of the sea, he didn't faint afterward. "And that's what Bogdana brought you north to try to fix?"

She hesitates.

"Shall I ask one of the Council to come and inspect what potions and powders you keep in your cabinet?"

She only laughs. "Would you really do such a thing to an old lady such as myself, to whom you already owe a debt? What bad manners that would be!"

He gives her an irritated look, but she's right. He does owe her a debt. And he is one of the Folk, brought up in Faerie enough to almost believe that bad manners outweigh murder in a list of crimes. Besides, half the Council probably buys from her. "Can you undo Wren's curse?"

"No," she says, relenting. "As far as I know, it cannot be undone. When the power of Mellith's death was used to curse Mab, Mellith's heart became the locus for that curse. How can you fill something that devours everything you put into it? Perhaps you can answer that. I can't. Now go back to the palace, prince, and leave Mother Marrow to her ruminations."

He's probably late for the banquet already. "If you see Bogdana," he says, "be sure to give her my regards."

"Oh," says Mother Marrow. "You can give her those yourself soon enough."

By the time he arrives in the brugh, the hall beneath the hill is full of Folk. He is, as he predicted, late.

"Your Highness," Tiernan says, falling into step behind him.

"I hope you rested," Oak says, attempting to seem as though he hasn't just been dumped, as though he hasn't a care in the world.

"No need." Tiernan speaks in a clipped fashion, and he's frowning, but since he's so often frowning, the prince can't tell if it indicates more disapproval than usual. "Where were you this afternoon?"

"I took a quick trip to Mandrake Market," Oak says.

"You might have fetched me," Tiernan suggests.

"I might have," Oak agrees amiably. "But I thought you might be the worse for wear after almost drowning—or perhaps otherwise occupied."

Tiernan's frown deepens. "I was neither."

"I *hoped* you might be otherwise occupied." Oak glances around the hall. Cardan lounges on his throne on the dais, a goblet hanging off his fingers as though it may spill at any moment. *Cardan.* Oak has to speak with him, but he can't do it here, in front of everyone, in front of Folk who may be part of the conspiracy the prince needs to disavow.

Jude stands close to Oriana, who is gesturing with her hands as she speaks. He doesn't spot any of the other members of his family, although that doesn't mean they're not here. It's quite a crowd.

"Hyacinthe is a traitor thrice over," Tiernan says. "So you can cease speaking of him."

Oak raises a single eyebrow, a trick he is almost sure he stole from Cardan. "I don't recall mentioning Hyacinthe at all."

Not unexpectedly, that irritates Tiernan even more. "He betrayed you, helped imprison you. And struck you. He attempted to kill the High King. You ought to dismiss me from your service for how I feel about him, not inquire about it as though it were perfectly normal."

"But if I don't inquire, how will I know enough to dismiss you from my service?" Oak grins, feeling a bit lighter. Tiernan said *feel*, not *felt*. Maybe Oak's romance is doomed, but that doesn't mean someone else's can't succeed.

Tiernan gives him a look.

Oak laughs. "If anyone wants to torture you, all they need to do is make you talk about your feelings."

Tiernan's mouth twists. "On the ship, we...," he begins, and then seems to think better about the direction of that statement. "He saved me. And he spoke to me as though we could...but I was too angry to listen."

"Ah," Oak says. Before he can go further, Lady Elaine moves toward him in the crowd. "Ah, shit."

Her ancestry is half from river creatures and half from aerial ones. A pair of small, pale wings hangs from her back, translucent and veined in the manner of dragonfly wings. They shimmer like stained glass. On her brow, she wears a circlet of ivy and flowers, and her gown is of the same stuff. She is very beautiful, and Oak very much wishes she would go away.

"I will tell your family that you've arrived," Tiernan says, and melts into the crowd.

Lady Elaine cups Oak's cheek in one delicate, long-fingered hand. Through sheer force of will, he neither steps back nor flinches. It bothers him, though, how hard it is to steel himself to her touch. He's never been like that before. He's never found it hard to sink into this role of besotted fool.

Maybe it's harder now that he actually *is* a besotted fool.

"You've been hurt," she says. "A duel?"

He snorts at that but grins to cover it. "Several."

"Bruised plums are the sweetest," she says.

His smile comes more easily now. He is remembering himself. Oak of the Greenbriar line. A courtier, a little irresponsible, a lot impulsive. Bait for every conspirator. But it chafes worse than before to pretend to ineptitude. It bothers him that had he not pretended for so long, it was possible his sister would have entrusted him with the mission he had to steal.

It bothers him that he's pretended so long he's not sure he knows how to be anything else.

"You are a wit," he tells Lady Elaine.

And she, oblivious to any tension, smiles. "I have heard a rumor that you are being promised in marriage to some creature from the north. Your sister wishes to make an alliance with a hag's daughter. To placate the shy folk."

Oak is surprised by that story, which manages to be almost wholly accurate and yet totally wrong, but he reminds himself that this is Court, where all gossip is prized, and though faeries cannot lie, tales can still grow in the telling.

"That's not quite—" he begins.

She places a hand on her heart. Her wings seem to quiver. "What a relief. I would hate for you to have to give up the delights of Court, forever sentenced to a cold bed in a desolate land. You have already been away so long! Come to my rooms tonight, and I will remind you why you wouldn't want to leave us. I can be gentle with your cuts and scrapes."

It comes to Oak that he doesn't want gentle. He isn't sure how he feels about that, although he doesn't want Lady Elaine, either. "Not tonight."

"When the moon is at its zenith," she says. "In the gardens."

"I can't—" he begins.

"You wished to meet my friends. I can arrange something. And afterward, we can be alone."

"Your friends," Oak says slowly. Her fellow conspirators. He had hoped their plans had fallen apart, given how many rumors were flying around. "Some of them seem to be speaking very freely. I've had my loyalty questioned."

It is on that statement that Wren enters the brugh.

She wears a new gown, one that looks like nothing that could have come from Lady Nore's wardrobe. It is all of white, like a cocoon of spider silk, clinging to Wren's body in such a way that the tint of her blue skin shows through. The fabric wraps around her upper arms and widens at the wrists and the skirts, where it falls in tatters nearly to the floor.

Woven into the wild nimbus of her hair are skeins of the same pale spider silk. And on her head rests a crown, not the black obsidian one of the former Court of Teeth, but a crown of icicles, each an impossibly thin spiral.

Hyacinthe stands at her side, unsmiling, in a uniform all of black.

Oak has seen his sister reinvent herself in the eyes of the Court. If Cardan leads with his cruel, cold charm, Jude's power comes from the promise that if anyone crosses her, she simply cuts their throat. It is a brutal reputation, but would she, as a human, have been afforded respect for anything gentler?

And if he didn't wonder how much that myth cost Jude, how much she disappeared into it, well, he wonders now. He hasn't been the only one playing a role. Maybe none of his family has quite been seeing one another clearly.

Wren's gaze sweeps the room, and there's relief in her face when she finds him. He grins before he remembers her rejection. But not before she gives him a minute grin in return, her gaze going to the woman at his side.

"Is that her?" Lady Elaine asks, and Oak realizes how close to him she stands. How her fingers close possessively on his arm.

The prince forces himself not to take a step back, not to pull free of her grip. It won't help, and besides, what reason does he have to worry over sparing Wren's feelings? She doesn't want him. "I must excuse myself."

"Tonight, then," Lady Elaine says, even though he never agreed. "And perhaps every night thereafter."

As she departs, he is aware he has no one to blame but himself that she ignored his words. Oak is the one who makes himself appear empty-headed and easily manipulated. He is the one who falls into bed with anyone he thinks may help him discover who is betraying Elfhame. And, to be fair, with plenty of others to help forget how many of the Folk are dead because of him.

Even those he cared for, he hid from.

Maybe that's why Wren can't love him. Maybe that is why it seems so believable that he may have enchanted everyone in his life into caring for him. After all, how can anyone love him when no one really knows him?

CHAPTER

17

The crowd ought to be familiar, but the noise of the gathered Folk is loud and strange in his ears. He tries to shake it off and hurry. His mother will be annoyed he's late again, and not even Jude and Cardan are going to sit down to a feast in his honor without him, which means it can't officially begin until he gets to the table.

And yet, he keeps getting distracted by his surroundings. By hearing his father's name on certain lips. Hearing his own on others. Listening to knots of courtiers speculate about Wren, calling her the Winter Queen, the Hag Queen, the Night Queen.

The prince notes Randalin, the little horned man drinking from an enormous, carved wooden mug, chatting with Baphen, whose curling beard sparkles with a new selection of ornaments.

Oak passes tables with wines of different colors—gold and green and violet. Val Moren, the former Seneschal, and one of the few mortals in Elfhame, is standing beside one, laughing to himself and turning in circles as though playing the childish game of seeing how dizzy he can become.

"Prince," he calls out. "Will you fall with me?"

"Not tonight, I hope," Oak answers, but the question echoes eerily in his mind.

He passes a table with roasted pigeons, looking entirely too pigeon-y for Oak's comfort. Several leek and mushroom tarts rest beside them, as well as a pile of crab apples being set upon by sprites.

His friend Vier spots him and raises a flagon. "A toast to you," he cries, walking over to sling an arm over Oak's shoulders. "I understand you've won yourself a northern princess."

"*Won* is definitely overstating the case," Oak says, sliding out from his friend's arm. "But I ought to go to her."

"Yes, don't leave her waiting!"

The prince wades back into the crowd. He sees a flash of metal and spins, looking for a blade, but it is just a knight wearing a single sleeve of her armor over a frothy gown. Near her are several ladies of the Court with enormous, cloudlike clusters of baby's breath for wigs. He passes faeries in mossy capelets and dresses that end in branches. Elegant gentlemen in embroidered robes and doublets of birch bark. One green-skinned girl with gills has a train on her gown long enough to catch occasionally on roots as she passes. As he's looking, Oak realizes it isn't a train at all but the spill of her hair.

By the time he makes it to the High Table, he sees Wren standing before his sister and Cardan. He really should have gotten here sooner.

Wren catches his gaze as he approaches. Though her expression does not alter, he thinks he sees relief in her eyes.

Jude watches them both, calculating. Still, after two months away and a long rest to clear his head, what he notices most is how young Jude looks. She *is* young, but he can see a difference between her and Taryn. Perhaps it is only that Taryn has been to the mortal world more recently and has caught up to her years. Or that having a young child is tiring, and she doesn't look older so much as exhausted.

A moment later, he wonders if it was only the fancy of the moment that made him think that. But another part of him wonders if Jude is quite as mortal as she once was.

He bows to his sister and to Cardan.

"Wren was just telling us of her powers," says Jude, voice hard. "And we asked for the return of the bridle *you* borrowed."

He's missed something and not something good. Did she refuse them?

"I have sent one of my soldiers for it," Wren tells him, as though in answer to the question he did not ask.

Perhaps they are only annoyed at the reminder of how many traitors to Elfhame serve in the Court of Teeth. If so, they must be doubly annoyed when a falcon swoops into the room, becoming a man as he lands. Straun.

Oak's former prison guard gives him a smug look as he holds out the bridle to Wren.

The prince can still conjure the feeling of the straps against his skin. Can still remember the helplessness he felt when she commanded him to crawl. How Straun watched him, how he laughed.

Wren takes it from the soldier, letting it lie across her palm. "It's a cursed thing."

"Like all Grimsen's creations," Jude says.

"I don't want it," Wren says. "But I won't give it to you, either."

Cardan raises his brows. "A bold statement to make to your rulers in the heart of their Court. So what do you propose?"

In her hands, the leather shreds and shrivels. The magic departs from it like a thunderclap. The buckles fall to the dirt floor.

Jude takes a step toward her. Everyone in the brugh is looking at them now. The sound the destruction made drew their attention as surely as a shout.

"You unmade it," says Jude, staring at the remains.

"Since I have cheated you out of one gift, I will give you another. There's a geas on the High Queen, one that would be easy enough for me to remove." Wren's smile is sharp-toothed. Oak isn't sure what the nature of the geas is, but he is sure from the spark of panic in Jude's face that she doesn't want it gone.

The offer hangs in the air for a long moment.

"So many secrets, wife," Cardan says mildly.

The look Jude gives him in return could have peeled paint.

"Not only the geas, but half a curse," Wren tells his sister. "It winds around you but cannot quite tighten its grip. Gnaws at you."

The shock on Jude's face is obvious. "But he never finished speaking—"

Cardan holds up a hand to stop her. All teasing is gone from his voice. "What curse?"

Oak supposes the High King may well take a curse seriously, since he was once cursed into a giant, poisonous serpent.

"It happened a long time ago. When we went to the palace school," Oak's sister says.

"Who cursed you?" asks Cardan.

"Valerian," Jude spits out. "Right before he died."

"Right before you killed him, you mean," Cardan says, his dark eyes glittering with something that looks a lot like fury. Although whether it is toward Jude or this long-dead person, Oak isn't certain.

"No," Jude says, not seeming in the least afraid. "I'd already killed him. He just didn't know it yet."

"I can remove that and leave the geas alone," Wren says. "You see, I can be quite helpful."

"One supposes so," says the High King, his thoughts clearly on the curse and this Valerian. "A useful alliance."

Oak supposes that means Wren is still pretending she's willing to marry him.

Wren reaches her hand into the air, extending her fingers toward Jude and making a motion as though gripping something tightly. Then her hand fists.

His sister gasps. She touches her breastbone, and her head tips forward so that her face is hidden.

The High Queen's knight, Fand, unsheathes her blade, the glint of the steel reflecting candlelight. All around, guards' hands go to their hilts.

"Jude?" Oak whispers, taking a step toward her. "Wren, what did you—"

"If you've hurt her—" Cardan begins, his gaze on his wife.

"I removed the curse," Wren says, her voice even.

"I'm fine," Jude grates out, hand still pressing against her chest. She moves to a chair—not the one at the head of the table, not her own— and sits. "Wren has given me quite a gift. I will have to think long and hard about what to give her in return."

There's a threat in those words. And looking around, Oak realizes the reason for it.

It isn't just that Wren took apart the bridle without permission and the curse without warning, nor that she exposed something that Jude may have wanted to stay hidden, but she made the High King and Queen look weak before their Court. It's true they weren't up on the dais for all to see, but enough courtiers were listening and watching for rumors to spread.

The High King and Queen were helpless in the face of Wren's magic. That Wren did them a service and put them in her debt.

She did to Jude what Bogdana had done to her in the Citadel—and did it more successfully.

But to what purpose?

"You bring an element of chaos to a party, don't you?" Cardan says, his tone light, but his gaze fierce. He lifts a goblet from the table. "We obviously have many things to discuss regarding the future. But for now, we share a meal. Let us toast, to love."

The High King's voice has a ringing quality that enjoins people to pay attention. Nearby, many glasses are raised. Someone presses a silver-chased goblet into the prince's hand. Wren is given one by a servant, already filled to the brim with a dark wine.

"Love," Cardan goes on. "That force that compels us to be sometimes better and often worse. That power by which we can all be bound. That which we ought to fear and yet most desire. That which unites us this evening—and shall unite the both of you soon enough."

Oak glances at Wren. Her face is like stone. She is clutching her own goblet so tightly that her knuckles are white.

There is a half smile on Cardan's face, and when his gaze goes to Oak, he gives a small extra tip of his goblet. One that may be a challenge.

I do not want your throne, Oak wishes he could just say aloud and not care if anyone hears, not care if it makes the moment awkward. But the conspirators will reveal themselves just after midnight, and it's worth waiting a single day.

The Ghost, standing near Randalin, raises his own glass in Oak's direction. Not far from them, standing by Taryn and Leander, Oriana does not toast and, in fact, appears to be contemplating pouring her wine onto the dirt.

Well, this is going great.

He turns toward Wren and realizes how pale she's grown.

He thinks of her feverish gaze aboard the ship and how he had to carry her to her bed. If she passes out now, all her work—the way she forced herself upright to walk on the shore, this exchange with his sister—will be undone. The Court will see her as weak. He hates to admit it, but his family may see her that way, too.

But she can't be well. She was weak from breaking the troll kings' curse before they left. Then she took apart that monster, and now this. He thinks of Mother Marrow's words, about how Wren's own hag power—a power of creation—has been turned inside out.

"I would have a moment with my betrothed," Oak says, reaching a hand toward her. "A dance, perhaps."

Wren looks at him with wild eyes. He's put her in a difficult position. She can't very well turn him down, and yet she is probably wondering how much longer she can stay upright.

"We're soon to eat," his mother objects, having come closer without his noticing.

Oak makes a gesture of carelessness. "It's a banquet, and now that the toast is made, we're not needed here to sample every dish."

Before anyone else can weigh in, he puts his arm around Wren's waist and escorts her to the floor.

"Perhaps," Oak says, when they've gone a few steps, "we continue on to a corner and sit for a moment."

"I will dance," she says, as though meeting his challenge. Not what he intended, but it was so ill-done that it may as well have been.

Cursing himself, he takes one of her hands in his. Her fingers are cool, her grasp on him tightening. He can feel her force herself to relax.

He guides her through the steps he taught her, back in the Court of Moths. The dance isn't quite appropriate for the music, but it hardly matters. She barely remembers the steps, and he barely cares. Her skin has that same pale, waxy look it had aboard the ship. The same bruises around her mouth and eyes.

He presses her to him so no one can see.

"I will be well enough in a moment," she says as he turns with her in his arms. She missteps, and he catches her, holding her upright.

"Let's sit in some dark corner," he says. "Take a moment to rest."

"No," she tells him, although he's holding her whole weight now. "I see the way they look at me already."

"Who?" Oak asks.

"Your family," she says. "They hate me. They want me gone."

He wants to contradict her, but he forces himself to consider what she's saying. As he does, he moves through the dance, one hand at her waist, another against her back, holding her feet above the ground, pressing her body to his. So long as she doesn't pass out entirely, so long as her head doesn't loll, they will seem like they're moving together.

There's some truth to Wren's fears. His mother would spit at Wren's feet if she could find a way to do it that would reconcile with her rigid sense of etiquette. And while Jude seems conflicted, she would murder Wren herself if she thought Wren's death would shield people she cares about. Jude wouldn't need to dislike her to do it.

"My family believes they must protect me," he says, the words sour in his mouth.

"From me?" she asks, her face no longer looking so pale and bruised. She manages to even seem a little amused.

"From the cruel, terrible world," he says.

Her lip turns up at the corner. Her gaze rests on him. "They don't know what you're capable of, then?"

He takes a deep breath, trying to find his way to the answer. "They love me," he says, knowing that's not enough.

"How many people does your sister Jude believe you've killed?" Wren asks.

There was the bodyguard who turned on him. There was no hiding that. And that duel he was in with Violet's other lover. *Two.* Jude could have guessed some of the others, but he doesn't think she did.

Of course, he didn't want her to guess. So why did it bother him so much? And how many people *had* he killed? Two dozen? More?

"Your father?" Wren asks into his silence.

"He knows more," Oak says, a betrayal in and of itself.

That is the problem with being Madoc's son. The redcap understands people, and he understands his children best of all. When he isn't consumed by rage, he is horribly insightful.

He sees in Oak what no one else has. He sees the desperate and impossible desire to repay all that he owes his family. Has Madoc used that to manipulate Oak? Oh, most definitely. Many times over.

He smiles at Wren. "*You* know what I am capable of."

"A terrifying thought," she says, but doesn't sound displeased. "I should have understood better—what you did for your father and why. I wanted it to be simple. But my sis—Bex—" A choking fit stops her speech.

"Perhaps you might like a glass of something. Watered wine?"

She smiles tremulously in return. "A goblet of only water, if that will cause no one offense. What I drank during the toast seems to have gone to my head."

They both know that isn't the reason she feels faint, but he carries on the pretext. "Of course. Will you—"

"I can stand now," she says.

He maneuvers them close to a chair, then sets her on her feet. If nothing else, she can hold on to the chair back. He remembers how weak he felt after leaving her dungeons. Something to lean against helped.

Then, leaving her reluctantly, he heads toward the nearest table where drinks have been set. Food is still being brought out from the kitchens, though at the High Table, most everyone is seated. As he pours water into a glass, he notes that a few courtiers have crowded around Wren and seem intent on charming her. He watches her give a smile that is perfectly polite, watches her eyes narrow, watches her listen.

He cannot help but think of Madoc's words. *They will sidle up to your little queen tonight. They will introduce themselves and curry her favor. They will attempt to ingratiate themselves with her people and compliment her person. And they will gauge just how much she hates the High King and Queen.*

"Prince," the Ghost says, hand on Oak's shoulder, making him startle. "I need to speak with you a moment."

Oak raises his eyebrows. "I haven't asked Taryn about Liriope yet, if it's about that."

Garrett does not meet his gaze. "Other things have taken up my attention as well. I overheard something, and I have been following the path of it, but I want to warn you not to go wandering out alone. Keep Tiernan by your side. No assignations. No heroics. No—"

The Ghost bites off the words as Jack of the Lakes approaches, the kelpie looking relieved and as unamused as he did when he swore his allegiance to Oak.

"Forgive the interruption," says the kelpie. "Or don't. I don't care. I have need of the prince."

"You presume much," the Ghost says.

"I often do," says Jack silkily.

Probably the kelpie doesn't know he's baiting a master assassin. Probably.

"I have heard your warning," Oak tells the Ghost.

The Ghost sighs. "I will have more information for you tomorrow, although perhaps not what you will want to hear." With that, he walks off into the crowd.

The prince looks over at Wren. She's speaking to another courtier, her hand heavy on the back of the chair.

Oak drags his attention to the kelpie. "I think I can guess the purpose of this conversation. Yes, I will help. Now, I must get back to my betrothed."

Jack snorts. "I haven't come to complain. Your sister terrorized me only a little."

"Then what is it you want?"

"I saw a most interesting meeting last night," Jack says. "Bogdana and a man with golden skin. He was carrying a large trunk. He opened it to show her the contents, then shut it again and took it away."

Oak remembers the hag with the golden skin from the Citadel. He was the one who didn't give Wren a present. "And you have no idea what was inside?"

"No, indeed, prince. Nor did he seem the sort who would take kindly to being followed by one such as myself."

"I appreciate your telling me," says Oak. "And it's good to see you."

Jack grins. "I share that sentiment, yet I would be away from this place if you put in a good word with your sister for my release."

At that, Oak laughs. "So you wish to complain after all?"

"I would not wish to turn your good nature ill," says Jack, looking around him uncomfortably. "Nor would I wish that ill nature directed at me. But I am not well suited to your home."

"I'll talk to my sister," Oak promises.

On his way back to Wren, he spots Taryn speaking with Garrett. Oak's gaze picks out Madoc in the crowd, leaning heavily on his cane. Leander is telling a story, and the redcap is listening with what seems rapt attention to his grandchild.

It occurs to him how strange a family they all are. Madoc, who murdered Jude and Taryn's parents—and yet somehow, they consider him their father. Madoc, who almost killed Jude in a duel. Who might have used Oak to get to the throne and then ruled through him.

And Oriana, who was cold to his sisters, even to Vivi. Who didn't trust Jude enough to leave Oak alone with her when they were young, but asked her to lay down her life to protect him just the same.

And Vivi, Taryn, and Jude, each different, but all of them clever and determined and brave. Then there is Oak, still trying to figure out where he fits in.

As the prince approaches Wren, he clears his throat.

"Your water," he says when he's close, his voice loud enough that the courtiers surrounding her make their excuses. He offers her the goblet of water, which she drinks thirstily.

"I was waylaid," he says by way of apology.

"As was I," she tells him. "We should go back to your family's table."

He hates that she's right but offers her his arm.

She takes it, leaning on him with some force. "When you said you loved me..." It begins as a question, but one she cannot seem to complete.

"Alas that I cannot lie," he tells her as he guides her through the hall, the smile easy on his lips now. "I hope you will try to find the humor in my feelings. I shall endeavor to do so myself."

"But... don't you want revenge?" she asks, her voice even softer than before.

He glances at her swiftly and takes a moment to decide how to answer. "A little," he admits finally. "I wouldn't mind if there was some dramatic reversal where you pined while I remained aloof."

Wren laughs at that, a startled sort of sound. "You are the least aloof person I know."

He makes a face. "Alas once again, my dreams crushed."

She stops smiling. "Oak, please. I've made a mistake. I've made several and I need..."

He stops. "What do you need?"

For a moment, it seems as though she will answer. Then she shakes her head.

Just then, the musicians cease playing their instruments. The rest of the courtiers begin to move toward the banquet tables.

Oak guides Wren back to her chair. Predictably enough, the leaf place card with her name on it is set across the table from him, in the place of honor, beside Cardan. His own seat is two down from Jude, next to Leander. A snub.

He's almost sure that's not where his chair was before he took off.

A servant comes with pies in the shape of trout.

"You'll like this," Taryn says to him and Leander both. "There's a coin inside one of the dishes, and if you find it, you'll receive a boon."

The High King is speaking to Wren, perhaps telling her about the coin as well. Oak can see the effort she's making not to shrink in on herself.

Slabs of mushroom, grilled and shiny with a sweet sauce, are brought out. Then stewed pears alongside platters of cheese. Seed cakes. Sweet, fresh cream. Broad beans, still in their pods. More fanciful pies arrive. They're shaped like stags and falcons, swords and wreaths—each with a different filling. Partridge stewed in spices. Blackberries and hazelnuts, pickled sloes, mallow fruit.

When he looks over at Wren again, he can see that she is covering her mouth as she eats, as though to hide the sharpness of her teeth.

There is a sound at the entrance, a clatter of armor as guards leap to attention. The storm hag has arrived, hours late, wearing a tattered black dress that hangs off her like a shroud and a smile full of menace.

Bogdana thrusts her hand into the pie in the shape of a stag. Her hand is stained red with the juice of sloes as she pulls it out, her fingers gripping a coin. "I shall have my boon, king. I want Wren and your heir married tomorrow."

"You requested three days," Cardan reminds her. "To which we gave no answer."

"And three days it will be," says Bogdana. "Yesterday was the first, and tomorrow will be the third."

Oak sits up straighter. He glances across the table, waiting for Wren to stop this. Waiting for her to say she doesn't want to marry him.

Her gaze meets his, and there is something like pleading in it. As though she wants to both break his heart publicly and have some guarantee he won't hold it against her.

"Go ahead," he mouths.

But she remains silent.

A glance passes between Jude and Cardan. Then Jude stands and raises her glass, turning to Oak. "Tonight, we feast in the hall in celebration of your betrothal. Tomorrow, we will have a hunt in the afternoon, then dance on Insear. At the end of the night, I will ask your bride a question about you. Should she get it wrong, you will delay your marriage for seven days. Should she answer rightly, we will marry you both on the spot, if such is still your desire."

Bogdana scowls and opens her mouth to speak.

"I agree to those conditions," Wren says softly before the storm hag can answer for her.

"So do I," Oak says, although no one asked him. Still, this is all a performance. "Provided that I am the one who comes up with the question for my betrothed."

Wren looks panicked. His mother looks as though she'd like to stab him with her fork. Jude's expression is impossible to read, so rigidly does she keep her features set.

Oak smiles and keeps smiling.

He doesn't think she'll contradict him in public. Not when Bogdana drew so much attention to them.

"So be it, brother," his sister says, sitting back in her chair. "The choice will be yours."

S hortly after that, Wren rises and makes her excuses.

On her way out, she stops by Oak whispers in his ear. "Meet me in the gardens at midnight."

He nods with a slight shiver. She's already moving away from the table, fingers resting briefly on his shoulder as she goes. The storm hag spots her leaving, rises, and follows, menace in her movement.

That's two assignations for Oak. The moon's zenith tonight is about an hour past midnight, so they're a little too close together for him to feel easy about moving between them. And yet, he's helpless to do anything but agree to see Wren. When they were alone on the floor of the brugh, he felt as though they were friends again. And something was obviously wrong. Wren said she made mistakes—could that have to do with allowing Bogdana to accompany her? The storm hag wants them to marry—and soon—but he isn't sure why Wren doesn't tell her that isn't going to happen. Is it because Wren's power is at such a low ebb that she's afraid she will lose if she has to fight?

He can postpone the betrothal easily enough. Pose her a question to which she doesn't know the answer—or pose it in such a way that it's possible for her to pretend to guess wrong.

Who is my favorite sister?

What's my favorite color?

Can you ever forgive me?

Okay, maybe not that last one.

Out of the corner of his eye, he notices that Tiernan has walked up to Hyacinthe. Both of them stood near the High Table throughout dinner; Hyacinthe didn't follow Wren out. Instead, he had remained behind, looking uncertain.

"I want you," the prince hears Tiernan say. Oak feels some chagrin at overhearing that, but he is also surprised at the starkness of the admission. It sounds almost like an accusation.

"And what are you going to do about it?" Hyacinthe asks.

Tiernan snorts. "Pine, I suppose."

"Aren't you tired of that?" Hyacinthe could have said the words like a tease, but instead he sounds exhausted. A man offering a truce after a long battle.

"What else is there?" Tiernan's voice is harsh.

"What if I said you could have me? Have me and keep me."

"I could never compete with your rage toward Elfhame," Tiernan says.

"Eavesdropping, prince?" asks the Ghost, taking the seat on the other side of Leander.

Oak turns toward him guiltily. He would really like to have heard what Hyacinthe said next.

"I am behaving just as you wished," Oak says. "No going off on my own. No heroics. Even a little spy work."

Garrett rolls his eyes. "It's been a mere handful of hours—barely that. Manage to last the night, and I will actually be impressed."

Since Oak didn't plan on lasting the night without sneaking out, he says nothing.

"Show me the trick," Leander says to the Ghost, interrupting them.

"Which trick?" Garrett's smile is indulgent. It's surprising to see the shift in his behavior. But then he's known Leander since the child was born. Garrett and Taryn became close before the Battle of the Serpent, possibly even before Locke's death. Vivi and Heather—and Oak himself—have long believed they're lovers, but after Taryn's disastrous first marriage, Taryn hadn't admitted it out loud.

"The one with the coins."

Oak grins. He knows a few of those. The Roach taught them to him when he was only a little older than Leander.

Garrett reaches into his pocket and comes out with a silver coin. Before he can demonstrate, though, Madoc walks up, leaning heavily on his twisted black cane.

"My lads," the redcap says, putting a hand on Leander's head. The boy turns to smile up at him.

The Ghost sets the coin before Leander. "Why don't you practice and show me what you learned," he instructs, then rises.

"But...," the boy protests, a whine coming into his voice.

"I will show you the trick again tomorrow." With a sharp look at Madoc, he leaves the table.

Oak frowns. He had no idea how uncomfortable the Ghost was around Madoc, but of course the redcap was in exile for years. Oak never saw them together before. Leander picks up the coin but does nothing more with it.

"So you're really going through with this marriage?" Madoc asks the prince.

"We'll all find out the answer to that tomorrow." And Oak will look more like the fickle and flighty courtier than ever when he asks Wren a question she can't answer and postpones their engagement.

The redcap raises his eyebrows. "And have you asked yourself why the storm hag is in favor of your union?"

Truly, his father takes him for a fool. "If you know, perhaps you ought to tell me."

Madoc looks in the direction where the Ghost went. "Hopefully, your sister's spies will turn up something. There are worse things, though, than to learn how to rule in the harsh north."

Oak doesn't argue with him. He's tired of arguing with his father.

When Madoc wanders off, though, he shows Leander all the coin tricks he knows. He runs the silver disc over his knuckles, makes it disappear behind the child's ear, makes it reappear in his glass of nectar.

"Did it seem to you that Garrett doesn't like your grandfather?" Oak says, handing back the coin.

Leander tries to roll the disc over his knuckles, but it slides off and onto the floor. He jumps down to scrounge for it. "He knows his name," the boy says.

For a moment, Oak isn't sure he heard right. "His name?"

"Garrett's secret name," Leander says.

"How do you know that?" Oak must have spoken too harshly, because Leander looks startled. The prince gentles his voice. "No, no one's in trouble. I was just surprised."

"I heard Mom and him talking," Leander says.

"Is the Ghost his secret name?" Oak asks, just to be sure.

Leander shakes his head. "That's just his code name."

Oak nods and shows Leander the trick again, his mind running in circles. There was absolutely no reason for Garrett to give his true name to Madoc.

But then the Ghost's words from the ship come back to the prince: *Locke had the answer you seek. He knew the name of the poisoner, much good it did him.*

Had Locke told Taryn during their disastrous marriage? Had she told Madoc? But no—surely the Ghost wouldn't have forgiven that. Maybe Locke gave Madoc the name directly—but why?

Oak looks across the table at Taryn, deep in conversation with Jude. How it happened didn't matter. What mattered was what it meant.

They knew Garrett was the one who murdered his mother. Who fed her blusher mushroom. He feels hot and cold all over, rage making him tremble.

Did they think he didn't deserve this answer? That he was too much a child?

Or did they not tell him because they didn't think there was anything wrong with what Garrett had done?

At midnight, the gardens are full of night-blooming plants, limned in moonlight. Wren's blue skin is the same color as the petals of a flower, and as she enters the clearing, she seems as remote as a star in the sky.

He is still reeling from what he has learned. From the idea that someone he knows—someone he likes—tried to kill him. From the betrayal of his family.

"You wanted to see me?" he asks Wren, and wonders if, in the state he's in, he should have come at all.

"I did," she says with a sly smile. "I do."

He remembers what it was like to be a child with her. He is half-tempted to propose a game. He wonders if he can get her to run wild through the grass with him.

"It was wrong to lock you away in my prisons," she says.

That's so unexpected that he laughs.

She makes a face. "Very well, I concede that's obvious."

"I am not sitting in judgment of you," he says. Not with all the blood on his hands. "Does this mean you forgive me?"

She raises an eyebrow but doesn't deny it.

"Shall I say instead that there's peace between us at last?"

At that, he does get a smile. "Peace?"

"Not even that?" Oak puts a hand to his chest, as if wounded. Under his fingers, he can feel the thrum of his heart.

"I am not a peaceful person," she says. "And neither are you."

He loves that she knows he's not peaceful. Loves that she doesn't think him kind. He doesn't know how, but from the first she seemed to recognize something in him that no one else does—that inner kernel of hardness, of coldness.

He never convinced her that he was a hero. He perhaps half-convinced her he was a fool, but never for long. She saw through his playacting and his smiles. Heard the riddles and schemes his charmed tongue tried to obscure.

And so, when she kissed him, it felt as though *he* was being kissed. Perhaps for the first time.

And he loves the way she's watching him now, as though he fascinates her. As though she's drawn to him. As though he's got a chance.

Even if she doesn't want to marry him. Even if she doesn't love him. Wren draws in a deep breath. "It's beautiful here."

Oak looks around the gardens, full of flowers. Golden evening primrose, carpets of night phlox with tiny white buds, pale moonflowers, the purple night-scented stock, and the large silvery flowers of the cereus. He cups one. "Did you know this is called Queen of the Night?"

Wren shakes her head, smiling. "I dreamed about this place sometimes."

He thinks about her comment that she would make new nightmares and is silent. When she looks at him, there is something vulnerable in her face, though her voice is sharp with sudden anger.

"You could have kept me here, in Elfhame, but you let your sister send me away." Wren turns her gaze to the flower, speaking to it instead of him. "You gave me the first safe place—the *only* safe place I had after I was stolen from my unfamily—and then you took it from me."

He wants to object and insist that he *helped* her. He interceded with his sister. He hid her from the Court of Teeth. But though he did those things, he didn't keep doing them. He helped a little, and then having done so, assumed he did enough.

"It never occurred to me that you didn't have a home to go back to." He didn't understand. He didn't ask.

"You were bored with me," she accuses, but there isn't much heat in her voice. He can tell that she believes it and that she has believed it for a long time. Maybe she doesn't even condemn him for it.

"I would have hidden you in my rooms forever if I thought that's what you wanted," he vows. "I thought about you a lot ever since. Which you must know, since I showed up in your forest a few years later."

She clearly wants to object.

"Whereupon you sent *me* away," he concludes, and watches her expression change to one of exasperation.

"You think I did that because I didn't like you?"

He gives her a steady look.

"I did it to help you! If you stayed in the forest with me, the best thing that could ever have happened was that your family came and dragged you back to Elfhame. I'd lose you again, and you'd gain nothing."

"So you thought—" he starts, but she cuts him off.

"And the worst thing, the more likely thing, was that one of the enemies you were telling me about would find you. And then you'd be dead."

Her logic is alarmingly sound, although he doesn't like to admit it. He must have seemed very dramatic, showing up in her woods like that. Very dramatic and very, very, *very* foolish. The typical spoiled, naive royal. "And you couldn't tell me that?"

"*What if you didn't listen?*" she shouts. There's a desperation in her voice that's out of step with the conversation they're having.

"I'm listening," he says, puzzled.

"It's not safe," she says. "Not then and not now."

"I know that," he tells her.

"*I'm* not safe," she says. "You can't trust me. I—"

"I don't need safe," he says, and leans down, putting his hands in her hair. She doesn't move, looking up at him with lips that are slightly parted, as though she can't quite believe what he's doing.

Then he kisses her. Kisses her like he's wanted to for days and weeks and what feels like forever.

It isn't a careful kiss. He can feel her teeth against his tongue, her dry lips. He can feel the sharp edges of her nails as they dig into his neck. He shivers with sensation. He doesn't want careful any more than he wants safe.

He wants *her*.

Wren pulls him down, lower, until they are kneeling in the gardens. Oak feels dizzy with desire. All around them, the petals of night-blooming flowers have opened, and their thick perfume scents the air.

"Do you want—?" he starts, but she is already pushing up her dress.

"I want," she says. "That's my problem. I want and I want and I want."

"What do you want?" he asks, voice soft.

"*Everything.* Charm me. Rip me open. Ruin me. Go too far."

He shudders at her words, shaking his head against them.

She goes on, whispering against his skin. "You cannot understand. I am a chasm that will never be full. I am hunger. I am need. I cannot be sated. If you try, I will swallow you up. I will take all of you and want more. I will use you. I will drain you until you are nothing more than a husk."

"Use me, then," he whispers, mouth on her throat.

Then her lips are against his, and there is no more talking for a long time.

Wren is lying against him, her head pillowed against his shoulder, when the shifting branches alert him.

"Someone's coming," Oak says, grabbing for his trousers and also his knife.

Wren springs to her feet, pulling on her gown, trying to make herself look less like she's been rolling around in the dirt.

For a moment, their gazes meet, and they both grin helplessly. There's something so silly about this moment, scrambling to get dressed before they're caught. Neither of them can pretend to anything but merriment.

"Your Highness," says Lady Elaine, taking in the situation with a frown as she steps into the clearing. "I see you had a surfeit of trysts planned for this evening."

Her words wipe the smile from Oak's face. He was supposed to meet her, and he didn't pay attention to the zenith of the moon. Didn't pay attention to anything but Wren. Didn't care about conspirators or schemes or even his family's lies.

After years of bending his whole self to be a lure for the worst of Elfhame, he simply *forgot* to be that person.

"Moonrise, sunrise, dawn, dusk, zeniths," he says as flippantly as he can manage. If anything can make this moment worse, it would be his acting as though he feels *caught*. "Regrettably, I can be imprecise about imprecise times. My apologies. I hope you didn't wait long."

Wren looks between Lady Elaine and Oak, no doubt coming to her own conclusions.

"You're the girl from the Court of Teeth," Lady Elaine says, the gossamer of her wings apparent in the moonlight.

"I am the queen of what was once the Court of Teeth." Wren's expression is stony, and despite her dress gaping open in the back and the leaves tangled in her hair, she looks quite fearsome. "Betrothed to the Prince of Elfhame. And you are?"

Lady Elaine looks as astonished as if she bit into a pear and found it full of ants. She walks to Oak and puts her arm around his. "I am Elaine. *Lady* Elaine, a courtier from the Court of Moss in the west and an old friend of the prince's. Isn't that right?"

"Despite my being a trial to her," agrees Oak, avoiding giving any real confirmation.

Wren offers up a chilly smile. "I will go back to the feast, I think. Might you do up the back of my dress?"

Lady Elaine gives her a scathing look.

"Of course." Oak has to hide his smile at that as he walks behind Wren and does up the laces of her gown.

As she makes ready to go, she looks back at Lady Elaine. "I hope he will give you half the delight he's given me."

Oak has to swallow a laugh.

As Wren leaves, Lady Elaine turns to Oak, hands on her hips. "Prince," she says, sterner than any instructor in the palace school.

He is so tired of being treated as though he is a fool, as though he is in need of—what did Randalin say about Wren—a *little guidance*. Maybe he is a fool, but he is a fool of a different sort.

"There was little I could do," he protests with a shrug, choosing his words carefully. "She is my betrothed, after all. It's not the easiest thing to get rid of someone."

Lady Elaine's mouth relaxes a little, although she's not going to let him out of this that easily. "You expect me to believe you wanted to be rid of her?"

Well, it would be *convenient* if she thought that. "I mean her no insult," Oak says, deliberately misunderstanding. "But you were going to introduce me to your friends—and, well, I haven't seen you in a long while."

"Perhaps it's time you explained this betrothal," she says.

"Not here." It's too strange to stand in the place he was with Wren and attempt to deceive Lady Elaine about her. "Where was it you were going to take me?"

"We were to meet at the edge of the Crooked Forest," she tells him, walking with him as he makes his way down one of the paths. "But they will be long gone. This is dangerous, Oak. They are putting themselves at great risk for your benefit."

He notes that she didn't say *for your sake*, although he's sure that's how she wants him to take her words. "Wren is powerful," Oak says, hating himself. "And would be useful."

"That point has been made to me before," Lady Elaine says bitterly, and to his surprise. "That you were clever to make this alliance, and having the storm hag with her puts us all in a better position."

For a moment, he is tempted to explain that Bogdana is never going to be on the side of anyone with his bloodline, but what would be the point? Let her believe anything that will have her accepting Wren and taking him to the rest of the conspirators.

"She will make you unhappy," Lady Elaine tells him.

"Not all alliances are happy ones," he says, and takes one of her hands in his.

"But you," she says, putting her hand to his cheek. "You, who have little experience of sacrifice. Who have always seemed filled with such joy. How will you bear it when that joy is dimmed?"

He laughs outright at her words and then has to think fast to cover up the reason. "See? I can yet be merry. And I shall be merry still, even if wed."

"Perhaps this plan asks too much of all of us," Lady Elaine says, and he understands. *Her plan*, to be by his side, at the very least a sort of ruling consort, would be in shambles were he to marry Wren. If she cannot have that role, then she doesn't want to risk her neck.

He turns toward her, and a kind of desperation rises in him. If she gives this up, then the conspirators scurry away—rats back into their holes—and he learns nothing.

Oak can fix this. He can use his honey-tongued words on her. He can feel them, sitting on his lips, ready to fall. If he says the right things, if he draws her into his arms, then she will believe in their plan once more. He will be able to convince her that Wren means nothing, that it will be her counsel he heeds once he is on the throne. He can even persuade her to take him to the conspirators, if perhaps not tonight.

But if he does nothing, then she gives up treason. Maybe the plan falls apart, becomes idle discontented conversation and nothing more. Then she will not be shut up in a tower, or cursed into a dove, or executed in a bloody spectacle.

He gives her hand a squeeze. Gives her one last sad smile. Maybe this can be over and everyone can live. "Perhaps you're right," he says. "Sadness just doesn't suit me."

O ak wakes with dread in his heart. As he lingers over a coffee-like substance that is made from roasted dandelions and picks at a plate of acorn cakes, his mind spins. His thoughts fly between Wren in his arms, her eyes bright and teeth sharp, kissing him as though they could crawl into each other's skin—then Lady Elaine and the capsizing of his plans—then circling back to what he learned about the Ghost.

Who gave Oak's mother poison.

Who gave Oak's mother poison so that Oak would die.

How could the Ghost *look* at Oak when, if not for Oriana, if not for *sheer luck*, he could have been the prince's murderer?

It galls Oak to think of Taryn and Jude watching him be trained, letting the Ghost clap him on the shoulder or reposition his arm to swing a sword.

Somehow, it's Taryn's betrayal that strikes Oak the most sharply. Jude has always been constrained by position and politics while Madoc has been constrained by his nature. Oak thought of Taryn as the kind-hearted one, the one who wanted a gentler world.

Maybe she just wanted an easier one.

Oak kicks one hoof against the low table, sending the coffeepot and the tray it was sitting on crashing to the floor, crockery smashing, cakes going everywhere. He kicks it again, splintering a wooden leg and causing the whole thing to collapse.

If his mother came in, she would frown, call him childish or petulant. Summon servants to clean up. Ignore any reason he may have for his anger.

That's what his family does. Ignores everything uncomfortable. Talks around betrayals and murders. Papers over bloodstains and duels. Brushes all the bones under the rug.

Since he was old enough to really understand why he had to be the one to put the Blood Crown on Cardan's head or live with Vivi and Heather in the mortal world, away from his parents, Oak wasn't able to think of his sisters without being aware of the debt he owed them. The sacrifices they made for him. Everything he could never repay. So it is entirely new for him to think of them and be absolutely *furious*.

Then his thoughts slide back to Wren. To her expression of horror when he told her he loved her. To her warning of the night before, after he kissed her, while she dug her nails into his nape.

He was playing fast and loose back in the Ice Needle Citadel, determined to win her over despite the danger. And then he came up with a desperate plan to avoid a conflict when it was clear that Elfhame considered Wren a dangerous enemy.

When she agreed to come home with him, he thought it might *help* to be away from the Citadel. Wren was focused on survival for so long—and whatever else you may say about the isles, they are full of wine and song and other lazy indulgences.

But ever since they arrived, she's been different. Of course, he could just as easily say that she's been different ever since he confessed his love.

You've always been clever, she told him when she asked him to break things off. *Be clever now.*

Does she think that if she is the one to dump him, Elfhame will take her crown for breaking his heart?

And yet, he can't shed the feeling there is a greater wrongness she was trying to communicate. Could someone be leveraging something against her in order to stop their marriage? Was it one of her retinue? One of his family? He didn't think it could be Bogdana, who was so vocal in support of their union.

Or perhaps it *was* the storm hag—maybe Bogdana threatened Wren if she strayed from that path? And yet, if that was the case, why not tell Oak outright?

A knock comes on the door. A moment later, it opens and Tatterfell enters. She frowns at him, her inkdrop eyes taking in the wreckage of the table.

"Leave it," he tells her. "And leave off lecturing me about it, too."

She presses her thin lips together. She's been a servant in Madoc's household, paying off some debt, and then moved to the castle with Jude, possibly as a spy for their father. He's never much liked her. She's impatient and prone to pinching.

"The hunt is today," she says. "And then that farce on Insear right after. There are tents for you to change in, but we still need to select what garb to send over."

"I don't need your help with that," he tells her. Her words *that farce on Insear* echo in his head.

The little faerie looks up at him with her shining black eyes. "You ought to clothe yourself as though you expect to exchange vows, even if there's little chance of that."

He frowns at Tatterfell. "Why do you think so?"

She snorts, going to his wardrobe and taking down a tunic of deep burgundy cloth embroidered with golden leaves and pants of a deep brown. "Oh, it's not my place to speculate on the plans of my betters."

"And yet," Oak says.

"And yet, were I Jude," Tatterfell says, pulling out riding clothes of mouse gray, "I might want to marry you to the new queen of the Undersea. It would be a better alliance, and if you *don't* marry her, the alliance goes to someone else."

The prince thinks of the contest he was told of for Nicasia's hand. The one that Cirien-Cròin was attempting to prevent with the attack. "Cardan courted her, didn't he?"

Tatterfell is quiet for a moment. "Another good reason for your sister to marry you to her. Besides, I hear she threw over the High King for Locke. You look something like him."

Oak scowls as she urges him out of his nightshirt. "Jude doesn't usually expect much from me."

"Oh, I don't know," Tatterfell says. "I hear you're widely considered to be a rake."

Oak wants to object, but he has to consider that maybe Jude *does* think a marriage of Oak to Nicasia would be possible and useful. Maybe it *did* seem like a good solution to Cardan, who's heard rumors of Oak's treachery.

And if Jude wanted him to compete to be King of the Undersea, would that lead Jude to move against Wren? Would Jude push her to break off the betrothal while pretending to allow it? Push Wren to hide her interference from Oak—and have enough power to back up any threat.

Well, given the secrets she's already kept, if that is what she's doing, he'd never know about it?

Dressed in mouse gray, with Tatterfell taking his evening clothes on to Insear, Oak heads to the stables. From there, he will ride out to the Milkwood, where he intends to determine the actual reason Wren wants Oak in particular to break off their betrothal.

As he heads toward Damsel Fly, he finds Jack of the Lakes waiting for him. The kelpie is in his person form, dressed all in brown and black, bits of seaweed hanging out of his breast pockets. A rough-beaten gold hoop hangs from one ear.

"Hullo," Jack says, brushing the hair back from his eyes.

"My apologies," Oak says, resting one hand on the needle of a sword he insisted on strapping to his belt. "I haven't yet managed to speak with my sister on your behalf."

He shrugs. "My obligation to you is greater than yours to me, prince. I've come to dismiss some of it, if I can."

"Observe another clandestine meeting?" Oak asks.

"I am a steed. Get on my back, and we'll ride to the hunt together."

Oak frowns, considering. Jack is capricious and a gossip. But the vow he once gave Oak was sincere, and at the moment, Oak is feeling short on allies. Someone he can even *mostly* trust seems a boon. "Concerned about something?"

"I mislike this place," Jack says.

"Viper nest," Oak agrees.

"It seems quite the trick to tell the friendly snakes from the other ones."

"Ah," Oak says. "They're all friendly snakes until they bite you."

"Perhaps you'll have no need of me today," the kelpie tells him. "But if you do, I will be there."

Oak nods. Jack's concern makes his own worries all the more real. He reaches for a saddle. "You really don't mind?"

"So long as there's no bit between my teeth," Jack says, transforming shape on the last word. Where once there was a boy, there is a sharp-toothed black horse. The sheen on his coat is murky green, and his mane ripples like water.

Oak swings up on his back and rides out. Tiernan is waiting for him outside the palace stables on a white steed of his own. He takes one look at Jack and raises both his brows. "Have you run mad, trusting him again?"

Oak thinks of what he promised Hyacinthe in the Citadel—the hand of the person responsible for Liriope's death. And the prince considers Tiernan, whose happiness he will rob if he gives that to Hyacinthe—even supposing he could. He considers how awful it would be and all the consequences that would follow.

"Oh, don't worry," Oak says. "I'm not sure I trust anyone anymore. Not even myself."

They arrive at the Milkwood, riding beneath pale, silvery boughs covered with bleached leaves. There, the gentry of the Court are assembling in their riding garb. Cardan sits atop a black steed with flowers braided into its mane. He himself is wearing a doublet with a high collar and a crisscrossing pattern sewn into the dark fabric. Aside from shining buttons in the shape of beetles, he looks positively staid.

Taryn is all in lilac—a jacket with long tulip sleeves, breeches, and boots—and astride a dappled pony. The Ghost is beside her in dark gray, and somehow seems more knight, clad in her livery, than partner.

Oak feels a spike of rage at the sight of him. Rage that he swallows. For now.

Beside the High King, Jude is mounted on a riding toad, wearing a dress the color of unskimmed cream with billowing sleeves. Over that, a thin vest, embroidered with gold, laces over her chest. Calf-high brown boots dig into the stirrups. No crown sits on her head, and her hair is pulled simply back.

He tries to judge from her expression, from her body language, if she is working against him. If she has gone around his back and threatened Wren. But Jude is a consummate liar. There's no way he can tell, and asking would be worse than useless. All that would happen is that she'd know Wren gave something away.

On that thought, he notes Cardan watching him. He cannot, in this moment, bring himself to explain his true role in this or the other conspiracies. He cannot bring himself to be vulnerable in front of either of them. And if he begins to tell the story, Lady Elaine will face the very fate she would have if she hadn't renounced her treachery the night before. She will certainly be interrogated.

He thinks of the cold stone slab and Valen standing over him and shudders.

He wishes he could trust his sister as he once did. He wishes that he could be sure she trusted him.

The prince turns away, his gaze going to the servants loading baskets and blankets onto ponies for the picnic the courtiers will have once the hunt grows dull.

"We cannot possibly catch the silver stag," says a man in a hat with a plume sticking out of it and a longbow. He rides a chestnut steed with dainty hooves. "Nor anything much with two mortals among us. They will frighten off the beasts with their noise."

He means for Jude to hear, and she has. She gives him a lethal smile. "Well," she says, "there are always birds in the trees to hunt. Even a few falcons."

The reference to Wren's soldiers is not missed. Some of the gathered Folk appear uncomfortable. Others seem eager.

"Or we could draw lots to play the fox," she continues with a grin. "That's a fine sport, and one I've played before."

She's *been* the fox, but they don't know that. The man with the plumed hat looks nervous. "A ride through the Milkwood is its own delight."

"I could not agree more," she tells him.

Randalin blows a horn, calling for them to all assemble.

Oak spots Lady Elaine, whispering something to Lady Asha, Cardan's mother. When she notices him, she turns away without meeting his gaze.

The attention of the crowd shifts, and voices still. He turns to see Wren and Bogdana ride in, not on steeds, but on creatures enchanted from sticks and twigs and brambles. They move like horses but remind Oak of ragwort ponies in their uncanniness.

Unconsciously, he leans back, urging Jack away. Their presence bothers Oak, not just because he fought creatures like them, not just because they were Lady Nore's beasts and conjured from Mab's bones, but because he was aboard the *Moonskimmer* and did not see them there.

Another secret.

Wren is in a dress of pale gold. A chain veil is on her head, set with shimmering aquamarines. It contains her hair and falls down over her cheeks and chin, almost to her waist. She holds the reins of a bridle made from a thin chain that wraps around the horse's mouth. Though she looks majestic and even bridal, she frowns at her hands, shoulders hunched. She looks haunted.

By contrast, Bogdana is in another dark shroud, tattered in places and flying behind her in the breeze. Her expression is the picture of satisfaction.

Their arrival is greeted with murmurs of admiration. Courtiers ooh and aah over the bramble beasts, running hands over twiggy flanks.

He may not get answers out of his sister, but that doesn't mean he can't get answers. Pressing his knee gently against the kelpie's flank, he guides him toward Wren.

"Is that...?" Wren frowns.

"Jack of the Lakes," Oak says, patting the kelpie's neck. "A merry wight."

Wren's lip lifts in something that could have become a smile but doesn't stay long enough.

"Tonight I must ask you a question," Oak says. "What if it's impossible to respond to what I ask incorrectly?"

"You would bind me to marriage unwilling?" Nothing in her tone acknowledges the night before, their tangled limbs and ragged breaths. Her eloquent, whispered wants.

He feels guilty that he's not telling her the truth—he won't make her do anything she doesn't wish. But he needs to know if something is actually wrong.

"Am I supposed to declare that I was swept away first by one whim and then another?" he asks, blithe as ever. If her shield is coldness, his is mirth.

"Would they not believe it? Besides, you could tell the Court we had an argument." Wren glances over her shoulder, as though afraid someone can hear her. "I would be more than willing to have one right now. A *spectacular* fight."

He raises his brows. "And what might this argument be about?"

"Lady Elaine, perhaps," Wren offers. "Your fickle nature. I could tell you about it, loudly."

He winces. "I needed information from her."

"And did you get it?" Her brows draw together.

"I am not what I pretend to be here at Court. I would have thought you knew that."

"Don't be such a fool," she snaps. "It doesn't matter what I believe, only that..."

"Yes?" He waits for her to finish the statement.

But she only shakes her head, smothering a cough. Bogdana glances back at them.

For a long moment, they ride in silence.

"I suppose you're going to tell me that argument was enough," Oak says finally. There's definitely something strange about this conversation. "Jack could spread around a few details, given his penchant for gossip."

The kelpie makes a horselike whinny and tosses his mane, objecting.

"And I suppose you're also going to tell me that last night means nothing," Oak goes on.

Wren stiffens. "What does it matter? Despite your declaration of love, can you really say you want to marry me?"

"And if I do?" he asks.

"That doesn't matter, either," she says, her voice the snap of a lash.

He takes a breath. "Tonight—"

"Tonight is too late," she says, anguished. "It may already be too late." With that, she pulls at the lead on her twig-and-branch steed, wheeling away from him.

He watches after her, certain that someone is manipulating or threatening her. Obviously, she can't tell him directly or she would have done so. But how can anyone constrain her, as powerful as she is?

He sees Taryn steer her horse to Wren's side, hears his sister tell her how well she likes what Wren is wearing. Watches Bogdana guide her bramble steed toward Randalin. He doesn't have the wit to be afraid of her and begins merrily chatting away.

Some of the courtiers have ridden fast, in search of game, but many more have ambled along on their mounts, deep in conversation. A few have parasols of flowers or feathers or even cobwebs.

Oak rides alongside them, deep in thought, until a horn blares, signaling the beginning of the picnic.

He swings down from Jack's back and follows the others to the campsite. Servants have set up an array of differently patterned blankets and baskets, along with parasols and even musicians. If the presence of mortals or the lot of them trooping around hasn't frightened off the silver stag, a few sets of murder ballads surely will.

There are duck hand pies, stoppered carafes of wine, blackberry tarts beside piles of roasted chestnuts, and bread so light and airy that cold butter spread across it would tear it like tissue.

Oriana walks to Oak, holding out a cup of red clover tea. "I barely spoke with you last night," she says.

"We sat at the same table, Mother," the prince reminds Oriana.

She puts her arm through his. She is so much smaller that it seems impossible she ever tossed him in her arms. "Have you come up with your question for the girl?"

He shakes his head.

"Ask her your fondest memory," she urges slyly. "Or perhaps your deepest secret."

"They're clever questions," Oak says. "They seem difficult, but she might well be able to guess both. Not a bad suggestion."

His mother frowns, and he takes perverse delight in having turned her words against her. But at least he's certain that if she's so obvious in urging him to walk away, she isn't engaged in a secret manipulation of Wren. "Hoping I will seek Nicasia's hand instead?" he asks, thinking of Tatterfell's theory.

Oriana's eyes go wide. "Of course not. That would be madness."

"You don't think my sister wants—"

"No," his mother says. "She wouldn't. You would never survive down there."

If Jude *does* plan on his marrying Nicasia, she hasn't started the process of suborning Oriana. And while, being the High Queen, she could do whatever she wants, you'd think she'd have brought it up once, at least.

He reminds himself that he can't be sure, though. Right now, he can't be sure of anything.

Taryn has stuck by Wren. They are speaking together, standing beside the Ghost's horse. For a moment, he thinks of going over there and dumping his red clover tea over his sister's head.

Hyacinthe walks toward Oak, signaling with raised brows.

The prince kisses his mother's cheek. "See? After considering the Undersea, nothing seems so bad." Then he leaves her and goes to where Hyacinthe is scowling at him.

"I heard you last night," Hyacinthe says, low-voiced.

That could mean a lot of things. "And?"

"*With your nephew*," he says.

Oak winces. He should have realized that if he could eavesdrop on Tiernan and Hyacinthe, it was equally possible for him to be eavesdropped upon.

"Were you going to deliver what I asked of you?" Hyacinthe asks. "Or are you the coward who lets your mother's murderer walk free?"

Oak has been asking himself about the closer betrayals, but eventually he would have to answer that question. "I thought you'd had enough of revenge."

"I am not speaking of myself," Hyacinthe reminds him. "And I told you that I did not release you from your vow."

Choosing the worst possible moment, the Ghost moves toward them, a skin of wine and two carved wooden cups in his hand. *Right*, because he was going to give Oak an update on whatever it was he was seeking to find out the night before.

"Send him away," Hyacinthe says.

"He knows something," Oak objects.

"Send him away or I will stab him through," hisses Hyacinthe under his breath.

"A cup of mead, prince?" offers the Ghost, pouring one for Oak and then one for himself. He glances at Hyacinthe. "I am afraid I only brought the two, but if you bring yours, I will pour."

Oak's cheeks feel hot, and there is a roaring in his ears the way there is when he gives in to instinct and fights without mercy. He takes the cup of honey wine and drinks it. It's too sweet and cloying in his mouth.

The Ghost takes his in a gulp, then winces. "Not good wine, but wine nonetheless. Now, if you will walk with me."

"I am afraid I can't talk right now," the prince tells Garrett.

The Ghost must hear something in his voice. Looking puzzled, he says, "Come find me when you're ready, but it must be soon. I will ride a little ways north so that we will be alone. When we're done, we will speak with your sister."

"You're gripping your sword," Hyacinthe tells Oak in a low voice as the spy departs.

Oak glances down at his hand, surprised to find it curled around the hilt of his blade. Surprised to find it shaking a little.

"I have to go after him," the prince says. "Someone's manipulating Wren."

"Manipulating? Who? How?" Hyacinthe asks.

"I don't know."

Hyacinthe glances in the direction that the Ghost went. Courtiers are still sitting on blankets, so there's no chance of the hunt starting up again immediately. Oak needs to find out what information the spy has.

Garrett already disappeared into the Milkwood, somehow slipping between the white trunks.

With a glance toward Wren and a reminder that he needs to keep his temper, Oak remounts the kelpie and heads in the direction the Ghost went. His head is swimming. He's got to keep himself under control. Surely whatever it is that the spy knows will help Oak understand the constraints on Wren and who put them there.

He rides a little farther and looks down at his hand, which has started to tremble. He still has the sensation of being underwater. And with it, he feels a rush of something entirely too familiar.

Blusher mushroom. He's been poisoned.

He thinks of the honey wine, sweet enough to hide the flavor. Honey wine, given into his hand by the Ghost.

The prince laughs out loud. Of all the things the Ghost knows about murder, apparently he doesn't know that this is the one poison to which Oak is immune. If the spy hadn't decided to go with the symmetry of finishing the job the way he'd begun it, Oak might really be dead.

The prince draws his sword.

Oh, he's going to *murder* the spy. The Ghost thinks he knows what Oak can do, but he isn't aware of his other lessons, from Madoc. Garrett doesn't know what Oak has become under his father's tutelage. Doesn't know how many people he's already slain.

The prince urges Jack north through the brambles, past the columns of pale trees. Finally, he comes upon a clearing. The kelpie stops short. For a moment, Oak doesn't understand what he's looking at.

There, in a tangle of vines, lies a body.

Oak slides down from the kelpie's back to draw closer. The man's mouth is stained purple. His eyes are open, staring up at the late afternoon sky as though lost in contemplation of the clouds.

"Garrett?" Oak says, leaning down to shake him.

The Ghost does not move. He does not even blink.

The prince's fingers close on his shoulder. The spy's body is hard beneath his hand, more like fossilized wood than flesh.

Dead. The man who murdered his mother. The spy who had trained him to move quietly, to wait. Who bounced Leander on his shoulders. Taryn's lover. Jude's friend.

Dead. Impossibly dead.

Which means that Garrett didn't poison Oak. He shared his poisoned wine, all unknowing.

Could *Hyacinthe* have done this? He might have thought dosing the Ghost with what killed Liriope to be fitting—a symmetry of a different kind. And if he knew that Oak wouldn't die from it, he wouldn't be kind enough to stop him from drinking a portion of the blusher mushroom. He wouldn't care if Oak suffered a little.

But if it *wasn't* Hyacinthe, then it came down to the question of what the Ghost had learned. What he wanted to tell Oak. What they needed to go to Jude with. What couldn't wait.

G uards and courtiers thunder up all around Oak. Did he cry out?
Did Jack? The kelpie is standing beside the prince now, but he
doesn't remember when Jack stopped being a horse. The noise and confusion mirror Oak's thoughts. People are shouting at one another, making Oak dizzy.

Or maybe that's the blusher mushroom still slowing his blood.

Jack is insisting they found the Ghost like this and someone is
saying *how horrifying* and a lot of other meaningless words that blend
together in Oak's mind.

Taryn is screaming, a high keening sound. She's on her knees beside
the spy, shaking him. When she looks up at Oak, her gaze is so full of
grief and accusation that he has to look away.

I hated him, Oak thinks. But he's not even sure that's true. He never
knew Liriope, and he knew Garrett. *I should have hated him. I wanted
to hate him.*

He didn't kill him, though.

He didn't kill him, but he might have. He could have. Could he have?

Jude moves to Taryn's side, one hand going to her twin's shoulders. Fingers pressing reassuringly.

The Roach leans down to check the body, and when one of the guards tries to stop him, it's Cardan who tells them to let him be. Oak didn't even realize the Roach was *at* the hunt.

Taryn lies down beside Garrett's corpse, her hair shrouding his face. One of her tears has pooled in the corner of his eye, wetting his lash.

Cardan kneels beside her, his hand going to Garrett's chest. Taryn looks up at him.

"What are you doing?" She doesn't sound happy, but they've never really gotten along.

"Blusher mushroom slows the body," he says, his gaze flickering to the Roach, who almost certainly taught him that. "But it slows it *slowly*."

"Do you mean he's not dead?" she asks.

"Is there something to be done?" Jude asks at almost the same time.

"Not in the way you mean," says Cardan, answering his wife's question and not Taryn's. He turns to Randalin and the crowd, then waves his beringed hand exaggeratedly. "Disperse. Go on."

Courtiers step away, heading to their horses, a buzz of rumors in the air. The Minister of Keys remains, glowering, standing beside Oriana. A few more Folk seem to believe this order doesn't apply to them. The Roach stays, too, but he's practically family.

Oak forces himself to scoot back, bracing against the trunk of a tree. For him, it was not much blusher mushroom, but he still feels the numbness tingling through his fingers and toes. Right now, he isn't certain whether he would fall back down if he tried to stand.

Wren crosses to his side. Bogdana stands at the edge of the clearing, half hidden by shadows.

"You're going to have to move as well," Cardan tells Taryn.

"What are you going to do to him?" she asks, shielding his body as though to protect it from the High King.

Cardan raises his eyebrows. "Let's just see if it works."

"Taryn," Jude says, reaching for her sister's hand and pulling her to her feet. "There isn't time."

Cardan closes his gold-rimmed eyes and, for all his extravagance, right then he looks like one of the paintings of the High Kings of old, somehow moved into the realm of myth.

All around them, wildflowers sprout, uncurling from buds. Trees shiver, sending down pale leaves. Brambles coil into unlikely shapes. There is a buzz of bees in the air, and then from the earth, roots rise, turning into the sturdy trunk of a tree around Garrett's body.

Taryn makes a sharp sound. The Roach lets out a breath, awe in his eyes. Oak feels it, too.

Bark wraps around Garrett and branches unfold, budding with leaves and fragrant blossoms the lilac of Taryn's clothing. A tree, unlike all that grow in the Milkwood, rises from the ground, shrouding the Ghost's body. Its limbs reach toward the sky, petals raining down around them.

Where Garrett stood, there is only the tree.

The High King opens his eyes, letting out a ragged breath. The courtiers that remained have taken several steps back. They are slack-jawed in surprise, perhaps having forgotten his command of the land beneath their feet.

"Will that—" Jude begins, her eyes shining.

"I thought that if the poison makes every part of him slow, then I could turn him into something that could live like that," says Cardan with a shudder. "But I don't know that it will save him."

"Will he be like this forever?" Taryn asks, her voice cracking a little. "Alive but imprisoned? Dying but not dead?"

"I don't *know*," Cardan says again, in a raw way that makes Oak think of being trapped in the royal bedchamber and overhearing him and Jude together. It's Cardan's real voice, the one he uses when he's not performing.

Taryn runs her hand over the rough bark, her tears coming on a sob. "He is still lost to me. He is still gone. And who knows if he's suffering?"

Oak feels Wren's hand in his, her fingers cool. "Come," she says, and at her tug, he finally rises. He's a little unsteady on his hooves, and she narrows her eyes at him. She's seen him poisoned before.

"We will discover who did this," Jude is telling her twin, voice firm. "We will punish them, I promise you that."

"Don't we know already?" Taryn says through tears, her voice breaking on the words. Her gaze goes to Wren. "I saw her by his horse."

"Wren had nothing to do with this," Oak snaps, squeezing Wren's fingers. "What possible motive could she have?"

"Queen Suren wants to destroy Elfhame," one of the remaining courtiers interjects. "Just as her mother did."

Jude does not speak, but Oak can tell she isn't unmoved by the argument that Wren may have had a hand in this. And to make it worse, Wren denies none of it. She says nothing. She just listens to their accusations.

Deny it, he wants to tell her. But what if she can't?

Just then, a cry fills the air. A vulture circles once to land heavily on Wren's shoulder. The storm hag.

"Prince?" Tiernan asks Oak, eyeing the vulture with misgiving.

"We should quit this place," says Randalin. "Our milling about cannot do anything in the way of helping."

The Bomb glares at everyone. "What did he eat or drink? We should isolate the poison."

"It was in the mead," Oak says.

The Bomb turns toward him, white hair a nimbus around her heart-shaped face. "How do you know that?"

The prince doesn't want to say this part out loud, not in front of even a small crowd, but he can't see a way out, either. "I drank some."

There is a ripple of shock through the remaining courtiers.

"Your Highness!" Randalin protests.

"And yet you're standing," says a pixie. "How is it that you're standing?"

"He must only have had the barest sip," Jude lies. "Brother, perhaps it's time to come away and rest."

Perhaps it would be better if they got out of the Milkwood. He's feeling somewhat unsteady on his feet. He's feeling somewhat unsteady, period.

"Do you think I'm responsible?" Wren whispers, her hand still in his.

No, of course not, Oak wants to say, but he isn't sure he can make his mouth spit out those words.

Did she poison the Ghost? Would she have done it for Hyacinthe's sake, if he asked her to help? Had he found out a secret so great she would protect it, even if it cost a life?

"I will believe whatever you tell me," Oak says. "Nor will I look for deceit in your words."

She watches the shifts of his expression, almost certainly looking for deceit in *his* words.

The vulture shifts, watching him with bead-black eyes. Bogdana's eyes, filled with rage.

"I'm sorry," Wren says. He sees the hag's talons sink into her shoulder hard enough to pierce flesh. A trickle of blood runs down her dress. But Wren's expression doesn't change.

He's sure she feels the pain. This is what she must have been like back in the Court of Teeth. This is how she endures all that she does. But he doesn't understand why she allows Bogdana to hurt her this way. She has the authority and power now.

Something is very, very wrong.

"You need to tell me what's going on," he says, keeping his voice low. "I can fix it. I can help."

"I'm not the one who needs saving." Wren lets go of his hand.

"It was *her*," insists Taryn. "Her or that witch she has with her or the traitorous knight who tried to kill Cardan. I want the knight arrested. I want the girl arrested. I want the witch in a cage."

Randalin blinks several times in surprise. "Well," he says to Wren. "Aren't you going to say anything? Tell them you didn't do it."

But again, she is silent.

The Minister of Keys sputters a bit as he tries to digest this. "My dear girl, you must speak."

Cardan turns toward Wren. "I'd appreciate it if you went with my knights," he says. "We have questions for you. Tiernan, show us your loyalty and accompany her. I am personally charging you with not letting her out of your sight."

Tiernan looks in Oak's direction in alarm.

Wren closes her eyes, as though her doom has come upon her. "As you command."

"Your Majesty," Tiernan begins, frowning. "I can't leave my charge—"

"Go," Oak says. "Don't let her out of your sight, as the High King said." He understands why Tiernan is concerned, however. Sending him away may mean that Cardan doesn't want Oak to have anyone to fight at his side when the High King questions him.

Randalin clears his throat. "If I may, I suggest we move to Insear. The tents are already set up and guards sent ahead. We will not be so out in the open."

"Why not?" says Cardan. "A perfect place for a party *or* an execution. Tiernan, take Queen Suren to her tent and wait with her there until I call on her. Keep everyone else out."

The vulture on her shoulder jumps into the sky, beating black wings, but Wren makes no protest.

Oak wonders if he could stop them. He doesn't think so. Not without a lot of death.

"Let me go with her," Oak says.

Jude turns toward him, raising her brows. "She didn't deny it. She isn't denying it now. You're staying with us."

"Furthermore," proclaims Cardan to the rest of his knights, "I want the rest of you to find Hyacinthe and bring him to *my* tent on Insear."

"Why not suspect me?" Oak demands, voice rising.

Taryn gives a little laugh, at odds with the tears staining her cheeks. "That's ridiculous."

"Is it? I found his body," the prince insists. "And I have a motive, after all."

"Explain," Cardan says, mouth a grim line.

Jude seems to sense what's coming. There are too many people around, guards, courtiers, Randalin, and Baphen. "Whatever Oak has to tell us, he can tell us in private."

"Then by all means," says Cardan, "let's depart."

But Oak doesn't want to be quiet. Maybe it's the blusher mushroom in his blood, maybe it's the sheer frustration of the moment. "He murdered my first mother. He's the reason she died, and you both—you all—hid it from me."

A hush goes through the courtiers like a gust of wind.

Oak feels the delirious abandon of breaking the rules. In a family of deceivers, telling the truth—out loud, where anyone could hear it—was a massive transgression. "You allowed me to treat him like a friend, and all the while you knew we were spitting on my mother's memory."

A drawn-out silence follows his last word. Oriana has a white-fingered hand pressing against her mouth. She didn't know, either.

Finally, Cardan speaks. "You make a very good point. You had an excellent reason to try to kill him. But did you?"

"I urge you all," interrupts Randalin, "if for no other reason than discretion, let us repair to the tents at Insear. We will have some nettle tea and calm ourselves. As the High Queen says, this is not a conversation to be had in public."

Jude nods. This may be the first time Randalin and Jude ever agreed on anything.

"If my family had their way," says Oak, "this isn't a conversation we'd have at all."

Then, from across the Milkwood, there's a scream.

Moments later, a knight steps into the clearing, looking as though she's run all the way there. "We found another body."

Most of the remaining knot of courtiers begin to move in the direction of the scream, and Oak goes along, though he still feels unsteady. They know he's poisoned, at least. If he falls down, no one will have many questions.

"Whose?" Jude demands.

They don't have to go far, though, and he sees the body before she gets her answer.

Lady Elaine, lying in a heap, one of her small wings half crushed when she fell from the horse that is nuzzling the end of her skirts. Lady Elaine, her cheek stained with mud. Her eyes open. Her lips purple.

Oak shakes his head, taking a step back. Hand coming up to cover his mouth. Two people poisoned—*three* people, counting himself. Because of the conspiracy?

Cardan is watching him with an unreadable expression. "Your friend?"

The Roach moves to Oak, puts one green clawed hand against the middle of his back. "Let's go ahead to Insear, as the Minister of Keys said. You're upset. Death's upsetting."

Oak gives him a wary look, and the goblin holds up his hands in surrender, his black eyes sympathetic. "I had no part in Liriope's murder nor these," the Roach says. "But I can't claim I've never done anything wrong."

Oak nods slowly. He can't claim that, either.

He mounts up again on Jack, who has obligingly become a horse again. The goblin rides a fat, spotted pony, low to the ground. Behind him, someone is saying that the festivities can't possibly go on as planned.

Oak thinks of Elaine, lying in the dirt. Elaine, who was dangerously ambitious and foolish. Had she told the rest of the conspirators that she was quitting and received this in answer?

His mind turns to Wren, with the vulture's talons digging into her skin. Her blank expression. He keeps trying to understand why Wren endures it without crying out or striking back.

Does it have something to do with Garrett and Elaine being poisoned?

Oak was a fool to bring Wren here. When he gets to the tents on Insear, he's going to find hers. Then he is going to get them both off the isles and out of this vipers' nest. Away from Bogdana. Away from his family. Maybe they could live in the woods outside her mortal family's home. She'd said, back when they were questing, that she'd like to visit her sister. What was her name? Bex. They could eat scavenged berries and look up at the stars.

Or maybe Wren wants to go back north, to the Citadel. That's fine, too.

"How long have you known?" the goblin asks.

For a moment, Oak isn't sure what he means. "About what Garrett did? Not long." Above them, the black bees of the Milkwood buzz, carrying nectar to their queen. Late afternoon sunlight turns the pale trees gold. He sets his jaw. "Someone should have told me."

"Someone clearly did," says the Roach.

Leander, he supposes, which hardly counts. And *Hyacinthe*, although he didn't know the whole of it. Oak doesn't want to blame either of them out loud, not to someone who will carry the tale to his sister. He understands what the Roach is doing, getting him alone like this, understands it well enough to avoid the trap. He shrugs.

"Did you poison him?" the Roach asks.

"I thought Garrett poisoned *me*," the prince says, shaking his head.

"Never," says the goblin. "He regretted what he did to Liriope. Tried to make it up to Locke by giving him his true name. But Locke's not the person to trust with that sort of thing."

Oak wonders if Garrett tried to make it up to him, too, in ways he never saw. Teaching him the sword, volunteering to go north when the prince was in trouble, going to Oak with information before taking it to Jude. He didn't like having a reason to be anything but angry, but that didn't mean it wasn't true.

"There was something he needed to tell me," Oak says. "Not about any of that. Something else."

"Once you're delivered to Insear, I'll check out his part of the lair. If he had any sense, he wrote it down."

At the edge of the Milkwood, they pass the Lake of Masks. Oak's gaze goes to the water. You never see your own face, always the face of someone else, someone from the past or future. Today he sees a blond pixie laughing as she splashes someone else—a man in black with salt-white hair. Recognizing neither of them, he turns away.

At the coastline, several boats await them, pale, narrow boats with high prows and sterns curving upward so that they look like crescent moons floating on their backs—all crewed by armored guards. As the sun dips beneath the ocean on the horizon, Oak looks across to Insear, outfitted with tents for the festivities to come, then to the sparkling lights of Mandrake Market, and beyond, to the Tower of Forgetting, stark black against the red-and-gold sky.

He and the Roach get into one of the boats, and Jack, having shifted into his bipedal form, gets in after them. A guard Oak doesn't recognize nods to them and then puts up the sail. A few moments later, they are speeding across the short stretch of sea.

"Your Majesty," says the guard. "There are tents for your refreshment. Yours is marked with your father's sign."

The prince nods, distracted.

The Roach stays in the boat. "I'll find out what the Ghost knew, if I can," he says gruffly. "You stay out of trouble."

Oak couldn't count how many times someone said that to him. He isn't sure he ever listened.

On Insear, there is a small forest of pavilions and other elaborate tents. He looks among them for Wren's, listening in vain for the sound of her voice or Tiernan's. He doesn't hear either of them, and he doesn't see Madoc's moon-and-dagger crest marking a tent for him, either.

Everything feels wrong. He can see individual threads but not make out the larger web, and there isn't much time.

It may already be too late. Wasn't that what Wren said?

Surely, she couldn't have been referring to the poison.

I'm not the one who needs saving.

He pushes the thought from his mind. No, she couldn't have been speaking about that. She couldn't have a hand in murdering Lady Elaine and probably killing Garrett, too, for all that turning him into a tree might help.

As Oak and Jack walk on, the prince spots a tent with the flap open and Tatterfell within. But it isn't Madoc's crest that's stamped on the outside. The prince frowns at the mark until he understands what he's looking at. *Dain's crest.* But people don't generally refer to Oak as Dain's son, even though at this point it's well known where his Greenbriar blood comes from. If she sees this, Oriana is going to have a fit.

Oak puzzles over who arranged things this way. Not his sister. Nor Cardan, unless this is some kind of backhanded way of reminding Oak of his place. But it seems a little too backhanded. Cardan is subtle but not *confusingly* subtle.

He steps inside. The tent is furnished with rugs covering the rock and patches of grass. He spots a table is crowded with bottles of water and wine and the pressings of fruit. Candles burn to chase away shadows. Tatterfell looks up from spreading his change of clothes out on a low couch.

"You're early," the imp says. "And who's this?"

Jack comes forward to take Tatterfell's hand and bow deeply over it. "His steed and sometimes companion, Jack of the Lakes. It is my honor, lovely lady. Perhaps we shall dance together this evening."

The little faerie blushes, looking very unlike her usual grouchy self.

Oak looks at the burgundy doublet, chosen hours earlier. He can still feel the disorientation of the blusher mushroom coursing through his system, but his movements are less stiff and more sure.

"You must dress for the festivities," she says.

He opens his mouth to tell her that they're probably not going to happen, then remembers her calling tonight a farce. Did she know something? Did she have a part in this?

He needs to think straight, but it's so hard with blusher mushroom still addling his mind. Almost certainly, Tatterfell was not planning any assassinations. But he wonders if the poisonings had to do with stopping the ceremony.

That theory didn't withstand much scrutiny, though. If they wanted it stopped, and had some power over Wren, couldn't they pressure her to end it? Whoever *they* were.

As his mind runs in circles, he strips off his hunting clothes and puts on the new, more formal ones. In moments, Tatterfell is dusting him off and polishing away any mud on his hooves. As though he really is going to his wedding.

The flap of the tent opens, and two knights step inside.

"The High King and Queen request your presence in their tent before the revel begins," one says.

"Is Wren there?" he asks.

The knight who spoke shakes his head. He looks to be at least part redcap. The other knight has more elven features and dark eyes. He seems twitchy.

"Tell them I will be along presently," Oak says.

"I'm afraid we're to escort you—*now*."

That explains the twitchiness, then. "And if I don't comply?"

"We must yet bring you to them," the elven knight says, looking unhappy about it.

"Well, then," Oak says, walking to them. He could, perhaps, use his charm to talk the knights out of it, but that seems hardly worth it. Jude would only send more soldiers, and these two would get in undeniable trouble.

The prince carefully does not look in the direction of Jack. Since the kelpie wasn't mentioned, he doesn't have to go and will be the safer for it.

Lightning slices across the sky, followed by a crack of thunder. No rain has started yet, though the air is thick with it. The wind is picking up, too, whipping the skirts of the tents. Oak wonders if Bogdana has something to do with this. Certainly, she is in a bad enough mood.

He thinks of Wren again, of the talons biting into her skin. Of her words in the gardens. *I'm not safe. You can't trust me.*

There is little for him to do but walk across Insear behind the knights, past where garlands of ferns and wisteria and toadstools have been slung from trees, and musicians are tuning their fiddles, while a few courtiers, arriving unfashionably early, are selecting drinks from a large table, loaded with bottles of all shapes and sizes and colors.

One of the knights pushes aside the flap of a heavy cream-and-gold tent.

Inside, two thrones sit, although neither is occupied. Jude and Cardan stand with Taryn and Madoc. Cardan has changed into clothes of white and gold while Madoc is in deep red, as though they were opposing suits in a deck of cards. Taryn still wears her hunting clothes, her eyes red and swollen, as though she hasn't stopped crying until just before this moment. Oriana sits in a corner, entertaining Leander. Oak thinks of his own childhood and how she pulled him away from so many dangerous conversations, hiding them in the back, distracting him with a toy or a sweet.

It was a kindness, he knew. But it made him vulnerable as well.

Three members of the Living Council are in attendance. Fala, the fool; Randalin; and Nihuar, representative of the Seelie Courts. All three of them look grim. Hyacinthe is there, too, sitting on a chair, stony-faced and defiant. Oak can sense the panic he is trying to hide.

Ringed around the tent are guards, none of whom Oak knows. All of whom wear the expressions of people expecting an execution.

"Oak," Jude says. "Good. Are you ready to talk?"

"Where's Wren?" he asks.

"What an excellent question," she says. "I thought perhaps you knew."

They stare at each other.

"She's gone?" he asks.

"And Tiernan with her." Jude nods. "You can see why we have a lot to discuss. Did you arrange her freedom?"

Oak takes a deep breath. There are so many things he should have told her over the years. To tell her now is going to feel like peeling off his own skin. "You may have heard some things about me and the company I was keeping before I went north with Wren. Lady Elaine, for example. My reasons were not what you might suppose. I'm not—"

Outside, there's a crash and a howl of wind.

"What's that?" Taryn demands.

Cardan narrows his eyes. "A storm," he says.

"Brother," Jude says. "Why did you bring her here? What did she promise you?"

Oak remembers being caught in the rain and thunder of Bogdana's power, remembers his ragwort steed being torn out from beneath him. This portends disaster.

"When we were on our quest, I tricked Wren," Oak says. "I kept back information that wasn't mine to keep." He cannot help hearing the echo of his own complaint in those words. His family hid things from him the same way he hid things from her.

"And?" Jude frowns.

Oak tries to find the right words. "And she was angry, so she threw me in prison. Which seems extreme, but I was handling it. And then you . . . overreacted."

"Overreacted?" Jude echoes, clearly incensed.

"I was handling it!" Oak repeats, louder.

There's movement out of the corner of his eye, and then two bolts fly across the tent toward Jude. Oak hits the floor, pulling his sword from its sheath.

Cardan whips up his cloak in front of Jude—the cloak made by Mother Marrow, the one that was enchanted to turn the blades of weapons. The arrows fall to the ground as though they've struck a wall instead of cloth.

A moment later, the High King staggers back, bleeding. A knife juts out from his chest. Falling to his knees, he covers the wound with his hands, as though the blood seeping through his fingers is an embarrassment.

Randalin steps back, smug and satisfied. It's his dagger in the High King's chest.

"Put down your weapons," a soldier shouts unsteadily, taking a step forward. For a moment, Oak isn't sure whose side they're on. Then he sees the way they're standing. Seven soldiers moving closer to the Minister of Keys, two of them the knights who came to Oak's tent.

Finally, the unfamiliarity of them makes horrible sense. This is a trap.

This is the conspiracy he hoped Lady Elaine would reveal. Had Oak not missed their meeting in the gardens, had he not been so willing to believe that it was over when Lady Elaine herself gave it up, had he not departed on the quest to save his father in the first place, perhaps he could have discovered this. Discovered it and foiled it.

Oak recalls the councilor extolling the wisdom of his betrothal to Wren, recalls his pushing the royal family to come immediately to Insear after the hunt. Remembers how Randalin maneuvered a conference alone with Bogdana and Wren.

The Minister of Keys was laying the groundwork while acting so pompous and irritating that he couldn't be taken seriously. And Oak fell for it. Oak underestimated Randalin in the most foolish way possible—by falling for the same trick he played on others.

Jude eases Cardan to the ground and kneels beside him, sword in her hand. "I will cut your throat," she promises Randalin.

"Stabbity stab, knife wife," says Fala, with feeling. "Traitor's blood is hot, but it still spills."

Taryn has a dagger out. Madoc, dangerous enough with just his claw-tipped hands, has moved into a fighting stance. Oak rises and moves to his side.

"You should have listened to me," Randalin tells Jude from the safe distance he has put between them, behind one of his soldiers. "Mortals are not meant to sit on our thrones. And Cardan, the least of the Greenbriar princes, pathetic. But all that will be remedied. We will have a new king and queen in your place. You see, none of your own knights are here to save you. Nor can they cross to this isle while the storm rages. And it will rage until you're dead."

Oak blinks. "You made a deal with Bogdana. That's what the Ghost was getting proof of, that's the thing he thought I wouldn't like."

Because of Wren. That's *why* the Ghost thought Oak wouldn't like it.

"You should be grateful," Randalin tells the prince. "I persuaded Bogdana to spare you, though you are of the Greenbriar line and her enemy. Because of me, you will sit on the throne with a powerful faerie queen by your side."

"Wren would never...," Oak begins, but he's not sure how to finish. Would she agree to the murder of his family? Did she want to be the High Queen?

You can't trust me.

I'm not the one who needs saving.

Randalin laughs. "She didn't object. And neither did you, as I recall. Didn't you tell Lady Elaine of your resentment of the High King? Didn't you encourage her plot to get you on the throne?"

Oak's stomach hurts, hearing those words. Knowing a storm is raging outside because of someone he brought here. Seeing Cardan's body lying in a pool of red, no longer conscious and maybe no longer alive. Thinking of the Ghost's open, staring eyes. Seeing the way Oak's sisters are looking at him now and how his mother is looking away.

"*You* poisoned Garrett," Oak says.

Randalin laughs. "I gave him the wine. He didn't have to drink it. But he got too close to uncovering our plans."

"And Elaine?" he asks.

"What could I do?" Randalin says. "She wanted out." And pouring her wine from the same urn as the spy's convinced him it was safe to drink.

Expressing the desire to get out was how Oak planned on getting Elaine and her friends to turn on him. The same way he'd defeated other conspiracies—courting an attempted murder and exposing them for that instead of as traitors. But she hadn't known it would doom her. He should have given her a warning.

And now his family thinks he was part of this. He can see it in their faces. And worse, in bringing Wren here, maybe he was.

Maybe this *is* what Wren wanted when she agreed to come to Elfhame. Revenge on him. Revenge on the High King and Queen, who stripped her of her kingdom and sent her away with no help and no hope. The crown that Mellith was promised.

Wren, whom he believed he loved. Whom he believed he *knew*.

He sees now that she learned the lessons of betrayal, learned them down to the marrow of her bones.

There is no apology Oak can give that could be believed, no way to explain. Not anymore.

Oak feels something snap inside him. He draws his sword.

"Don't be foolish," Randalin says with a frown. "This is all for *you*."

There is a familiar roaring in Oak's ears, and this time he gives in to it eagerly. His limbs move, but he feels as if he's watching himself from far away.

He stabs into the stomach of the guard nearest to him, cutting up under his breastplate. The man screams. The thought that these soldiers believed he was on their side, believed he would be their High King, makes him even angrier. He turns, stabbing out. Someone else is screaming, someone he knows, urging him to stop. He doesn't even slow. Instead, he knocks a bolt aside as two more guards crowd around him. He pulls a dagger from one of their sheaths and uses it to stab the other while he parries a blow.

Oak can feel his consciousness slipping away, falling deeper into the trance of the fight. And it is such a relief to let go, the way he does when he allows the right words to fall from his tongue in the right order.

The last thing the prince feels before his awareness slides entirely away is a knife in his back. The last thing he sees is his sword biting through the throat of an enemy.

He finds himself with his blade pressed against Jude's. "Stop it," she shouts.

He staggers back, letting the sword fall from his hands. There's blood on her face, a fine spatter. Did he strike her?

"Oak," she says, not yelling anymore, which is when he realizes she's scared. He never wanted her to be scared of him.

"I'm not going to hurt you," he says. Which is true. Or at least he believes it's probably true. His hands have started shaking, but that's normal. That happens a lot, after.

Does she still think he's a traitor?

Jude whirls toward Madoc. *"What did you do to him?"*

The redcap looks baffled, his gaze on Oak speculative. "Me?"

Oak scans the room, the adrenaline of battle still running through his veins. The guards are dead. All of them, and messily. Randalin too. Oak isn't the only one holding a bloody sword, either. Hyacinthe has one as well, standing near Nihuar as though they had very recently been back-to-back. Fala is bleeding. The Roach and the Bomb are beside each other, having appeared from the shadows, the Bomb's fingers curled around a curved, nasty-looking knife. Even Cardan, using the throne to prop himself upright, has a dagger in his hand with red on the blade, although his other hand, holding his chest, is stained scarlet, too.

Cardan's not dead. The relief almost makes Oak sag to his knees, except that Cardan is still bleeding and pale.

"What did you turn Oak into?" Jude demands of Madoc. "What did you do to my brother?"

"He's good with a sword," the redcap tells her. "What can I say?"

"I am losing patience almost as fast as I am losing blood," says Cardan. "Just because your brother killed Randalin, it doesn't mean we should forget he was at the center of this conspiracy—and that he is at the center of whatever Bogdana and Wren are planning. I suggest that we lock Oak up where he won't be so tempting to traitors."

The prince spots Oriana, her arms still protectively around Leander, holding him turned toward her skirts so he can't see the slaughtered bodies. She's wearing an anguished expression. The prince feels the overwhelming urge to go to her, to bury his face in her neck as he might have done as a child. To see if she would push him away.

You wanted them to know you, his mind supplies unhelpfully.

Wren once described what she was afraid of, if she revealed herself to her family. How she imagined their rejecting her once they saw her true face. Oak sympathized, but until this moment he didn't understand the horror of having all the people who loved you best in the world look at you as though you were a stranger.

Charm them. The thought is not just unhelpful but wrong. And yet the temptation yawns in front of him. *Make them look at you as they once did. Fix this before it is broken forever.*

A shudder goes through him. "It's not Dad's fault or anyone else's that I'm good at killing," he makes himself say, meeting Jude's gaze. "I chose this. And don't you dare tell me that I shouldn't have. Not after what you've done to yourself."

Clearly, Jude was about to say something very much like that, because she chokes off the words. "You were supposed to—"

"What? Not make the same choices the rest of you did?"

"To have a childhood," she shouts at him. "To let us protect you."

"Ah," says Cardan. "But he had loftier ambitions."

Madoc's gaze is impassive. Does *he* believe Oak to be a traitor? And if so, does he applaud the ambition or scorn the failure?

"I think it's time to get off this isle." Cardan's trying to sound casual, but he's unable to hide that he's in pain.

The rain is still battering the tent. Taryn walks to the flap and looks outside. She shakes her head. "I am not sure we can get through the storm. The councilor was right about that, if nothing else."

Jude turns to Hyacinthe. "And what was your role in all this?"

"As though I would give any confidences to you," Hyacinthe says.

"Kill him," orders Cardan.

"Hyacinthe fought on your side," protests Oak.

Cardan gives an exhausted sigh and waves one lace-cuffed hand. "Very well, truss up Hyacinthe. Find the girl and the hag and kill *them*, at least. And I want the prince locked up until we sort this out. Lock up Tiernan, too, if he ever comes back."

I'm sorry, Wren said before she left him in the Milkwood.

She warned him not to trust her, and then she betrayed him. She conspired with Randalin and Bogdana. She allowed Oak to delude himself into believing that someone was controlling her, when she had all the power.

It was clever, to keep him chasing shadows.

That had been the part of the puzzle he wasn't able to solve—what any of them could have over her, who could unmake them all. The answer should have been obvious, only he didn't want to believe it. They had *nothing* over her.

A mystery with a void at its center.

"Shoot her on sight," Jude says, as though it's going to be that simple.

"Shoot her? She'll unmake the arrows," Oak says.

Jude raises her brows. "*All* the arrows?"

"Poison?" his sister asks.

The prince sighs. "Maybe." If he wasn't so busy drinking all the poison in sight, he might know.

"We'll find her weakness," his sister assures him. "And we will bring her down."

"No," says Oak.

"Another protestation of her innocence? Or yours?" asks Cardan in a silky voice, sounding like the boy Taryn and Jude used to hate, the one who Hyacinthe wouldn't believe was any different from Dain. The one who ripped the wings off pixies' backs and made his sister cry.

"I make no defense of myself," Oak says, leaning down to pick up his sword from the floor. "This is my fault. And my responsibility."

"What are you doing?" Jude asks.

"I am going to be the one to end this," Oak says. "And you will have to kill me to stop me."

"I'm going with you," Hyacinthe tells him. "For Tiernan."

The prince nods. Hyacinthe crosses the floor to stand against the prince's back. As one, they move toward the door, blades bared.

Jude doesn't order anyone to block their way. Doesn't confront Oak herself. But in her eyes, he can tell she believes that her little brother—the one she loves and would do anything to protect—is already dead.

CHAPTER
21

Oak and Hyacinthe plunge into a storm of terrifying ferocity. The fog is so thick the prince can't even see the shore of Insmire, and the waves have become towering things, beating against the shoreline, biting off rocks and sand.

Bogdana has sealed off Insear from aid, keeping Elfhame's military and all else who would help them at bay. And now the storm hag waits with Wren for some signal that the royal family is dead.

There's a problem with their plan, though. Oak *hasn't* married Wren. Perhaps Randalin thought no one would find the Ghost's or Elaine's body—or that no one would care. Must have believed the evening's festivities wouldn't turn into an inquest. But since things didn't happen that way, the murder of the High King and Queen wouldn't automatically give Wren the throne. She still needed him.

As he walks along the beach, soaking wet, Oak is shaking so hard it's difficult for him to tell what's from the chill and what is from rage.

He's become the fool he's spent so long pretending to be. If he hadn't fallen in love, then no one would be in danger. If he didn't believe in Wren, promise to be on her side, make every excuse for her, then Randalin's schemes would have come to nothing.

He loves her still, more's the pity.

No matter, though. He owes his family his loyalty, no matter their secrets. Owes Elfhame itself. Whether or not he likes being the prince, he accepted the role with all its benefits and obligations. He cannot be the one to put his people in danger. And whatever Wren once felt for him, he cannot believe she could do all this unless that was gone. He ruined it, and he wasn't able to fix it. Some broken things stay broken.

The prince runs through the storm, the cold cutting through his thin courtier's clothes. "Come on," he calls to Hyacinthe over the rumble of thunder, making a sweeping gesture with his arm to indicate a tent he wants them to duck into.

Marked with the sigil of a courtier from the Court of Rowan, it's empty. Oak wipes some of the water off his face.

"Now what?" Hyacinthe asks.

"We find Wren and Bogdana. Can you guess where they might go? Surely you overheard something these past few days." As the adrenaline of the fight ebbs away, Oak realizes there's a raw line of pain down his back where he dimly recalls being stabbed. There may also be a shallow slash at his neck. It stings.

"And if we find them," Hyacinthe hedges. "Then what?"

"We stop them," Oak says, pushing away pain, pushing away the thought of what stopping them will really entail. "They can't be too far. Bogdana needs to be close enough to control this storm."

"I owe Wren a debt," says Hyacinthe. "I swore myself to her."

"She has Tiernan," Oak reminds him.

The man looks away. "They'll be on Insmoor."

"Insmoor?" Oak echoes. The smallest isle, besides the one they're standing on. The location of Mandrake Market and not much else.

"Bogdana turned the cottage back into a walnut before the hunt and tucked it away in her pocket. Told us we might have to meet her on Insmoor."

So the rest of her falcons would be there with them. That makes things more complicated, but Oak won't mind a chance to face Straun. And it isn't like Wren could unmake Oak unless she wants to unmake her plans for ruling as well.

"I know how we can get to Insmoor," the prince says.

Hyacinthe meets his gaze for a long moment, seeming to understand his scheme. "You cannot be serious."

"Never more so," Oak says, and plunges back out into the storm.

Oak's teeth are chattering by the time he comes to the tent marked with Dain's crest. Tatterfell and Jack are inside, huddled far from the flaps, which keep blowing apart, letting the cold rain inside.

"Jack, I'm afraid I need your help again," Oak tells him.

"At your service, my prince," Jack says, bowing his head. "I promised to be of use to you, and I shall."

"After this, your debt to me will be more than paid. You will owe me nothing. Perhaps you will even be the one with a favor to call in."

"I should enjoy that," Jack says with a sly smile.

"I want you to take me under the waves to the shore. Do you have a way to keep me breathing while we go?"

Jack looks at him with wide eyes. "Alas, I am no help to you there. My kind do not much worry over the lives of our riders."

Hyacinthe gives Oak an incredulous look. "No, you delight in their deaths and then devour them. Can you control yourself with the prince on your back?"

That wasn't something Oak worried over before, but he doesn't like the flash of delight that passes across Jack of the Lakes' face at the mention of devouring.

"I can keep my teeth from the prince's sweet flesh, but if you want to come along, there's no telling what I might do to you," Jack says.

"I'm coming," Hyacinthe says. "They've got Tiernan."

Oak hoped he would. He's not sure he can do this alone. "No snacking on Hyacinthe."

"Not even a small bite?" Jack asks petulantly. "You are making it hard to be merry, Your Highness."

"Nonetheless," Oak says.

"What fool thing is it that you intend to do in this storm?" Tatterfell asks, poking the prince in the gut. "And are you bleeding?"

"Maybe," he says, touching a finger to his neck. It hurts, but his back hurts worse.

"Take off your shirt," the little faerie commands, blinking up at him.

"There isn't time," he tells her. "But if you have some bindings, I'll use them for my sword. I seem to have dropped the sheath somewhere."

Tatterfell rolls her ink-drop eyes.

"I will swim as swiftly as I am able," Jack says. "But it might not be swiftly enough."

"You can surface partway there," Oak suggests. "Let us catch a breath, then go on."

Jack considers that for a long moment, as though it is not much in his nature. But after a moment, he nods. Hyacinthe frowns and keeps frowning.

Tatterfell binds up the sword and belts it to Oak's waist with torn strips of his old clothes. She sews up the wound on his back as well, threatening to press her finger into the gouge if he moves.

"You're ruthless," he tells her.

She smiles as though he's delivered an extremely charming compliment.

Then, bracing against the wind and rain, Oak, Jack, and Hyacinthe make their way to the shore.

At the beach, Jack transforms into a sharp-toothed horse. He lowers himself to his knees and waits for them to lash themselves to him. Oak wraps a rope scavenged from the tent around the kelpie's chest and then around Hyacinthe, tying him tightly to Jack's back. Then he straps himself on, looping the rope a final time around their middles so they are bound to one another.

When Oak looks at the crashing waves, he begins to doubt the wisdom of his plan. He can barely make out the lights of Insmoor in the storm. Can he really hold his breath for as long as Jack is going to believe he needs?

But there's no going back. Nothing even to go back to, so he tries to inhale deeply and exhale slowly. Open up his lungs as much as he can.

Jack gallops toward the waves. The icy water splashes against Oak's legs. He grips the rope and takes one last breath as Jack plunges them all into the sea.

The cold of the ocean stabs the prince's chest. For a moment, it almost forces the breath from his lungs, but he manages to keep himself from gasping. Opens his eyes in the dark water. Feels the increasing, panicked pressure of Hyacinthe's grip on his shoulder.

Jack swims swiftly through the water. After a minute, it's clear it isn't fast enough. Oak's lungs burn; he feels lightheaded.

Jack needs to surface. He needs to do it now. *Now.* The prince presses his knees hard against the kelpie's chest.

Hyacinthe's hold on Oak's shoulder goes slack, his fingers drifting away. Oak concentrates on the pain of the rope cutting into his hand. Tries to stay alert. Tries not to breathe. Tries not to breathe. Tries not to breathe.

Then he can't hold on anymore, and water comes rushing in.

CHAPTER

22

They surface abruptly, leaving Oak choking and coughing. He can hear Hyacinthe hacking behind him. A swell comes along and slaps him in the face, sending seawater down his throat, making him cough worse.

Jack's head is above the waves, his mane plastered to his neck. Some kind of membrane has closed over his eyes, causing them to appear pearlescent. A glance toward the shore reassures Oak they are more than halfway to Insmoor. He can't even catch his breath, though, no less hold it again. His chest hurts and he's still coughing and waves keep crashing over him.

"Oak," Hyacinthe manages to wheeze. "This was a bad plan."

"If we die, he's going to eat you first," Oak gets out. "So you better live."

Too soon, the kelpie begins to descend, slowly enough for Oak to suck in a breath, at least. It's a shallow one, and he is almost certain he can't hold it until the shore. His lungs are burning already.

This is the only way across, he reminds himself, closing his eyes.

Jack surfaces once more, just long enough for Oak to gulp down another breath. Then they race for the shore, only to hit the crashing waves there.

The kelpie is hurled forward, thrown against the sandy bottom. Oak and Hyacinthe are dragged along. A sharp rock scrapes against Oak's leg. He wriggles against the rope, but it is pulled tight.

Somehow Jack fights his way higher onto the beach. Another wave knocks against his flank, and he staggers, then transforms into a boy. The rope slackens. Oak slips down onto the sand. Hyacinthe falls, too, and the prince realizes he's not conscious. Blood is seeping from a cut above his brow where he may have struck a rock.

Oak puts his shoulder under Hyacinthe's arm and attempts to haul him away from the shoreline. Before he can get clear, a stray wave trips the prince, and he falls to his knees. He throws his body over Hyacinthe's to keep him from being sucked back into the sea.

A moment later, Oak is up and dragging Hyacinthe behind him. Jack grabs Hyacinthe's other arm, and together they pull the man up onto soft grass before collapsing beside him.

Oak starts coughing again, while Jack manages to turn Hyacinthe onto his side. The kelpie slaps him on the back, and he vomits up seawater.

"How—?" Hyacinthe manages, opening his eyes.

Jack makes a prim face. "You both get soggy rather fast."

Above their heads the sky is a clear and steady blue, the clouds pale and puffy as lambs. It is only when Oak looks back at Insear that he sees the storm, a thick fog surrounding the isle, crackling with lightning and a sheet of rain that blurs everything beyond it.

After a few minutes of lying on the grass, convincing himself that he's still alive, Oak pushes himself to his hooves. "I know this place. I am going to scout around and see if I can find them."

"What are we supposed to do?" Hyacinthe asks, although he looks too half-drowned to do much of anything.

"Wait here," says Oak. "I'll tell you if I find Tiernan."

Hyacinthe nods in what seems a lot like relief.

Insmoor is called the Isle of Stone because of how rock-covered and wild it becomes away from Mandrake Market. This is where treefolk wander among thick vines of ivy, their bark-covered bodies slow as sap. Birds cry from the trees. It is a good place for Wren and Bogdana to hide. Few soldiers and fewer courtiers are likely to stumble over them in this place. But Oak has lived in Elfhame much of his life, and he knows the paths. His hooves are soft on the moss and swift over the stone. He's quiet as he moves through the shadows.

Some distance off, he sees falcons roosting on trees. He must be getting close. Sticking to shadows, he hopes he won't be spotted.

A few steps more, he halts in surprise. Wren sits on a boulder, legs drawn up to her chest, arms encircling them. Her nails are digging into the skin of her calves, and her expression is anguished, as if, though she planned the royal family's doom, she isn't *enjoying* it. It's nice, he supposes, that betraying him isn't fun.

His honey-mouthed charm comes easily this time, the burr in his tone just right. "Wren," he says softly. "I was looking for you."

She looks up, startled. Her headpiece is gone; her hair loose down her back. "I thought you were—"

"On Insear, waiting for our wedding?"

Her expression turns puzzled for a moment, then clears. She slides down off the rock and takes a step toward him, as though in a trance.

He can't make himself hate her, even now.

But he can make himself kill her.

"We can exchange our vows right here," he says.

"We can?" There's a strange wistfulness in her voice. But why wouldn't there be? She needs to marry him if she intends to be the High Queen of Elfhame. He's promising her exactly what she wants. That's how his power works, after all.

He brings his hand to the side of her face, and she rubs her cheek against his palm as though she were a cat. The rough silk of her hair slides over his fingers. It is agony to touch her like this.

His sword is at his belt, still tied in its makeshift sheath. All he needs to do is slide it out and stab it through her ancient heart.

"Close your eyes," he says.

She looks up at him with a bleakness that makes him catch his breath. Then she closes them.

Oak's hand drops to the hilt of his needle blade. Curls around the cold, wet pommel. Draws.

He looks down at the shining steel, bright enough to see Wren's face reflected in it.

He can't help thinking of the Ghost's words when they were aboard the *Moonskimmer*, flying above the sea. *You're very like Dain in some ways.*

Nor can he forget that he once thought, *If I love someone, I won't kill them*, a vow too obvious to need to be made aloud.

Oak doesn't want to be like his father.

He wishes his hand was still trembling, but it is remarkably steady.

You've always been clever. Be clever now. That's what Wren told him when she urged him to break off their betrothal. She needs their marriage if she intends to rule once Cardan and his sister are dead. And yet, if he'd ended the betrothal when she asked him to, there would be no way to accomplish that.

You can't trust me.

Why warn him? To send him in circles? To set him to one puzzle so he didn't notice another? That was a complicated and risky plan, while merely expecting him to do his duty and marry her the way he'd said he would was a shockingly simple plan, one with a high chance of success.

Oak remembers Wren standing in the Milkwood over the body of the Ghost. Taryn accused her of poisoning him. Why not deny it? Why make everyone suspicious of her? Randalin admitted to having done it, and he'd urged her to declare her innocence. And the storm hag sank her talons into Wren's skin. All that it bought was a good excuse for the royal family to ask more questions.

I'm not the one who needs saving.

That had seemed the most damning statement, when bolts started flying on Insear. But if it wasn't a taunt about the murder of his family that Randalin was planning, then someone else needed saving. Not Oak, who was a necessary cog. The Ghost? Lady Elaine?

He recalls something else, from the banquet. *I should have understood better—what you did for your father and why. I wanted it to be simple. But my sis—Bex—*

Wren didn't finish speaking because of a coughing fit. Which could have been because she made herself sick using her magic. Or it could have been that she was trying to say something she made a vow not to say.

My sister. Bex.

I'm not the one who needs saving.

Maybe Oak has this all wrong. Maybe she's not his enemy. Maybe she's been given an impossible choice.

Wren loves her mortal family. She loves them so much she slept in the dirt near their house just to be close. Loves them so much that there might be nothing she wouldn't do to save her mother or father or sister. No one she wouldn't sacrifice, including herself.

He knows what love like that feels like.

Oak had wondered why Lady Nore and Lord Jarel left Wren's mortal family alive, given what he knew of their cruelty. Wouldn't it have been more to their taste to remove any chance at Wren's happiness? To butcher her family members one by one in front of her and drink her tears?

But now he sees what use they could have been. How could Wren ever rebel when there was always something else to lose? A hatchet that never fell. A threat to be delivered over and over again.

How pleased Bogdana must have been to find Bex still alive and usable.

Wren opens her eyes and looks up at him. "At least it will be you," she says. "But you better hurry up. Waiting is the worst part."

"You're not my enemy," he says. "You were never my enemy."

"Yet you're standing there with a bare blade," Wren reminds him.

Fair point. "I just figured it out. She has your sister, doesn't she?"

Wren opens her mouth, then closes it. But the relief in her expression is answer enough.

"And you can't tell me," he guesses. "Bogdana made you vow all sorts of things to make sure you couldn't give away her game. Made you vow to go through with the marriage, so the only way out was if I refused you. Hid Bex away, so you couldn't simply unmake everyone and free her. Left word with someone to do away with Bex if the storm hag turns up dead. All you could do was try to stall. And try to warn me."

All she could do was hope he was clever enough.

And perhaps, if he wasn't, she hoped that at least he would stop her from having to do the worst of what Bogdana commanded. Even if the only way to stop her was with a blade.

She, who never wanted to trust him again, having to do exactly that.

Wren's eyes are wet as she blinks, her lashes black and spiky. She reaches into a pocket of her dress and takes out the white walnut. "Tiernan is trapped in the cottage. Take it. This is all I can offer you." Her fingers brush the palm of his hand. "I am not your enemy, but if you can't help me, the next time we meet, I might be."

It's not a threat. He understands now. She's telling him what she fears.

The prince practically runs into Jack and Hyacinthe as they're coming off the beach. The kelpie yelps and glares at him accusatorily.

"I have Tiernan," Oak says, out of breath.

Hyacinthe raises both eyebrows and looks at the prince as though he must have fallen on his head, hard.

"No, not with me," he says. "He's in my pocket."

Inside of the cottage must have been how they brought the bramble horses without their being on the ship. And any other sinister supplies they may have needed. Arms and armor, certainly. And there was no reason for Wren to have even known.

"And your queen? Is she ...?" Jack makes a throat-slashing motion.

"Bogdana has her mortal sister," Oak says. "She's being blackmailed."

"Has her where?" Hyacinthe asks. "And when is a single thing you are saying going to start making sense?"

The first is the important question. And Oak thinks he may have the answer.

As Oak approaches Mandrake Market, he has a startlingly good view of the storm lashing Insear. The lanes are empty. Merchants huddle in their homes, probably hoping the waves don't rise too high, that lightning doesn't strike too close. Hyacinthe follows the prince, carrying the walnut in his pocket, while Jack brings up the rear.

Together, they come to Mother Marrow's cottage, the thatch roof overgrown with moss. Oak stands in front of the door while the other two go around the back. Looking inside, he can see her sitting on a stump before a fire, poking at a bucket hanging over the flames.

Oak pounds on the hag's front door. Mother Marrow frowns and goes back to her fire. He bangs his fist again. This time she stands. Scowling, she waddles to the door on her bird talons.

"Prince." She squints. "Aren't you supposed to be at a party?"

"May I come in?"

She steps back so he can make his way into the room. "Quite a storm we're having."

Mother Marrow closes the door behind him and bolts it. He goes to the window, looking across at Insear while his fingers undo the latch. He can see nothing but rain and fog and hopes fervently that his family is no worse than he left them.

"You're holding Wren's sister for Bogdana, aren't you?" he asks, turning and walking toward the back of her cottage. "Your friend with the gold skin picked her up, but you're the one with the place here, so you're the one who's keeping her, right?"

Her eyebrows rise. "Beware, Prince of Elfhame, what you accuse Mother Marrow of doing. You want to keep her as your friend, don't you?"

"I'd rather discover her treachery," he says, pushing open the door to a back room.

"How dare you?" she says as he enters her bedroom. A canopied bed rests against one wall, bedsheets smoothed out over it. A few bones lie in a corner, old and dry. There's a little desk with a skull resting on top of several tomes. A cup of tea sits beside her bed, old enough that a dead moth floats atop the liquid.

Ignoring her, he pushes past to open one of the two other doors. It's a bathing chamber, with a large wooden tub in the middle of the room and a pump beside it. A drain rests off to one side. And a large trunk, like the one Jack described.

He flips it open. Empty.

Mother Marrow presses her lips together. "You are making a mistake, boy. Whatever you think I have, is it worth the curse I will put on you?"

As angry as he is, he doesn't hesitate. "Have you not already betrayed me once, when you knew exactly where Mellith's heart was and sent me on a fool's errand anyway? I am Prince Oak of the Greenbriar line, kin to the High Queen and King, heir to Elfhame. Perhaps you should be afraid."

Surprise flashes across her features. She stands in the hall, staring after him as he opens the final door. Another bed, this one piled with pillows in sloppy needlepoint, as though done by a child. Shelves on the wall, with books on them, a few that look as ancient as the tomes piled up in Mother Marrow's room, a few that are newer and less dusty. There are even a few paperbacks that obviously came from the mortal world. This must be the daughter's room.

But no Bex.

"Where is she?" he demands.

"Come," Mother Marrow says. "Sit. You're shivering. Some tea will cure that."

Oak feels as though his blood is boiling. If he is shivering, it is not from cold. "We don't have time for this."

Nonetheless, she busies herself, fussing with the bucket over her fire. Something floats in the water that might be kelp. The hag dunks the wooden ladle and dishes up two servings of tea into ceramic mugs. His has a screaming face on it.

Mother Marrow sips at her tea. Oak's nerves spark like live wires underneath his skin. Randalin is dead, and whatever signal he planned to give Bogdana that he murdered the royal family will never come. Eventually, Bogdana will realize that and execute the next stage of her plan. Wren will be helpless to stop her. She may have to help her. And he must find Bex before that happens.

The room is as it was before—stumps and a wooden chair before the fire and a threadbare chair off to one side. The same painted curio cabinet with its collection of beetle wings, potions, and poisons. The same nuts rattling in the bowl. The passageway to the rest of the empty cottage.

"What can you possibly offer Mother Marrow in exchange for what you seek?" the hag asks mildly.

Oak considers hags unfathomable beings, different from other Folk. Creators of objects, casters of curses. Part witch, part god. Solitary by nature, according to his instructors. But he heard the story of Bogdana and Mellith. And he remembers Mother Marrow's desire for Cardan to wed her child.

Maybe not always so solitary. Maybe not entirely strange.

"I want to save Wren," he says.

"A little bird," she says. "Caught in a storm."

Oak gives her a steady look. "You have a daughter. One you wanted to marry to the High King. You told me about her."

Mother Marrow gives a small grunt. "That was some time ago."

"Not so much time, I will wager, that you've forgotten the insult of the courtly Folk thinking that a hag's daughter wasn't fit for a throne."

There's a growl in her voice. "You best be careful if you expect to get something from me. And you best not try honey-mouthing me, either. I enjoy sweet words, but I will enjoy eating your tongue even more."

He inclines his head in acknowledgment. "What is it you want in exchange for Bex?"

She snorts. "You found no girl. What if none is here?"

"Give me three guesses," he says, though he is far from certain he can succeed at this. "Three guesses to where you put her, and if I'm right, you give her to me."

"And if you fail?" Her eyes glitter. He knows she is intrigued.

"Then I will return here at the new moon and serve for a year and a day. I will wash your floors. I will scour your cauldron and trim your toenails. So long as it harms no one, I will do whatever you ask as a servant in your household."

He can feel the air shift around him, feel the rightness of these words. He isn't using his charm in the usual way, but he allows himself to feel the contortions that power urges on him, the way it wants him to reshape himself for Mother Marrow. The gancanagh part of him knows that she will believe herself to be more wily than he, that her pride will urge her to take the bet.

"*Whatever* I ask of you, Prince of Elfhame?" Her grin is wide and delighted at the anticipation of his humiliation.

"So long as I guess wrong three times," he says.

"Then guess away," she says. "For all you know, I've turned her into the lid on a pot."

"I would feel very stupid if I didn't guess that first, then," Oak says.

Mother Marrow looks extremely pleased. "Wrong."

Two guesses. He's good at games, but it's hard to think when it feels as though there's no time left, when he can hear the storm in the background and the rattling of the . . .

He thinks of the white walnut cottage and Tiernan. And he recalls who gave Wren that gift. Getting to his feet, Oak walks to the cabinet. "She's trapped in one of the nuts."

Rage washes across Mother Marrow's face briefly, only to be replaced by a smile. "Very good, prince," she says. "Now tell me which one."

There has to be a half dozen in the bowl. "I guessed correctly," Oak protests. "I got the answer."

"Did you?" she says. "That would be like saying I turned her into a flower and not being sure if it was a rose or a tulip. Choose. If you're wrong, you lose."

He opens the cabinet, takes out the bowl, then goes to her kitchen for a knife.

"What are you doing?" she shouts. "Stop that!"

He selects a filbert and jams the point of the blade into the seam. It bursts open, scattering an array of dresses around the room, each in a different diaphanous color. They drift gently to the floor.

"Put that one down," she says as he reaches for a hazelnut. "Immediately."

"Will you give me the girl?" Oak demands. "Because I don't need you to get her out now. I will open every one of these and destroy them in the process."

"Foolish boy!" Mother Marrow says, then intones:

> *Be trapped inside with no escape*
> *Your fate is cast in acorn shape*
> *In the shadows, you'll dwell and wait*

The world seems to grow larger and smaller at the same time. Darkness rushes up and over him. He does, in fact, feel quite foolish. And very disoriented.

Inside of the nut are curved walls, polished to a high mahogany-like shine. The floor is covered in straw. Thin light seems to emanate from everywhere and nowhere at once.

He hears a sharp gasp from behind him. His hand goes automatically to his sword as he turns, and he has to force himself not to draw it from the rag sheath.

A mortal girl stands among baskets and barrels and jars, against the curved wall of her prison. In the dim glow, her skin is the pale brown of early fall leaves, and she wears a white puffer coat, which swallows her up. Her arms are crossed over each other as though she's holding herself for comfort or warmth or to keep herself from coming apart.

"Don't scream," Oak says, holding up his hands to show that they're empty.

"Who are you, and why are you here?" the girl asks.

Oak takes a breath and tries to think of what he ought to say. He doesn't want to frighten her, but he can see from the way she's looking at his hooves and horns that it's possible that ship has already sailed. "I'd like to believe that we're going to be friends," he says. "If you tell me who you are, I will do the same."

The mortal girl hesitates. "There was a witch, and she brought me here to see my sister. But I haven't seen her yet. The witch says she's in trouble."

"A witch...," he echoes. He wonders how aware the girl has been of the passage of time. "You're Wren's sister, Bex?"

"Bex, yes." A small smile pulls at her mouth. "You know Wren?"

"Since we were quite young," he says, and Bex relaxes a little. "Do you know what she is? What I am?"

"Faeries." *Monsters*, her expression says. "I keep rowan on me at all times. And iron."

When Oak was a child, living in the mortal world with his oldest sister, Vivi, he was super excited to show her girlfriend, Heather, magic. He took his glamour off and was crushed when she looked at him in horror, as though he wasn't the same little boy she took to the park or tickled. He thought of the news as a surprise present, but it turned out to be a jump scare.

He didn't realize then how vulnerable a mortal in Faerie can be. He should have, though, living with two mortal sisters. He should have, but he didn't.

"That's good," he says, thinking of the burn of the iron bars in the Citadel. "Rowan to break spells, and iron to burn us."

"Your turn," Bex says. "Who are you?"

"Oak," he says.

"The prince," Bex says flatly, all the friendliness gone from her voice. He nods.

She takes two steps forward and spits at his feet. "The witch told me about you," Bex says. "That you steal hearts, and you were going to steal my sister's. That if I ever saw you, I ought to run."

Used to people liking him, or at least used to having to court dislike, Oak is a little stunned. "I would never—" he begins, but she's already moving across the room, flattening herself against the curved wall as though he's going to come after her.

There's a sound in the distance, loud and sharp. The walls shake.

"What's that?" she demands, stumbling.

"My friends," Oak says. "I hope."

Bright light flashes, and the prison tilts to one side. Bex is thrown against him, and then they're both on the floor of Mother Marrow's cottage.

Hyacinthe has a crossbow pointed at Mother Marrow. The window Oak unlatched is open, and Jack is inside. The kelpie stoops down to lift an acorn, unbroken.

Mother Marrow glowers. "A bad-mannered lot," she grouses.

"You found her!" says Jack. "And what a toothsome morsel—I mean *mortal*."

Bex jumps up and pulls an antique-looking wrench from her back pocket—that must be the iron to which she was referring. She appears to be considering hitting the kelpie over the head with it.

In two strides, Oak is across the room. He claps his hand against the girl's mouth hard enough for her teeth to press against his palm.

"Listen to me," he says, feeling like a bully almost certainly because he was behaving like one. "I am not going to hurt Wren. Or you. But I don't have time to fight you, nor do I have time to chase you if you run."

She struggles against him, kicking.

He leans down and whispers in her ear, "I am here for Wren's sake, and I am going to take you to her. And if you try to get away again, remember this—the easiest way to make you behave would be to make you love me, and you don't want that."

She must really not, because she goes slack in his arms.

He takes his hand from her mouth, and she pulls away but doesn't scream. Instead, she studies him, breathing hard.

"I should have known something was wrong when you knew my name," Bex says. "Wren would have never told you that. She says that if you know my name, it would give you power over me."

He gives a surprised laugh. "I wish," he says, then winces. He should have found a better way to phrase that, one that didn't make him sound quite so much like an actual monster. But there is little for him to do but forge on. "You need someone's full name, their true name. Mortals don't have those. Not in the way that we do."

Bex's gaze shifts to the door of the cottage and then back, calculation in her eyes.

"Wren is in trouble," he says. "Some people are using your safety to make her do what they want. Which is going to mean killing a lot of my people."

"And you want to use me to stop her," Bex accuses.

That's a harsh way of putting it, but true. "Yes," he says. "I don't want my own sisters hurt. I don't want anyone hurt. Not Wren and not you."

"And you'll take me to her?" Bex asks.

He nods.

"Then I'll go with you," she says. "For now."

Oak turns his gaze to Mother Marrow. "I am going to grant you this, for whatever I owe you. Should I survive, I will not tell the High King and Queen that you took Bogdana's part against them. But now my debt is dismissed."

"And if she wins, what then?" Mother Marrow says.

"Then I will be dead," Oak tells her. "And you are more than welcome to spit on the moss and rocks where my body fell."

It is at that moment that the front door cracks in two. The smell of ozone and burning wood fills the air. The storm hag stands there as though summoned by the speaking of her name.

Lightning crackles between her hands. Her eyes are wild. "You!" cries Bogdana as she spots Bex beside the prince.

"Take the mortal to Wren," Oak shouts to Jack and Hyacinthe, drawing his sword. "Go!"

Then he rushes at the storm hag.

Electricity hits his blade, scorching his fingers. Despite the pain, he manages to swing, slashing through her cloak.

Out of the corner of his eye, Oak sees Jack lift Bex and push her feet through the window. From the other side, Hyacinthe grabs hold of her.

Bogdana reaches for Oak with her daggerlike fingers. "I am going to enjoy stripping the skin from your flesh."

He swings, blocking her grab. Then he ducks to her left. She takes another step toward him.

By now, Hyacinthe and Jack are out of sight, Bex with them.

A move occurs to Oak—a risky move, but one that might work. One that might get him to Wren faster than anything else. "What if I surrender?" he asks.

He can see her slight hesitation. "Surrender?"

"I'll sheathe my sword and go with you willingly." He shrugs, lowering his blade a fraction. "If you promise to bring me straight to Wren with no tricks."

"No tricks?" she echoes. "That's a fine thing coming from you."

"I want to see her," he says, hoping he seems convincing. "I want to hear from her lips what she's done and what she wants. And you don't want to leave her alone too long."

Bogdana regards him with a sly expression. "Very well, prince." She reaches out and runs her long claws over his cheek so lightly that they only scrape his bruises. "If I can't have the sister, then you'll be my prize. And I'll have you well-seasoned by the time I end you."

Bogdana has one clawed hand around his wrist as she tugs him toward the water and the storm.

"I thought we were going back to Wren," he says.

"Ah, did you think she was still here on Insmoor? No, I brought her to Insear. We were there together when Mother Marrow signaled me."

He should have suspected Mother Marrow had a way to let Bogdana know her hostage was being released and regrets his generosity with her. All he is likely to get in the way of gratitude is a curse. "On Insear?" he says, staying with the part that matters. If Wren and Bogdana made it to Insear, what did that mean for his family?

"Come," Bogdana says, stepping off the edge of the rocks. A swirling wind catches and lifts her, as it caught and lifted the ship. The storm hag's robes billow. She gives a sharp tug on Oak's wrist. He follows her, his hooves walking on what seems like nothing but knots and eddies of air.

The fog parts, and droplets of rain do not fall in their path as the wind carries them over the sea.

Minutes later, they drop onto the black rocks of Insear. Oak slips and nearly falls, attempting to find his footing.

And in front of him, he sees Wren and Jude.

They are squared off, his sister holding a sword in one hand, her eyes shining. Most of her brown hair has come out of its braids and hangs loose and wet around her face. Her cheeks are pink with cold, and the bottom of her dress is raggedly cut away, as though she wants to be sure it won't trip her.

Wren wears the clothes she wore at the hunt, the same clothes she wore on Insmoor. They hang on her, as though there is even less of her now, as though more of her has been eaten away. Her cheekbones are sharper, the hollows beneath them more pronounced. Her expression is as bleak as the rain-streaked sky. As bleak as when she was going to let him stab her.

Behind his sister are four other Folk. The Roach, a dagger in one hand and a fresh wound on his brow. Two archers—knights that Oak recognizes, holding longbows. And a courtier, dressed in velvet and lace, hair and beard in braids, hands gripping a hammer. They are all soaked to the bone.

On Wren's side are more than a dozen of her soldiers—armored, swords at their belts and bows in their hands.

"*Jude*," Oak says, but she doesn't even seem to hear him.

As he watches, Wren lunges toward Jude, grabbing for her unsheathed blade. Wren's blood smears over the bare steel where the edge catches her palm. But before the sword can bite more deeply, before Jude can wrench it from her grip, the metal begins to melt. It pools on the ground, hissing where it hits water, cooling into jagged metal shapes. Unmade.

Jude takes a step back, dropping the hilt as though it bit her.

"Nice trick." Her voice isn't quite steady.

"I see you have things well in hand, daughter," Bogdana calls to Wren. "I have the prince. Now, where is the High King?"

"Shoot them," Jude snaps, ignoring Bogdana's words and instead focusing on the falcons transforming into soldiers. "Shoot *all* our enemies."

Arrows fly, soaring through the air in a beautiful and deadly arc.

Before they can fall, Wren raises a hand. She makes a small motion, as though brushing away a gnat. The arrows break and scatter like twigs caught in a harsh wind.

Jude has pulled two daggers from her bodice, both of them curved and sharp as razors.

Oak steps away from Bogdana, hand on the pommel of his own sword. "Stop!" he shouts.

The storm hag sneers. "Don't be foolish, boy; you're surrounded."

Several of the falcons have notched their own bows, and though Oak believes Wren doesn't want more death, if they fire, he isn't at all sure she'd stop her own archers' arrows from striking. It would be a drain on her power, and her falcons would take it much amiss.

"I have your sister," he calls, because that's the important thing. That's what she needs to know. "I have Bex."

Wren turns, her eyes wide, hair plastered to her neck. Lips parted, he can see her sharp teeth.

"He's stolen her from us," Bogdana shouts. "Believe nothing he says. He would use her to fetter you, child."

Jude looks across at them, eyebrows raised. "Blackmail, brother? Impressive."

"That's not—" he starts.

"You have some decisions to make," Jude tells him. "The falcons follow your lady. But perhaps she wants your head on a pike as much as the storm hag does. Give her an inch, and she might take your life."

Bogdana answers before Oak can. "Ah, Queen of Elfhame, you see how useless your weapons are. You're married to the faithless child of a faithless line. Your crown was secured with my daughter's blood."

"My crown was secured with a lot of people's blood." Jude turns to her archers. "Ready another volley."

"You cannot so easily hurt us with sharp sticks," Wren says, but her gaze keeps drifting to Oak. She must be aware that this is his family and he has hers.

Wren's magic harrowed her before they got to Elfhame. She sagged in Oak's arms just the day before. She cannot stop arrows endlessly. He's not sure what she can do.

"Randalin is dead," the prince tells the storm hag. "He conspired against Elfhame. He poisoned the Ghost. He planned this coup long before he tried to involve you in it. There is no reason to let him drag you down, too."

"Don't let him manipulate you," Bogdana says, as though it's Wren he's trying to convince. "He's using you just as Randalin hoped to— Randalin, who wanted to help put Prince Oak on the throne. See how the councilor was rewarded for his loyalty? And this is the person you would trust not to use your sister against you?"

Once Bex was safe, Oak thought Wren would be free of Bogdana's control. And she is, but that doesn't mean she's free. *He* has Bex. *He* can control Wren the way Bogdana did. He could make her crawl to him as assuredly as if strips of the bridle were digging into her skin.

He doesn't know how to convince her that's not what he intends to do. "You care for your sister. And I, mine. Let's end this. Tell Bogdana to stop the storm. Tell your falcons to stand down. This can be over."

Bogdana sneers. "He gave the mortal to Jack of the Lakes. Jack's likely drowned her by now."

Wren's eyes widen. "You didn't."

"He's bringing her to you," Oak says, realizing how bad it sounds. Not only that, but he isn't sure it's possible for Jack to bring Bex here, if he even guesses where they are. Oak nearly drowned, getting across.

"You believe that, girl?" snaps Bogdana. "They would have delighted if one of their arrows had pierced your heart. Let's find the High King and cut his throat. Your falcons can watch the prince."

Oak may be able to draw and strike before Bogdana can stop him, but if Wren tells her archers to fire, he'll be dead. He has no magical cloak to hide behind.

Jude shifts her stance. "Anyone who goes toward that tent, kill them," she orders her remaining Folk. "And you, little queen, better not interfere. If Oak has your sister, I assume you want her back in one piece."

"That's not helping, Jude," he says.

"I forgot," she says. "We're not on the same side."

"You're hiding the High King from me?" Bogdana asks. "He must be the coward everyone says, letting you fight his battles."

Oak sees rage flash across Jude's face, watches her swallow it. "I don't mind fighting."

Cardan *isn't* a coward, though. Hurt though he was, he picked up a weapon when Randalin's knights turned on them. How badly wounded must he be not to be here now—not to even have given Jude his cloak. Cardan was bleeding when Oak left—but he was conscious. He was giving orders.

"So before this battle happens and we all have to pick sides, I have a question." Jude's gaze sharpens. She's stalling, Oak realizes but has no idea what she can gain from it. "If you wanted the throne for Wren so badly, why not let her marry him? She was supposed to marry Prince Oak this very evening, isn't that so? Wouldn't that have given her a straight path to the throne? After she became High Queen, all she'd have to do is what she intended all those years ago—bite out his throat."

Perhaps Jude just meant to remind him not to trust Wren.

"As though *you* would ever let Prince Oak come to his throne," Bogdana sneers.

"Generally speaking, one doesn't have to *let* one's heir do the inheriting," says Jude. "Of course, perhaps you're acting now because you had no choice. Maybe Randalin moved ahead without consulting you. You meant for the marriage to happen, but he set the thing in motion before you managed it."

Bogdana's lip curls. "Do you think I care about the treason of one of your ministers? Your courtly intrigues are of little consequence. No, with Wren by my side, I can return Insear to the bottom of the sea. I can sink all the isles."

It would destroy Wren to do that. The magic would unmake *her* along with the land.

"We can all die together," Oak says. "In one grand, glorious final act of stupidity fit for a ballad."

Wren's hands tremble, and she presses them together to conceal it. He notices how purple her lips have gone. The way her skin looks pale and mottled, such that even the blue color of it cannot hide that something is wrong.

Unmaking the sword and the arrows must have cost her—and he was uncertain if that was all she'd done since the hunt.

"I was the first of the hags," Bogdana returns, her voice like the crash of waves. "The most powerful of the witches. My voice is the howl of the wind, my hair the lashing rain, my nails the hot strike of lightning that rends flesh from bone. When I gave Mab a portion of my power, it came with a price. I wanted my child to have a place among the Courtly Folk, to sit on a throne and wear a crown. But that's not what happened." Bogdana pauses. "I was tricked by a queen once. I will not be tricked again."

"Mab is gone," Oak says, trying to reason with her. Hoping that he can find the real words, the *true* words, ones that will be persuasive because they are right. "You're still here. And you have Wren again. You're the one with everything to lose now and nothing to—"

"Quiet, boy!" Bogdana says. "Do not try your power on me."

"It lets me know what you want." He glances at Wren. "I don't need to charm you to tell you this isn't the way to get it."

Bogdana laughs. "And if Wren wants her throne? Will you stand aside as she plans to take it? Will you help? Let your sister die to prove this love you claim to have for her?" She turns to Jude. "And you? Bluff all you want, but you have only four Folk behind you—half of them probably contemplating turning on you. And a brother whose loyalty is in question.

"Surely your people do not want to face three times as many soldiers, all of whom can shoot at will while you return no volley. I would greatly reward boldness. Should one of them kill the King of Elfhame—"

"What if I give you Oak's head instead of Cardan's?" Jude asks suddenly.

The prince turns toward his sister. She can't really mean that. But Jude's eyes are cold, and the knife in her hand is very sharp.

"And why would I accept such a poor offer?" asks the storm hag. "We had him for months. We could have executed him anytime we wanted. I could have killed him on Insmoor less than an hour ago. Besides, wasn't it you who reminded me how much easier to establish Wren as the new High Queen if she marries your heir?"

"If Oak were dead, that would thin the Greenbriar line by half," says Jude. "Mere chance might do the rest. Cardan was hurt—he might not survive the night. I schemed my way to the throne, despite being mortal. Make me your ally instead of him. I am the better bet. I know Elfhame politics, and I am mercenary enough to make practical choices."

He knows she's not serious about her offer. But that doesn't mean she's not serious about wanting to kill him.

How foolish Oak has been, making himself seem like Cardan's enemy. How can he prove to Jude now, here, that he has always been on her side? That he never plotted with Randalin. That he was trying to catch the conspirators so that something like this could never happen.

But how could Jude ever guess what Oak was planning to do when she has no idea what he's already done?

"Oak wouldn't fight you," Wren says.

Bogdana's eyes glitter. "Oh, I think he will. What if I make the prince this bargain—win, and I will let Wren keep you as a pet. I will let you live. I'll even let you marry her, if she so desires."

"That's very generous," he says. "Since Wren can already marry whomsoever she wants."

"Not if you're dead," says Bogdana.

"You want me to fight my own sister?" he asks, voice unsteady.

"I very much do." Bogdana's lips pull into a grim, awful smile. "High Queen, I will not merely accept the prince's head, struck off by one of your soldiers. Just as I was tricked into murdering my own kin, it will be justice to see you kill yours. But I will spare the one of you who kills the other. Let the High Queen abdicate her throne, and I won't chase her. She may return to the mortal world and live out the brief span of her days."

"And Cardan?" Jude asks.

The storm hag laughs. "How about this? Take him, and I'll give you a head start."

"Done," Jude says. "So long as you'll let me take my people, too."

"If you win," Bogdana says. "If you run."

"Don't do this," Wren whispers.

Oak takes a step forward, his head spinning. He ignores the way Wren is looking at him, as though he is a lamb come straight to the slaughter, too stupid to run.

As he walks closer to his sister, an arrow hits the ground beside him from Jude's camp. A warning shot.

He really hopes that was a warning shot and not a miss.

"Prince Oak," says Jude. "You're making some very dangerous decisions lately."

He takes a deep breath. "I understand why you'd think I was planning to betray—"

"Answer me on the field," Jude says, cutting him off. "Ready for our duel?"

Wren steps forward. The rain has plastered her long, wild hair to her throat and chest. "Oak, wait."

Bogdana grabs her arm. "Leave them to sort out their own family affair."

Wren wrenches free. "I warned you. You can't keep me your thrall. Not without Bex."

"You think not?" says the storm hag. "Child, I will have my revenge, and you are too weak to stop me. We both know that. Just as we know that the falcons will listen to me once you collapse. And you will—you overextended yourself when you broke the curse on the troll kings and again on the ship, and you've used your power twice today already. There's not enough of you left to face me. There's barely enough of you to remain standing."

Jude is adjusting her dress, slicing it so that she can tie the sides of the skirt into makeshift pants. What is her game?

Had they not been isolated on Insear, the army of Elfhame would have easily cut down Bogdana and Wren and her falcons. But so long as Bogdana's storm keeps them isolated, so long as Wren stops arrows, Jude won't be able to keep them from Cardan's tent forever.

Jude will never abdicate, though. She will never run, not even if Cardan is dead.

Of course, if Cardan *is* dead, Jude might well blame Oak.

He wants to see hesitation in his sister's face, but her expression reminds him of Madoc's before a battle.

Someone is going to kill you. Better it be me.

Oak thinks about being a child, spoiled and vain, making trouble. It shames him to think of smashing things in Vivi's apartment, crying for his mother, when they took him there for his protection. It shames him more to think of ensorcelling his sister and the delight he felt at the red sting of her cheek after she slapped herself. He knew it hurt and, later, felt guilty about it.

But he didn't understand Jude's pride and how he shamed her. How that was the far worse crime.

Jude attributes most of her worst impulses to their father, sparing Oak's provocation. Sparing Oriana, too, who never made room in her heart for a little mortal girl who lost her mother.

Still, that anger and resentment have to be in her somewhere. Waiting for this moment.

"I heard that Madoc offered the High King a duel," says Bogdana. "But he was too much a coward to accept."

"My father should have asked me," Jude says, unbothered by the insult to her beloved.

"I don't want to fight with you," Oak warns.

"Of course you do," Jude says. "Van, bring me my favorite sword since Wren ruined the other one. I left it where I changed clothes."

The prince looks over to see the Roach, his mouth grim, walk toward the tent. A few moments later, he returns with a sword wrapped in heavy black cloth.

"I wasn't part of Randalin's conspiracy," Oak tries again.

But Jude only gives her brother a grim smile. "Well, then, what a wonderful opportunity for you to prove your loyalty and die for the High King."

The Roach unwraps a blade, but Oak can barely pay attention. Panic has taken hold of him. He cannot fight her. And if he does, he absolutely cannot lose control.

"There are twin swords," Jude says. "Heartseeker and Heartsworn. Heartsworn can cut through anything. It once cut through an otherwise invulnerable serpent's head and broke a curse. You can see why I'd like it."

"That hardly seems fair," Oak says, his eye on the sword at last. It's finely crafted, as beautiful as one might expect one made in a great smith's forge to be. And then he understands. He lets out his breath in a rush.

Jude moves into an easy stance. She's good. She's always been good. "What makes you think I am interested in fairness?"

"Fine," says Oak. "But you won't find me an easy opponent."

"Yes, I saw you inside. That was impressive," says his sister. "As was your cleverness. Apologies for not noticing what I should have long before."

"Apology accepted," says Oak with a nod.

Jude rushes at the prince. Oak parries, circling. "Cardan's okay, then?" he asks as quietly as he is able.

"He'll have an impressive scar," she returns, voice low. "I mean, not as impressive as several of mine, obviously."

Oak lets out a breath. "Obviously."

"But what he's really doing is getting the courtiers and servants off Insear," Jude goes on softly. "Through the Undersea. His ex-girlfriend is still queen there. He's leading them through the deep."

Oak glances toward the tents. The ones that Jude threatened to murder anyone who went near. The ones that are empty.

"Swordplay is a dance, they say." Jude raises her voice as she slashes her blade through the air. "One, two, three. One, two, three."

"You're terrible at dancing," Oak says, forcing himself to stay in the moment. He will not lose himself in the fight. He will not let himself go.

She grins and moves in, nearly tripping him.

"Wren was being blackmailed," he tells her, dodging a blow almost a moment too late, distracted by trying to think of what he can say to make her understand. "The thing with her sister."

"I am not sure you know your enemies from your allies."

"*I* do," Oak says. "And the falcons follow her."

"Tell me that you're sure of her," Jude says. "Really sure."

Oak thrusts, parries. Their swords clang together. If Jude really were fighting with Heartsworn, it would have sliced his blade in half. But Oak recognized the sword the Roach brought—it was Nightfell, forged by her mortal father.

As soon as Jude lifted it, Oak understood her game at last.

With as few soldiers as they had, she knew they had to get close to their enemy. Knew they needed the edge of surprise.

"I'm sure," says Oak.

"Okay." Jude presses her attack, forcing Oak back, closer and closer to the storm hag. "This dance I'm good at. One. Two. *Three.*"

Together they turn. Oak presses the tip of his sword to one side of Bogdana's throat. Jude's goes to the other.

The falcons turn their weapons toward Oak and Jude. Pull back bowstrings. On the other side, Elfhame's knights are ready to return a volley of arrows. If anyone fires, as close as they are to Bogdana, the storm hag is likely to be hit. But that doesn't mean they won't be hit, too.

"He tells me we can trust you," Jude says to Wren.

"Hold," Wren tells the falcons, her voice shaking a little. He can see in her face that she, despite everything, expected to find one of their blades to her throat. "Lower your weapons, and the High Court will do the same."

"Get away from her!" a voice comes from one of the tents, and Bex steps into view. She's soaked through and shivering, and when she sees them, her eyes go wide. "Wren?"

Horror clouds Wren's expression as Bex steps out of the shelter of the canvas into the rain. One hand goes to cover her mouth automatically, to hide her sharp teeth. Wren never wanted her family to look at her and see a monster.

Oak notes her swaying a little with nothing nearby to grasp to keep her upright. Wren has been drinking up far too much magic. She must feel as though she is fraying at the edges. She may *be* fraying at the edges.

"Bex," Wren says so quietly that he doubts the girl can hear the words over the storm.

The mortal takes a step toward her.

"She's actually here," Wren says, sounding awed. "She's okay."

"Oh no," says Bogdana. "That girl isn't your kin. You're my child. Mine. And you, boy—"

Lightning arcs down out of the sky, toward Oak. He steps back, lifting his sword automatically, as though he could block it like a blow. For a moment, everything around him goes white. And then he sees Wren lunge in front of him, her hair wild and wind-tossed around her head, electricity flashing inside her as though fireflies are trapped beneath her skin.

She caught the bolt.

Her lips curve, and she gives an odd, uncharacteristic laugh.

Bogdana's lips pull back in a hiss of astonishment. But she's accomplished this—Oak no longer has his sword to her throat, and even Jude has taken a step back.

The storm hag shakes her head. "You *imprisoned* the prince. You threw him into your dungeon. He tricked you. You *can't* trust him."

Wren slumps to her knees, as though her legs collapsed beneath her.

"This is done," Oak warns Bogdana. "You're done."

"Do not think to choose him over me," Bogdana snaps, ignoring him. "Your sister is a game piece. He'll use that mortal girl to manipulate you to do exactly what he wants, rather than use her, as I did, to help you take what is yours. And she is in more danger from him than she could ever be from me."

Wren's hands still spark with the aftereffects of the bolt. "You keep telling me that others will do to me what you have already done. I know what it is to want something so much that you would rather have the shadow of it than nothing, even if that means you will never have the real thing. And love is not that.

"You could have trusted me to choose my allies. Could have trusted how I would decide to use my powers. But no, you had to bring my unsis—my *sister* here and show her all the things I was afraid she would see. Show her the *me* that I was afraid for her to know. And if she spurns me, I am certain you will glory in it, the proof that I have no one but you."

Wren looks across the mud at Bex. "Prince Oak will make sure you get home."

"But—" the girl begins.

"You can trust him," Wren says.

"No, child," Bogdana snaps. Thunder rumbles. Dust devils begin to swirl around her, sucking up sand. "We have come too far. It's too late. They will never forgive you. He will never forgive you."

Oak shakes his head. "There is nothing to forgive. Wren tried to warn me. She would have given up her life to keep from being your pawn."

Bogdana remains focused on Wren. "Do you really think you're a match for my power? You caught one bolt of lightning, and you're already coming apart."

The falcons move toward their queen, turning their weapons on the storm hag for the first time.

Wren gives a wan smile. "I was never meant to survive. If we went through with this battle and the one that would inevitably come next, if you forced me to annihilate all the magic thrown at us, there would be nothing left of me. The magic that knits me together would have been eaten away."

"No—" Bogdana begins, but she can't say the rest. Can't, because it would have been a lie.

"You're right about one thing, though. It's too late." Wren opens her arms, as though to embrace the night. As she does, it seems that the whole storm—the spiraling wind, the lightning—recognizes her as its center.

Oak realizes what she's doing, but he has no idea how to stop her. And he understands now the despair that others have felt at the sight of him throwing himself at something, not caring for the consequences. "Wren, please, no!"

She takes the storm into herself, drinking down the rain that pelts her, letting it be absorbed into her skin. Wind whips her hair, then stills. Dark clouds dissipate, blowing away on her breath until they are no more.

The pale moon shines down on Elfhame again. The wind is still. The waves crash no more against the shores.

With the last of her might, Bogdana sweeps her hand at Wren.

A bolt of lightning cracks through the sky to strike her in the chest.

Wren staggers back, bending over with the pain of it. And when she looks up, her eyes are alight.

She glows with power. Her body rises into the air, hair floating around her. Her eyes open wide. Hovering in the sky, she's lit from within. Her body is radiant, so bright that Oak can see the woven sticks where bones ought to be, the stones of her eyes, the jagged pieces of shell used to make her teeth. And her black heart, dense with raw power.

He can feel it like a gravitational force, pulling him toward her. And he can feel when it stops.

CHAPTER

24

Wren collapses, her skin bruised and pale, her hair plastered across her face. Her eyes closed. The stillness of her is too profound for sleep.

Oak cannot seem to do anything but look at her. He cannot move. He cannot think.

Bex kneels beside Wren, pressing on her chest, counting under her breath. "Come on," she mutters between compressions.

Bogdana leans down to place her overlong fingers on Wren's cheek. Without her power, she looks old. Even her long nails look brittle. "Get away from her, human girl."

"I'm trying to save my sister," Bex snaps.

Jude stands behind the mortal. "Is she breathing?"

"*You destroyed her,*" Oak snarls at Bogdana, holding his sword pommel so hard that he feels the edge of the hilt dig into his hand. "You had a chance to undo what you did, to save your only daughter. No one tricked you this time. You did the very thing you knew would kill her."

"She betrayed me," Bogdana says, but there is a hitch in her voice.

"You cared nothing for her," Oak shouts. "You terrorized her so that she would come into a power that you could use. You let those monsters in the Court of Teeth hurt her. And now she's dead."

The hag narrows her eyes. "And you, boy? Are you so much better? You're the one who brought her here. What would you do to save her?"

"Anything!" he shouts.

"No!" Jude says, nearly as quickly, putting her body between his and the storm hag's. "No, he would not." She takes Oak by the shoulders and shakes him. "You can't just keep throwing yourself at things as though you don't matter."

"She matters more," he says.

"It's possible that Wren can be woken," says Bogdana.

"Deceive me in this, and I will bury you, so do I vow," Oak says.

"Her heart is stopped," says Bogdana. "But hag children don't need beating hearts. Just magical ones."

Oak recalls the Ghost giving him a warning when they were aboard the ship. *It is said that a hag's power comes from the part of them that's missing. Each one has a cold stone or wisp of cloud or ever-burning flame where their hearts ought to be.*

He'd dismissed it as a piece of superstition. Even Faerie found hags and their powers troubling enough to make up legends about them. And the Ghost had clearly been worried over Oak's plan to marry one.

The prince lowers himself back to the ground. He kneels in the wet sand on the other side of where Bex is working. She scowls at him as she counts. He puts his hand on Wren's chest. Desperately hoping the storm hag is right. But he feels not a single thrum of a pulse nor the movement of breath in her lungs. What he does feel is magic. There's a deep well of it, curled up inside her body.

Pulling back his hand, he doesn't know what to think.

Mother Marrow told him that Wren's magic was turned inside out. A power meant to be used for creation, warped until all it could do was destroy, annihilate, and unmake. Twisted on itself, a snake eating its own tail. But perhaps taking apart the storm and being struck twice by lightning was more than even her magic could devour. Maybe some of it spilled over.

Though she set all her matches alight and burned up with them, maybe something new could emerge from the ashes.

How many girls like Wren can there be, made from sticks and imbued with a cursed heart? She's made of magic, more than any of them.

"What will wake her?" he demands.

"That I do not know," Bogdana says, not meeting his eyes.

Jude raises both brows. "Helpful."

Oak remembers the story Oriana told him long ago about his mother. *Once upon a time, there was a woman who was so beautiful that none could resist her. When she spoke, it seemed that the hearts of those who listened beat for her alone.*

But how could he persuade someone who might not even be able to hear him?

"Wren," Oak says, letting the burr come into his voice. "Open your eyes. Please."

Nothing happens. Oak tries again, letting loose the full force of his honey-tongued charm. The nearby Folk watch him with a new, strange intensity. The air seems to ripple with power. Bex sucks in a breath, leaning toward him.

"Come back to me," he says.

But Wren is silent and still.

Oak lets go of his power, cursing himself. He glances up helplessly at Jude, who looks back at him and shakes her head. "I'm sorry." It is a very human thing for her to say.

He lets his head fall forward until his forehead is touching Wren's.

Gathering her in his arms, he studies the hollowness of her cheeks and the thinness of her skin. Presses a finger to the edge of her mouth.

Oak thought his magic was just finding what people wanted to hear and saying it in the way they wanted, but since he's let himself really use the power, he discovered that he can use it to find truth. And for once, he needs to tell her the truth. "I thought love was a fascination, or a desire to be around someone, or wanting to make them happy. I believed it just happened, like a slap to the face, and left the way the sting from such a blow fades. That's why it was easy for me to believe it could be false or manipulated or influenced by magic.

"Until I met you, I didn't understand to feel loved, one has to feel known. And that, outside of my family, I had never really loved because I hadn't bothered to know the other person. But I know you. And you have to come back to me, Wren, because no one gets us but us. You know why you're not a monster, but I might be. I know why throwing me in your dungeon meant there was still something between us. We are messes and we are messed up and I don't want to go through this world without the one person I can't hide from and who can't hide from me.

"Come back," he says again, tears burning the back of his throat. "You want and you want and you want, remember? Well, wake up and take what you want."

He presses his mouth against her forehead.

And startles when he hears her draw in a breath. Her eyes open, and for a moment, she stares up at him.

"Wren?" Bex says, and smacks Oak on the shoulder. "What did you do?" Then she pulls the prince into her arms and hugs him hard.

Jude is staring, hand to her mouth.

Bogdana stays back, glowering, perhaps hoping that no one noticed she rent her garments with her nails as she watched and waited.

"I'm cold," Wren whispers, and alarm rings through him like the sounding of a bell. She could walk barefoot through the snow and not have it hurt her. He never heard her complain of even the most frigid temperatures.

Oak stands, lifting Wren in his arms. She feels too light, but he is reassured by her breath ghosting across his skin, the rise and fall of her chest.

He still cannot, however, hear the beat of her heart.

With the storm stopped, it seems that all of Elfhame has forded the distance between Insear and Insmire. There are boats aplenty, and soldiers. Grima Mog's second-in-command is barking orders.

Bex scavenges a blanket from one of the tents, and Oak manages to bundle Wren in it. Then he carries her to a boat and commandeers it to take him back across so he can bring her to the palace. The journey is a blur of panic, of frantic questions, plodding steps. Finally, he carries her into his rooms. By then, her body is shivering, and he tries not to let terror leak into his voice as he speaks to her softly, explaining where they are and how she will be safe.

He puts Wren in his bed, then pushes it close by the fire and piles blankets on top of her. It seems to make no difference to her shuddering.

Herbalists and bonesetters come and go. *Like a banshee*, one of them says. *Like a sluagh*, says another. *Like nothing I've ever seen before*, says a third.

Wren's skin has become dry and oddly dull. Even her hair looks faded. It seems as though she is sinking so deeply into herself that he cannot follow.

Oak sits with her throughout that night and all through the next day, refusing to budge as people come in and out. Oriana tries to prize him from Wren's side to eat something, but he won't leave.

Bex comes and goes. That afternoon, she sits for a while, holding her sister's hand and crying as though she were already gone.

Tiernan brings them both hard cheese, fennel tea, and some bread. He also brings news of Bogdana, who is being held in the prisons of Hollow Hall, soon to be moved into the Tower of Forgetting.

Bex makes up a bed for herself on the floor out of scavenged cushions. Oak gives her one of his robes, all of gold and spider silk, to wear.

As night comes on, Wren seems like a husk of herself. When he touches her arm, it feels papery under his fingers. A wasp's nest instead of flesh. He draws his hand back and tries to convince himself of something other than the worst.

"She's not getting better, is she?" the mortal girl says.

"I don't know," Oak says, the words hard to get out, so close to being a lie.

Bex frowns. "I think I met your, uh, father. He was telling me about the Court of Teeth."

Well, he should know all about that place, Oak thinks but doesn't say.

"I guess I can see why Wren thought she couldn't come back to my family, and it wasn't because—I don't know, not because she didn't want to see us."

"She was willing to do a lot for your sake," Oak says, thinking of all the ways Wren must have struggled to free them from Bogdana's trap, how despair must have closed in around her when she realized she was going to have to choose between an agonizing death for her sister and the deaths of many others.

"I just wish—" Bex says. "I wish I'd talked to her when I first saw her sneaking into the house. I wish I'd followed her. I wish I'd done more, done *something*."

Over the past few days, Oak has been making a comprehensive and damning list of all the better choices he could have made. He's wondering whether he ought to admit them out loud when Bex screams.

He rockets to his feet, not sure what she's seeing.

And then he does. Inside of the husk of Wren, something is moving. Shifting beneath her skin.

"What is that?" Bex says, scuttling back until she hits the wall.

Oak shakes his head. The dullness of Wren's skin suddenly makes him think of the shed casings that spiders leave behind. He reaches out an unsteady hand—

Wren moves again, and this time, the papery flesh tears. Skin emerges, vibrant blue. Her body cracks open like a chrysalis.

Bex makes an alarmed sound from the floor.

From within, a new Wren emerges. Her skin the same cerulean blue, her eyes the same soft green. Even her teeth are the same, sharp as ever when she parts her lips to take a breath of air. But on her back are two feathered wings, light blue gray at the tips, with darker feathers closer to her body, and when they unfurl, they are large enough to canopy him, Bex, and Wren.

She stands, naked and reborn, looking around the room with the sharp gaze of a goddess, deciding whom to bless and whom to smite.

Her eyes settle on the prince.

"You have wings," he says, awestruck and foolish. He sounds as though he took a hard blow to the head. That isn't far from how he feels.

Astonished joy has robbed him of all cleverness.

"Wren?" Bex whispers.

Wren's attention swings to her, and he can see the mortal girl flinch a little under the weight of it.

"You don't have to be afraid," Wren says, although she looks positively terrifying right then. Even Oak is a little frightened of her.

Bex draws in a breath and pushes herself off the floor. Picking up a fallen blanket, she hands it to her sister, then gives Oak a pointed look. "You should probably stop staring at her like you never saw a naked girl with wings before."

Oak blinks and turns away, shamefaced. "Right," he says, heading for the door. "I'll leave you both."

He looks back once, but all he sees are feathers.

In the hall, a guard comes immediately to attention.

"Your Highness," he says. "Tiernan went to rest a few hours ago. Shall I send for him?"

"No need," says Oak. "Let him be."

The prince moves through the palace like a stunned sleepwalker, desperately happy that Wren is alive. So happy that when he finds Madoc in the game room, he can't contain his smile.

His father stands from behind a chess table. "You look pleased. Does that mean—"

Time—never particularly well calculated by the Folk—has blurred at the edges. He's not sure how long he's been in that room. "Awake. Alive."

"Come sit," Madoc says. "You can finish Val Moren's game."

Oak slips into the chair and frowns at the table. "What happened?"

In front of Madoc are several captured pawns, a bishop, and a knight. On Oak's side, only a single pawn.

"He wandered off when he realized he was going to lose," says the redcap.

Oak blinks at the game, too exhausted to have any move in mind, no less a good move.

"Your mother isn't particularly happy with me right now," Madoc says. "Your sisters, either."

"Because of me?" It was perhaps inevitable, but he felt guilty to hasten it along.

Madoc shakes his head. "Maybe they're right."

That's alarming. "Everything okay, Dad?"

Unlike Oriana, Madoc smiles at his use of the human term. *Dad*. Perhaps he likes it better because when Jude and Taryn used it, it meant they cared about him in a way he might not have thought they ever would.

"That mortal girl being around made me think."

It has to be strange for him to be back in Elfhame, and yet no longer the grand general. To be back in his old house, without his kids there. And to be away from Insear when the rest of them were in danger. "About my sisters?"

"About their mother," Madoc says.

Oak is surprised. Madoc doesn't usually speak of his mortal wife, Eva. Possibly because he murdered her.

"Oh?"

"It's not easy for mortals to live in this place. It's not easy for us to live in their world, either, but it's easier. I shouldn't have left her so much alone. I shouldn't have forgotten that she could lie, or that she thought of her life as brief, and would risk much for happiness."

Oak nods, sensing there's more, and advances his pawn out of the range of being taken by another.

"And I shouldn't have told myself that cultivating a killing instinct I couldn't control had no chance of bringing me tragedy. I shouldn't have been so eager to teach the same to you."

Oak thinks of the fear he'd felt when his father struck him to the ground all those years ago, of the hard kernel of shame he carried at that terror and his own softness, at how his sisters and mother protected him. "No," Oak says. "Probably not."

Madoc grins. "And yet, there are few things I would change. For without all my mistakes, I would not have the family I do." He moves his queen, sweeping across the board to rest in a place that doesn't seem imminently threatening.

Since Madoc would almost certainly have the crown if not for one of Eva's mortal daughters, that was quite an admission.

Oak moves his knight to take one of his father's undefended bishops. "I'm glad you're home. Try not to get banished again."

Madoc shifts his castle. "Checkmate," he says with a grin, leaning back in his chair.

On his way back to his rooms, Oak stops at Tiernan's. He taps lightly enough that if Tiernan is really asleep, the sound won't rouse him.

"Yes?" comes a voice. Hyacinthe.

Oak opens the door.

Tiernan and Hyacinthe are in bed together. Tiernan's hair is rumpled, and Hyacinthe is looking quite pleased with himself.

Oak smirks and comes to sit at the foot. "This won't take long."

Hyacinthe shifts so he's leaning against the headboard. His chest is bare. Tiernan shifts up, too, keeping a blanket over himself.

"Tiernan, I am formally dismissing you from my service," Oak says.

"Why? What did I do?" Tiernan leans forward, not worrying about the blanket anymore.

"Protected me," Oak says with great sincerity. "Including from myself. For many years."

Hyacinthe's looks outraged. "Is this because of me?"

"Not entirely," says Oak.

"That's not fair," Hyacinthe says. "I fought back-to-back with you. I got you out of Mother Marrow's. I practically got you out of the Citadel. I even let you persuade me to be half-drowned by Jack of the Lakes. You can't still think I would betray you."

"I don't," Oak says.

Tiernan frowns in confusion. "Why *are* you sending me away?"

"Guarding a member of the royal family isn't a position one is supposed to quit," Oak says. "But you should. I have been throwing myself at things and not caring what happens. I didn't see how destructive it was until Wren did it."

"You need someone—"

"I did need you when I was a child," Oak says. "Although I wouldn't admit it. You kept me safe, and trying not to put you in danger made me a little more cautious—although not nearly cautious enough—but more, you were my friend. Now both of us need to make decisions about our future, and those might not follow the same paths."

Tiernan takes a deep breath, letting those words sink in.

Hyacinthe gapes a little. Of all the things he has resented Oak for, what he seemed to feel most keenly was the fear that Tiernan was being taken from him. The idea that Oak might not actually want that clearly never occurred to him.

"I hope you'll always be my friend, but we can't *really* be friends if you're obliged to throw away your life for my bad decisions."

"I'll always be your friend," Tiernan says staunchly.

"Good," Oak says, standing up. "And now I will get out of here so Hyacinthe doesn't have a new reason to be angry with me and you can both—eventually—sleep."

The prince heads for the door. One of them throws a pillow at his back on his way out.

At the door to his rooms, Oak knocks. When neither Wren nor Bex answers, he goes in.

It takes him a few turns through the sitting area, the bedroom, and the library to realize she's not there. He calls her name and then, feeling foolish, sits on the edge of the bed.

A sheet of paper rests on his pillow, one ripped out of an old school notebook. On it in an unsteady hand is a letter addressed to him.

Oak,

I have always been your opposite, shy and wild where you are all courtly charm. And yet you are the one who pulled me out of my forest and forced me to stop denying all the parts of me I tried to hide.

Including the part of me that wanted you.

I could tell you how easy it was to believe that I was monstrous in your eyes and that the only thing I could have of you was what I took. But that hardly matters. I knew it was wrong, and I did it anyway. I exchanged the certainty of possession for what I most wanted—your friendship and your love.

I am going with Bex to visit my family and then return to the north. If I can no longer only take things apart, then it's time to learn how to create. It would be cruel to hold you to a promise made in duress, a marriage proposal given to prevent bloodshed. And crueler still to make you bid me a polite farewell, when I have already taken so much from you.

Wren

The prince crumples the paper in his hands. Didn't he make her an entire speech about how she taught him about love? About knowing and being known. After that, how could she—

Oh, right. He made that speech while she was *unconscious*.

He slumps down in a chair.

When Jude sends for him, he has spent the better part of the afternoon staring out a window miserably. Still, she's the High Queen and also his sister, so he makes himself somewhat presentable and goes to the royal chambers.

Cardan is lying on the bed, bandaged and sulking, in a magnificent dressing gown. "I hate being unwell," he says.

"You're not *sick*," Jude tells him. "You are recovering from being stabbed—or rather, throwing yourself on a knife."

"You would have done the same for me," he says airily.

"I would not," Jude snaps.

"Liar," Cardan says fondly.

Jude takes a deep breath and turns to Oak. "If you really want, you have our formal permission, as your sovereigns, to abdicate your position as our heir."

Oak raises his brows, waiting for the caveat. He's been telling her he didn't want the throne for as long as he can remember having a reason to say the words. For years, she acted as though he'd eventually come around. "Why?"

"You're a grown person. A *man*, even if I'd like to think of you as forever a boy. You've got to determine your own fate. Make your own choices. And I have to let you."

"Thank you," he forces out. It's not a polite thing to say among the Folk, but Jude ought to hear it. Those words absolve him of no debt.

He's let her down and possibly made her proud of him, too. His family cares about him in ways that are far too complex and layered for it to come from enchantment, and that is a profound relief.

"For listening to you? Don't worry. I won't make it a habit." Walking to him, she puts her arms around him, bumping her chin against his chest. "You're so annoyingly tall. I used to be able to carry you on my shoulders."

"I could carry *you*," Oak offers.

"You used to kick me with your hooves," she tells him. "I wouldn't mind a chance for revenge."

"I bet." He laughs. "Is Taryn still angry?"

"She's sad," Jude says. "And feels guilty. Like this is the universe punishing her for what she did to Locke."

If that were true, so many of them deserved greater punishment.

"I didn't want—I don't *think* I wanted Garrett dead."

"He isn't dead," Jude says matter-of-factly. "He's a tree."

He supposes it must be some comfort, to be able to visit and speak with him, even if he can't speak in return. And perhaps someday the enchantment could be broken when the danger was past. Perhaps even the hope of that was something.

"And you had every reason to be mad. We did keep secrets from you," Jude goes on. "Bad ones. Small ones. I should have told you what the Ghost had done. I should have told you when Madoc was captured. And—you should have told me some things, too."

"A lot of things," Oak agrees.

"We'll do better," Jude says, knocking her shoulder into his arm.

"We'll do better," he agrees.

"Speaking of which, I would speak with Oak for a moment," Cardan says. "Alone."

Jude looks surprised but then shrugs. "I'll be outside, yelling at people."

"Try not to enjoy it too greatly," says Cardan as she goes out.

For a moment, they are silent. Cardan pushes himself up off the bed. Messy black curls fall over his eyes, and he ties the belt of his deep blue dressing gown more tightly.

"I am sure she doesn't want you getting up," Oak says, but he offers his arm. Cardan is, after all, the High King.

And if he slipped, Jude would like that even less.

Cardan leans heavily on the prince. He points toward one of the low brocade couches. "Help me get over there."

They move slowly. Cardan winces under his breath and occasionally gives an exaggerated groan. When he finally makes it, he lounges against one of the corners, propped up with pillows. "Pour me a goblet of wine, won't you?"

Oak rolls his eyes.

Cardan leans forward. "Or I could get it myself."

Outmaneuvered, Oak holds his hands up in surrender. He goes to a silver tray that holds cut crystal carafes and chooses one half-full of plum-dark liquor. He pours it into a goblet and passes that over.

"I think you know what this is about," Cardan says, taking a long slug.

Oak sits. "Lady Elaine? Randalin? The conspiracy? I can explain."

Cardan waves his words away. "You have done enough and more than enough *explaining*. I think it is my turn to speak."

"Your Majesty," Oak acknowledges.

Cardan meets his gaze. "For someone who cannot outright lie, you twist the truth so far that I am surprised it doesn't cry out in agony."

Oak doesn't even bother denying that.

"Which makes perfect sense, given your father...and your sister. But you've even managed to deceive her. Which she doesn't like admitting—doesn't like, period, really."

Again, Oak says nothing.

"When did you start, with the conspiracies?"

"I don't want—" Oak begins.

"The throne?" Cardan finishes for him. "Obviously not. Nor have you waffled on that point. And if your sisters and your parents imagined you'd change your mind, that's for their own mad reasons. It's the only thing on which you have remained steadfast for more than a handful of years. And, I will have you know, I thought the same thing when I was a prince."

Oak can't help recalling the part he had in taking that choice away from Cardan.

"No, I don't suspect you of wanting to be High King," Cardan says, and then smiles a wicked, little smile. "Nor did I believe you wanted me dead for some other reason. I never thought that."

Oak opens his mouth and closes it. *Isn't* that what this is about? *Wasn't* that what Cardan believed? He overheard the High King tell Jude as much, back in their rooms in the palace, before he left to try to save Madoc. "I am not sure I understand."

"When your first bodyguard tried to kill you, I ought to have asked more questions. Certainly after one or two of your lovers died. But I thought what everyone else thought—that you were too trusting and easily manipulated as a result. That you chose your friends poorly and your lovers even more poorly. But you chose both carefully and well, didn't you?"

Oak gets up and pours himself a glass of wine. He suspects he is going to need it. "I overheard you," he says. "In your rooms, with Jude. I overheard you talking about Madoc."

"Yes," Cardan says. "Belatedly, that became obvious."

If I didn't know better, I might think this is your brother's fault. Oak tries to remember the exact words the High King chose. *He's more like you than you want to see.* "You didn't trust me."

"Having spent a great deal of time playing the fool myself," Cardan says, "I recognized your game. Not at first, but long before Jude. She didn't want to believe me, and I am never going to tire of crowing about being right."

"So you didn't think I was really allied with Randalin?"

Cardan smiles. "No," he says. "But I wasn't certain which of your allies were actually on your side. And I was rather hoping you'd let us lock you up and protect you."

"You could have given me some sort of hint!" Oak says.

Cardan raises a single brow.

Oak shakes his head. "Yes, well, *fine.* I could have done the same. And *fine,* you were losing blood."

Cardan makes a gesture as though tossing off Oak's words. "I have little experience of dispensing brotherly wisdom, but I know a great deal about mistakes. And about hiding behind a mask." He salutes with his wineglass. "Some might say that I still do, but they would be wrong. To those I love, I am myself. Too much myself sometimes."

Oak laughs. "Jude wouldn't say that."

Cardan takes a deep swallow of plum-dark wine, looking pleased with himself. "She *would,* but she'd be lying. But, most important"—he raises a single finger—"*I* knew what you were up to before she did." Then a second. "And if you decide you want to risk your life, perhaps you could also risk a little personal discomfort and let your family in on your plans."

Oak lets out a long sigh. "I will take that under advisement."

"Please do," says Cardan. "And there is one more thing."

Oak takes an even bigger slug of his wine.

"You may recall that Jude gave you permission to abdicate? Well, that's all well and good, but you can't do it immediately. We'll need several months more of your being our heir."

"Months?" Oak echoes, completely puzzled.

The High King shrugs. "More or less. Maybe a little longer. Just to make the Court feel as though there's some kind of backup plan if something happens while we're away."

"Away?" After so many surprises, Oak seems unable to do more than repeat the things Cardan tells him. "You want me to stay the heir while you two go off somewhere? And *then* I can step down, be de-princed, whatever?"

"Exactly that," says Cardan.

"Like on a vacation?"

Cardan snorts.

"I don't understand," Oak says. "Where are you going?"

"A diplomatic mission," says Cardan, leaning back on the cushions. "After that last little rescue, Nicasia has demanded we honor our treaty, meet her suitors, and witness the contest for her hand and crown. And so Jude and I are headed to the Undersea, where we will go to a lot of parties and try very hard not to die."

CHAPTER
25

Oak steps onto the crust of ice, his breath clouding in the air.
He is dressed in thick furs, his hands wrapped in wool and then in leather, even his hooves wrapped, and yet he can still feel the chill of this place. He shivers, thinks of Wren, and shivers again.

The Stone Forest is different from what he remembers, lush instead of menacing. He is not pulled toward it now, nor does he feel pursued by it. As he passes, he attempts to see the troll kings, but the landscape has swallowed them up. All he can see is the wall they built.

When he approaches it, he finds that a great ice gate—newly built—stands open. He passes through. As he does, some falcons fly into the air from the top, probably to announce his arrival.

Beyond, he expects to see the same Citadel that he invaded with Wren, the one in which he was imprisoned, but a new structure has taken its place. A castle all of obsidian instead of ice. The rock shines as though it were made of black glass.

If anything, it looks more forbidding and impossible than what was there before. Certainly more pointy.

Hag Queen. He thinks of those whispered words and is more aware than ever why Folk are afraid of this kind of power.

Oak trods past copses made entirely from ice, animals sculpted from snow peering out from their branches. It makes him think, eerily, of the forest in which he found Wren. As though she has re-created parts of it from memory.

She made all of this with her magic. The magic that should have always been her inheritance.

The doors to the new castle are high and narrow, without a knocker nor any handles. He pushes, expecting resistance, but the door swings open at the touch of his gloved hand.

The black hall beyond is empty but for a fireplace large enough to cook a horse, crackling with real flames. No servants greet him. His hooves echo against the stone.

He finds her in the third room, a library, only a portion of it stocked with books, but clearly built for the acquisition of more.

She is in a long dressing gown of a deep blue color. Her hair is down and falls over her shoulders. Her feet are bare. She sits on a long, low couch, novel in hand, wings spread. At the sight of her, he feels a longing so sharp that it is almost pain.

Wren sits up.

"I didn't expect you," she says, which is not encouraging.

He thinks of visiting her in the forest when they were young and how she sent him away for his own good. Perhaps wisely. But he isn't about to be sent away easily again.

She goes to one of her shelves and returns the book, sliding it back into place.

"I know what you think," Oak says. "That you're not whom I should want."

She ducks her head, a faint flush on her cheeks.

"It's true you inspire no safe daydream of love," he tells her.

"A nightmare, then?" she asks with a small, self-deprecating laugh.

"The kind of love that comes when two people see each other clearly," he says, walking to her. "Even if they're scared to believe that's possible. I adore you. I want to play games with you. I want to tell you all the truths I have to give. And if you really think you're a monster, then let's be monsters together."

Wren stares at him. "And if I send you away even after this speech? If I don't want you?"

He hesitates. "Then I'll go," he says. "And adore you from afar. And compose ballads about you or something."

"You could *make* me love you," she says.

"You?" Oak snorts. "I doubt it. You're not interested in my telling you what you want to hear. I think you might actually prefer me at my least charming."

"What if I am too much? If I need too much?" she asks, her voice very low.

He takes a deep breath, his smile gone. "I'm not good. I'm not kind. Maybe I am not even safe. But whatever you want from me, I will give you."

For a moment, they stare at each other. He can see the tension in her body. But her eyes are clear and bright and open. She nods, a slow smile growing on her lips. "I want you to stay."

"Good," he says, sitting on the couch beside her. "Because it's very cold out there, and it was a long walk."

She lets her head fall against his shoulder with a sigh, lets him put his arm around her and pull her into an embrace.

"So," she says, her lips against his throat. "If everything had gone well that night on Insear, what would you have asked me? A riddle?"

"Something like that," he says.

"Tell me," she insists, and he can feel the press of her teeth, the softness of her mouth.

"It's a tricky one," he says. "Are you sure?"

"I'm good at riddles," she says.

"What I would have asked you—if somehow I wasn't trying to manipulate the situation so that you could wriggle out of it—is this: Would you consider actually marrying me?"

She looks up at him, obviously surprised and a little suspicious. "Really?"

He presses a kiss to her hair. "If you did, I would be willing to make the ultimate sacrifice to prove the sincerity of my feelings."

"What's that?" she asks, peering up at him.

"Become a king of some place instead of running away from all royal responsibility."

She laughs. "You wouldn't rather sit by my throne on a leash?"

"That does seem easier," he admits. "I would make an excellent consort."

"Then I'll have to marry you, Prince Oak of the Greenbriar line," Wren says, with a sharp-toothed smile. "Just to make you suffer."

ACKNOWLEDGMENTS

I am grateful to all those who helped me along on the journey to the novel you have in your hands, particularly Cassandra Clare, Leigh Bardugo, and Joshua Lewis, who helped me plot this the first time (surrounded by cats), Kelly Link, Sarah Rees Brennan, and Robin Wasserman, who helped me replot and reconsider my plot (though with fewer cats). Also to Steve Berman, who gave me notes and encouragement throughout and who has been critiquing my books since before *Tithe.*

Thank you to the many people who gave me a kind word or a bit of necessary advice, and who I am going to kick myself for not including right here.

A massive thank-you to everyone at Little, Brown Books for Young Readers for returning to Elfhame with me. Thanks especially to my amazing editor, Alvina Ling, and to Ruqayyah Daud, who provided invaluable insight. Thank you to Crystal Castro for dealing with all my delays. Thank you as well to Marisa Finkelstein, Kimberly Stella, Emilie Polster, Savannah Kennelly, Bill Grace, Karina Granda, Cassie Malmo, Megan Tingley, Jackie Engel, Shawn Foster, Danielle Cantarella, and Victoria Stapleton, among others.

In the UK, thank you to Hot Key Books, particularly Jane Harris, Emma Matthewson, and Amber Ivatt.

Thank you to my publishers and editors all over the world—those who I have had the pleasure of meeting in the past year and those I have not. And thank you to Heather Baror for keeping everyone on the same page.

Thank you to Joanna Volpe, Jordan Hill, and Lindsay Howard, who read versions of this book as well and kept me feeling as though I was on the right track. And thank you to everyone at New Leaf Literary for making hard things easier.

Thank you to Kathleen Jennings, for the wonderful and evocative illustrations.

And thank you, always and forever, to Theo and Sebastian Black, for keeping my heart safe.

MORE FROM HOLLY BLACK

THE NOVELS OF ELFHAME

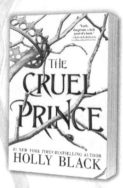

DIGITAL NOVELLA